Amazing nights of passion...
and a child!

Tall, Dark &
Handsome

Three fabulous novels
from international bestselling author

CAROLE MORTIMER

CAROLE MORTIMER'S
TALL, DARK & HANDSOME COLLECTION

August 2013

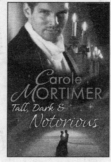

September 2013

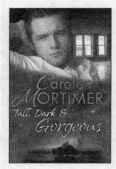

October 2013

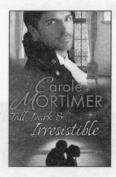

November 2013

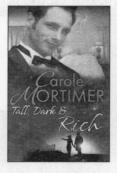

December 2013

January 2014

A beautiful collection of favourite Carole Mortimer novels.
Six seductive volumes containing sixteen fabulous
Modern™ and Historical bestsellers.

Carole MORTIMER

Tall, Dark &
Handsome

MILLS & BOON

Published in Great Britain 2013
by Mills & Boon, an imprint of Harlequin (UK) Limited, Eton House, 18-24 Paradise Road, Richmond, Surrey TW9 1SR

TALL, DARK & HANDSOME
© Harlequin Enterprises II B.V./S.à.r.l. 2013

The Infamous Italian's Secret Baby © Carole Mortimer 2009
Pregnant by the Millionaire © Carole Mortimer 2006
Liam's Secret Son © Carole Mortimer 2001

ISBN: 978 0 263 91010 0

024-0813

Harlequin (UK) policy is to use papers that are natural, renewable and recyclable products and made from wood grown in sustainable forests. The logging and manufacturing processes conform to the legal environmental regulations of the country of origin.

Printed and bound by
CPI Group (UK) Ltd, Croydon, CR0 4YY

Carole Mortimer was born in England, the youngest of three children. She began writing in 1978 and has now written over one hundred and eighty books for Mills & Boon. Carole has six sons, Matthew, Joshua, Timothy, Michael, David and Peter. She says, 'I'm happily married to Peter senior; we're best friends as well as lovers, which is probably the best recipe for a successful relationship. We live in a lovely part of England.'

The Infamous Italian's Secret Baby

CAROLE MORTIMER

PROLOGUE

'THE party is outside by the pool.'

Bella froze in the doorway, searching the shadows of the unlit room she had entered by mistake, a study or den if the book-lined walls and desk were any indication. Her hand tightened about the door-handle as she finally saw the outline of the large, imposing figure seated behind that desk.

The man was totally unmoving, and yet his very stillness was an implied danger, an echo of the challenge in his tone. By the light from the hallway behind her, Bella was just able to make out the fall of long dark hair that grew onto a pair of wide shoulders, those shoulders and a powerful chest encased in a dark top of some kind.

She swallowed hard before speaking. 'I was looking for the bathroom...'

'As you can see, this is not it,' he responded, his amused voice slightly accented. As he spoke some of the tension left his upper torso and he relaxed back in the high-backed chair, head tilted slightly sideways as the glitter of his gaze moved slowly over Bella standing silhouetted in the doorway. 'Or perhaps you cannot see...'

Bella barely had time to realise that the husky voice

sounded vaguely familiar before there was the click of a switch and a light illuminated the desk in a soft warm glow. And the man seated behind it. Bella recognised him instantly.

Gabriel Danti!

Bella felt her heart plummet in her chest as she looked at the wickedly handsome man in front of her. His thick dark hair and chocolate-brown eyes were almost black in their intensity. His olive-skinned face boasted a perfectly straight aristocratic nose, high cheekbones, a mouth that was full and sensual, and a square, arrogant chin, softened only by the slight cleft in its centre.

It was the face that thousands, no, *millions* of women all over the world sighed over. Daydreamed over. Drooled over!

Italian by birth, Gabriel Danti was, at the age of twenty-eight, the defending champion of the Formula One racing car championship currently in its fifth month. This man was the darling of the rich and the famous on both sides of the Atlantic—and, as if that weren't enough, he was also the only son and heir of Cristo Danti, head of the Danti business and wine empire, with vineyards in both Italy and America.

Even while she registered all those things about him Bella was also aware of the fact that this house in the Surrey countryside was Gabriel Danti's English home, and that he was actually the host of the noisy party taking place outside by the pool. So what was he doing sitting up here alone in the dark?

She moistened suddenly dry lips. 'I'm terribly sorry for disturbing you. I really *was* looking for the bathroom.' She gave a small self-conscious grimace. How awful that the first and probably only time she had the opportunity to speak to Gabriel Danti it was because she needed to find the bathroom!

Gabriel made a lazy study of the tiny, dark-haired woman who stood in the doorway of his study. A young woman totally unlike the tall, leggy blondes that he usually escorted—and totally unlike the traitorous Janine, he acknowledged grimly to himself.

She had very long, straight hair, as black as ebony and falling soft and silky about her shoulders. A dark fringe of that same silky softness lay on her forehead, and her small, heart-shaped face was pale and smooth as alabaster—and totally dominated by a pair of the most unusual violet-coloured eyes Gabriel had ever seen. Her gently pouting lips were unknowingly sensuous and inviting.

His gaze dropped lower, to the soft woollen top she wore, which was the same violet colour of her eyes. The top two buttons were undone to reveal surprisingly full breasts—completely naked breasts beneath the thinness of her sweater, if Gabriel wasn't mistaken, which made her slender waist look even more so in comparison. Her narrow hips and legs were clearly defined in figure-hugging jeans.

That long, leisurely glance told Gabriel that he didn't know her.

But he wanted to!

Bella took an involuntary step back as Gabriel Danti stood up from behind the desk, revealing that the top he wore was in fact a black silk shirt that rippled as he stood before resettling softly against the muscled hardness of his shoulders and chest. The sleeves were turned back to just below his elbows, revealing muscled forearms lightly dusted with dark hair.

At least a foot taller than her own five feet two inches, Gabriel Danti at once dominated the space around him. And she, Bella realised in some alarm as she found herself rooted to the spot, was totally unable to move as the tall Italian sauntered across the room in long feline strides to stand mere inches in front of her. The raucous noise of the party outside instantly became muted as all Bella could see or hear was him.

She had been wrong, Bella mused as she found herself in a daze, unable to look away from the dark beauty of his face. Gabriel Danti wasn't handsome. He was stunningly gorgeous.

Bella could feel the heat radiating from his body, could smell his tangy aftershave, the male scent of him that invaded and claimed the senses, filling her with a warm lethargy, a need to move closer to all that heady maleness.

A need Bella was unable to resist as she felt herself swaying towards him. She made an effort at the last moment not to do so, lifting a hand to stop herself from curving her body along the length of his. Instead she found the palm of her hand against the black silk of his shirt, her fingers curling against the warm hardness of the chest beneath as she felt the hot, heady thrum of his heart against her fingertips.

What was happening to her?

She never reacted to men like this. At least, she never had before…

She had to—

Bella froze, every part of her immobilised as Gabriel Danti raised one of his long elegant hands that so capably handled the wheel of a racing car travelling at unimaginable speeds, and cupped her chin, the soft pad of his thumb caressing lightly across her bottom lip. The tingling warmth that ensued travelled down her throat and spine to pool hotly between her thighs.

Dark brown eyes held her own captive. 'You have the most beautiful eyes I have ever seen.' His voice was low, husky, as if he were aware that anything else would break the spell that surrounded them.

'So do you,' Bella breathed, her chest rising and falling sharply with the effort it took to breathe at all.

His throaty laugh was a soft rumble beneath her fingertips before it faded; the darkness of his gaze suddenly became intense, searching. 'Did you come here with someone?'

Bella blinked, trying to think through the slow insidiousness of his seduction. 'I—I'm here with a group of friends, Mr Danti.' She gave a self-conscious shake of her head as his eyes compelled her answer. 'Sean is the nephew of one of your mechanics.'

It didn't surprise Gabriel that this beautiful young woman knew who he was. Even if she hadn't recognised him from the photographs of him that appeared almost daily in the newspapers at the moment, the fact that this was his house and he had been sitting in the study where several framed photographs of him winning races also adorned the walls would have given him away.

'Sean is your boyfriend?' There was a slight edge to his voice that hadn't been there seconds earlier.

'Heavens, no!' she denied with a smile, her long hair falling forward across her breasts as she shook her head. 'We're just at university together. I hope you don't mind

that Sean brought some friends with him, Mr Danti?'
She was frowning now, her eyes almost purple. 'His
uncle said—'

'I do not mind,' Gabriel cut in reassuringly. 'And
please call me Gabriel.'

A slight flush darkened her cheeks. 'And I'm Bella,'
she invited huskily.

'Bella?'

'Isabella.' She grimaced. 'But everyone just calls me
Bella.'

Gabriel wasn't sure he wanted to be grouped with
'everyone' where this fascinating woman was concerned. He raised one dark brow. 'You are Italian?'

'No,' she laughed softly, her teeth small and white
against the fullness of her lips. 'My mother allowed my
father, who's a doctor, to choose my own and my
younger sister's names, so he named us after two of his
favourite models and actresses: Isabella and Claudia.
When my brother was born six years ago my mother had
the choice of names. She chose Liam. After the actor.
A tall Irishman, with what my mother describes as "very
sexy blue eyes"—'

'I know him,' Gabriel admitted.

'You know of him or you know him?' Bella was
aware that she was talking too much. About things
that could be of absolutely no interest to a man like
Gabriel Danti. It was nerves, that was what it was.
That and the fact that she couldn't think straight with
Gabriel's fingers still curled possessively around the
softness of her chin!

The Italian smiled. 'I know him. I cannot confirm the
sexiness of his blue eyes, of course, but—'

'You're mocking me now,' Bella reproved self-consciously.

'Only a little,' Gabriel murmured, his gaze once more intense on hers. 'You said you are at university?'

'Was,' Bella corrected ruefully. 'I left last month.'

Telling Gabriel that Bella was probably aged twenty-one or twenty-two to his twenty-eight. 'What subject did you study?'

'Art and History,' she supplied.

'With a view to teaching, perhaps?'

'I'm really not sure yet. I'm hoping something that involves both subjects.' She shrugged slender shoulders, the movement giving Gabriel, with his superior height, a delicious glimpse of the fullness of her breasts.

Gabriel could never remember being so instantly attracted to a woman before. So attracted that he was sure her appraisal of him earlier had raised his body temperature by several degrees, at the same time making him totally aware of every muscle and sinew of his own body as well as hers. Rousing a need, a hunger, inside him that demanded the slender curves of Bella's body be placed against his much harder ones. Intimately. Preferably with no clothing between them.

Bella gave a slightly nervous laugh as she saw the way the Italian's eyes had suddenly darkened. 'If you'll excuse me, I think I'll just go and find the bathroom—'

'The bathroom is the room next to this on the right,' Gabriel interrupted, his fingers firming against her chin. 'While you are gone, I suggest I find a bottle of champagne and some glasses and then we can find somewhere more comfortable in which to continue this conversation, hmm?'

What conversation? Bella wondered, slightly bemused. She was pretty sure that Gabriel Danti didn't want to hear more about her degree in art and history or her family! 'Shouldn't you be returning to your guests?' She frowned.

His laugh was slightly wicked. 'Does it sound as if they are missing me?'

Well…no, the party outside sounded noisier and more out of control than ever. Which was some feat considering several of the guests had already thrown off their clothes and jumped into the pool naked before Bella had left to go in search of the bathroom. Which had hastened her need to go in search of the bathroom, if she was honest; the party looked in danger of disintegrating in a way Bella wasn't at all comfortable with.

It had sounded like a fun thing to do when Sean Davies had invited several of his fellow ex-students to the party being given at the Surrey home of Gabriel Danti. A chance to mix with the rich and the famous.

The fact that most of those 'rich and famous' were behaving in a way Bella would never have imagined if she hadn't seen it with her own eyes had come as something of a shock to her. It wasn't that she was a prude, it was just a little disconcerting to have a man she had last seen reading the evening news, a respected middle-aged man, jumping stark naked into Gabriel Danti's swimming pool. Admittedly it was a warm summer's evening, but even so!

'Come, Bella.' Gabriel removed his hand from her chin only to place it about her waist, his arm warm and spine-tingling as it rested against the slenderness of her back. 'Do you have any preference in champagne?'

'Preference?' she echoed. Champagne was champagne, wasn't it?

'White or pink?' he elaborated.

'Er—pink will be fine.' As a student, the only preference Bella had when it came to wines was that it not cost a lot of money! 'Are you sure you wouldn't rather just rejoin your guests?' Bella hesitated in the hallway, rather confused that this gorgeous man, a man any of his female guests would scratch another woman's eyes out in order to spend time alone with, appeared to want to spend that time with *her*...

'I am very sure, Bella.' Gabriel turned her in the curve of his arm so that she now faced him, his hands resting lightly against her waist. 'But perhaps you would rather return to your friends...?'

Bella swallowed hard as Gabriel made no effort to hide the hot sensuality burning in his eyes. 'No, I—' She stopped as she realised her voice was several octaves higher than normal. She cleared her throat before trying again. 'No, I think I would enjoy drinking champagne with you more.'

Those dark eyes gleamed with satisfaction as he raised his hands to cup either side of her face before slowly lowering his head to take possession of her mouth. Sipping, tasting, his tongue was a warm sweep against her lips as he tacitly asked her permission to enter. Then he claimed her mouth, groaning low in his throat as Bella gave in to temptation, parting her lips and inviting his tongue to surge inside.

His mouth was hot against hers now, Bella feeling slightly dizzy from the warm rush of desire that instantly claimed her. Her breasts were firm and aching and she moved instinctively to rub that ache against the hardness of Gabriel's chest, that friction affording her some relief even as she felt more desire pooling between her thighs.

Oh, how she wanted this man. Wanted him as she had never known it was possible to want any man, the hot demand of his kiss, the hardness of his thighs against hers, telling her that he returned that need.

Gabriel had never tasted anything as sweet as the response of Bella's mouth beneath his. Never felt anything so lush, so perfect, as his hands moved down over her hips and then down to clasp her bottom as he pulled her into him, his arousal now nestled demandingly against the flatness of her stomach.

Gabriel dragged his mouth from Bella's to cast a searching look down at her. Those beautiful violet-coloured eyes were so darkly purple it was almost impossible to distinguish the black of her pupils. Her cheeks were flushed, her lips swollen from their kisses, and she looked more erotically enticing than ever. Her breasts were firm against his chest, and Gabriel was able to feel the hardness of her nipples through the soft silk of his shirt.

'Go. Before I lose all sense and make love to you out here in the hallway!' He grasped the tops of her arms tightly and turned her in the direction of the bathroom she had been seeking. 'I will return in two minutes with the champagne and glasses.'

Bella was completely dazed and disorientated as she entered the bathroom and closed the door behind her before leaning weakly back against it.

She was twenty-one years of age, had dated dozens

of boys in the last five or six years, but never before had she known anyone or anything as lethal—as potent—as Gabriel's kisses!

Bella straightened to look at herself in the mirror on the door of the bathroom cabinet over the sink. Her cheeks glowed with the warmth of her arousal. Her mouth—oh, dear, her lips were swollen and slightly parted as if in invitation! Her eyes were deep pools of liquid violet, the pupils enlarged. As for her breasts... Well, if she had any sense she would leave now! If she had any will power at all, she would *make* herself leave now.

Even as she told herself these things Bella knew she wasn't going anywhere but back into Gabriel Danti's arms...

'Nice?'

'Mmm.'

'Would you like more?'

'Please.'

'Come a little closer, then. Now hold out your hand.'

Bella lifted the hand holding her glass to allow Gabriel to pour her more champagne as she sat on the sofa beside him, at the same time noting that he hadn't touched any of the bubbly wine in his own glass since placing it on the coffee table in front of them. The two of them were seated in a sitting-room at the front of the house on the first floor, well away from the noisy party downstairs.

'You aren't drinking,' she pointed out in an effort to cover up the slight shaking of her hand as she once again raised her glass to her lips and took a sip of the delicious pink champagne.

He shook his head, his arm along the back of the sofa as he sat very close beside her, that hand playing with the silken strands of her hair. 'I'm going to the track for a practice session tomorrow, and I never drink if I am going to drive the next day.'

Bella's eyes widened. 'You shouldn't have bothered opening a bottle of champagne just for me.'

'It is not just for you,' Gabriel assured her, dipping his finger into her champagne glass before running his finger lightly behind Bella's ear and along her jaw. 'I said I do not drink champagne before driving, Bella, not that I do not intend enjoying its taste,' he murmured softly, his breath warm against her ear lobe as his lips moved to follow the trail of champagne left by his finger, his tongue rasping against her already sensitised skin.

The combination of Bella and champagne was more intoxicating to Gabriel's senses than drinking a whole bottle of the expensive wine could ever have been, her skin so smooth to the touch, its sweet taste driving the heat through Gabriel's already roused body until he throbbed with the need to touch her more intimately. All of her.

He held her gaze as he deliberately dipped his finger back into the champagne before leaving a moist trail from her chin, down the delicate curve of her throat, to the exposed swell of the fullness of her breasts, his lips instantly following that heady trail.

Bella squirmed pleasurably as the warmth of his mouth lingered on her breasts. 'Gabriel—'

'Let me, Bella,' he pressed huskily. 'Let me bathe you in champagne. All of you. So that I might drink from your body.' His hand moved to cup her cheek as his thumb moved across her parted lips once more. 'Will you allow me to do that, Bella?'

Bella had accepted exactly where this was going the moment she had agreed to accompany Gabriel up the stairs to what had turned out to be the private sitting-room that adjoined his bedroom. Although thankfully the bedroom door had remained closed, otherwise she might have panicked long before now.

Not that she was panicking. Quivering with delicious anticipation more described her present state of mind! Just the thought of Gabriel dribbling champagne over her totally naked body, before slowly licking away each drop with the rasp of his arousing tongue, was enough to heat every inch of her to a tingling awareness that suddenly made the few clothes Bella was wearing feel tight and restrictive.

'As long as I can reciprocate.' She dipped her own finger into the champagne before running that finger over the firm sensuality of Gabriel's slightly parted lips. 'May I?' She paused expectantly with her mouth only centimetres away from his, violet eyes looking deeply into dark brown.

'Please do,' he encouraged.

What Bella lacked in experience she hoped she made up for in her delight at being given the freedom to explore the sculptured perfection of Gabriel's mouth in the same way he had hers. She heard his ragged intake of breath as she gently sucked his top lip into her mouth and her tongue slowly licked the heady champagne from that softness. His hand moved up to entangle his fingers into her hair as she gave the same treatment to his bottom lip, knowing as those fingers tightened in her hair that these caresses were arousing Gabriel as deeply as they were her.

Gabriel's body hardened more with each heated sweep of Bella's tongue against his lips, the throb of his thighs becoming an urgent demand. In fact, he wasn't even sure he was going to make it as far as the bedroom before stripping Bella's clothes from her deliciously responsive body and surging hotly, satisfyingly inside her!

He moved back abruptly, a nerve pulsing in his tightly clenched jaw as he stood up to hold out his hand to her. 'Come with me, Bella,' he invited as she looked up at him uncertainly.

Gabriel continued to hold that gaze as Bella placed her hand in his and rose gracefully to her feet, her breasts quickly rising and falling beneath the thin wool of her sweater.

She was like a small, wild thing, Gabriel acknowledged with growing wonder. So tiny. So delicate. So absolutely, potently desirable.

Gabriel felt his stomach muscles tighten with the force of that desire, continuing to keep a firm hold of her delicate fingers as he picked up the chilled bottle of champagne with his other hand, neither of them speaking as they went into his bedroom.

'Please don't...' Bella protested shyly as Gabriel would have turned on the bedside light.

A four-poster bed! A genuine antique if Bella wasn't mistaken, as were the drapes of deep gold brocade that could be pulled around the four sides of the bed.

What did it matter whether or not the bed and drapes were genuinely old? It was still a bed. A bed Bella had no doubts she would shortly be sharing—very shortly, if the heat of his gaze was any indication!—with Gabriel Danti.

This was madness. Sheer, utter, delicious madness!

'I want to be able to look at you as I make love to you, Bella,' Gabriel said, once again standing very close to her, but not touching her, the warmth of his body alone acting on Bella's senses like a drug. 'Will you allow me to do that?' he encouraged throatily. 'I will undress first if you would be more comfortable with that…?'

God knew Bella wanted to look at him in all his naked glory! 'Please do,' she begged breathlessly.

He reached out to turn on the bedside lamp, to bathe the room in a muted golden glow before he reached up and began to unfasten the buttons down the front of his black shirt.

Bella found her gaze fixed on the movements of those long, elegantly slender hands as they slowly slipped each button from its fastening, the silk falling back to reveal the muscled hardness of Gabriel's chest covered in another dusting of dark hair. Dark hair that thickened as it reached his navel before disappearing below the waistband of his black tailored trousers.

It was instinct, pure compulsion that caused Bella to reach out and touch his chest, to feel the tautness of his flesh beneath her fingertips as it stretched tightly across those muscles. His skin felt hot and fevered, those muscles tightening as Bella's hands moved up to slide the shirt from his shoulders before she dropped the garment to the carpeted floor.

Gabriel was as beautiful as the angel he was named for. Achingly, temptingly gorgeous as his eyes burned hotly in the chiselled beauty of his face.

Bella wanted to see more. Wanted to see all of him!

Her hands trembled slightly as she unfastened his trousers to slide the zip down slowly, her fingers skimming lightly across Gabriel's arousal beneath black underpants, causing him to draw in a sharp breath.

His hand moved down to clasp hers against him. 'Feel how badly I want you, Bella,' he grated fiercely. 'Feel it!'

She looked up at him, their gazes fusing hotly, Bella never more sure of anything in her life as she slowly, deliberately, peeled away Gabriel's last item of clothing to release his pulsing erection.

He was long and thick, incredibly hard, that hardness moving against her hand as Bella reached out to touch him.

Gabriel felt his control slipping, groaning softly, lids closing, his jaw clenching, as his pleasure centred totally on the caress of Bella's fingers against his arousal. Selfishly he wanted those caresses to continue to their pleasurable conclusion. But more than that he wanted to see Bella, to touch her with the same intimacy as she was now touching him.

His gaze held hers as he stepped back slightly before reaching out to grasp the bottom of her thin sweater and draw it slowly up over her breasts and then her head before adding it to the pile of clothes on the carpet. Gabriel's breath caught in his throat as he gazed at the firm thrust of her breasts, the nipples a deep, dusky rose, and a waist so small and slender Gabriel felt sure he would be able to span it with his hands.

He slowly bent his head to kiss those uptilting breasts, able to see and feel Bella's response as his tongue moved moistly across one nipple before he drew it deeply into his mouth.

Bella was lost. Totally, utterly lost as her hands moved up to clasp Gabriel's head to her, her fingers tangling in the heavy thickness of his hair as the pleasure created by his lips and tongue washed over her in dark, sensuous waves, pooling achingly between her thighs. An ache that Gabriel helped to assuage as his hand moved to cup her there, pressing lightly, Bella gasping weakly as he unerringly found the centre of her arousal.

She had no idea which one of them removed her jeans and panties, any more than she could remember how they came to be lying on the bed, bodies pressed close together, legs entwined as they kissed hotly, fiercely, feverishly.

Bella stopped breathing altogether as Gabriel's hand parted her thighs before his thumb began to touch, to stroke, the hardened nub that nestled there. Her senses became saturated with the intensity of her arousal, her hips rising off the bed to meet the thrust of Gabriel's fingers as they moved deeply, rhythmically inside her and Bella exploded with spasm after spasm of unimagined pleasure, her head moving from side to side on the pillow, her fingers curled into the sheets beneath her as that pleasure seemed never ending.

It didn't end as Gabriel moved above her, his gaze holding hers as he slowly, inch by inch, entered her still quivering body until he claimed her completely. He began to move inside her, his thrusts slow and measured, and then increasing in depth, Gabriel groaning low in his throat as he surged fiercely inside her. Bella met the fierceness of his thrusts as she—amazingly, in-credibly!—felt her own release building for a second time in as many minutes.

Her eyes widened, deeply purple, as that release grew, the pleasure so achingly deep now it was almost painful in its intensity as Gabriel deliberately slowed the strokes of his erection inside her, holding her on the edge of that plateau, refusing to release her as he watched her pleasure.

'Please!' Bella gasped restlessly as her body burned and ached for that release. 'Oh, God, please!'

He continued to watch her even as he moved up onto his arms, his thrusts deepening, becoming harder, quicker, his cheeks flushed with his own pleasure, eyes glittering like onyx as Bella's second release took him over that edge with her.

Gabriel closed his eyes at the force of his release, surging, pumping, hot and fierce, his hips continuing to move against Bella's long after he had completely spilled himself as he remained hard inside her and the quivering pleasure still washed over and through him.

Finally, when he could take no more, when he felt as if he would die if the intensity of it didn't stop, Gabriel collapsed weakly onto Bella's breasts, turning only to pull the bedclothes over them both as they fell into a deep, exhausted sleep, their bodies still joined.

'It's time to wake up, Bella.'

Bella was already awake, had woken up several minutes ago in fact, and was trying to come to terms with who she was here with.

Gabriel Danti…

Just thinking of his name conjured up images of the night that had just passed. Of waking up in the early hours of the morning to find Gabriel once more hard inside her, his gaze silently questioning as he looked down at her. A question Bella had silently answered by the slow, languorous thrust of her thighs as her mouth became fused with his.

If anything, the second time they had made love had been even more intense than the first—and Bella hadn't believed that anything could possibly match their first time together!

But, having woken up alone in the four-poster bed a few minutes ago, the sound of the shower running in the adjoining bathroom telling her where Gabriel was, instead of the happy euphoria Bella should have been feeling after such a night of pure pleasure, she had instead been filled with a sense of trepidation.

Last night she had made love with Gabriel Danti. Number one driver of the Formula One racing championship. Playboy son and heir of the Danti business and wine empire.

Whereas she was the eldest daughter of an English country doctor, hopefully with a forthcoming degree in art and history.

Not only that, but Bella knew she was far from the tall, leggy blonde models or actresses that Gabriel usually escorted to the glitzy parties and film premieres he seemed to attend on a regular basis. The glossy magazines were constantly showing photographs of him with those women, most recently the model Janine Childe.

So she and Gabriel had absolutely nothing in common! Out of the bedroom, that was…

In the cold light of dawn Bella blushed to the roots of her tangled hair as she relived each and every one of their intimate caresses of the night before.

Of course, she should have thought of all the reasons she shouldn't be here with Gabriel before she went to bed with him. She probably would have done so if she hadn't been quite so mesmerised by all that brooding Latin charm. If she hadn't been held in thrall by the hard beauty of Gabriel's face and body…

'Bella…?' Gabriel prompted again as he moved to sit on the side of the bed. 'Wake up, *cara*, so that I can say goodbye properly.'

Goodbye?

Bella's lids flew open wide as she turned her head to look at Gabriel sitting on the bed beside her. She was grateful that she had the sheet draped over her to hide her nakedness when she saw that Gabriel was fully dressed in a black polo shirt that emphasised the width of his shoulders and chest, and faded jeans that rested low down on his hips, his hair still wet from the shower he had just taken.

Gabriel's smile was quizzical as he looked down at Bella, once again fascinated by how beautiful she was. How tiny and curvaceous. How responsive…

He felt his body stir, his thighs hardening, as he recalled just how responsive Bella had been the previous evening and once again during the night. How his own response had been deepened, intensified, to match hers.

He reached out to smooth the fringe of dark hair from her brow, his gaze holding hers as he bent to kiss her, slowly, his expression regretful when he finally raised his head. 'I really do have to go now, Bella, or I am going to be late getting to Silverstone,' he murmured huskily. 'But I will call you later, okay?'

'Okay,' she whispered.

Gabriel stood up reluctantly, as aware of the minutes ticking by as he was of Bella's nakedness beneath the sheet, and knowing he had to remove himself from the temptation she represented. 'My housekeeper will call a taxi for you when you are ready to leave.' He spoke abruptly as he fought the urge he had to say to hell with the practice session and remain here in bed with Bella instead. 'As I cannot drive you home myself I have left you some money on the dressing-table to pay for the taxi,' he added lightly, remembering that Bella had only recently ceased being a student.

She frowned slightly. 'That won't be necessary.'

'Bella…?' Gabriel lowered his own brows darkly as he could read none of her thoughts in those violet-coloured eyes.

'It's fine, Gabriel.' Bella forced a lightness to her tone that was completely contradicted by the heaviness that had settled in her chest at the suddenness of Gabriel's departure.

'I will call you later, Bella,' he repeated firmly. Gabriel bent once again to kiss her on the lips before turning to leave, pausing at the door to turn and add, 'Take your time showering—there is no hurry for you to leave.'

CHAPTER ONE

Five years later...

'AS PARTIES go this one is pretty amazi—I don't believe it!' Claudia gasped incredulously.

'What don't you believe?' Bella prompted indulgently, her sister having exclaimed over one wonder or another since the family's arrival in San Francisco two days ago.

Although Bella had to admit that the view of the San Francisco evening skyline from this private function room at the top of one of its most prestigious hotels was pretty spectacular. She could even see the Golden Gate Bridge lit up in all its splendour.

'Wow! I mean—wow!' Claudia wasn't looking out of the window but across the crowded room where the private party, to introduce the two families of their cousin Brian and his American fiancée Dahlia Fabrizzi, was taking place on the eve of their wedding. 'But it can't really be him, can it?' she queried as she frowned. 'Of course Aunt Gloria has been dropping huge hints the last few days about Dahlia's mother being well con- nected, but, still, I can't believe—'

'Claudia, will you for goodness' sake stop waffling

into your champagne and just—?' Bella broke off abruptly as she turned to see who was holding her sister so enrapt, and instantly recognised the 'him' Claudia had to be referring to.

Bella hadn't seen him for five years. Five years! And yet she had no trouble whatsoever in recognising Gabriel Danti!

No! Claudia was right; it couldn't possibly be him, Bella assured herself. Not here, of all places. It had to be an illusion.

Or perhaps just a waking nightmare!

'It *is* him!' Claudia exclaimed excitedly as she clutched Bella's arm. 'It's Gabriel Danti, Bella! Can you believe it?'

No, Bella couldn't believe it. She didn't *want* to believe it!

Maybe it wasn't him, just someone who looked a lot like him?

The height was the same, but the dark hair was much shorter than Bella remembered. The eyes, although dark, were cold and aloof despite the smile that curved those chiselled lips as he was introduced to several other guests. The cleft in the chin was also the same, but this man had a scar running from beneath his left eye to his jaw to mar the harsh, sculptured beauty of his face.

Bella remembered that Gabriel Danti had been photographed sporting a long scar down the left side of his face when he was discharged from hospital three months after the horrendous crash that had put an end to his own racing career and killed two of his fellow drivers.

Months after his accident, Gabriel Danti had returned to Italy on the family owned jet, had been photographed as he left the hospital, and then again as he entered the plane, but had rarely been seen in public since. His racing career over, he had turned his concentration on the Danti wineries and seemingly retired from the playboy lifestyle he had once so enjoyed.

'Do you remember those posters of him I had stuck all over my bedroom walls when I was younger?' Claudia laughed.

Of course Bella remembered those posters—they had given her the shivers for months following that night Bella had spent with him, her relief immense once Claudia took them down and replaced them with posters of one of the bad-boy actors of Hollywood.

'He's gorgeous, isn't he?' Claudia sighed dreamily.

'Lovely,' Bella answered insincerely, watching the man standing across the crowded room now talking to her uncle Simon.

He was several inches taller than her uncle, and had to bend slightly in order to hear the older man's conversation. He looked dark and mesmerising, his body lithe and obviously fit in the black evening suit and snowy white shirt with a black bow tie.

Could it really be Gabriel?

From the way his mere presence had ensnared the attention of all the female guests at the party Bella could well believe it was him. She just didn't want it to be!

'His hair's shorter, of course— Oh, look, he favours his left leg…' Claudia sympathised as their cousin Brian moved with the man to introduce him to several members of his own family who had made the trip over for the wedding tomorrow.

'His legs were badly crushed in the accident five years ago, remember,' Bella murmured with a frown.

'You would have thought that all the Danti millions could have fixed that,' her sister mused. 'You know, Bella,' she added slowly, 'he reminds me of someone...'

'Probably Gabriel Danti!' Bella said sharply as she finally came out of the dazed stupor that had held her firmly in its grip, linking her arm with her sister's in order to turn Claudia in the direction of the bar. 'Let's go and get some more champagne.'

'Aren't you in the least intrigued to know if it *is* him?' Claudia looked at her teasingly. She was of a similar height to Bella, but her hair was a short, wispy cap of ebony, the blue of her figure-hugging knee-length gown a perfect match in colour for her eyes.

'Not in the least,' Bella dismissed firmly, deliberately going to the farthest end of the bar away from the crowd of people where the man who looked like Gabriel Danti was now the centre of attention, several other people having drifted over to join the group, obviously as intrigued as Claudia.

Claudia gave a husky chuckle of affection as they stood at the bar waiting for their champagne glasses to be refilled. 'My big sister, the man hater!'

Bella raised dark brows. 'I don't hate all men—just those that have gone through puberty!'

'Exactly.' Claudia grinned, her face arrestingly pretty rather than classically beautiful. 'I wonder if I should go over and say hello to Brian and see if he can introduce me to— No, wait a minute...' Her attention noticeably sharpened as she looked over Bella's shoulder. 'I do believe our darling cousin is bringing him over to meet us!' Her face brightened excitedly.

No!

Bella couldn't believe this was happening!

She didn't even want to look at a man who resembled Gabriel Danti, let alone be introduced to him—

'And last, but not least, I would like you to meet the two most beautiful women I know after Dahlia,' Brian said affectionately behind her. 'Bella, Claudi, can I introduce you to Dahlia's cousin, Gabriel Danti? Gabriel, my cousins, Claudia and Isabella Scott.'

It truly *was* Gabriel Danti!

Bella couldn't breathe. Her mind had gone completely blank. Her knees had turned to jelly. In fact no part of her seemed to be functioning properly.

Luckily for her Claudia had eagerly grasped on to the introduction, and was even now enthusing to Gabriel how much she had enjoyed watching him during his career in Formula One racing, giving Bella a little time to catch her breath as she heard the familiar husky accented tones as he murmured a polite but dismissive response.

Perhaps Gabriel wouldn't remember her? Bella thought frantically.

Of course he wouldn't remember her!

Why should he remember the student of art and history called Bella who had once shared his bed for the night?

From his lack of a phone call, she could only assume he had forgotten her instantly!

'Bella...?' Brian prompted lightly as she still kept her back firmly turned towards both him and his guest.

Bella drew in a deep, steadying breath, knowing that she had no choice but to turn and face the man she so longed to forget, as he had her.

* * *

Gabriel's expression was blandly polite as Isabella Scott turned to face him. 'Miss Scott,' he greeted evenly as he briefly took the cool slenderness of her hand in his before releasing it. 'Or may I call you Isabella?'

'I—'

'Everyone calls her Bella,' Claudia put in helpfully.

'May I?' The icy darkness of Gabriel's gaze easily held Bella captive.

Violet-coloured eyes were surrounded by thick dark lashes the same colour as that wild cascade of hair down the slender length of her spine...

Bella blinked before abruptly breaking the intensity of Gabriel's gaze to focus on something across the room. 'Bella is fine,' she answered him evenly.

Isabella Scott looked self-assured and incredibly beautiful in an off-the-shoulder gown of the exact colour of her eyes, and, if Gabriel was not mistaken, her small, pointed chin was slightly raised in challenge as her gaze returned questioningly to meet the intensity of his...

'More guests to greet,' Brian Kingston murmured apologetically as he glanced across the room. 'Excuse me, won't you, Gabriel? I'm sure Bella and Claudi will be only too pleased to keep you entertained.' He shot a teasing glance at the younger of the two cousins before turning and making his way back across the crowded room to his fiancée's side.

Gabriel's gaze was hooded as he continued to look steadily at Bella. 'Will you?'

An irritated frown appeared between her eyes. 'Will I what?' she prompted sharply.

'Be pleased to keep me entertained?' he drawled with cool mockery.

Purple lights flashed in the depths of her eyes. 'Do you need entertaining, Mr Danti?'

'In truth, I doubt I will be staying long enough for that to be necessary,' he conceded.

Gabriel hadn't intended attending this party at all this evening, but at the last moment his father had asked him to represent the Danti side of the family, as he didn't feel well enough to attend the party of his niece this evening as well as her wedding tomorrow. Gabriel had reluctantly agreed to come in his place, his intention to only stay long enough to satisfy the proprieties.

At least, it had been...

Gabriel Danti wasn't staying long, Bella triumphed with inward relief. 'I'm sure Claudia and I can manage a few minutes' polite conversation, Mr Danti.'

Gabriel Danti gave a mocking inclination of his head before turning his attention to Claudia. 'Are you enjoying your visit to San Francisco, Claudia?'

Bella allowed her breath to leave her lungs in a soft, shaky sigh as she at last felt herself released from the intensity of Gabriel's dark, compelling gaze, and she took those few moments of respite to study him more closely.

The man she had met five years ago had possessed the broodingly magnetic good looks of his heavenly namesake. Along with a lazy self-confidence and charm that was utterly captivating, and a warm sensuality in those chocolate-brown eyes that undressed a woman at a glance.

Or, in Bella's experience, made a woman want to undress for him at a glance!

The man talking oh-so-politely to Claudia still possessed those broodingly magnetic good looks—the livid scar down the left side of his face only added a dangerous edge to that attraction!—but his eyes were no longer that warm and sensual colour of melted chocolate but were instead a flat, unemotional brown, and the lazy charm and self-confidence had been replaced with a cold and arrogant aloofness.

As far as Bella was aware, Gabriel had never married—although, in all honesty, Bella hadn't particularly gone out of her way to learn anything about his life in the five years since they had parted so abruptly.

What would have been the point? The two of them had shared nothing more than a night of unimaginable and unrepeatable passion.

'Would you care for a drink?'

Bella raised startled eyes to Gabriel's, frowning slightly as she saw the glass he held out to her. Champagne. It would have to be champagne, wouldn't it?

'Thank you,' she accepted stiltedly.

Gabriel watched beneath hooded lids as Bella's cheeks warmed with colour as she took the fluted glass from him with a deftness that prevented her fingers from coming into contact with his.

His mouth twisted derisively as he asked, 'Is this your first visit to San Francisco, too, Bella?'

'Yes.'

'You like the city?'

'Very much.'

'Have you done much sightseeing since your arrival?'

'Some, yes.'

Gabriel's gaze narrowed at the economy of her replies. 'Perhaps—'

'Excuse me for interrupting, Gabriel,' his cousin Dahlia, tomorrow's bride, cut in lightly as she joined them, 'but my brother Benito is anxious to become re-acquainted with Claudia,' she added indulgently.

'Really?' The younger of the two Scott sisters glanced across the room to where Benito stood watching her intently.

Bella felt herself begin to tremble as she was over-whelmed with an impending sense of doom. If Claudia left then Bella would be completely alone with—

'You don't mind, do you, Bella?' Claudia's eyes were glowing with excitement. She had confided in Bella earlier today, after being introduced to Benito the previous evening, that she definitely wanted to get to know Dahlia's older brother better.

Obviously the attraction was reciprocated—which didn't help Bella in the least when she had no inclina-tion whatsoever to be left alone with Gabriel Danti!

'I assure you, Claudia, your sister will be perfectly safe with me,' Gabriel replied with dry mockery before Bella had a chance to say anything.

Bella shot him a glance beneath her long lashes. She still had absolutely no idea whether or not Gabriel re-membered her from their night together five years ago—and she didn't want to know, either.

She remembered *him*, and that was bad enough!

But before she could add anything to his reply Claudia gave her arm a grateful squeeze. 'Thanks, Bella,' she whis-pered before moving away to accompany Dahlia over to where the dark and handsome Benito stood waiting.

The sudden silence the two women left in their wake seemed deafening to Bella.

The room was full of people, at least a hundred or so of the guests invited to the wedding tomorrow, all of them chatting or laughing as they either renewed old acquaintances or met new ones. And yet as far as Bella was concerned she and Gabriel could have been alone on an island in the Arctic—the air between them was certainly frigidly cold enough for them to be on one!

'There is a more—private sitting area next to this one in which we might talk,' Gabriel bit out abruptly.

Bella raised apprehensive eyes, knowing that wariness was justified as Gabriel looked down his nose at her with a glacial brown gaze, his mouth—the mouth she had once found so sensually mesmerising!—flattened to a thin, uncompromising line above that cleft chin.

She moistened suddenly dry lips. 'I'm perfectly happy where I am, thank you, Mr Danti.'

His eyes became even more icy as he reached out and curled his fingers compellingly about the top of her arm. 'It was a statement of intent, Bella, not a question,' he assured her grimly as he began to walk towards the exit, Bella firmly anchored to his side, the stiffness of his left leg barely noticeable.

'But—'

'Do you really want to have this conversation here, in front of Dahlia and Brian's other guests?' he asked harshly as he came to a halt halfway across the crowded room to look down at her through narrowed lids.

Bella swallowed hard as she saw the unmistakeably angry glitter in that dark gaze. 'I have absolutely no idea what conversation you're referring to—'

'Oh, I think that you do, Bella,' he retorted menacingly.

Bella thought that she did, too!

She only wished that she didn't. But Gabriel's behaviour since Claudia and Dahlia's departure all
pointed to the fact that he *did* remember her from five
years ago, after all…

CHAPTER TWO

'I REALLY have no idea what the two of us could possibly have to talk about, Mr Danti,' Bella told him stiltedly as he sat perfectly relaxed in the armchair across from hers in the quiet of the otherwise deserted small reception-room just down the hallway from where the family party was being held.

Gabriel's eyes narrowed on the paleness of her face as she sat stiffly upright in her own chair. 'Considering our—past acquaintance, shall we say?—I believe re-fraining from addressing me as "Mr Danti" in that superior tone would be a good way to begin.'

She raised her brows in what she hoped was a querying manner. 'Our past acquaintance…?'

Gabriel's mouth thinned. 'Do not play games with me, Bella!'

She shot him another glance before looking sharply away again. 'I wasn't sure you had remembered we'd met before…'

'Oh, I remember,' he growled.

She swallowed hard before speaking. 'As do I— Gabriel,' she conceded tightly.

He gave a humourless smile. 'You had absolutely no idea I would be here tonight, did you?'

Those eyes flashed deeply purple at his mocking tone. 'Why should I have done? Dahlia's name is Fabrizzi.'

'Her mother, my aunt Teresa, is my father's younger sister,' Gabriel supplied evenly.

Bella's mouth twisted. 'How sweet that you flew all the way from Italy to attend your cousin's wedding!'

Gabriel's mouth thinned at her obvious mockery. 'I no longer live in Italy, Bella.'

She looked startled. 'You don't?'

Gabriel shook his head. 'I spend most of my time at the Danti vineyards about an hour's drive away from here, but I also have a house right here in San Francisco.'

Bella could easily guess exactly where in San Francisco that house was!

She and the rest of her family had gone for a tour of the city earlier today, and part of that tour had been through an area known as Pacific Heights, where the houses were grand and gracious—and worth millions of dollars!

'Do you like living in America?' she asked curiously.

Gabriel shrugged. 'It has its—advantages.'

Bella just bet that it did! She also couldn't help wondering if Gabriel's move to America didn't have something to do with the fact that Janine Childe, the woman Gabriel had once been in love with—perhaps was still in love with?—now lived in California, too…

'Have you now finished with the polite exchange of information?' Gabriel asked.

Bella forced her gaze to remain level on his. 'What do you want from me, Gabriel?'

What did he want from her? That was an interesting

question, Gabriel acknowledged grimly. Until he had arrived at the party earlier, and seen Bella across the room as she chatted with the young woman he now knew to be her sister, Gabriel would have liked to believe he had cast Bella from his mind after that single night together. But having recognised her instantly, he knew he could no longer claim that to be the case...

If anything, Isabella Scott was even more strikingly lovely than she had been five years ago, maturity having added self-assurance to a beauty that had already been breathtaking. Her violet eyes were still as stunning as ever, her hair was still long and the colour of ebony, but styled now in heavy layers so that it swung silkily against her cheeks and her throat, before cascading wildly down the length of her back. And the close fit of her violet gown revealed that her waist was still delicately slender beneath the full thrust of those perfect breasts...

What did he want from her?

He wanted not to have noticed any of those things!

His mouth set in a grim, uncompromising line. 'What do you have to give, Bella?'

Her gaze was searching as she eyed him warily, and Gabriel knew that Bella would see that he, at least, was visibly much changed from their last meeting.

The darkness of his hair was styled several inches shorter than it had once been, but the scar that ran the length of his left cheek—a constant reminder, when Gabriel looked in the mirror to shave each morning, of the guilt he carried inside—was a much more visible reminder of how much he had changed in the last five years.

Was Bella repulsed, as Gabriel was himself, by the livid ugliness of that scar?

'What do I have to give to you, in particular?' Bella repeated incredulously. 'Absolutely nothing!' she scornfully answered her own question.

Gabriel's hand moved instinctively to the jagged wound that marred his cheek. 'That, at least, has not changed,' he rasped coldly.

Bella eyed him frowningly. Why was he looking at her so contemptuously? He was the one who had seduced her only because the woman he had really wanted—the beautiful supermodel, Janine Childe—had told him their relationship was over, and that she was involved with one his fellow Formula One drivers.

That Formula One driver had been Paulo Descari. Killed in the crash that had occurred only hours after Gabriel had left Bella in his bed.

Janine Childe had tearfully claimed at the time that Gabriel had deliberately caused the accident out of jealousy, because of Paulo Descari's relationship with her.

While not convinced Gabriel would have deliberately caused that crash, five years later Bella still cringed whenever she thought that being on the rebound had been Gabriel's only reason for spending the night with her.

So how dared Gabriel now look at her with such contempt?

'I've changed, Gabriel,' she told him pointedly.

'For the better?'

Bella frowned. 'What the—'

'Did you ever marry, Bella?' Gabriel cut icily across her protest, his mouth twisting derisively as his dark gaze moved over the bareness of her left hand. 'I see not. Perhaps that is as well,' he added insultingly.

Bella took an outraged breath. 'Perhaps it's as well

that you have never married either!' She came back in just as cutting a tone.

He gave a humourless smile. 'Perhaps.'

'I don't think the two of us sitting here exchanging insults is in the least harmonious to Brian and Dahlia's wedding tomorrow, do you?' she challenged.

Bella's heart sank every time she thought of attending that wedding.

She had been looking forward for weeks to this trip to San Francisco. But meeting Gabriel again, knowing he was going to be at the wedding tomorrow, too, now made it an ordeal Bella didn't even want to attempt to get through.

But she had no idea how to get out of it, either…

Gabriel watched the emotions as they flickered across Bella's beautiful and expressive face, taking a guess at the reason for her look of trepidation. 'Your parents and brother are here for the wedding also?'

'Yes,' she confirmed quietly.

He gave a ruthless smile. 'And they, like your sister just now, have no idea that the two of us have ever met before.' It was a statement, not a question.

'No,' she sighed.

Gabriel gave a mocking inclination of his head. 'And you would prefer that it remain that way?'

Bella sent him a narrow-eyed glance. 'Yes!'

'They would not understand our having spent the night together five years ago?'

'*I* don't understand it, so why should they!' Bella exclaimed. 'That night was totally out of character for me. Totally,' she added vehemently as she remembered just how eager, how *gullible* she had been.

Gabriel almost felt a hint of sympathy for Bella as he noticed that her hands were trembling slightly as she wrapped her fingers about her fluted glass sitting on the table in front of her. Almost. The fact it was champagne that bubbled inside the glass, the same wine that Gabriel had once dribbled all over this woman's body, before slowly licking it from the sensuous softness of her skin, precluded him feeling in the least sorry for Bella's obvious discomfort with this unexpected encounter.

He shrugged unsympathetically. 'I am sure that we all have things in our past that we wish had not happened.'

Bella wondered briefly if he could possibly be talking about that horrific car crash and Janine Childe's accusations, but then she saw the hard glitter in Gabriel's eyes as he looked at her, and the contemptuous curl of his top lip, and Bella realised he had been referring to her, that she was something he wished had not happened in his life, either.

She swallowed before speaking. 'Then we're both agreed that it would be better for everyone if we both just forgot our—past acquaintance?' She deliberately used his own description of that night five years ago.

The grimness of his smile lacked any genuine humour. 'If only it were that simple, Bella...'

If only.

But it wasn't. Bella, more than anyone, knew that it wasn't.

Much as she hated meeting Gabriel again like this, let alone having to sit through this insulting conversation, she also thanked God that this initial meeting had taken place this evening. It could have been so much more disastrous if it had happened at the wedding tomorrow instead...

She straightened, pushing her wine glass away from her so that she didn't risk knocking it over. 'Let's make it that simple, Gabriel,' she offered. 'We'll both just agree to stay well away from each other for the rest of my stay in San Francisco.' Which was only three more days, thank goodness; her father hadn't been able to take any longer than a week away from his medical practice.

Gabriel's gaze narrowed as he took in the smooth creaminess of Bella's skin as she flicked her hair back over her shoulders. Deliberately drawing attention to the full swell of her breasts above the fitted purple gown? Somehow, going on their previous conversation, Gabriel didn't think so.

'One dance together, Bella, and then perhaps I will consider your suggestion,' he murmured huskily.

Her eyes widened. 'One dance?'

'They have begun dancing at the party now that all of the guests have arrived,' he pointed out dryly, the earlier soft strains of background music having given way to louder dance music.

Bella looked confused. 'You want to *dance* with me?'

'Why not?' Gabriel wanted to know.

Her cheeks were very pale. 'Because—well, because— Can you dance? I mean—'

'You mean considering I am so obviously disadvantaged?' Gabriel rasped harshly, his expression grim as he acknowledged that she had obviously noticed that, as well as the scar on his face, he also favoured his left leg when he walked.

Not that the disability was anywhere near as bad as it had been five years ago. Gabriel had spent several months in a wheelchair after the accident, several more painful months after that learning to walk again. That he now had the scar and a slight limp as the only visible sign of the car crash, even if unsightly, was a miracle.

Bella gave an impatient shake of her head. 'You're about as *disadvantaged* as a stalking tiger!'

'I am pleased that you realise that,' he growled—and had the satisfaction of seeing the heated colour that instantly flooded her cheeks. 'I am definitely able to dance, Bella. As long as the music is slow,' he added challengingly.

Slow…! Bella inwardly groaned. What Gabriel really meant by that was he could dance to the sort of music where a man held the woman closely in his arms… Her mouth firmed. 'I was actually thinking of excusing myself and going to bed—'

'Was that an invitation for me to join you?' he smoothly inserted.

'No, it most certainly was not!' She flushed slightly as she almost screeched her indignation with the suggestion. Definitely an overreaction to that sort of temptation…

He shrugged. 'Then I believe I will return to the party once you have left and ask that Brian introduce me to your parents.'

Bella glared across the table at him. 'You rat! You absolute, unmitigated—'

'I will tolerate the name calling once, Bella.' Gabriel's tone was steely. 'But only once,' he warned coldly. 'It is your choice.' Then his tone softened almost to pleasantness as he relaxed back in his chair to once again look across at her with mocking eyes. 'Consent to one dance with me or I will ask to meet your parents.'

'Why?' she groaned protestingly. 'Why do you even want to dance with me?'

'Curiosity, perhaps…?'

'Curiosity about what?' She voiced her bewilderment.

His gaze roamed over her slowly, from the darkness of her hair, across her face, and then lower, to the swell of her breasts.

Bella could barely breathe as she suffered that slow perusal, rising abruptly to her feet when she could no longer bear the deliberate insult of that gaze. 'One dance, Gabriel,' she said, abruptly giving in. 'After which, I would prefer it if you didn't so much as speak to me again!'

He smiled before rising more leisurely to his feet. 'I will let you know how I feel about that after we have danced together.'

Bella shrugged off the hold Gabriel would have taken of her arm, instead walking several feet away from him as they returned down the hallway to the function room where the party was being held.

She was nevertheless aware of everything about him, from the mocking gleam in those dark eyes, the smile of satisfaction that curved those sculptured lips and that sexy cleft in the centre of his arrogant chin, to the lithe grace of his body as he easily compensated for the injury he had sustained in the crash five years ago.

According to the newspaper reports at the time, Gabriel's injuries had been horrific. Both legs and his pelvis crushed. Burns over much of his torso. Numerous cuts on his body, the worst of them that terrible gash to his left cheek. But as far as Bella was concerned, those scars only added to the air of danger Gabriel had already possessed in such abundance!

'Perfect,' Gabriel murmured with satisfaction when a slow ballad began to play as they entered the crowded function room. The lights had been dimmed and several couples were already dancing in the space that had been cleared in the centre of the room, including Claudia Scott and his cousin Benito. 'A pity there is not a song about a lady in purple,' Gabriel mocked, taking hold of Bella's hand as they stepped onto the dance floor.

'I would prefer it if we danced formally,' she told Gabriel stiffly as he deliberately placed his arms about her waist to draw her against him, her hands crushed against his chest.

'Did no one ever tell you that life is full of disappointments?' he murmured, a hand against her spine continuing to hold her body moulded against his as they began to move slowly in time to the music.

She pulled back slightly, her eyes glittering with anger. 'Oh, yes,' she snapped scathingly. 'Someone taught me that only too well!'

Gabriel raised dark brows. 'Then it will not surprise you to know that I prefer that we continue to dance exactly as we are.'

Bella was past being surprised by anything that happened this evening!

In fact, she was too busy fighting her complete awareness of the hardness of Gabriel's body pressed so close to her own, his cheek resting lightly against her hair, the warmth of his hand against her spine, his other hand enveloping one of her own as he held it against his chest, to be able to concentrate on anything else.

Much as she wished it weren't so, Bella was aware of everything about Gabriel as they danced. His heat.

His smell. The warmth of his breath against her temple. The sensuality of his body against hers as he moved them both to the slow beat of the music.

And Bella was also supremely aware of her own response to all of those things, her breathing soft and uneven, her skin sensitised, her breasts swelling, the nipples hardening, and a deep hot ache pooling between her thighs.

This was torture. Absolute torture.

Nor was her discomfort helped by the fact that Claudia had spotted the two of them dancing so closely together, her encouraging nods and smiles showing Bella that one member of her family, at least, was totally fooled by Gabriel's marked interest in her.

Bella pulled slightly away from him, releasing her hand from his as she deliberately put several inches between them. 'I think we've danced quite long enough, don't you?' she said stiffly, her gaze fixed on the third button of his white evening shirt.

Gabriel's mouth tightened, his gaze becoming glacial as he inwardly acknowledged that he had definitely danced with Isabella Scott 'quite long enough'. Long enough for him to confirm that his body still responded to the voluptuousness of Bella's breasts and the warmth of her thighs pressed against his. Which was all he had wanted to know...

'Perhaps you are right,' he said and immediately stepped away from her in the middle of the dance floor.

Bella looked uncomfortable at his abrupt withdrawal, and she glanced about them self-consciously as several of the other people dancing gave them curious glances. 'You're deliberately trying to embarrass me,' she muttered irritably before she turned and walked off the dance floor, her cheeks warm with colour.

'You expressed a wish that we stop dancing.' Gabriel followed at a more leisurely pace.

'Go away, Gabriel. Just *go away*,' she repeated wearily.

Gabriel looked down at her searchingly, the glitter in those purple eyes no longer looking as if it was caused by anger. 'Are you *crying*, Bella?'

'Of course I'm not crying,' she snapped, her chin once again rising in challenge as she now met his gaze defiantly. 'It would take more than the misfortune of having met you again to make me cry!' she said scathingly. 'Now, if you will excuse me? I really would like to go to my room.'

He raised dark brows. 'You are staying here at the hotel?' It was a possibility that hadn't occurred to him.

Her eyes narrowed. 'And so what if I am?'

'I was just curious, Bella,' he pointed out.

'Are you?' She gave a mocking smile. 'I don't remember you being curious enough five years ago to be interested in anyone but yourself.'

Gabriel's mouth thinned warningly. 'Are you accusing me of having been a selfish lover?' He sounded outraged.

'No, of course not!' Bella's cheeks blazed with colour. 'This is a ridiculous conversation!' she added resentfully. 'It's time I was leaving. I won't say it's been a pleasure meeting you again, Gabriel—because we both know that isn't true!' she added before turning and walking away, her head held high.

Gabriel watched Bella as she crossed the room to make her excuses to his aunt and uncle before leaving, her hair long and gloriously silky down the length of her spine, the movements of her hips provocative beneath the purple gown, her legs appearing slender and shapely above the high heels of her purple sandals.

No, Gabriel agreed, it had certainly not been a pleasure to meet Isabella Scott again.

But it had been something…

Bella forced herself to move slowly, calmly, as she made her excuses to her hosts, Teresa and Pablo Fabrizzi, before leaving the function room to walk down the hallway to the lift, refusing to give Gabriel Danti the satisfaction of seeing her hurrying down that hallway in order to escape being the focus of his intense gaze.

She breathed easier once inside the lift, leaning weakly against one of the mirrored walls as she pressed the button to descend to the sixth floor where her room was situated.

Could anything worse than Gabriel Danti being related to her cousin's fiancée possibly have happened?

Bella couldn't think of anything.

Nor had she yet been able to think of a way to avoid being at the wedding tomorrow. But she would have to come up with something. She had to.

'You're back early,' Angela, Dahlia's younger sister, greeted warmly as Bella let herself into the sitting-room of the suite she was sharing with her siblings.

Bella put her evening bag down on the table just inside the door. 'I have a bit of a headache,' she dismissed.

'That's a pity.' Angela stood up, as tall and lithely beautiful as her older sister.

'I also thought that you've been babysitting long enough this evening and perhaps you might like to go up and join in the party for a while?' Bella added warmly, Angela having very kindly offered to take the half a dozen younger members of the English contingent of the wedding party out to a pizza restaurant for the evening, before bringing them back to the hotel and ensuring they all settled down in bed for the night.

'If you're sure you don't mind?' Angela smiled.

'Not at all,' Bella assured her. 'The dancing has only just started,' she added encouragingly.

'Take something for that headache, hmm?' Angela encouraged lightly before letting herself out of the suite.

Bella heaved a shaky sigh, taking several minutes to calm herself before going into the adjoining bedroom where her young brother lay in bed, the bedside lamp still on as he read a book. 'Everything okay, Liam?' she enquired softly as she paused beside him.

Her twelve-year-old brother grinned up at her. 'Fast asleep, as you can see.'

Bella turned, her expression softening as she looked down at the occupant of the second bed.

Her four-year-old son, Toby.

His curls were dark against the pillow, lashes of the same warm chocolate resting on his baby cheeks, his lips slightly parted as he breathed deeply, an endearing dimple in the centre of his chin.

A dimple that Bella knew would one day become a firm cleft.

Just like the one in his father's chin.

CHAPTER THREE

'YOU do not feel a woman's usual need to cry at weddings?'

Bella's back stiffened at the softly taunting sound of Gabriel's voice directly behind her as she stood with all the other wedding guests outside the church, watching the bride and groom as they posed for numerous photographs.

Hard as Bella had tried to find a reason for Toby and herself not to attend the wedding today, including a headache for herself and possible signs of a fever for Toby, ultimately she had had no choice but to concede defeat when her father had declared them both fit and well. Other than throwing herself down a flight of stairs, Bella knew she had lost that particular battle! The most she had been able to hope for was that Gabriel Danti would heed her advice from last night and just stay away from her.

The fact that he was standing behind her now showed that he hadn't!

Bella had seen him when she and the rest of her family arrived for the wedding an hour or so ago, seated in a pew further down the church. Sitting next to him was a silver-haired man whose height and facial likeness to Gabriel indicated that this was probably his father, the aristocratic Cristo Danti.

Her heart had given a jolt as she watched the two Italians unobserved before glancing down at the small boy fidgeting on the pew beside her, instantly recognising how like his father and grandfather Toby was.

As Claudia had also innocently noted the previous evening when she remarked that Gabriel reminded her of someone…!

Thank goodness Toby had disappeared with his adored uncle Liam once the service was over, and was even now playing beneath an oak tree further down the churchyard, with the group of children who had gone out for pizza the evening before.

A fact Bella took note of before she slowly turned to face Gabriel, her response to how handsome he looked in a tailored dark suit and snowy white shirt hidden behind a deliberately neutral expression as she rather wickedly responded to his comment about women usually crying at weddings. 'I'd only cry in sympathy, I'm afraid!'

Gabriel gave an appreciative smile as his hooded gaze swept admiringly over her in the knee-length dress that fitted smoothly over the curves of her slender body, a silk flower pinned behind her left ear and holding back the long length of her dark hair.

She looked cool and beautiful—and utterly self-contained.

It was an assurance that Gabriel perversely wanted to shatter. 'Perhaps that is because no man has so far asked you to become his bride?' he taunted.

Delicate colour warmed her cheeks at the intended

insult. 'What on earth makes you assume that, Gabriel?' she retorted. 'Maybe I've simply chosen not to marry because I'm only too aware of how fickle a man's interest can be?' she added sweetly.

Gabriel's mouth thinned at her riposte. 'Perhaps you have been—*meeting* the wrong men…?'

'Perhaps I have.' Her gaze was openly challenging now as it met his.

Enjoyable as it was, this constant bickering with Bella would not do, Gabriel recognised ruefully. It was his cousin's wedding day, an entirely inappropriate time for open dissent between two of her guests.

Bella had obviously come to the same conclusion. 'If you'll excuse me, Gabriel? I have to rejoin my family—' She looked up at Gabriel with sharp enquiry as the fingers he had placed about her arm prevented her from leaving.

A nerve pulsed in his jaw as he looked down at her. 'We need to talk, Bella.'

'We talked yesterday evening, Gabriel—for all the good it did either of us!' she exclaimed.

'Exactly,' he agreed. 'We cannot possibly continue this estrangement between us, when our two families are now united—'

Bella's unamused laugh cut him off. 'My cousin is now married to your cousin—that hardly makes our families united!' she pointed out impatiently. 'In fact, I can't think of another occasion when the two of us will ever have to meet again!'

It was what Bella fervently hoped, at least. At the moment she would just think herself lucky if she could get through the rest of today without this whole situation blowing up in her face.

It really was unfortunate that her father happened to be a doctor, and as such perfectly able to dismiss the illnesses Bella had imagined earlier for both herself and Toby. Although, her previously mythical headache was rapidly becoming a reality during this latest conversation with Gabriel!

How could it be otherwise when she still had absolutely no idea how she was going to prevent Toby and Gabriel from coming face to face at some time during the wedding reception? If that should happen Bella had no idea what Gabriel's reaction would be… After his rejection of her, there was no way she was going to risk Toby being rejected, too, and Gabriel's menacing looks did nothing to calm her fears.

She glanced past Gabriel now as she easily recognised the sound of her young son's giggle, knowing the reason for his joyful laughter as she saw that Liam was tickling him.

Toby was a happy child, totally secure in the adoration of his mother and his indulgent grandparents, as well as his doting aunt and uncle. And Bella wished for him to remain that way.

The last three days had shown her how close the members of the Danti family were, how much they valued and loved their children. She literally quailed at the thought of what Gabriel might do if he were to ever realise that Toby was the result of their single night together five years ago, and how much of his young son's life he'd already missed out on…

'I really do have to go, Gabriel.' Her gaze avoided meeting his now as she stepped away from him to release herself from his hold on her arm.

Gabriel watched Bella with frowning intensity as she walked away from him, that frown turning to a scowl as he heard the softness of her laughter as she was surrounded by the group of laughing children, some of them the offspring of his own cousins, the likeness to Bella of the tallest of the group making him easily recognisable as her brother Liam.

How strange it was that the people she had talked of so affectionately five years ago—her parents, her sister Claudia and her brother Liam—should now be a reality to him.

'A friend of yours…?'

Gabriel's smile stayed in place as he turned to face his father, revealing none of his inner concern as he saw the unhealthy grey pallor to the older man's face. 'I doubt Bella would think so,' he answered wryly.

'Bella?' Cristo raised silver brows before he glanced across to where Bella was now walking down the pathway chatting with her brother and another of the children.

'Isabella Scott. I met her yesterday evening at Dahlia's party,' Gabriel enlarged.

Again, he could have added. But didn't, knowing that to do so would only arouse his father's insatiable curiosity.

Cristo was the patriarch of the Danti family, and, at sixty-five and ill in health, he had begun to make definite murmurings about Gabriel marrying and producing children to continue the dynasty that Gabriel's great-grandfather had begun with the vineyards in Italy a hundred years ago, and which each succeeding generation had added to. It was Gabriel's own grandfather who had instigated the planting of the vineyards in America seventy years ago.

Gabriel had taken over the running of the California vineyards four years ago, after his father suffered a minor heart attack. But, at the age of thirty-three, unhappily for his father, Gabriel as yet felt no inclination to marry and produce the heirs necessary to continue that dynasty.

As a consequence, Cristo tended to look at every woman Gabriel so much as spoke to as a possible mother to his grandchildren.

How Bella Scott would have laughed if she had known Cristo had briefly considered her for that role!

Bella began to breathe a little easier once the wedding breakfast and speeches were over, and the guests began to wander through to the adjoining room where the evening's dancing was to begin and the socialising to continue. Giving her an ideal opportunity, she hoped, in which to excuse herself and Toby.

Her luck in keeping Toby well away from Gabriel had held during the reception, with Gabriel and his father seated at a dining-table on the furthest side of the room from where Bella sat with her own family.

Dahlia's family being Italian, there were a lot of children present, and the happy couple had chosen to seat all the children at four tables separate from their parents, both allowing the children the freedom to be themselves, and the parents to eat their meal in peace and enjoy socialising with the other adults. This arrangement had also made it impossible to know which children belonged to which parents.

Or, in Bella's case, which parent...

Taking a quick mental note of Gabriel's presence on the other side of the reception room, Bella made her excuses to her own family before slowly making her way towards the door where Dahlia and Brian stood greeting the last of their evening guests, her intention to collect Toby from where he was running riot with the other children, before making—hopefully!—an unnoticed exit.

'You are leaving so soon, Bella?'

She had counted her chickens far too early, Bella acknowledged with a sinking sensation in the pit of her stomach, looking up to see Gabriel Danti's challenging expression as he blocked her progress to the door. 'I have a headache,' she excused tightly.

He raised a mocking eyebrow. 'Weddings really do not agree with you, do they?'

'It's only the prospect of ever having to attend one of my own that I'm allergic to,' she assured him dryly.

Gabriel gave an appreciative smile. He had watched narrow-eyed as Bella made slow but determined progress down the room as she took her leave of several of the other guests, easily guessing that it was her intention to leave early.

It amused him to challenge that departure. 'I trust my own presence has not added to your—discomfort?'

'Not at all.' Those violet-coloured eyes gazed steadily into his. 'My headache is probably a delayed reaction to jet lag.'

'Of course,' Gabriel drawled. 'My father expressed a wish earlier to be introduced to you,' he added not quite truthfully.

No doubt his father would enjoy the introduction, and would draw his own—erroneous—conclusions about it, but he certainly hadn't asked for it.

'Your father?' Bella looked startled by the suggestion. 'Oh, I don't think so, Gabriel—I mean—what would be the point?' she concluded, obviously flustered.

Gabriel studied her beneath hooded lids. 'Politeness, perhaps?' he suggested blandly. 'He is, after all, now the uncle-in-law of your cousin.'

Bella didn't look convinced by that argument. 'As I told you earlier, it's doubtful that any of us will ever meet up again after today.'

He raised dark brows. 'Not even at the christening of Dahlia and Brian's first child?'

Bella hadn't thought of that! This situation really was getting extremely complicated. So much so that she wasn't sure how much longer Gabriel would remain in ignorance of the fact that she had a small son—or, more crucially, that he had one, too!

Nevertheless, she didn't feel able to make that explanation right now, so... 'That's probably years away,' she dismissed sharply. 'Who knows what any of us will be doing then?'

Personally, Bella was thinking of emigrating to Tasmania!

She tried again. 'I really do have to go, Gabriel—'

'Perhaps, as you obviously do not feel inclined to meet my father this evening, you and your family might like to visit the Danti vineyards tomorrow?'

Bella froze, a frown on her brow as she turned to look up at Gabriel with uncertain eyes. 'Why are you doing this?' she asked.

'I merely asked if you and your family would care to come to the Danti vineyards tomorrow,' he reiterated.

'You didn't "merely ask" anything, Gabriel, and you

know it,' she argued. 'Just as you know that you are the very last man I wish to spend any more time with!' She was trying not to breathe hard, hoping to conceal the worst of her agitation from him.

'The very last man?' he repeated softly, eyes narrowed suspiciously. 'Why is that, Bella? What did I do to merit such a distinction? Or perhaps it is my scars that you now find so repulsive?' he added harshly.

'I'm insulted that you believe me to be so shallow,' Bella snapped to hide the fact that she had made yet another mistake where this man was concerned.

Yet when had she ever done anything else...?

Toby hadn't been a mistake!

Bella had been stunned five years ago, and not a little frightened, when she'd realised she was pregnant. But that shock and fear had quickly given way to the wonder of the new life growing inside her. Her parents' support, as well as that of Claudia and Liam, had also helped. Especially in the early months when Bella had wondered what she was going to do, how she was going to cope, and especially how she would be able to earn a living once she had a small baby to care for.

Again her parents had been wonderful, insisting that Bella remain living at home with them during her pregnancy, and for some time after Toby was born, by which time Bella had been earning enough money to be able to support them both.

Her parents' attitude to her pregnancy was doubly admirable when Bella considered that they had done all of that without her ever telling them, or their insisting, on knowing the name of her baby's father...

But how long would they remain in ignorance of his

identity if Gabriel went ahead with his intention of inviting her family to the Danti vineyards tomorrow?

She looked at Gabriel searchingly, easily noting his similarity to Toby: the darkness of his hair, the same facial structure, those dark eyes, the cleft in his chin. But was Bella only seeing those similarities because she knew of Toby's paternity? Would her parents, her siblings, see them, too?

Claudia had already seen Gabriel's likeness to 'someone', so Bella obviously couldn't risk it!

'Okay, Gabriel, I'll stay long enough for you to introduce me to your father,' she capitulated suddenly, before turning and preceding him across the room to where Cristo Danti sat in conversation with his sister.

Bella hadn't completely answered his question about being put off by his scar, Gabriel noted with a scowl as he closely followed her to make sure she didn't manage to slip away. But there had been no doubting the vehemence of her claim that he was the very last man she wished to spend any more time with.

Interestingly, Gabriel had once felt exactly the same way about Bella...

His father broke off his conversation and stood up at their approach, Gabriel frowning slightly as he noted the increased pallor in his father's face. The long flight from Italy earlier in the week, and attending Dahlia's wedding today, had obviously taken more of a toll on his father's health than was wise.

Gabriel would suggest that the two of them leave, too, once the introductions were over. 'Papa, may I present Isabella Scott? Bella, my father, Cristo Danti.'

Bella's breath caught in her throat as she looked up

into that stern, aristocratic face that was so much like Gabriel's. So much like Toby's, too…

'Mr Danti,' she greeted with a coolness she was far from feeling, only her cheeks echoing her inner warmth as the older man took her hand in his before raising it gallantly to his lips.

'You are well named, Miss Scott,' Cristo Danti murmured appreciatively as he slowly released her hand.

Bella gave an awkward smile. 'Thank you.'

'You are enjoying your stay in San Francisco?'

'Very much, thank you.'

He nodded. 'I have always liked San Francisco.'

'It's certainly an interesting city,' Bella came back non-committally, very aware of Gabriel's broodingly silent presence beside her.

No doubt he was enjoying her discomfort in this stilted conversation with his father. Just as he had enjoyed being able to force this introduction on her in the first place by the veiled threat of inviting her family to the Danti vineyards when she so obviously didn't want his company at all.

'It was a beautiful wedding,' Cristo Danti continued lightly.

'Bella does not enjoy weddings.' Gabriel spoke for the first time. Dryly. Dark brows raised mockingly as Bella shot him a frowning glance.

Bella gave him another quelling glance before answering the older man. 'Dahlia is a lovely bride.'

'Yes, she is.' Cristo Danti's expression was slightly quizzical now as he glanced at his son and then back to Bella. 'Are you remaining in San Francisco long, Miss Scott?'

'Just another couple of days. And please call me Bella,' she invited.

The older man nodded. 'Perhaps before you leave you might care to—'

'Mummy, Nanny and Grandad said we're leaving now!' Toby complained irritably as he suddenly appeared at her side, the excitement of the last week, and his late night yesterday evening, obviously making him tired and slightly querulous.

Bella froze at the first sound of her son's voice, like a nocturnal animal caught in the headlights of an oncoming car.

This couldn't be happening! Not here. Not now!

Bella couldn't breathe. She couldn't move. Couldn't speak.

This was worse than anything she could ever have imagined. Worse than any of the nightmares that had plagued her dreams since she had met Gabriel again yesterday evening.

'Mummy?' Gabriel echoed beside her with soft incredulity.

Bella forced herself to move as she slowly turned to look at him, the colour draining from her cheeks as she saw the way he was staring down so intently at Toby.

But it was Cristo Danti, the man standing at Bella's other side, who broke their frozen tableau as, his breath rasping in his throat, he slowly, but graciously, began to collapse, his eyes remaining wide and disbelieving on Toby as he did so.

As he stared at the little boy who was unmistakeably his grandson…

CHAPTER FOUR

'DO NOT speak! Not one word!' Gabriel warned harshly as he paced the hallway where he and Bella waited to hear news of his father.

Gabriel had managed to halt his father's collapse before he hit the floor. Bella had reminded Gabriel that her father was a doctor before rushing off to get him as Gabriel helped Cristo from the room with as little fuss as was possible in the circumstances.

Even so several concerned wedding guests, including the bride and groom, had followed them to hover outside the doorway of the small unoccupied room Gabriel had found to take his father to further down the hallway.

Henry Scott, Bella's father, had dealt firmly with those onlookers when he joined them a couple of minutes later, by ordering those guests back to the wedding reception and Gabriel and Bella out into the hallway while he examined his patient.

At last giving Gabriel the opportunity to deal with, to think of, the reason for his father's collapse!

That small boy—Bella's son—

His son, too…?

Bella flinched as Gabriel stopped his pacing to look down at her with dark, accusing eyes, knowing it would do no good now to deny what had been so patently obvious to Cristo Danti that he had collapsed from the shock of suddenly being confronted by his grandson.

She drew in a ragged breath. 'His name is Toby. Tobias,' she enlarged shakily. 'He's four years old.'

Gabriel's hands clenched into fists at his side. 'Four years and four months to be exact!'

Bella swallowed hard. 'Yes.'

Those dark eyes glittered menacingly. 'Where is he now?'

Bella straightened defensively. 'I took him back to sit with my mother and Liam. I— It frightened him when your father collapsed in that way.'

Gabriel looked at her coldly. 'Shock is apt to do that to a man who has already suffered three minor heart attacks in the last four years!'

Bella hadn't known that about Cristo Danti. Not that it would have made a lot of difference if she had known. Neither Gabriel nor his father were part of her own or Toby's lives.

At least, they hadn't been until now…

Gabriel, she had no doubt, wanted—no, he would demand—some answers from her concerning that. Just as the look on her own father's face, as he had looked first at Cristo Danti and then Gabriel, had told Bella he would no doubt like some answers, too, once he had finished examining his patient!

She gave a shaky sigh. 'I don't think this is the time or place to discuss this, Gabriel—'

'The time and place to discuss this would have been

almost five years ago when you first discovered you were pregnant!'

'As I recall you were no longer around to talk to almost five years ago!'

His mouth tightened. 'It was well publicised that I was in Italy at the time, at the Danti vineyards, recovering from the injuries I sustained in the car crash!'

Bella's eyes flashed deeply purple. 'And you seriously think that I was going to follow you there and tell you the news!'

'You had no right to keep my son's existence from me!' A nerve pulsed in Gabriel's tightly clenched jaw.

She shook her head. 'You gave up any right you had to know about Toby by the fact that you never phoned me as you promised and only slept with me that night out of jealousy and spite because of your ex-girlfriend's relationship with Paulo Descari!'

Gabriel's face darkened dangerously. 'I—'

'Could the two of you please save your—*discussion*—until later?' Henry Scott had opened the door of the room where Gabriel could see his father lying back on one of the sofas. 'I think your father has merely suffered a severe shock rather than another heart attack, Mr Danti, but to be on the safe side I would like to get him to a hospital for a check-up.'

'Daddy…?' Bella looked across at her father uncertainly.

He gave her a reassuring smile. 'It's okay, Bella,' he said gently. 'For the moment let's just concentrate on getting Mr Danti to hospital, hmm?'

Bella didn't need to be told any plainer that her father had guessed Toby's relationship to the two Danti men.

What must her father think of her?

More to the point, what must he think of the fact that Gabriel Danti, of all men, was unmistakeably the father of his grandson?

'I would like to see my son.'

Bella had remained behind at the hotel to put Toby to bed when Gabriel and her father had accompanied Cristo Danti to the hospital. But she hadn't made any attempt to go to bed herself. Had known—had been absolutely certain, in fact—that Gabriel would return once he had assured himself of his father's recovery.

It was almost two o'clock in the morning, but nevertheless Bella had been expecting the knock on the door of the sitting-room between the bedroom she shared with Claudia and the one Liam shared with Toby. She had changed out of the dress she had worn to the wedding, and into fitted jeans and a black T-shirt, in anticipation of this meeting.

Gabriel looked grim, to say the least, that scar down his left cheek more noticeable in his harshly set features, his eyes fierce as he looked down at her challengingly.

Bella opened the door wider so that Gabriel could step inside the suite. 'Toby is asleep,' she told him calmly as she closed the door behind him before turning to face him.

That scar on Gabriel's cheek seemed to pulse as he clenched his jaw tightly. 'Nevertheless, I wish to see him.'

'How is your father?'

'Tests have shown your father's original diagnosis to be the correct one. It was shock that caused my father's collapse and not a heart attack. He is to remain in hospital overnight for observation, but they expect to discharge him in the morning. Isabella—'

'Did my father return with you from the hospital?' Bella had already had one long, uncomfortable conversation with her mother this evening, she wasn't sure she would be up to another one with her father once Gabriel had left.

Gabriel gave a terse nod. 'He told me to tell you he will speak with you in the morning.'

Her eyes widened. 'He knew you were coming here?' Even as she asked the question Bella knew the answer; how else would Gabriel have known which suite to come to in order to see her if her father hadn't told him?

Gabriel's mouth thinned. 'He realised I would want to see my son again before I left, yes.'

Bella flinched every time he said that. No matter what his biological make-up might be, Toby was her son, not Gabriel's.

She gave a firm shake of her head. 'I don't think that's a good idea—'

Gabriel's scornful laugh cut across her refusal. 'Any concern I might have felt for your wishes died the moment I discovered you had kept my son's existence from me for over four years!' He made no effort to hide his contempt.

He had a son!

Gabriel still found it incredible that such a person existed. That there was a small, tousle-haired boy in the adjoining bedroom with his dark curls and eyes, and a small dimple in the centre of his still-babyish chin…

Having been denied all knowledge of him for over four years, Gabriel had no intention of letting that continue a minute—even a second—longer!

'Where is he, Isabella?' he rasped furiously, her panicked glance towards the door to the right of the room enough for Gabriel to stride towards it determinedly.

'Where are you going?'

Gabriel ignored Bella's protest as he gently pushed that door open, recognising the sleeping boy in the first bed as Liam Scott before he turned his attention to the much smaller child in the second bed.

His breath caught in his throat as he looked down at the little boy he now knew to be his own son. Toby. Tobias.

He was beautiful, Gabriel acknowledged achingly. Absolutely beautiful. A perfect combination of his two parents.

Toby had Gabriel's hair colour and that dimple on his chin that would one day become a cleft exactly like those of his father and grandfather. The smoothness of Toby's brow and the long lashes that swept his cheeks were his mother's, as was that perfect bow of a mouth with its fuller top lip.

His!

This beautiful child was of his loins. Of his blood.

Bella could only stand helplessly by as Gabriel dropped to his knees beside Toby's bed, her protest strangling in her throat as Gabriel reached out a hand to touch the little boy, the stroke of his fingers against one slightly chubby cheek so gentle, so tender, that Toby didn't even stir.

Her heart felt as if it were breaking, shattering, as she watched the rush of love that softened Gabriel's harshly hewn features. As she saw that love glowing in his broodingly dark gaze as he continued to stare at his son in wonder.

And she knew without a doubt that the last four years of sharing Toby only with her family were over...

'I need a drink,' Gabriel stated flatly some time later when he had reluctantly left his son's bedside to return to the sitting-room, not waiting for Bella's reply but moving to the mini-bar to help himself to one of the small bottles of whisky before pouring it into a glass and drinking most of it in one swallow. 'So, Isabella,' he stated as he looked across at her grimly. 'What do you suggest we do about this situation?'

'What situation?' she repeated sharply, her stance wholly defensive as she stood across the room.

Gabriel looked at her through narrowed lids. He had made love with this woman a little over five years ago. That lovemaking had resulted in a child. A child whose existence she had deliberately kept from him. For that alone Isabella deserved no mercy from him.

His mouth thinned. 'The situation that Toby, despite what you may have decided to the contrary, deserves to know both of his parents rather than just one!'

Her throat moved convulsively, but otherwise she maintained her defensive stance. 'As I have already explained—'

'As far as you are concerned, I gave up the right to know my own child because *you* believe I only went to bed with you out of jealousy and spite over my ex-girlfriend's relationship with Paulo Descari,' Gabriel coldly repeated her earlier accusation. 'Neither jealousy nor spite were part of my emotions that night, Isabella,' he added curtly. 'And I certainly wasn't feeling those emotions at the time of the accident the following day either,' he bit out deliberately.

Bella moistened lips that had gone suddenly dry as she sensed the leashed violence in him. 'I didn't suggest they were, Gabriel. You did.'

He gave a scathing snort. 'It is impossible not to do so considering Janine's claims following the accident,' Gabriel snarled. 'The official enquiry proved my innocence in the matter. But perhaps you would prefer to believe that I am responsible for the accident that caused the death of two other men, rather than take my word for what happened that day?'

Bella felt the colour drain from her cheeks even as she stared at Gabriel. No, of course she didn't prefer to believe that Gabriel had deliberately caused the accident that had killed two other men. She didn't believe it!

Gabriel might be guilty of many things, but Bella certainly hadn't ever believed him to be guilty of that.

Gabriel looked at her coldly. 'I did *not* cause the accident, Isabella,' he repeated firmly. 'That was only the hysterical accusation of a woman who took advantage of the fact that I was unconscious for several days following the crash, and so was unable to deny those accusations.'

And that accusation hadn't been the reason Bella had made no effort to contact Gabriel following the car crash, either…

How could she possibly have just arrived at the hospital and asked to be allowed to see Gabriel when they had only spent a single night together?

If Gabriel wanted to see her again, Bella had reasoned, then he would contact her just as he'd said he would. Until he chose to do that—if he chose to do that!—she would just have to get on with her life as best she could.

Her pregnancy had been something Bella simply hadn't taken into account when she had made that decision.

Weeks later, after her pregnancy was confirmed, Bella had been forced to make choices, both for herself and her baby. Gabriel's failure to phone had simply reinforced Bella's suspicion that he would want nothing to do with them. Or if he did, he had the power to take her baby away from her. Something Bella would never allow to happen. It was too late now, far too late, for her to explain or undo any of those choices...

Gabriel watched the emotions that flickered across Bella's beautiful and expressive face, too fleeting for him to be able to discern any of them accurately. 'I did not cause the accident, Isabella, but that does not mean I have not carried the guilt of Paulo and Jason's deaths with me every day since.'

'But why?' She looked totally confused now.

Gabriel turned away to look out of the window at the San Francisco skyline.

How could he ever explain to her how he had felt five years ago when he'd regained consciousness and learnt of Paulo Descari and Jason Miller's deaths? Of Janine's hysterical accusations?

Added to that, Gabriel had felt utter despair, even helplessness, at the seriousness of his own injuries.

The cuts and burns to his body that were still visible, five years later, in the scar on his face and those that laced across his chest, back, and legs. The crushing of his pelvis and legs had kept him confined to bed for months, with the added possibility that he might never walk again.

Worst of all, worse even than Paulo and Jason's

deaths, Janine's duplicity, had been the knowledge that their night together had meant so little to Bella that—

No!

Gabriel refused to go there. He had not thought of Bella's desertion for almost five years. He would not— could not—think of it now.

Now he would think only of Toby. Of his *son*. And Bella's second betrayal…

He turned back to face Bella, his expression utterly implacable. 'Toby is all that is important now,' Gabriel told her icily. 'I will return at ten o'clock tomorrow— or rather, today,' he corrected, 'at which time you and Toby will be ready to accompany me—'

'I'm not going anywhere with you, Gabriel, and neither is Toby,' Bella cut in immediately.

'At which time,' he repeated in, if possible, even icier tones, 'you and Toby will be ready to accompany me on a visit to my father. Toby's grandfather,' he added harshly.

Bella's second denial died unspoken on her lips.

She had talked with her mother earlier tonight. Or rather, her mother had talked with her. A conversation in which her mother had assured Bella that the relationship between herself and Gabriel was their own affair, and for the two of them alone to unravel. However, speaking as a grandmother, she had added, she had nothing but sympathy for Cristo Danti and the fact that he had only learnt this evening of his grandson's existence. That knowledge had been obviously so emotionally profound it had resulted in the older man's collapse.

An irrefutable fact against which Bella had no defence. Either earlier or now.

Her shoulders were stiff with tension. 'Firstly, let

me tell you that I deeply resent your use of emotional blackmail in order to get me to do what you want—'

'Would you rather I pursued a legal claim, instead?' Gabriel challenged contemptuously.

Bella swallowed hard even as she refused to lower her gaze from his. 'That would take months, by which time I would be safely back in England.'

'I will have my lawyers apply for an immediate injunction to prevent you, or Toby, from leaving this country,' Gabriel warned scathingly. 'I am a Danti, Isabella,' he reminded her.

Her eyes flashed darkly purple at his underlying threat. 'Secondly,' she pointedly resumed her earlier conversation, 'despite the fact that I resent your methods, I am nevertheless perfectly aware of your father's claim as Toby's grandfather—'

'But not my own as his father!' Gabriel was so furiously angry now that there was a white line about the firmness of his mouth and his body was rigid with suppressed emotion.

Bella looked at him sadly, knowing this conversation was achieving nothing except to drive a distance between the two of them that was even wider than the gaping chasm that already existed.

She had known when she met Gabriel again yesterday that he wasn't the same man she had been so attracted to five years ago that she had forgotten, or simply put aside, every vestige of caution in order to spend the night in his arms.

This Gabriel was scarred on the inside as well as the outside and the coldness of his anger concerning her having kept Toby's existence a secret from him was worse than any emotional accusations might have been.

She sighed. 'Ten o'clock, I believe you said?'

Gabriel's eyes narrowed on her, searching for any sign of deception in her eyes or expression. He could see none. Only a weary acceptance of a situation she could do nothing to change.

The tension in his shoulders relaxed slightly. 'We will sit down together with Toby first and explain my own and my father's relationship to him.'

'Isn't that a little premature?' Bella protested.

'In my opinion it is almost four and a half years too late!' Gabriel snapped.

'It will only confuse Toby when you have no active role in his life—'

His scornful laugh cut off her protest. 'Do you *seriously* believe that is going to continue?'

Bella looked at him, knowing by the implacability in Gabriel's expression as he looked down the length of his arrogant nose at her—the same implacability in his tone whenever he now referred to her as *Isabella*—that it wasn't. That it was Gabriel's intention to take an extremely active role in Toby's life in future.

Precisely where that left her, Bella had no idea…

CHAPTER FIVE

'DOES Grandad live in one of these big houses?'

'He certainly does, Toby,' Gabriel answered him indulgently.

Bella would never cease to be amazed by the resilience of children and by her own child's in particular.

Having lain awake long into the night dreading, planning, how best to break the news to Toby that Gabriel Danti was his father and Cristo Danti was his grandfather, she had been totally surprised by Toby taking the whole thing in his four-year-old stride.

Even his initial shyness at suddenly being presented with a father had quickly given way to excitement as he was strapped into the back of Gabriel's open-topped sports car to make the drive over to the house where his grandfather was anxiously waiting to meet him after being discharged from the hospital earlier this morning.

Bella's own emotions were far less simplistic as she stared out of the car window, seeing none of the beauty of the Pacific Ocean in the distance, her thoughts all inwards.

Her life, and consequently Toby's, was back in England. In the small village where she had bought a cottage for the two of them to live in, once she had been financially able to do so, after living with her parents for the first two years of Toby's life. She liked living in a village, as did Toby, and he was due to start attending the local school in September.

This situation with Gabriel, his veiled threats of the night before, made Bella wonder exactly when she could expect to return to that life.

Not that she was able to read any of Gabriel's thoughts or feelings this morning. He was wearing sunglasses now, and his mood when he had arrived at the hotel earlier had been necessarily upbeat for Toby's benefit, his attitude towards Bella one of strained politeness. Only the coldness in Gabriel's eyes earlier, whenever he had chanced to look at her, had told Bella of the anger he still felt towards her.

The anger he would probably always feel towards her for denying him knowledge of his son for the first four years of Toby's life…

'Here we are, Toby,' Gabriel turned to tell his son after steering the car into the driveway, smiling as he saw the excitement on his son's face as they waited for the electrically operated gates to open so that he could drive them down to the house.

His son…!

Even twelve hours later Gabriel still had trouble believing he had a son. A bright, happy, and unaffected little boy who had taken the news of Gabriel being his father much more pragmatically than Gabriel had responded the evening before to learning that he had a son.

Gabriel glanced at Bella now from behind his dark sunglasses, his mouth thinning as he noted the pallor to her cheeks, the lines of strain beside her eyes and mouth.

Deservedly so!

Whatever claims Janine Childe had made against him five years ago did not change the fact that Bella hadn't so much as attempted to inform him she was expecting his child, that she had actually borne him a son, or that she had then brought Toby up with no knowledge whatsoever of his father or his father's family.

'Your own family are all aware now of Toby's paternity?'

Bella was glad she was wearing sunglasses to hide the sudden tears that had welled up in her eyes at the emotional breakfast she had shared earlier with her parents and siblings.

There had been no words of rebuke or disapproval from her parents, only their gentle understanding as she explained the situation of five years ago to them—and Claudia's demand, as the two sisters had returned to their hotel suite once the meal was over, that Bella 'tell all' about the night she had spent in Gabriel's bed. A curiosity Bella had chosen not to satisfy.

She didn't even want to think about that night, let alone relive, even verbally, how completely she had been infatuated with the darkly seductive Gabriel Danti five years ago!

'Yes,' she confirmed huskily.

Gabriel nodded in satisfaction as he accelerated the black sports car down the driveway to the house that was just as grand as Bella would have expected of this prestigious area of San Francisco. It was large and gabled, slightly Victorian in style, with its redbrick structure and the white frames to the stained-glass windows.

'You're sure this...visit...isn't going to give your

father a relapse?' Bella hung back reluctantly on the gravelled driveway once they were all out of the car.

Gabriel had removed his sunglasses and left them in the car, his expression mocking as he glanced down at her. 'On the contrary, I believe its possibilities will achieve the opposite.'

Bella looked up at him, a little confused by the cryptic comment. 'Sorry?'

His mouth tightened. 'Later, Isabella,' he said curtly. 'You and I are going to talk again later.'

Bella didn't much like the sound of that.

And she was really starting to dislike the way Gabriel kept calling her *Isabella* in that coldly contemptuous way!

Once Gabriel had left the previous night Bella had thought long and hard about his claim that he hadn't made love with her five years ago, or spent the night with her, in an effort to make Janine Childe jealous. After hours and hours of going over the situation in her head, Bella had finally come to the conclusion that it really didn't matter what Gabriel's reasons had been.

They had spent only that single night together. Admittedly it had been an intensely passionate, even erotic night, but nevertheless that was all it had been. On Gabriel's side, anyway. That Bella had experienced strong feelings for him after that night didn't change the fact that Gabriel hadn't felt that way about her.

As the last five years of silence on Gabriel's part showed...

He had never made any attempt to contact her again after that night although that had been his promise. Admittedly Gabriel had been involved in the car crash later that day, but he hadn't suffered memory loss. Once he had recovered enough to be able to talk, to receive visitors, that needn't have stopped him from getting in touch. Not too much to ask if Gabriel really had been interested in seeing her again. Which he obviously hadn't... That was not the kind of man she wanted as a father for her child!

She shook her head. 'I don't think we have anything left to talk about, Gabriel,' she told him firmly.

Gabriel gave a brief, humourless smile. 'We have not even begun to talk yet, Isabella!'

His father was waiting for them in the warmth of the plant-filled conservatory at the back of the house, Gabriel appreciating that the informality of such surroundings was exactly what was needed to put a four-year-old boy at his ease.

That his father found the meeting highly emotional Gabriel had no doubts, Cristo's voice husky with suppressed tears as Toby joined him and he allowed the little boy to water the orchids for him.

'I am neglecting your mother, Toby,' Cristo apologised some minutes later as he straightened. 'You may continue to water if you wish, Toby, or you may come and sit with us while your mother and I talk.'

Bella knew exactly which choice her young son would make; like most small boys, Toby had absolutely no interest in the conversation of adults!

'Bella.' Cristo Danti's voice was deep with emotion as he crossed the room to where she had sat in one of the half a dozen cane chairs watching him and Toby together. He took her hand in his to raise it to his lips as she stood up. 'Thank you for bringing Toby to see me,' he told her, his eyes slightly moist as he looked at her.

Bella felt her own tears clogging her throat as she looked at Gabriel's father, not able to discern any reproach in the directness of that brown gaze, only the slight sheen of the tears that he made no effort to hide from her.

Bella was very aware of the menacingly silent Gabriel standing beside her. 'I—' she moistened her lips nervously '—I really don't know what to say,' she stuttered, aware that statement was painfully inadequate and yet totally true.

'Gabriel has already explained all that needs to be explained.' Cristo Danti smiled at her reassuringly. 'All that really matters is that you and Toby are here now.'

Bella, besides feeling the heavy weight of guilt at Cristo Danti's complete acceptance of a situation that yesterday evening had caused his collapse, also wondered exactly what Gabriel had explained...

'You're very kind,' she told the older man as she squeezed his hand before releasing it.

'Obviously Isabella and I have much to talk about yet, Papa,' Gabriel spoke abruptly beside her. 'If you and Toby will excuse us for a few minutes...?'

Bella felt a sense of rising panic at the suggestion, not sure she was up to another confrontation with Gabriel at the moment. She hadn't slept much during what had been left of the previous night, and the morning had already been traumatic enough with the conversation with her family, followed by Gabriel's arrival at the hotel and their explanation to Toby, and now this meeting with Cristo Danti.

But a single glance at the grim determination of Gabriel's set expression was enough to tell Bella that she didn't have any choice in the matter!

'Toby…?' she prompted lightly to gain her young son's attention from watering the plants. 'Will you be okay while I just go and have a little chat with—with—your father?' That didn't get any easier with actually saying out loud!

'Of course.' Toby beamed across at her unconcernedly.

Bella wished at that moment that her young son weren't quite so gregarious; obviously she wasn't going to get any help at all from Toby in avoiding another confrontation with Gabriel.

To Toby, Bella knew, this was obviously all just a big adventure; he had absolutely no idea of the underlying tensions—or the possible repercussions!—of Gabriel Danti being his father and Cristo Danti being his grandfather.

Bella wanted to make sure it remained that way…

'I am sure Toby and I will be able to keep each other amused, Bella,' Cristo assured her.

She gave him a grateful smile, that smile fading as Gabriel stood back politely to allow her to precede him into the main house. Polite, even coldly polite, Bella could deal with—she just didn't think that politeness was going to last for very long once she and Gabriel were alone together!

'He'll probably drown your poor father's orchids for him,' Bella murmured ruefully as Gabriel moved ahead to open a door further down the hallway.

Gabriel glanced back at her, his gaze hooded. 'I doubt my father will mind, do you?' he said pointedly as he pushed open the door to the room before standing back to allow her to enter.

It was a book-lined room, Bella noted with dismay,

much like the study in the Danti's English home in Surrey where she and Gabriel had first met.

Gabriel was also aware of the irony of their surroundings as he quietly closed the door behind them before moving to sit behind the green leather-topped desk, his gaze narrowed on Bella as she chose not to sit in the chair facing that desk—and him!—but instead moved to look out of the huge picture-window, her back firmly turned towards him.

She had pulled her hair back today and secured it up in a loose knot at her crown, her exposed neck appearing fragile in its slenderness, her shoulders narrow beneath the soft material of the cream blouse she wore with black fitted trousers.

She appeared slight, even delicate, but Gabriel knew that appearance to be deceptive—Isabella Scott was more than capable of defending both herself and Toby if the need should arise. In Toby's case, as far as Gabriel was concerned, it didn't. Bella herself was a different matter, however...

His mouth firmed in exasperation. 'Ignoring me will not make me go away, Isabella!'

She turned, her smile rueful. 'If only!'

Gabriel regarded her coldly. 'You have had things completely your own way for the last five years—'

'What *things*?' she came back tartly, her body tense. 'I was twenty-one years old at the time, Gabriel. Only twenty-one!' she emphasised. 'Having a baby wasn't in my immediate plans back then, let alone one whose father wasn't even living in the same country as me when that baby was born!'

'It does no good to get angry, Isabella—'

'It does *me* good, Gabriel!' she contradicted him vehemently. 'You have made it clear you disapprove of my actions five years ago, so I'm just trying to explain to you that I did what I thought was best—'

'For whom?' Gabriel sat back in his chair to look at her intently.

'For everyone!'

Gabriel's jaw clenched. 'In what way was it *best* for Toby that he was not even aware of his father or his father's family? In what way was it *best* for him that he did not have the comforts that being a Danti could have given him—?'

'Toby hasn't gone without a single thing—'

'He has gone without a *father*!' Gabriel's voice was icy cold, his accusation indisputable.

Bella drew in a controlling breath, very aware that letting this conversation dissolve into another slanging match would settle none of the things that stood between herself and Gabriel. The main one, of course, being Toby…

She shook her head. 'I assure you that my own parents have been wonderful,' she told him huskily. 'Claudia and Liam, too. And once I was able to work I made sure that Toby wanted for nothing.'

'At what did you work?' Gabriel asked.

Bella gave a grimace. 'I was completely at a loss as to what job I could do once I discovered I was pregnant. But I had written my thesis at university on the life of Leonardo da Vinci. My tutor thought it might be good enough for publishing, so during the months of my pregnancy I approached a publishing company to see if they were interested. With a lot more hard work, and another fifty thousand words, they accepted it. I was fortunate in that its publication coincided with a fiction book on a similar theme that was very popular at the time.' She gave a rueful shrug. 'I've had two books at the top of the non-fiction bestseller list in the last three years,' she added quietly.

Gabriel realised now where Bella's self-assurance and that air of quiet self-containment came from. In spite of her unexpected pregnancy, and the difficulty involved with being a single mother, Bella had still managed to achieve success in her chosen career.

'That is—commendable.'

Bella gave a tight smile. 'But unexpected?'

Gabriel couldn't deny that Bella's obvious financial independence was something he hadn't taken into consideration when contemplating a solution to their present problem.

Although perhaps he should have done?

Her suite at the hotel would have been costly, and Bella's clothes were obviously designer-label, as were the T-shirt and shorts Toby was wearing today.

'Perhaps,' he allowed after a pause. 'But ultimately it changes nothing,' he pointed out.

Bella gave a puzzled frown. 'I'm sorry…I don't understand?'

'Toby is *my* son—'

'I believe I've already acknowledged that fact,' she snapped.

Gabriel eyed her mockingly. 'Undeniable, is it not?' he murmured with satisfaction, Toby's likeness to both himself and his father so obvious it had caused his father to collapse with the shock of it. Gabriel's mouth tightened.

'The only solution open to us is that we will be married as soon as I am able to make the arrangements—'

'No!' Bella protested forcefully, her expression one of horror. 'No, Gabriel,' she repeated determinedly, her chin once again raised in the familiar air of challenge. 'I have no intention of marrying you, either now or in the future.'

Bella was absolutely astounded that Gabriel should have suggested marriage to her. Suggested it? Gabriel hadn't *suggested* anything—he had stated it as a foregone conclusion!

Five years ago Bella had considered all of the options, despite the complication of Gabriel's feelings for Janine Childe, if she were to go to Gabriel and tell him of her pregnancy.

The offer of his financial help was obviously one of them, and Bella had rejected that on principle; no matter how hard a struggle it might be for her to manage on her own, she did not want to be beholden to Gabriel Danti in that way.

That he might want to marry her, for the sake of the baby, had been a less likely option considering they had only had a one-night stand, and one that Bella had rejected even more vehemently than she had the idea of Gabriel's financial help.

She didn't want to marry anyone just because they had made a child together.

'Do you not want to marry me because you lied when you said you are not repulsed by my scars?' Gabriel rasped harshly, his eyes narrowed to dangerous slits, a nerve pulsing in his tightly clenched jaw.

Bella shook her head. 'I'm not in the least repulsed by them,' she insisted quietly.

His gaze was glacial. 'Most women would be.'

'Well I'm not "most women",' Bella said, furiously. 'Gabriel, acknowledge Toby as your son, by all means, but please leave me out of the equation,' she pleaded.

Gabriel's mouth twisted. 'That might be a little difficult when you are Toby's mother.'

She shook her head. 'I'm sure we can work out some sort of visiting—' She broke off as Gabriel stood up abruptly.

'Is that what you want for Toby?' he asked harshly, the scar on his cheek seeming to stand out more severely. 'You want him to become nothing more than a human parcel that passes between the two of us?'

'It doesn't have to be like that,' she protested emotionally.

'If the two of us do not marry that is exactly what it will be like,' Gabriel insisted impatiently.

Bella swallowed hard, her expression pained. 'You think Toby will fare any better as the only lynchpin between two people who don't love each other but are married to each other?'

'You have said you do not find my more obvious scars—unacceptable.' Gabriel moved close enough now to see the slight flush that slowly crept into her cheeks, and the rapid rise and fall of her breasts beneath the cream blouse.

'I don't.' She frowned. 'But that doesn't mean I like the idea of marrying you!'

Bella couldn't think straight when Gabriel was standing so close to her. Couldn't concentrate on anything with the heat of his dark gaze moving slowly over her body to linger on the firm thrust of her breasts,

breasts that responded in tingling awareness, the nipples suddenly hard against the soft material of her bra and blouse. A warm, aching surge between her thighs made her shift uncomfortably.

She moistened lips that had gone suddenly dry. 'Physical attraction is not a basis for marriage, either.' Even as she said the words Bella was aware that her denial lacked any force.

'Surely you will agree it is a start?' Gabriel murmured huskily, a look of deep satisfaction in his eyes.

She could barely breathe as Gabriel easily held her gaze with his, allowing her to see the warmth burning deep within those dark brown eyes. Then he stepped close enough for her to be aware of the hard press of his arousal against her and his head lowered with the obvious intention of claiming her mouth with his own...

It was like a dam bursting as their mouths fused hotly together. Bella's fingers became entangled in the dark thickness of Gabriel's hair as their bodies pressed demandingly against each other. Their kiss deepened fiercely, spiralling out of control when Gabriel's tongue moved to duel with hers as he enticed her to claim him as he was claiming her.

Bella was so hungry for this. The aching emptiness inside her was completely filled when Gabriel pushed the soft material of her blouse aside to cup and hold her breast, the soft pad of his thumb moving urgently, arousingly, over the hardened nub.

Bella almost ripped Gabriel's shirt undone as she satisfied her own need to touch his naked flesh. The hard ripple of muscle. The dark silkiness of the hair that covered his chest. Fingers tracing the fine lines of the scars he still bore from his accident five years ago, Gabriel responding to those caresses with a low groan in his throat.

She offered no resistance as Gabriel snapped the back fastening to her bra to release her breasts to his questing hands, her throat arching, breath gasping as Gabriel's lips parted from hers to draw one hardened nipple into the hot, moist cavern of his mouth, and his tongue flickered and rasped over that sensitive nub as his hand cupped and caressed her other breast.

The ache between Bella's thighs became hot and damp, an aching void needing to be filled as she felt the hardness of Gabriel's arousal, rubbing herself against him as the hardness of his thighs pulsed with the same need. She offered no resistance when Gabriel's hands moved to cup her bottom and he lifted her so that she was sitting on the front of the desk, parting her legs so that he could move inside them, his hardness now centred on the throbbing nub that nestled there.

Bella groaned with satisfaction as Gabriel lay her back on the desktop so that he could suckle the nakedness of her breasts with the same heated rhythm as his erection thrust against the hardened nub between her thighs. Bella's breathing became shallow, a husky rasp, as her release began to burn, to explode, taking her over the edge of reason—

A soft knock on the study door sounded before Cristo Danti informed them, 'Toby and I will be outside in the garden when you have finished talking.'

Gabriel had moved sharply away from Bella the moment the knock sounded on the door, his mouth tightening now as he saw Bella's horrified expression before she pushed up from the desk and moved away from him to turn her back and rearrange her clothes. 'Isabella and I will join you shortly,' he answered his father distractedly as he pulled his shirt together.

'There is no rush,' his father assured pleasantly before he could be heard walking back down the hallway.

Gabriel frowned at Bella's back as she tried, and failed, to refasten her bra with fingers that were obviously shaking too badly to complete the task. 'Here, let me,' he rasped before moving to snap the hook back into place.

'Thank you,' she said stiffly, making no effort to turn as she quickly buttoned her blouse. 'I—I don't know what to say! That was— I'm not sure what happened...'

'Oh, I think you are well aware of what almost happened, Bella,' he drawled. 'It pleases me that you did not lie concerning my scars,' he added huskily.

Bella hadn't lied about Gabriel's physical scars; his inner ones were another matter, however...

She shook her head. 'I don't usually behave in that—in that way!'

'It is perhaps some time since you last had a man,' Gabriel pointed out dryly.

Bella turned sharply, a frown between her eyes as she glared at him. Exactly what sort of woman did Gabriel think she was?

The sort of woman who allowed herself to almost be made love to on a desktop, apparently!

The sort of woman who had almost ripped Gabriel's shirt from his back in her need to touch his naked flesh!

Bella closed her eyes in self-disgust as she tried to reassemble her thoughts. She most certainly was *not* that sort of woman! Gabriel probably wouldn't believe her even if she were to tell him—which she had no intention of doing; it was bad enough that she knew how out of character her response to Gabriel had been without him knowing it, too!—that there hadn't been a man in her life on an intimate level since that single night she had spent with Gabriel five years ago.

How could there have been? For nine months of that time she had been pregnant with Toby. And since Toby's birth Bella had centred all of her attention on him. She certainly hadn't wanted to add any more confusion to his young life by giving him a succession of 'uncles'!

She drew in a deep controlling breath before opening her eyes to glare at Gabriel. He had pulled his shirt back onto his shoulders, but hadn't bothered to refasten it, and Bella could now see the fine pattern of scars that marred the smoothness of the olive-coloured skin. With his dark hair in disarray from her recently entangled fingers, and that unbuttoned shirt revealing his scarred chest, Gabriel looked more piratical than ever. Certainly more rakishly attractive than Bella felt comfortable with!

She raised dark, mocking brows. 'I'm sure it's been much longer for me than the last time you "had" a woman!'

Gabriel continued to look at her levelly for several tense seconds, and then a humourless smile curved those sculptured lips. 'Not all women are as—understanding, about physical imperfection, as you appear to be,' he said dryly.

Bella couldn't believe that. If Gabriel were any more perfect she would be a gibbering wreck!

'I believe that what took place just now proved that we would not lack physical gratification in our marriage,' he commented wickedly.

Bella's mouth tightened. 'We are *not* getting married,' she repeated firmly.

Gabriel looked unconcerned by her vehemence. 'Oh, I think that we are.'

'Really?' She frowned her uncertainty, not liking the assurance in Gabriel's tone at all.

Any more than she liked the smile that he now gave her. 'Really,' he drawled confidently. 'I am sure you must be aware of the benefits to you in such a marriage—'

'If you're referring to what happened between us just now, then forget it!' Bella glared at him. 'I can find that sort of "benefit" with any number of men!'

Gabriel's mouth compressed. 'There will be no other men in your life once we are married, Isabella. Now I am assured of your response, we will be married in the fullest sense of the word. As an only child myself, I am hoping it will be a marriage that will result in us having more children together. Lots of brothers and sisters for Toby.'

Bella was thrown momentarily off balance by that last claim as she easily imagined having more sons and daughters that looked exactly like Gabriel.

She gave a fierce shake of her head. 'You can't seriously want to spend the rest of your life married to a woman who doesn't love you—'

'Any more than you would wish to be married to a man who does not love you,' he acknowledged curtly. 'But the alternative is even less palatable. A long—and no doubt very public—legal battle for custody of Toby,' Gabriel said grimly.

Bella gasped as her greatest fear was made a possibility. 'You would do that to Toby?'

Gabriel gave a shrug. 'If you leave me with no other choice, yes.'

Bella looked at him searchingly, knowing by the utter implacability of Gabriel's expression that he meant every word he had just said. Marriage to him, or Gabriel would involve them all in a very messy legal battle.

She breathed in deeply. 'All right, Gabriel, I'll think about marrying you—'

'Thinking about it is not enough, Isabella,' he cut in harshly. 'Especially,' he added more softly, that dark gaze narrowed on her speculatively, 'when I suspect you are only delaying the inevitable in order that you and Toby might return to England tomorrow, as originally planned, with your family, yes?'

That was exactly the reason Bella was delaying giving Gabriel a definite answer!

She chewed on her bottom lip. 'I don't believe it's inevitable that the two of us will marry—'

'I beg to differ, Isabella.'

Her eyes flashed deeply purple. 'You've never begged in the whole of your privileged life!'

He lifted an autocratic eyebrow. 'And I am not about to do so now, either,' he said. 'I want your answer before you leave here today.'

'You'll have my answer when I'm damned well ready to give it!' she flashed back heatedly.

Although Bella already had a feeling she knew what that answer was going to be.

What it *had* to be…

CHAPTER SIX

'WILL I see you in the morning, Daddy?'

Bella's breath caught in her throat as she waited for Gabriel to answer Toby. She was standing at the bottom of her son's bed watching the two of them as Toby lay tucked snugly beneath the duvet, Gabriel sitting at his side.

She had absolutely no doubts that Toby had enjoyed his day with his father and grandfather. The three of them had spent most of the morning out in the garden, Gabriel keeping Toby occupied with a number of ball games while Bella sat on a lounger watching them, dark sunglasses perched on the end of her nose as she allowed her thoughts to wander. The problem was, they kept coming back to the same place—Gabriel's insistence that she marry him...

As the day had progressed—a drive out to look at the Danti vineyard, and lunch eaten outside on the terrace at the magnificent villa there, and then dinner later that evening at a wonderful fish restaurant at Pier 39—it was impossible for Bella to deny that Gabriel was wonderful with Toby.

That he already loved Toby with the same fierceness that Bella did...

And that Toby loved Gabriel right back!

Looking at the two of them sitting together now on Toby's bed, so alike with their dark curling hair and chocolate-brown eyes, and that cleft in the centre of their chins, Bella couldn't help feeling that she was fighting a losing battle. That even attempting to fight this harder, more arrogant Gabriel was a waste of her time and emotions.

Gabriel glanced down at her now, the expression in his eyes unreadable. 'I think that depends on Mummy, don't you?' he murmured.

'Mummy?' Toby prompted eagerly.

Bella drew in a ragged breath before answering. 'We'll see,' she finally said non-committally.

'That usually means yes,' Toby confided as he looked up at Gabriel conspiratorially.

'It does?' The darkness of Gabriel's gaze was mocking as he glanced across at Bella.

'It means we'll see,' she insisted. 'Now it's time for you to go to sleep, young man,' she told her son firmly as she moved to tuck him more comfortably beneath the covers. 'G—Daddy and I will just be in the other room if you should need us, Toby,' she added reassuringly before bending down to kiss him.

Toby reached up to wrap his arms about her neck as he hugged her. 'It was a lovely day, wasn't it, Mummy?'

Emotion caught in Bella's throat as she looked down into her son's happily beaming face.

Could she endanger that unclouded happiness by subjecting Toby to the trauma that a legal battle with Gabriel was sure to cause? Could she really put Toby into a position where he would almost be forced to choose between the mother he had lived with all of his young life and the father he had only just met? Could she do that to him?

Surely the answer to all of those questions was no...

'Lovely,' she answered Toby brightly before kissing him again.

'I'll see you in the morning, darling.' She ruffled his dark curls before stepping away from the bed.

'We will both see you in the morning, Toby,' Gabriel added pointedly as he moved to receive Toby's hug goodnight.

Gabriel's arms were gentle, but his emotions were not. Toby, his son, now represented everything to him, the past, the present, and most definitely the future.

'Sleep now, little one,' he said huskily as he released Toby to step back.

'You promise you'll come back in the morning?' Toby's eyes were anxious.

Gabriel doubted that Toby heard the sob in his mother's throat as she stood just behind him, but Gabriel certainly did. 'I will come back in the morning,' he assured the little boy. Whatever it took, Gabriel was determined to be in Toby's life every morning!

'What would you have done about this situation if you had already been married to someone else when you learnt of Toby's existence?' Bella challenged once the two of them had returned to the sitting-room.

Gabriel's mouth tightened. 'Fortunately, that problem does not arise.'

'But if it had?' she insisted.

He shrugged. 'I refuse to answer a "what if" question, Isabella.'

She gave a little huff of frustration. 'Doesn't it bother you that I don't want to marry you?'

It should, and it did. But Gabriel knew from Bella's response to him earlier today that on one level, at least, she did want to be with him…

Other marriages, he was sure, had begun with less.

'Not particularly,' Gabriel dismissed curtly.

Bella continued to glare at him for several more seconds before she gave a sigh of defeat. 'All right, Gabriel, I will agree to marry you—'

'I thought that you would,' Gabriel murmured as he moved to sit in one of the armchairs.

'If you will allow me to finish…?' She raised dark, expressive brows as she stood across the room from him.

'By all means.' Gabriel relaxed back in the armchair. He had won the first battle—and the most difficult, he hoped—and so could now afford to be gracious in victory.

'Thank you,' she accepted dryly. 'I will agree to marry you,' she repeated, then went on more firmly, 'but only on certain conditions.'

Gabriel's gaze narrowed as he easily guessed, from the calmness of Bella's expression, that he wasn't going to like those conditions. 'Which are?'

'Firstly, if we married I would like to continue living in England—'

'I am sure that can be arranged.' He nodded, having already considered this problem earlier today when he had decided that marriage between himself and Isabella was the only real solution to Toby's continued welfare.

It would be a simple enough process to put a manager in charge of the vineyards here, with the occasional visit from him to make sure they were being run properly.

'The Danti business interests are international, Isabella,' he informed her. 'I will simply take over the running of our London office. Your second condition...?'

'Toby will attend schools of my choice—'

'As long as that choice eventually includes Eton and then Cambridge, I do not foresee that as being a problem,' Gabriel drawled.

'Eton and Cambridge?' Bella echoed disbelievingly.

'The Dantis have been educated at Eton and Cambridge for several generations.'

Bella shook her head. 'Toby will begin attending the local school in September. Following that he will be a day-pupil at another local school.'

Gabriel quirked one dark brow. 'Then I suggest we ensure that we have already moved into a house close enough so that he can attend Eton school as a day-pupil.'

He looked so damned smug, Bella fumed inwardly. So sure of himself.

As he had no doubt been sure of what her answer to his marriage proposal would be. Proposal? Hah! Gabriel didn't ask, he ordered; he was arrogance personified!

But, while Toby had been enjoying himself as the centre of Cristo Danti and Gabriel's attention, Bella had spent most of the day considering her options. Her limited options, she had very quickly realised, considering there was no way now of denying that Toby was Gabriel's son—even if Bella did attempt to deny it, a simple blood test would prove her a liar!

Just as there was no denying that the Dantis were a very rich and powerful family, both here and in Europe. In reality, what possible chance did she have of ensuring that she and Toby—especially Toby!—came out of a legal battle unscathed? The answer to that was only too clear. Against Gabriel Danti she had no chance.

But if she was forced to agree to this marriage, then Bella was determined to have at least some say in what she would and would not agree to!

'Thirdly,' she snapped, 'the marriage will be in name only.' She looked across at him challengingly, her eyes widening in alarm as he suddenly stood up.

Gabriel slowly shook his head. 'I am sure that you are already well aware that will not be possible.'

Because of their response to each other earlier today!

A response that still made Bella cringe whenever she thought about it—which she had tried very hard not to do all day. She never responded to men in that totally wild and wanton way. At least…she never had until Gabriel. Both five years ago and then again today…

Which was why Bella was making this the last condition to their marriage. She could imagine nothing worse than becoming a slave to the desire that Gabriel seemed to ignite in her so easily.

Even now, feeling angry and trapped, Bella was still totally aware of Gabriel in the black shirt and faded jeans. Clearly remembered pushing that shirt from his shoulders earlier so that she might touch the warm, muscled flesh beneath it. Unfortunately, she remembered even more distinctly the way that Gabriel had touched her…

She would not, could not allow her emotions, her life, to be ruled by the desire Gabriel made her feel!

She straightened her shoulders. 'Without your agreement to that last condition I couldn't even contemplate the idea of the two of us marrying each other.'

Gabriel looked at her from under hooded lids, knowing by the steadiness of Bella's gaze, the sheer determination in her expression, that she thought she meant every word she was saying, at least. Considering their response to each other in his study earlier today, Gabriel found that very hard to believe. Or accept.

Bella had come alive in his arms. Wildly. Fiercely. Demandingly. How could she possibly imagine they could live together, day after day—night after night!—and not take that lovemaking to its inevitable conclusion?

His mouth tightened. 'You wish for Toby to be an only child?'

She shrugged. 'He was going to be that, anyway.'

Gabriel studied her closely. 'You are a beautiful woman, Isabella; if we had not met again you would no doubt have married one day and had other children.'

'No,' she answered flatly. 'I decided long ago that I would never subject Toby to a stepfather who may or may not have accepted him as his own,' she explained simply as Gabriel frowned at her.

The mere thought of Toby or Bella ever belonging to another man filled Gabriel with uncontrollable fury. Toby was his. Bella was his!

His hands clenched at his sides. 'I agree to your last condition, Bella—'

'I thought that you would,' she dryly echoed his earlier comment.

'Like you, Bella, I have not finished,' Gabriel replied. 'I agree to your last condition on the basis that it can be nullified, by you, at any time.'

Bella eyed him warily. 'What exactly does that mean?'

His smile was mocking. 'It means that I reserve the

right to—*persuade* you, shall we say, into changing your mind.'

Bella had no doubt that what Gabriel meant by that remark was that he reserved the right to try and *seduce* her into changing her mind any time he felt like it!

Would she be able to resist him? Living with Gabriel twenty-four hours a day, every day, would she be able to withstand a Gabriel bent on seduction?

Did she have any real choice other than to try?

'You took me by surprise earlier, Gabriel,' she stated bravely. 'In future I will be on my guard against—well, against any attempt on your part to renew such attentions!'

She sounded so serious, so firm in her resolve, Gabriel acknowledged with a grudging admiration. 'I will allow no other men in your life, Isabella,' he warned her seriously.

'And will that rule apply to you, too?' she snapped.

Gabriel eyed her mockingly. 'My own tastes do not run in that particular direction—'

'You know very well what I meant!' She glared her exasperation.

He shrugged. 'There will be no other women in my bed but you, Isabella,' he taunted.

'I'm not going to be in your bed, either, Gabriel!'

Bella did not believe she was going to be in his bed, which, as far as Gabriel was concerned, was a totally different matter. 'You have named your own conditions for our marriage, Isabella,' he rasped. 'Now I wish to tell you mine.'

Her eyes widened. 'You have conditions, too?'

'But of course.' His mouth quirked. 'You did not think that I would allow you to have everything your own way?'

'Forcing me into marrying you is hardly that!' she scorned.

Gabriel gave another shrug. 'You have a choice, Isabella.'

'Not a viable one!'

'No,' he acknowledged simply. 'But it is, nevertheless, still a choice.'

Bella sighed her frustration, just wanting this conversation over and done with now. She was tired, both emotionally and physically, and she needed time and space alone now in which to sit and lick her wounds. While she came to terms with the idea of marrying Gabriel Danti!

How different it would have been if this had happened five years ago. How different Bella would have felt if their night together had been the start of something that had eventually resulted in Gabriel asking her to marry him. She had been so infatuated with him then, so totally seduced by Gabriel's lovemaking, that Bella had absolutely no doubts she would have said yes.

Instead, what they were now proposing was nothing more than a business transaction. A marriage of convenience because both of them wished to ensure that Toby's life, at least, continued in happiness and harmony.

'What's your condition, Gabriel?' she asked.

He didn't answer her immediately, but instead walked slowly towards her, only coming to a halt when he stood mere inches away from her.

Bella eyed him warily, her nails digging into the palms of her hands as she knew herself to be totally aware of the warmth of Gabriel's body, the clean male smell of him, the golden lights that now danced in the warm darkness of his eyes as he looked down at her.

'What do you want?' she snapped apprehensively, to which he gave a slow, seductive smile. A smile Bella took exception to. 'I was referring to your condition, Gabriel,' she added hastily.

'My condition at this moment is one of—'

'Your verbal condition to our marriage!' Bella could see for herself, by the languorous desire burning in that dark gaze as it roamed slowly over the firm thrust of her breasts, and the hard stirring of his body, exactly what Gabriel's physical condition was!

'Ah. Yes. My verbal condition, Isabella,' he murmured, 'is that, in order to ensure the continued harmony of both your own family and mine, I suggest it would be better if they were all to believe that our marriage is a love match.'

Bella gasped in disbelief. 'You want me to *pretend* to be *in love* with you?'

'Only in public,' he qualified.

She glared at him. 'And in private?'

'Oh, simply in lust will do for the moment,' he said softly.

Bella's gaze narrowed. 'You arrogant son-of-a—'

'Insulting my mother will achieve nothing except to annoy me intensely, Isabella,' he warned her.

'I'm so sorry,' she came back sarcastically. 'My intention was to insult *you*, not your mother!'

Gabriel was aroused, not insulted. Marriage to Isabella promised to be a feast for the senses—all of them!

She had been beautiful five years ago, like a delicate and lovely flower that blossomed to his slightest touch. But, Gabriel now realised, he had plundered only one of her petals then. Motherhood and a successful career had ensured there was now so much more to Isabella Scott, and he found it all desirable…

He smiled slowly. 'I am not insulted, Isabella,' he assured huskily. 'Intrigued, perhaps, but not insulted.'

'Pity,' she muttered.

Gabriel's smile widened. 'You agree to my condition, then?'

She eyed him, totally frustrated with her lack of anything resembling control of this situation. 'I assure you I no more want my parents and siblings upset about the choice I'm making than you want to distress your father.'

'And so…?'

She glared her dislike of him, then grudgingly conceded. 'And so, in public at least, I will try to ensure that it appears as if our marriage is something I want.'

'Good.' Gabriel murmured his satisfaction as he lifted his hand and curved it about the delicate line of Bella's jaw, instantly feeling the way she tensed at his lightest touch before moving sharply away. 'Neither your family or my own will be convinced of our—ease with each other, if you react in that way when I touch you!' he growled disapprovingly as his hand fell back to his side.

She gave a dismissive snort. 'I promise I'll try to do better when we have an audience!'

'To merely try is not good enough,' Gabriel told her coldly.

'It's the only answer I can give you for now,' she told him wearily.

Gabriel studied her through narrowed lids, easily able to see that weariness, along with the air of defeat Bella no longer tried to hide from him.

Yes, he had won the battle by forcing Isabella's compliance in the matter of marrying him, and in claiming Toby as his son.

But Gabriel felt little triumph in that victory as he sensed that, in doing so, he might have put the success of the entire war he was waging in jeopardy...

CHAPTER SEVEN

'YOU make a stunning bride, Bella!' Claudia smiled at her tearfully as she put the finishing touches to the veil before stepping back to admire her sister's appearance.

Bella could only stare numbly at her own reflection, in a beautiful white satin wedding gown and lovely lace veil, in the full-length mirror on the door of the wardrobe in the bedroom that had been hers as a child.

Whoever would have thought, having agreed to Gabriel's marriage proposal, that only five weeks later Bella would be standing here dressed in this beautiful white wedding gown and veil, preparing to drive to the church with her father, on her way to becoming Gabriel's bride?

Gabriel's bride.

Gabriel Danti's bride.

Oh, God!

'You can't be having second thoughts about marrying a man as gorgeous as Gabriel, Bella?' Claudia teased her obvious nervousness.

'No, I can't, can I?' she agreed with forced lightness. 'Go and tell Daddy that I'm ready to leave, hmm?' she asked, waiting until Claudia had left the bedroom before turning back to look at her reflection in the mirror.

What would be the point in having doubts about marrying Gabriel when he had already legally claimed Toby as his son? The name Danti had been enough to ensure that Gabriel's claim was dealt with quickly and positively. Toby Scott was now Tobias Danti.

As Bella would very shortly become Isabella Danti.

Even that name sounded alien to her, not like her at all. Which was pretty apt when Bella hadn't felt like herself for the last five weeks. Even less so today!

The woman reflected in the mirror wearing the white satin gown and delicate lace veil over the dark cascade of her hair certainly looked like her, but Bella could feel no joy in her appearance, or at the thought of becoming Gabriel's wife.

They had shared the news of their engagement with their delighted families five weeks ago. Bella and Toby had then remained in San Francisco for two more days to give Gabriel the time to settle his affairs before he flew back to England with them.

Since arriving in England, Gabriel had been staying in the house in Surrey where Bella had first met him, but coming to the cottage every day in order to spend time with Toby.

When in the company of her family and Gabriel's they had, as agreed, given every impression that they were happy in each other's company.

Not an easy thing on Bella's part when the more time she spent in Gabriel's company, the more physically aware of him she became. Until now, on their wedding day, she felt so tense with that physical awareness it was a constant painful ache. So much for her condition that this was to be a marriage in name only…

This was her wedding day, Bella accepted heavily.

And she couldn't have felt more miserable!

'Where are we going?'

'On our honeymoon, of course,' Gabriel said with satisfaction as he drove the black sports car to the private airfield where the Danti jet was fuelled and waiting to take off, the two of them having just been given a warm send-off by their wedding guests.

'What honeymoon?' Bella frowned as she turned in her seat to look at him, still wearing her wedding gown and veil. 'At no time in the last five weeks did we discuss going away on a honeymoon!'

'We did not discuss it because I knew this would be your reaction if we had,' Gabriel told her unrepentantly.

She scowled her frustration with his high-handedness. 'If you knew that then, why—?'

'It was meant to be a surprise,' Gabriel growled.

Her mouth compressed. 'Oh it's certainly that all right.'

'It is Toby's surprise, Bella,' he elaborated softly.

She looked at him sharply. 'Toby's?'

Gabriel nodded. 'Our son confided in me several weeks ago that newly married people go away on honeymoon together after the wedding.'

Bella's cheeks were flushed. 'You should have explained to him—'

'Should have explained *what* exactly to him, Isabella?' Gabriel grated harshly. 'That although his mother and father are now married, they are not in love with each other? That his mother has no desire whatsoever to spend time alone with his father?'

Bella winced. When he put it like that…!

They had spent the last few weeks, individually and together, convincing Toby that they were all going to be happy as a real family. Obviously they had succeeded as far as Toby was concerned, which was why he had decided his parents going away on honeymoon together was what a 'real family' did…

'I don't have any other clothes with me—'

'Claudia was kind enough to pack a suitcase for you,' Gabriel explained. 'It is in the trunk of the car with my own.'

Well, that explained the mischievous glint Bella had seen in Claudia's eyes earlier as her sister had stood with the other wedding guests outside the hotel to wave them off!

'Toby also arranged to stay with your parents for the week we are away,' Gabriel supplied. 'With my father remaining in England and visiting him often.'

'He's certainly been busy, hasn't he?' Bella sighed as she raised her hands to take the pins out of her hair and remove the veil, her head throbbing. 'That's better.' She threw the veil onto the back seat before sitting back more comfortably.

This really had been the most difficult day of Bella's life. Starting with the conversation her father had insisted on having with her early this morning…

He had been alone in the kitchen drinking coffee when Bella had come downstairs at six-thirty, his conversation light as she had made herself a cup of coffee.

Once Bella had sat down at the kitchen table with him it had been a different matter, however.

He had gently voiced his own and her mother's worries about the haste with which Bella and Gabriel were getting married. Was she doing the right thing? Was she really sure this was what she wanted? There was no doubting Toby's excitement but was Bella going to be happy?

Lying to her father had possibly been the hardest thing Bella had ever done.

Even now, thinking of his gentle concern for her happiness, Bella could feel the tears prick her eyes. 'So, where have you decided we're going on our honeymoon?' she asked Gabriel heavily.

Gabriel's mouth tightened at the fatigue in Bella's tone as she made no effort to hide the fact that today had been no more than a trial she'd had to get through.

She had looked stunningly beautiful as she had walked down the aisle towards him. A vision in white satin and lace.

A vision in white satin and lace who had avoided so much as meeting his gaze. Whose voice had quivered with uncertainty as she made her vows, her hand trembling slightly as she allowed Gabriel to slide the thin gold wedding band in place. Her fingers had been cold as she'd placed the matching gold band Gabriel had insisted on upon his own finger, her mouth stiff and unresponsive as Gabriel kissed her to seal their vows. Although admittedly she had made an effort to smile and acknowledge their guests as they'd walked back down the aisle together as husband and wife.

Probably because looking and smiling at their guests

was preferable to looking at him, Gabriel acknowledged grimly to himself.

'We are flying to your island in the Caribbean,' Gabriel told her.

'Don't you mean *your* island in the Caribbean?' she corrected.

'No, I mean yours,' Gabriel said. 'It is my wedding gift to you.' He hadn't meant to tell her that quite so abruptly; had intended surprising her with his gift once they arrived at their destination. He would have stuck to that plan, too, if he weren't feeling quite so frustrated with her distant behaviour.

Bella was absolutely stunned as she stared at Gabriel in complete disbelief. Gabriel was giving her a whole island in the Caribbean as a wedding present?

His mouth quirked as he obviously read some of her incredulity. 'Do not look so concerned, Isabella. It is only a small island.'

'Isn't even a *small* island a little overkill when I only gave you a pair of cufflinks?' A frown marred her brow.

Bella had only bought the cufflinks at the last moment because Claudia, as Chief Bridesmaid, said she had to; until then Bella hadn't even thought of giving Gabriel a gift to mark their marriage. What could she possibly give to the man who had everything?

Although Bella had noted, as they stood together in the church, that Gabriel was wearing the diamond and onyx links in the cuffs of the pristine white shirt he wore beneath the dark grey frock coat…

'You have given me so much more than that, Isabella,' Gabriel assured her huskily.

She looked at him warily, but she was unable to read

anything from his expression. 'I don't know what you mean,' she finally murmured uncertainly.

'I am talking of Toby, Isabella. You have given me a son,' he explained evenly.

A man who had everything—except that…

'Wow, a wedding ring and an island in the Caribbean,' she mocked. 'What would you have given me if I had only produced a daughter? A monthly allowance and visiting rights, perhaps?'

'No, I would have given you a wedding ring and an island in the Caribbean!' A nerve pulsed in Gabriel's cheek as he answered her. 'I would value a daughter no less than a son, Isabella, and I have no idea why you would ever think that I might. Or why it is you take such delight in insulting me!'

Why *did* Bella take delight in insulting him?

Because she was angry with him. Because she was angry with herself. Because she was just plain angry!

She was angry with Gabriel for forcing her into this marriage.

She was angry with herself for allowing him to do so.

She was angry because a part of her had thrilled at the sight of Gabriel as he'd stood down the aisle waiting for her, looking so devastatingly handsome in the dark frock coat and white shirt and red bow tie. She was angry because her voice had quivered with emotion as she had made her vows to him and because her hand had trembled at his slightest touch as he'd placed his wedding ring upon her finger.

Bella was angry for all of those reasons and more!

'I'm sorry,' she sighed wearily. 'It's been a long and—and difficult day.'

'For both of us,' Gabriel pointed out.

'Yes.' Bella turned her head to look at him.

Gabriel looked as strained as she felt, Bella acknowledged ruefully, lines beside his eyes and the grimness of his mouth, his skin slightly pale beneath his naturally olive complexion.

How different this could all have been if Gabriel hadn't been in love with another woman five years ago. How different today could have been if the two of them had married because they were in love with each other now.

Instead they were two strangers who had married to protect and sustain their young son's happiness.

Bella swallowed hard. 'I think, if you don't mind, that I would like to just sit here quietly for a while.' She closed her eyes.

Gabriel did mind. If Bella thought the last five weeks had been any less of a strain for him, then she was mistaken.

In company, Bella had managed, as agreed, to maintain an air of tranquil happiness, but once they were alone it had been a totally different matter. She had shown a total lack of interest whenever he had tried to discuss the wedding arrangements with her. Had been uncommunicative on the three Sunday mornings they had attended church together in order to hear the reading of their Banns.

Worst of all, once they were alone, Bella had avoided so much as touching him...

If Bella wished to punish him for forcing this marriage on her then she could not have chosen a better way to do it than with her icy silence and her obvious aversion to his lightest touch!

* * *

'You and your father certainly know how to travel in style,' Bella commented lightly as she sat across the table from Gabriel in the luxurious cabin of the Danti jet, only now beginning to appreciate the wealth and power behind the Danti name.

Well…apart from earlier when Gabriel had informed her he had given her an island in the Caribbean as a wedding gift!

Bella shied away from even thinking about what she was going to do with an island in the Caribbean and instead turned her attention back to her present surroundings.

The Danti-owned jet was the height of luxury, only six ultra-comfortable seats in the spacious and carpeted main cabin, with a bar at the cockpit end, and a door to another private compartment at the other.

Gabriel had given instructions to the captain to take off as soon as they were on board and their luggage had been stowed in the cabin at the back of the plane. A male steward had then placed two long-stemmed fluted glasses on the glass table in front of them before pouring the bubbly champagne, leaving the bottle cooling in a bucket of ice beside Gabriel and then disappearing back into the galley behind the bar and closing the door discreetly behind him.

Bella had totally avoided even looking at her own glass of champagne as it reminded her all too forcibly of that night with Gabriel five years ago. The last thing she needed to think about at the moment was that!

Gabriel nodded now. 'As you and Toby will also do now that you are Dantis.'

The sinking feeling in Bella's stomach owed nothing

to air-sickness and everything to the realisation that that was who she really was now.

Isabella Danti. Wife of Gabriel.

'No doubt Toby will be impressed,' she answered.

'But not you?'

Bella was more nervous than impressed. Nervous of being really alone with Gabriel for the first time in five weeks. A quivering wreck just at the thought of spending a week alone with him on *her* Caribbean island.

She shook her head. 'I'm not four years old, Gabriel.'

'No, you are not, are you?'

Bella shot Gabriel a swift glance, not in the least re-assured by the intensity of his chocolate-brown eyes as his gaze met hers and held it captive.

She physically had to turn her head away to break that gaze before she could stand up abruptly. 'I—I think I would like to go into the other room and take off this wedding gown.'

'An excellent idea, Isabella,' Gabriel murmured huskily.

Bella frowned up at him as he rose slowly to his feet, his height and the width of his shoulders at once dominating the cabin. 'I think I'm quite capable of changing my clothes on my own, thank you,' she told him sharply.

Gabriel gave a mocking inclination of his head. 'I thought you might need some help with the zip at the back of your gown.'

Good point, Bella realised. The wedding gown was medieval in style, with long, close-fitting lace sleeves that tapered to a point at her wrist, their snug fit making it impossible for Bella to reach the zip that ran the whole length of her spine without risking ripping the sleeves at the seams. It hadn't been a problem earlier today, because Claudia had helped her to dress, but Bella couldn't say she was exactly comfortable now with the thought of Gabriel helping her to *un*dress...

Comfortable? The thought of Gabriel touching her at all was enough to send her already fractured nerves into a complete tailspin!

She was never going to wear this gown again anyway, so what did it matter if she *did* rip the sleeves?

'I'm sure I can manage, thank you,' she replied distantly as she turned away.

'I need to change into less formal clothing, too,' Gabriel insisted quietly as he reached the door to the back compartment before Bella and held it open for her to enter.

Bella looked up at him uncertainly, knowing by the hard challenge she could see in his eyes that Gabriel expected to continue—and that he was actually enjoying!—arguing with her. On the basis that some sort of response from her was better than none, perhaps? Probably, Bella acknowledged wryly, even as she experienced a perverse desire not to give him that satisfaction.

'Fine,' she accepted airily before striding past him into the cabin at the back of the plane.

Only to come to an abrupt halt as she found herself, not in another sitting-room as she had supposed, but in a room totally dominated by the king-size bed in its centre!

Gabriel's eyes darkened with amusement when he saw Bella's stunned expression as she took in the luxuriously appointed bedroom with its fitted wardrobes, gold thick-piled carpet, and the deep gold and cream silk linen that covered the bed, several throw cushions of the same rich material against the sumptuous pillows.

Unfortunately Bella didn't stay stunned for very long as she turned to look up at him accusingly. 'I hope you don't have any ideas about adding my name to the list of women you've no doubt seduced in here!' she snapped.

Gabriel's humour faded at the deliberate insult. 'You have the tongue of a viper!'

She raised mocking brows. 'It's a little late for second thoughts, don't you think, Gabriel? We were married earlier today, remember?'

'Oh, I remember, Isabella,' he rasped harshly. 'Perhaps it is time that I reminded you of that fact also!' He closed the door gently behind him.

Bella took a step back as she obviously read the intent in his eyes. 'I meant what I said, Gabriel—I am not about to become another notch on your mile-high bedpost!'

Gabriel's jaw clenched as he took that same step forward. 'I meant what I said five weeks ago, too, concerning the right to change your mind about our marriage being in name only!'

Her eyes widened in alarm. 'Not here!'

'Wherever and whenever,' he promised.

She backed away from him. 'I told you I will not become another notch—'

'If you look at the bed again, Isabella, you will see that there is no bedpost.' Gabriel's voice was dangerously soft. 'And we are at least three miles high.'

'Your three-mile-high club, then,' she persisted as she faced him bravely, only the uncertainty Gabriel could read in her eyes telling him of the nervousness Bella was trying so desperately to hide.

Gabriel took another step forward, standing only inches away from Bella now, and able to see the nerve pulsing at the base of her throat and the slight trembling of her lips.

Full pouting lips that were slightly parted, that perfect bow of a top lip a temptation, the bottom one becoming a lure as the tip of Bella's tongue moved moistly between them.

An invitation, whether Bella meant it to be so, that Gabriel had no intention of resisting!

'Turn around, Isabella, so that I can unzip your gown,' he suggested gruffly.

She swallowed hard. 'I don't—' She broke off with a gasp as Gabriel ignored her protest and stepped behind her. She felt the touch of his fingers as he slowly began to slide the zip down.

Bella's second protest went unspoken, her back arching involuntarily as she felt the delicious ripples of awareness through her whole body as that zip slowly—so very slowly—moved down the length of her spine, her breath catching in her throat as Gabriel parted the satin material and she felt the warm caress of his lips against the bareness of her shoulder.

Desire. She instantly felt a hot, burning desire that ripped through her body at the first touch of Gabriel's mouth against her heated flesh, the moist rasp of his tongue as he licked and tasted her only intensifying that burning heat.

Much as she denied it, much as she fought against it, Bella knew she wanted him.

Wanted Gabriel passionately.

Knew that she had been fighting that want, that need, for the last five weeks, afraid to even touch him in case she revealed that ever-escalating desire. With the result that each minute she spent in his company had been torture, and full of an aching desire that had always seemed only seconds away from release.

It was a passion that Bella had only been able to keep in check by presenting Gabriel with a veneer of icy coldness. An icy veneer that had melted with the force of an avalanche the moment his mouth touched her naked flesh!

Her neck arched, her head resting back against Gabriel's shoulder as his hands slid inside the unzipped gown to move about her waist and then higher as he cupped the nakedness of her breasts beneath the satin gown, her own hands moving up to rest on top of his as she pressed him into her, wanting his caresses.

She cried out, desire surging between her thighs as Gabriel's thumbs moved across her turgid nipples, her body taut with expectation, not able to breathe as she waited for the second caress, gasping, almost sobbing as Gabriel's lips moved heatedly, moistly against her throat as he took those throbbing peaks between his thumbs and fingers and squeezed rhythmically.

'Gabriel?' Bella groaned as her bottom moved against the hardness of his arousal. 'Gabriel, please…!'

'Not yet, Bella,' Gabriel refused huskily even though his own body throbbed with that same need for release.

They had a long flight ahead of them, hours and hours before they reached their destination, and before that happened Gabriel intended to discover and fulfil every one of Bella's fantasies, as he hoped that she would fulfil every one of his.

Stripping the white satin wedding gown from Bella's

body was only the first of the fantasies that had kept him awake night after night for the last five weeks!

Gabriel heard her moan of protest as he slowly moved his hands from inside her gown, her breath catching in her throat seconds later as she realised he had only done so in order to slide the gown from her shoulders and down her arms before he bared her to the waist and then slowly allowed the gown to pool on the floor at her feet.

Bella's eyes were closed and Gabriel stared down at how beautiful she looked in only a pair of brief white lace panties and white stockings.

Her throat was exposed, her lips slightly parted and moist, her lids half closing over eyes of deep purple as Gabriel's arms moved about her and his hands once again cupped her breasts before his thumbs moved to caress the deep rose nipples.

'Yes!' she exclaimed. 'Oh, God, yes, Gabriel…!'

Gabriel pulled her back against him so his lips could roam freely, erotically up the length of her throat to the sensitivity of her ear lobe, his teeth nibbling on that lobe even as one hand continued to caress the firmness of a perfect nipple and his other hand moved lower still.

Bella's skin felt like velvet as his fingers splayed across the bare expanse of her waist and down over the jut of her hip. Gabriel opened his eyes to look down to where his hand cupped and teased her breast, his own skin so much darker than the creamy magnolia of hers.

His teeth bit the softness of her ear lobe even as his gaze moved lower to where his fingers quested beneath the silk of her panties to the dark curls he could see clearly through the sheerness of the material, parting the dampness of those curls and seeking the sensitive nub nestled amongst their darkness. Seeking and finding as his fingers began to stroke her there.

She was so hot and slick, her sensitive folds swollen with need, a need Gabriel intended building until Bella cried out, begged for him to give her the climax her body craved.

Bella moaned low in her throat as she felt the brush of Gabriel's fingers against her, her legs parting to allow him greater access, an invitation he accepted as he plunged one long, satisfying finger deep inside her, followed by another as his thumb continued to stroke against her swollen nub and his other hand squeezed and caressed her breast in the same mind-blowing rhythm.

Again and again.

Those caresses becoming fiercer. Deeper. Faster.

The heat rose unbearably, building, growing ever stronger as Bella's hips moved to meet the deep thrust of Gabriel's fingers inside her.

'Don't stop, Gabriel!' she gasped breathlessly. 'Please don't stop!'

'Let go, Bella!' he groaned hoarsely against her throat. 'Give yourself, *cara*!'

'Yes…' she breathed raggedly. 'Oh, yes! Oh, God, yes…!' Bella gasped and writhed against Gabriel's hand as her climax surged out of control and wave after wave of burning, shattering pleasure rippled through her.

Gabriel held her captive as his fingers continued to pleasure her, Bella climaxing again and again, her body quivering and shaking at Gabriel's slightest touch.

'No more, Gabriel!' she finally sobbed as she collapsed weakly in his arms.

CHAPTER EIGHT

BELLA woke slowly, slightly disorientated as she looked around the unfamiliar room.

And then she remembered.

Not just where she was, but everything that had happened since she had entered this bedroom.

Bella turned her face into the pillows, the aching protest of her body as she curled into a foetal position reminding her all too forcefully of the way Gabriel had touched and caressed her.

So much for her claim, her determination, that her marriage to Gabriel would be in name only—they hadn't even left British airspace before she'd succumbed to his caresses!

It was—

She looked sharply towards the door as she heard the handle turning softly before it was opened, her expression becoming defensive as she saw Gabriel standing in the doorway.

The cream polo shirt and jeans he wore showed that he had remained in the bedroom long enough to change his clothes after Bella—after she— After she what? Collapsed from the sheer ecstasy Gabriel had given her time and time again until she simply couldn't take any more?

Oh, God…!

Her mouth tightened. 'If you've come to gloat—'

'I came to see if you were awake yet,' he corrected coldly. 'We will be landing shortly, and you need time to dress before we do.'

Which reminded Bella all too forcibly that she was completely naked—apart from her panties and hold-up stockings—beneath the bedclothes.

It also reminded her that although she had been almost naked Gabriel had remained completely dressed throughout their earlier— Their earlier what? Sexual encounter? Lovemaking? It could hardly be called the latter when there was no love for each other, on either side.

Sexual encounter, then.

How awful did that sound?

'Thank you,' she accepted with polite dismissal.

Gabriel scowled across the cabin at Bella for several long seconds. Knowing her as he did, he hadn't been expecting her to fall lovingly into his arms when she awoke, but her coldness, her accusation that he had come here to gloat over her earlier capitulation, was unforgivable.

His expression was grim as he crossed the cabin in three long strides to stand beside the bed and look down at her. 'It is not me you are angry with, Isabella—'

'Don't presume to tell me what I'm feeling,' she said resentfully, her eyes glittering with suppressed emotion as she glowered up at him.

Gabriel sat down on the side of the bed, trapping her beneath the bedclothes as he put a hand either side of her to lean over her. 'We are husband and wife, Isabella; there is absolutely no reason for you to feel embarrassed because of what happened between us earlier—'

'I'm not *embarrassed*, Gabriel—I'm *disgusted*. With myself as much as with you!' she added, her expression defiant as she met his gaze squarely.

Gabriel wanted to reach out and shake her out of this mood of self-recrimination. But if he were to touch her again now, even in anger, he knew that he wouldn't be able to stop himself from making love with her again.

Just looking at Bella, her hair a cloud of darkness against the gold colour of the pillows, her mouth a sensual pout, and knowing her body was almost completely naked beneath the bedclothes was enough to make Gabriel shift uncomfortably as his thighs became engorged with arousal. His own lack of release earlier had become an aching throb he'd remained totally aware of while Bella slept.

He stood up abruptly, needing to put some distance between himself and Bella before speaking again, but before he could do so she got in first. 'Just don't count on a repeat performance, Gabriel,' she snapped.

Where Bella was concerned Gabriel didn't take anything for granted. Not one single thing. 'We will be landing in ten minutes, Isabella, so I suggest that before we do you get some clothes on,' he bit out tersely.

She kept the covers pulled up against her as she sat up, her hair falling silkily about her shoulders. 'I thought you said it was a small Caribbean island?'

'It is,' Gabriel confirmed. 'We will complete the rest of our journey by helicopter.'

Bella had never been in a helicopter before, and wasn't sure how she was going to respond to being in such a small aircraft.

She was even less comfortable when she realised that Gabriel intended piloting the small black wasp-looking craft himself!

She looked at him uncertainly as he climbed into the seat beside her after stowing their cases in the back. 'Are you sure you know how to fly one of these things?'

'Very sure,' he drawled. 'I assure you, Isabella, you will be completely safe in my hands,' he added mockingly as she still didn't look convinced.

Bella shot him a narrow-eyed glare before turning away to look out of the window beside her at the bright sunshine reflecting on the beautiful blue-green ocean beyond a beach of white-gold sand.

A relaxed pose that didn't last any longer than it took for Gabriel to start the engine and move the controls to lift the helicopter from the ground!

Bella reached out to clutch at Gabriel's arm as the helicopter bucked and swayed as it rose into the air. 'I think I'm going to be sick!' she cried frantically.

'You will not be sick if you look out at the sea and not down at the ground,' he instructed.

Easy enough for him to say, Bella groaned inwardly as her stomach continued to heave in protest for several long minutes, only settling down to a slight queasiness as the helicopter levelled out and she could finally appreciate the beauty of the scenery.

The sun was bright and very hot, the sea so blue and clear that Bella could see the sandy bottom in several places, even more so as they began to approach a small island edged by unspoilt beautiful beaches and covered in lush green foliage and trees.

Gabriel flew the helicopter over the beach, almost but not quite touching the tops of the trees, Bella's eyes widening as she saw he was heading towards a white-painted villa on top of a hill, only slightly inland and surrounded by more trees and huge brightly coloured flowers.

'Home.' Gabriel nodded in answer to Bella's questioning look as he began to lower the helicopter onto the patch of flat green grass next to the villa. 'What did you expect, Bella?' He turned to her once they were down on the ground. 'That I was bringing you to a shack in the middle of nowhere?'

Bella hadn't really given a lot of thought as to where they would stay once they reached the island. The fact that Gabriel had given her an island as a wedding gift had seemed fantastic enough!

'It is slightly primitive in that there are no servants here to wait on us,' Gabriel warned.

Bella smiled wryly. 'I won't miss what I've never had, Gabriel.'

'A Frenchman owned the island previously, and he had the villa built several years ago,' Gabriel told her as he climbed out of the helicopter. 'Obviously, if you want to change the décor then you must do so.'

'It's beautiful as it is,' Bella murmured as she took her sunglasses off to follow him inside the villa.

The floors were cool cream-and-terracotta-coloured marble, the cream furniture in the sitting-room kept to a minimum, with several glass-topped tables placed conveniently beside the armchairs and sofa. The kitchen was even more surprising, everything white, including the cooker and huge refrigerator and freezer.

'We have our own generator and fresh water supply,' Gabriel told her as she moved slowly about the room. 'Or rather, you have your own generator and fresh water supply,' he corrected ruefully.

Bella blinked, totally overwhelmed now that she was actually here. 'This really is all *mine*?'

Gabriel nodded. 'Do you like it?' His expression was guarded.

Almost as if he expected her to throw his gift back in his face. Not literally, of course, but verbally at least. Not surprising considering her remarks when Gabriel had first told her about the island!

'I love it!' Bella assured him emotionally. 'I—thank you, Gabriel,' she added slightly breathlessly.

Gabriel stood across the kitchen, his own sunglasses pushed up into the darkness of his hair. Hair that he hadn't bothered to have cut the last five weeks, its longer length making him look more like the man Bella had met and briefly fallen for five years ago.

She turned away abruptly. 'How on earth did everything get here? The materials to build the villa? The furniture?' she quickly asked to cover her sudden and complete awareness of Gabriel as he stood there so still and yet so lethally attractive.

Gabriel shrugged. 'The same way that the food in the freezer and refrigerator got here.' He opened the fridge door to show her all the food stored on the shelves. 'By boat,' he supplied ruefully as Bella still looked puzzled.

Bella eyes narrowed. 'Are you telling me that I didn't

have to suffer that helicopter flight at all? That we could have come here by *boat*, instead?'

Gabriel held back a smile at her slightly indignant expression. 'I thought it would be more...dramatic...to arrive by helicopter,' he admitted.

'Oh, you did, did you...?' Bella said quietly as she placed her bag down on one of the work-surfaces.

'I did, yes,' Gabriel muttered warily, not able to read Bella's mood at all as she strolled over and opened the freezer door, taking out a tray of ice cubes before moving over to the sink. 'Of course, you must be thirsty,' he acknowledged. 'There is a selection of drinks in the— What are you doing?' He frowned as Bella approached him brandishing a handful of ice cubes before reaching out to grasp the collar of his polo shirt and dropping them inside. 'Bella!' Gabriel gasped in protest at the first uncomfortable touch of the icy-cold cubes against the heat of his flesh.

'I thought you were looking a little hot, Gabriel,' she drawled as he stepped back to shake the frozen cubes out of his clothing, several of them shattering on the marble floor.

'Damn it, Bella—' Gabriel broke off as Bella began to laugh at his discomfort.

It was the first time, Gabriel realised, that he had heard her laugh without cynicism or sarcasm since they'd met again five weeks ago.

His breath caught in his throat as he stared at her, those gorgeous violet eyes shining with good humour, her teeth tiny and white against her pale pink lip gloss, a healthy colour in her cheeks.

Bella was the most beautiful woman Gabriel had ever seen!

'Perhaps I deserved that,' he allowed gruffly.

'Perhaps you did,' she confirmed unrepentantly. 'Next time we come by boat, yes?' she said as she moved to pick up the shattered ice cubes.

Gabriel remained silent as he hunkered down on his haunches to help her, unwilling to break the sudden truce by making any comment that Bella might take exception to, satisfied for the moment that there would be a next time…

'What are you doing, Gabriel?'

He threw his cheroot to the ground, grinding it beneath the sole of his shoe before turning slowly to look at Bella as she stood behind him in the moonlight.

Their uneasy truce had continued while they walked along the beach earlier, and through the dinner they had prepared together and then eaten outside on the terrace that overlooked the moon-dappled ocean. The two of them had returned outside after they had cleared the dishes away, the silence between them companionable rather than awkward as they finished drinking the bottle of red wine Gabriel had opened to accompany their meal.

Bella had excused herself half an hour or so ago in order to go to the master bedroom to prepare for bed, Gabriel opting to stay outside a little longer, still reluctant to say or do anything that might shatter even the illusion of the companionship they had found together since the ice-cube incident.

They were due to stay here for a week, and Gabriel

would prefer that they not spend all of that time at loggerheads!

Looking at Bella now, in a pale-lilac-coloured night-gown, the silk material clinging to her breasts and moulding to the gentle curve of her hips, Gabriel knew that he wanted to strip even that flimsy garment from her before making love with her.

Something, after her comments earlier on the plane, that was sure to shatter even the illusion of companion-ship that they'd shared so far!

He thrust his hands into the pockets of the black trousers he had changed into before dinner. 'I thought you would prefer your privacy after such a long and tiring day.'

Bella looked at him searchingly, but was totally unable to read Gabriel's mood beneath the remoteness of his expression. 'Aren't you coming to bed?' she finally prompted hesitantly.

'Later, perhaps,' he rasped dismissively. 'I am not tired yet.'

Bella hadn't exactly had sleep in mind when she'd asked that question!

The island was beautiful, and totally unspoilt, she had discovered as she and Gabriel had strolled bare-footed, if slightly apart, along the shoreline before dinner. The water had lapped gently against their feet, the smell of the exotic blossoms wafting in the warm softness of the breeze, and all adding to the seduction of the evening.

To the air of awareness that lay hidden just below the surface of even the slightest glance that Bella and Gabriel exchanged.

At least, she had thought it had.

Gabriel's reluctance to come to bed now seemed to imply that only she had felt that aching awareness.

Because Gabriel's lovemaking earlier had only been a way of showing her that he really could make love to her wherever and whenever *he* felt like it, as he had put it so bluntly?

That, having already proved his point once today, Gabriel now felt no urgency to repeat the experience?

How utterly ridiculous of her to have imagined that, because the two of them hadn't argued for the last few hours, they could have actually reached some sort of understanding in their relationship. Gabriel had never made any secret of his reason for marrying her—his only reason for marrying her!—and that reason was Toby.

Bella felt the humiliated colour burn her cheeks. 'You're right, Gabriel, I would prefer my privacy,' she said. 'As such, it would be better if you used one of the other bedrooms, and kept out of mine, for the duration of our stay here.'

Gabriel's gaze narrowed on the pale oval of her face in the moonlight, her chin raised in challenge, that same challenge reflected in the deep purple of her eyes.

'Don't come any closer, Gabriel!' she warned as he took a step towards her.

A warning Gabriel chose to ignore as he came to stand only inches away from her, his eyes glittering darkly as he looked down the length of his arrogant nose at her, and his hands clenched at his sides as he obviously fought the urge to reach out and shake her until her teeth rattled.

Bella felt her own anger starting to fade as she

instead found herself fascinated by the nerve that pulsed beside that livid scar on Gabriel's tautly clenched left cheek.

He looked so gloriously handsome with his long hair slightly tousled onto his shoulders, the black silk shirt and tailored trousers only adding to that darkness, his eyes also appearing a glittering black in the moonlight.

Bella had never known another man with the grace and beauty of Gabriel. Had never been as physically aware of another man in the way she was Gabriel. Had never wanted another man in the way she constantly seemed to want Gabriel.

As, God help her, she wanted him even now…!

She swallowed hard. 'You're right, Gabriel, it's been a long and tiring day. Far too long and tiring for this conversation,' she said huskily. 'I—I'll wish you a goodnight.'

His mouth twisted self-derisively. 'I very much doubt that it will be that!'

Bella looked at him searchingly for several seconds before shaking her head ruefully. 'We really must try to find a way to stop insulting each other, Gabriel.'

He winced. 'The only time we manage to do that is when we are making love together, but…' He shrugged. 'Goodnight, Isabella. I will try not to wake you when I come to bed.'

Bella was frowning as she turned and walked slowly back inside the villa, too utterly weary to fight him any more concerning their sleeping arrangements. Especially as Gabriel had already made it plain she would lose!

She very much doubted that she would be able to fall

asleep when she knew that at any moment Gabriel would be coming to share what was now *their* bed.

Very much doubted that she would be able to sleep at all with Gabriel in bed beside her…

CHAPTER NINE

'Do you know how to scuba-dive, Isabella?'

'No.' Bella looked up from eating her piece of toast as she and Gabriel sat outside on the veranda eating their breakfast. 'Do you?'

As Bella had already guessed, it had not been a restful night's sleep, and she had still been awake but pretending not to be when Gabriel had joined her in the bedroom half an hour or so after she had gone to bed. That Gabriel had fallen asleep within minutes of his head resting on the pillow had made absolutely no difference to her own feelings of tension, and Bella had lain awake for hours after the even tenor of Gabriel's breathing told her he remained fast asleep beside her.

Bella's only consolation was that Gabriel was already up and making breakfast when she finally woke up shortly after nine o'clock. But her eyes still felt gritty from lack of sleep, and all she really felt like doing was going back to bed!

'I would hardly have asked otherwise,' Gabriel pointed out before taking a sip of his coffee. 'Would you like to learn?'

He looked disgustingly well rested this morning in a

white short-sleeved shirt and white trousers, Bella noted, disgruntled. Much more relaxed than he had a right to be, as far as she was concerned.

'I suppose I could try,' she agreed irritably. 'As long as you aren't one of those awful teachers who gets cross with their student.'

'I have no doubts you will be a very attentive pupil, Isabella,' Gabriel teased, knowing by the heavy look to her eyes and the weary droop of her mouth that she hadn't slept well.

Gabriel had known she was still awake when he joined her in the bed the night before, her back firmly turned towards him as she had tried to give every appearance of being asleep. A deception Gabriel had allowed her to keep; it was enough for the moment that she accepted that they would be sharing a bed in future.

She gave him a sharp glance. 'I sincerely hope you were referring to scuba-diving!'

'What else?' he taunted.

Bella continued to eye him suspiciously for several long seconds, and then she gave a dismissive shrug. 'Why not? I obviously have nothing else to do today.' She stood up suddenly.

Gabriel looked up at her searchingly. 'Perhaps you would have preferred to go somewhere a little more… entertaining…for our honeymoon?'

Bella raked him with a scathing glance. 'Oh, I think this is entertaining enough, don't you?'

He laughed softly. 'Let us hope so.'

Bella refused to meet the challenge in his gaze. 'I'll go and get changed.'

Although she wasn't too sure about that once she saw

the skimpiness of the bikinis that Claudia, obviously in on the secret of their honeymoon destination, had packed for her!

There were two of them. A black one that consisted of two very small scraps of material that barely covered anything, top or bottom. And a pink one, which admittedly had a little more material in the bottom half, but unfortunately the top plunged deeply at the front, meaning that when she put it on her breasts spilled over it revealingly.

Quite what Claudia had been thinking of when she chose them, Bella had no idea—but she could take a good guess.

Bella forgot her own self-consciousness in the pink bikini the instant she came out onto the terrace and saw that Gabriel was wearing the briefest—and sexiest—pair of black swimming trunks she had ever seen!

Fitting low down on his hips, the material barely covered that revealing bulge in the front of the trunks. A bulge Bella found it difficult to look away from...

Gabriel looked up from checking the scuba gear, his expression hardening as he saw the way Bella was staring at him. 'Do my scars bother you, after all?' he ground out harshly.

'Scars?' she repeated vaguely, trying to concentrate on something other than those skimpy bathing trunks. 'Oh. Those scars.' She nodded as she took in the revealing criss-cross of scars that marked his chest and back, several deeper marks that looked like surgical incisions on his left leg, both below and above the knee. 'I've already told you they don't bother me, Gabriel,' she said with a frown.

'That was before you had seen the full extent of them,' he said stiltedly. 'Some women would be bothered by their unsightliness.'

Some women *would*? Or they already *had*? Perhaps Janine Childe, for instance…?

Bella stepped outside. 'We all have scars, Gabriel. It's just that some of us have them on the inside rather than the outside. Besides,' she continued as he would have spoken, 'what does it matter to you how I feel about them?'

Gabriel's eyes were narrowed to dark slits. 'You are the woman who will have to look at them for the rest of your life.'

The rest of her life?

She took a deep breath as she realised she hadn't actually thought about her marriage to Gabriel with exactly that time-frame in mind before…

She suddenly realised she hadn't said anything and Gabriel was still waiting… 'I wouldn't worry about it, Gabriel. All men look the same in the dark—' She broke off as Gabriel's hands suddenly closed firmly about her upper arms. 'Let go of me!' she gasped.

His grasp didn't relax in the slightest. 'I am not interested in what you think of other men, Isabella. In the dark or otherwise!' He shook her slightly, his expression now distinctly dangerous.

Bella stared up at him, unable to see anything but the darkness of his anger as he glared down at her. 'Your scars don't bother me, Gabriel, and that's the truth,' she finally said evenly.

His gaze remained dark and stormy on her face for several more seconds before he released her so suddenly that Bella stumbled slightly. 'I will be several more minutes checking the scuba equipment, so perhaps you would like to go for a swim while you are waiting,' he suggested abruptly.

Bella gave one last, lingering glance at the stiffness of his scarred back before turning away to walk in the direction of the beach.

Another day in paradise…

'That was the most wonderful experience of my life!' Bella gasped excitedly once she had waded out of the sea and removed her breathing mask.

'The *most* wonderful?' Gabriel arched mocking brows as he removed his own scuba gear before sitting down on the blanket spread on the white-gold sand, the long darkness of his hair pushed back from his face, rivulets of sea-water dripping enticingly down his shoulders and back.

'Well…one of them,' Bella corrected hastily. 'Holding Toby in my arms seconds after he was born was probably the most wonderful,' she added huskily.

A frown darkened Gabriel's brow. 'I would have liked to have shared that experience with you.'

'It's been a lovely day, Gabriel, let's not spoil it with another argument.' Bella sighed as she dropped down onto the blanket beside him before slipping her arms out of the straps of the scuba gear and dropping it back on the sand behind them. She pushed the dampness of her hair back over her shoulders and sat forward to clasp her arms about her knees and rest her chin on her bent knees. 'Besides, I very much doubt even you would have been allowed into the delivery-room.'

Gabriel arched one dark brow. 'Even me…?'

She nodded. 'Not even the Danti name would have got you in there,' she teased. 'There was a bit of a scare at the last moment,' she explained as Gabriel continued to look at her enquiringly. 'My blood pressure went off the scale, Toby became distressed, and they had to rush me off to Theatre to deliver Toby by Caesarean section.'

Gabriel tensed. 'Your life was in danger?'

'I think both our lives were in danger for a while,' Bella admitted. 'But luckily it all turned out okay in the end.'

The frown between Gabriel's eyes didn't lessen. 'Is that likely to happen with a second pregnancy?'

Bella gave him a surprised glance. 'I don't know. It never occurred to me to ask. Gabriel?' She stared at him as he stood up abruptly to walk the short distance to the water's edge. 'Gabriel, what's wrong?'

Gabriel's hands clenched at his sides. Bella could ask him that, when she might have lost her life giving birth to Toby? When they might both have lost their lives and he, Gabriel, Bella's lover and Toby's father, would not have even known!

'The way I see it, both you and I have almost died and have the scars to prove it—' Bella broke off abruptly as Gabriel turned, his expression fierce. 'I was only trying to make light of the situation, Gabriel,' she reasoned.

His eyes narrowed to steely slits. 'You think the risk to your life is a subject for humour?'

She grimaced. 'I think it's something that happened four and a half years ago. It's nothing but history now. We're all still here, after all.'

Gabriel knew that Bella was right, but having just learnt that she might have died giving birth to Toby made him wonder—fear?—that a second pregnancy might be as dangerous...

'May I see your scar?'

Bella looked up at Gabriel warily as he loomed over her and blocked out the sun, his face darkly intense.

He wanted to see her scar from the Caesarean section? Her below-the-bikini-line scar?

She swallowed hard. 'Can't you just take my word for it that it's there?'

There was a slight easing of the tension in his expression. 'No.'

'Oh.' Bella chewed on her bottom lip. 'I would really rather not.' Her arms tightened protectively about her knees.

'Why not?'

Because it was far too intimate, that was why! Because she already felt totally exposed, vulnerable, in the brief bikini, without baring any more flesh!

'Maybe later,' she said, turning away.

'Now.'

Bella frowned her irritation as she looked back at him. 'Gabriel, we don't have to literally bare all of ourselves to each other in the first few days of marriage!'

He gave a hard smile. 'You have seen *my* scars, now I would like to see yours.'

'I would rather not,' she came back crossly.

'Men and women all look alike in the daylight, too, Isabella,' Gabriel murmured throatily.

No, they didn't!

There was simply no other man like Gabriel. No other man with his broodingly dark good looks. No other man with the power to make Bella's knees tremble with just a glance from the warmth of those chocolate-brown eyes. No other man who made her feel so desirable. No other man who could make her totally lose control at the merest touch of his hand...

There just was no other man as far as Bella was concerned.

Oh, God!

Bella felt her cheeks pale even as she stared up at Gabriel with a feeling of helplessness. She loved him. Loved Gabriel.

Had she *ever* really stopped loving him?

Probably not, Bella acknowledged with a feeling akin to panic. She had fallen in love with Gabriel that night five years ago, and even though she had never seen him again she had continued to love him.

That was the reason she had never been interested in even going out with another man for all these years.

That was the reason she had never felt even remotely attracted to another man in that time.

Because she was already in love with Gabriel Danti, and always would be!

And now she was married to him. Married to the man she loved, would always love, and yet could never tell him of that love because it wasn't what Gabriel wanted from her. It had never been what Gabriel wanted from her, and even less so now. All Gabriel wanted was his son; Bella just happened to come along with the package.

She stood up abruptly. 'I think not, thank you, Gabriel,' she told him stiffly. 'I'm tired. I'll go back to the villa and take a nap before dinner.'

Gabriel remained on the beach, his gaze narrowed in thought as he watched Bella walk into the trees and up towards the villa, her hair a black silky cloud down the slenderness of her back, the gentle sway of her hips wholly enticing.

What had happened just now?

One minute Bella had been challenging him as she always did, just as he had been enjoying that challenge as he always did, and the next it seemed she had completely shut down all her emotions.

Perhaps that was as well when Gabriel knew he daren't risk another pregnancy for Bella until he was sure she would be in no danger...

'Tell me what happened five years ago, Gabriel.'

'As in...?' Gabriel's expression was guarded as he looked across the dinner table at Bella.

'As in the accident, of course,' she said impatiently.

'Ah.' Gabriel sat back to take a sip of the white wine that he had opened to accompany the lobster and salad they had prepared together and just eaten.

Bella frowned. 'What did you think I meant?'

Gabriel looked at Bella beneath lowered lids as he admired her and thought how lovely she looked in her simple black knee-length gown. Its thin shoulder straps and the bareness of her arms revealed the light tan she had attained at the beach earlier, the heavy cloud of her dark hair cascaded loosely over that golden hue, and her face was bare of make-up except a pale peach lip gloss.

Bella had never looked more beautiful. Or more desirable.

'What did I think that you meant?' Gabriel repeated slowly. 'The night we spent together, perhaps?'

'I think we're both already well aware of what

happened that night!' Bella pointed out tartly. 'Impressionable student meets sexy racing-car driver,' she enlarged as Gabriel raised questioning brows. 'And the rest is history, as they say!'

'What do *you* say, Bella?'

What should Bella say?

She could say that she had behaved like a complete idiot five years ago. She could say that she should have had more sense than to fall for all that rakish charm and spent that one glorious night in his arms. She could say that she should never have committed the complete folly of falling in love with a man like Gabriel Danti!

'Oh, no, you don't, Gabriel.' Her smile was tight. 'You're not going to distract me from my original question by annoying me.'

'I'm not?'

'No, you're not!'

He quirked dark brows. 'I am curious as to why our talking about the night we spent together five years ago should cause annoyance.'

'Gabriel!' she protested.

'Bella…?'

Maybe if he had continued to call her Isabella in that cold and distant way then Bella would have refused to answer him. Maybe. But when he said her name in that sexy, husky way she had no chance!

She sighed. 'I really don't want to argue with you again tonight, Gabriel.'

He nodded. 'Fine, then we will not argue.'

'We can't seem to do anything else!'

He shrugged his shoulders beneath the cream silk shirt he wore.

'We are here together for a week, Bella, with no other distractions. We have to talk about something.'

'I've already told you what happened that night. I'm more interested in what happened afterwards,' she said firmly.

Gabriel's mouth tightened. 'You are once again referring to the car crash in which two men died.'

The sudden coolness in his gaze, the slight withdrawal Bella sensed in his manner, told her how reluctant Gabriel was to talk about the accident.

At least as reluctant as Bella was to talk about that night they had spent together!

She gave him a direct look. 'I assure you I'm not going to be hurt by anything you have to say concerning your feelings for Janine Childe.'

'No?' Gabriel's eyes glittered in the moonlight that shone in the ever-encroaching darkness.

'No,' Bella said. 'You aren't the first man to go to bed with one woman when you're actually in love with another one. I very much doubt that you'll be the last, either!' she added with a rueful smile.

Gabriel's jaw tensed. 'You believe me so utterly dishonourable?'

'I believe you were a man surrounded by Formula One groupies who were only too happy to go to bed with defending champion Gabriel Danti, whether he was in love with someone else or not,' Bella explained practically.

'Formula One *groupies*?' Gabriel exclaimed.

'Oh, stop being obtuse, Gabriel,' Bella teased gently. 'Women of all ages find that macho image as sexy as hell, you know that.'

'Did you?' He sounded amused now.

'We weren't talking about *me*—'

'Why did you go to bed with me that night, Bella?'

He had called her Bella again! Her defences were already in tatters after the momentous recognition earlier of her love for this man, without that!

'Because you were sexy as hell, of course,' she said brightly. 'Now could you just—'

'Past tense, Bella?' Gabriel cut in softly, an edge to those husky tones. 'You no longer find me sexy?'

If Bella found Gabriel any sexier she would literally be drooling down her chin at how gorgeous he looked this evening with the dark thickness of his hair flowing onto his shoulders and the way that cream silk shirt emphasised every muscled inch of his chest.

If Bella found him any sexier she would be ripping that shirt from his back just so that she could touch bare flesh.

If she found Gabriel any sexier she would be on her knees begging him to make love to her again!

And again.

And again…

Just thinking about it made Bella's breasts firm and swell, the nipples hardening against the soft material of her dress, and an aching warmth begin to start between her thighs.

She shot him an irritated glance. 'You should have a public health warning stamped on your forehead!' She scowled as he began to smile. 'I'm glad *you* think it's funny,' she muttered.

Gabriel continued to smile as he regarded Bella across the width of the table. Without Bella realising it—or particularly wanting it?—they were becoming easier together in each other's company.

He sat forward slightly. 'Your public health warning should be on your breasts.'

Colour suffused Bella's cheeks. 'My *breasts*...?' she choked.

Gabriel nodded. 'They are beautiful, Bella. Firm. Round. A perfect fit in my hands. And your nipples are—'

'I'm not sure this is altogether polite after-dinner conversation, Gabriel!' she gasped when she could once more catch her breath.

Gabriel allowed his gaze to lower to the part of her anatomy under discussion as they pressed firm and pouting against the material of her gown. A clear indication that their conversation had roused Bella as much as it had him.

Yet he could not—no, he dared not—make love to her. The fear of further loss and trauma in his life made Gabriel determined not to put Bella's life at risk with a possible second pregnancy.

His mouth tightened as he realised the disastrous predicament he'd landed them both in. 'You are right, Isabella, it is not.' He stood up suddenly.

'I— Where are you going?' Bella frowned as Gabriel strode off towards the beach.

He turned on the pathway, the moonlight turning his hair to ebony and reflecting in his eyes. 'I require some time to myself,' he said distantly.

Gabriel needed some time to himself...

He couldn't have told Bella any more clearly that after only two days alone together he was already bored in her company!

'Fine.' She nodded abruptly. 'I'll see you in morning,

then,' she added lamely, still slightly stunned by the way Gabriel's mood had changed so swiftly from seduction to a need to go off by himself. After spending so many weeks resisting him, Bella was also shocked by the fierce desire that she *wanted* to be seduced.

'No doubt,' he answered curtly.

And, Bella realised painfully, he looked far from pleased at the prospect...

The two days it had taken Gabriel to find himself bored with her company was the same two days it had taken Bella to realise she was more in love with him than ever!

CHAPTER TEN

'BREAKFAST, Bella.'

Bella felt as if she were fighting through layers of fog as she roused herself from a deep and troubled sleep, inwardly wincing as she remembered exactly where she was. And who she was with...

Once again Bella had pretended to be asleep the previous night when Gabriel had finally come to bed about two hours after her, and had known by the restlessness of Gabriel's movements as he lay beside her that he was no more asleep than she was.

Still they hadn't spoken. Hadn't touched. Had just lain there, side by side, awake but totally uncommunicative.

'Your coffee is becoming cold, Bella,' Gabriel told her sharply.

Bella could smell that coffee, and warm buttery croissants, finally opening her eyes to frown up at Gabriel as he stood beside the bed holding a breakfast tray. He was already fully dressed, his hair still damp from the shower, evidence that he had been up for some time.

'Why the breakfast in bed, Gabriel?' Bella sat up against the sumptuous pillows, having decided attack was her best form of defence after the way the two of them had parted the previous evening.

He shrugged. 'It seemed like something a new husband should do for his bride.' He placed the tray across her knees and stepped back.

'No one has ever brought me breakfast in bed before,' Bella muttered uncomfortably, keeping her gaze averted from him to instead look down at the pot of coffee and the freshly warmed croissants with a deliciously tempting pot of butter.

'As we are leaving later this morning I thought it best if I ensure you have something to eat—'

'Leaving?' Bella cut in incredulously, the breakfast tray forgotten as she stared up at Gabriel. 'As in going back to England leaving?'

He gave a haughty inclination of his head. 'As in going back to England leaving,' he confirmed evenly.

Bella was completely stunned as she watched Gabriel begin to take his clothes from the wardrobe obviously in preparation for packing them.

Gabriel had decided they were leaving. After only two days of their planned week-long honeymoon!

She gave a confused frown. 'This is all rather sudden, isn't it?'

What on earth were her family going to make of them cutting their honeymoon short like this? Especially Toby!

Gabriel saw the doubts flickering across Bella's face. A face that showed the strain of the last few days and nights in the heavy tiredness of her eyes and the unhappy slant to her mouth.

The same strain that Gabriel was feeling. Although

he doubted that Bella's strain was for the same reason as his own!

He shook his head. 'You are unhappy here, Isabella.'

'So are you!' she shot back.

His mouth tightened. 'We were not talking about me.'

'No, we weren't, were we?' Bella said. 'Why is that, Gabriel? Why is it that you can never give me a straight-forward answer to a straightforward question?'

Those dark eyes narrowed warningly. 'Perhaps because the questions you ask have no straightforward answer.'

She sighed in disgust. 'You're doing it again!'

Gabriel was well aware of what he was doing. But he could not tell Bella of his fears, of his need to leave here, before he once again put her life at risk if she conceived a second time. 'If you think that your family will be concerned at our early return from our honeymoon, then I suggest you go straight to your cottage. That way no one even has to know we are back.'

Bella frowned. 'What's the difference between us staying here for another five days or hiding out in my cottage?'

Gabriel gave a humourless smile. 'I said that *you* could go straight to your cottage, Isabella, not that I would be joining you there.'

Her face blanked of all expression. 'I see...'

'Do you?' Gabriel said grimly.

'Oh, yes,' Bella snapped as she placed the breakfast tray on the bedside table before swinging her legs to the floor and sitting up. 'I can be ready to leave in half an hour or so, if that's okay with you?'

Gabriel had thought Bella would be pleased at the idea of leaving the island today. That she would be even happier at the idea of being relieved of his company once they were back in England. But instead she merely looked angry.

'There is no rush,' he told her. 'I have radioed ahead and instructed that the plane be fuelled and ready to leave as soon as we arrive.'

'Now I know where Toby gets his organisational skills from!' Bella huffed as she stood up. 'I would like some privacy to get showered and dressed, if you wouldn't mind, Gabriel?' She looked at him challengingly.

'Would it matter if I did?' he growled.

Her eyes flashed violet fire at him. 'Not in the least!'

His mouth thinned to a severe line. 'As I thought. Eat some of the breakfast, Isabella,' he instructed. 'You will feel less sick on the helicopter if you have eaten.'

'No—I'll just have something to be sick with!' she contradicted him mutinously.

'That is true, also,' Gabriel murmured dryly.

Bella glared. 'Please don't attempt to try and sugar-coat it for me!'

She looked so beautiful as she faced him across the room, her face flushed with anger and the darkness of her hair a wild tangle about her shoulders, the long, pale cream nightgown clinging to the lushness of her curvaceous figure.

It was all Gabriel could do to stop himself from taking the few steps that separated them before gathering Bella into his arms and making love to her until she screamed for mercy!

Instead he stepped towards the bedroom door. 'I will be outside if you should need me.'

'I won't,' she assured him firmly.

No, she probably wouldn't, Gabriel acknowledged ruefully as he strode outside into the sunshine to take deep, calming breaths of the fragrant air.

Much as he had done the previous evening as he walked along the moonlit shoreline and reminded himself all the reasons he dared not make love to Bella again...

'I thought you said you had to leave?' Bella reminded Gabriel many hours later as, having driven her to her cottage, he now lingered in the sitting-room.

The helicopter flight to the mainland had been less traumatic than the one going to the island, Bella having been prepared for the uneven flight this time.

The long flight on the Danti jet back to England had been free of incident, too—probably because neither of them had suggested going anywhere near the temptation of the bedroom at the back of the plane!

Once they'd landed in England Bella had protested the need for Gabriel to drive her back to the cottage. She could find her own way, she'd said. But it had been a battle she had lost. As she lost all of her battles against Gabriel...

But having been delivered here safely, Bella now expected him to leave. In fact, she was counting on it. Mainly because if Gabriel didn't soon go and leave her to her privacy, Bella knew she was going to give in to the hot tears that had been threatening to fall all day!

'Are you not going to at least offer me a cup of coffee?' Gabriel asked.

Her eyes widened. 'It's late, Gabriel, and I thought you had somewhere else to go.'

He frowned. 'I did not say that.'

'You implied it.'

Gabriel was well aware of what he had implied. As he was aware, now the time had come to part from Bella, that he was reluctant to do so.

'I am not sure it is the right thing to do, to just leave you here on your own.'

She laughed humourlessly. 'I've lived on my own for two years, Gabriel—'

'You have lived here with Toby,' he cut in firmly. 'That is not the same thing.'

No, it wasn't, Bella accepted ruefully, already aware of how quiet, how empty, the cottage seemed without her small son's presence.

'I'm a big girl now, Gabriel; I'm sure I'll manage,' she said dryly.

His eyes darkened in intensity, that familiar nerve pulsing in his clenched jaw. 'I am well aware of the fact that you are a big girl, Isabella.'

'Then I suggest you stop treating me like I'm six years old rather than twenty-six!'

His mouth flattened into a disapproving line. 'Showing concern for your welfare is treating you like a child?'

Bella shook her head impatiently. 'No, actually treating me like a child is doing that!'

'How would you have me treat you, Isabella?' Gabriel glowered his frustration with this conversation.

Bella became very still, very aware of the sudden tension in the room. She could almost feel the crackle of electricity that arced between herself and Gabriel...

She swallowed hard. 'I think you should just go.'

Gabriel thought so, too. In fact, he knew so! Before he did something he would later regret. Something they might both have reason to regret.

Except…

Bella looked tired after their long journey, her eyes purple smudges in a face that was pale with exhaustion, and the fullness of her lips bare of lip gloss. But nevertheless there was a beguiling determination to the stubborn lift of her chin, that challenge reflected in the brilliance of her eyes and the proud stance of her tiny body.

Gabriel felt the throb of his arousal just looking at her. Telling him it was definitely time that he left!

'I should go, yes,' he acknowledged huskily.

'Yes.'

'Now.'

'Yes.'

'Bella—'

'Gabriel…?'

He drew in a ragged breath. 'I need to go!'

'You do.'

Except Gabriel moved *towards* Bella rather than away from her as he crossed the room in two long strides to pull her hard against him even as his head lowered and his mouth claimed hers in a need as primitive and as old as time.

As wild and primitive as his fierce, uncontrollable desire to possess Bella again…

Gabriel's hands moved to become entangled in her hair as he kissed her hungrily, fiercely, his lips parting hers and allowing his tongue to plunge deeply into the heat beyond. Bella's mouth tasted of honey, and was hot, so very hot, as she drew him deeper inside her.

Gabriel curved her body into the hardness of his as he continued to kiss and claim her. His hands spread over her bottom as he pulled her against him and pressed her to the ache in his thighs, his arousal hard and pulsing, demanding, the need to possess her so strong that Gabriel could think of nothing else, feel nothing else but Bella.

He wrenched his mouth from hers to bury his face against the satin smoothness of her throat, licking, tasting, biting. 'We should stop this now, Bella!'

'Yes,' she breathed shakily.

'I cannot be gentle with you!' Gabriel groaned, knowing it was true. He had waited too long. Wanted her for far too long!

Bella already knew that, had felt his urgency the moment he took her in his arms. An urgency that she echoed, that had ignited the moment he'd touched her. No, even before he'd touched her! This physical awareness had been there between them all day, Bella realised now, burning just below the surface of even the most mundane of conversations.

'I won't break, Gabriel,' she encouraged, her throat arched to the erotic heat of his questing mouth, her fingers entangled in the silky softness of his hair. 'Just don't stop. Please don't stop...' She quivered with longing, several buttons ripping off her blouse as Gabriel parted it to bare her breasts to his lips and tongue, drawing one swollen tip into the heat of his mouth hungrily as one of his hands cupped and squeezed its twin.

Bella sobbed low in her throat as the pleasure ripped through her, to become centred as a hot ache between her thighs. She was so swollen there, so needy as she pressed against Gabriel's arousal, she could barely think straight.

He moved against her, his hardness, his length and

thickness, a promise of even greater pleasure. A pleasure Bella had no intention of letting Gabriel deny either of them. She wanted him inside her. Wanted to look up at Gabriel, to watch his face as he stroked long and hard inside her. Wanted to hear his groans of pleasure as they matched her own. To hear his cries as they reached that pinnacle together.

'Not this time, Gabriel.' She moved away as his hand went to open the fastening of her jeans. 'I want to touch you first. Kiss you. All of you,' she added huskily, her gaze deliberately holding his as she unbuttoned his shirt before slowly slipping it down his arms and dropping it onto the carpeted floor. Her fingers looked much paler than the darkness of Gabriel's skin as she touched the hard wall of his chest. 'You're so beautiful, Gabriel…!' she whispered before she began to kiss each and every one of his scars, her tongue a delicate rasp against the heat of his skin as she tasted him.

Gabriel knew that his scarred body was far from beautiful, but he ceased to care about anything else as Bella's lips roamed across him freely, her tongue flickering against him even as her hand flattened against the hardness of his arousal, his erection responding immediately as that hand moved against him slowly, rhythmically. Gabriel felt his blood pulsing, pounding, increasing in urgency.

They had spent five weeks together before their wedding and two days alone on a romantic Caribbean island. And yet it was here, and now, in Bella's tiny cottage, when he knew they would be apart for several hours, that Gabriel completely lost control!

'I need—Bella, I need—' He broke off with a groan

as Bella unfastened his jeans and pushed them out of the way so that she might fulfil that need.

Her mouth was so hot as she took him inside her, her tongue moist and her fingers curling about him as she caressed the length of him.

Gabriel became lost in the pleasure of this dual assault upon his senses, his neck arched, his muscles tensing, locking, as he fought to maintain control.

Just a little longer. He wanted—needed to enjoy being with Bella just a little longer, and then he would leave, Gabriel promised himself silently as Bella manoeuvred him gently backwards so that he sat down in an armchair, her hair a wild tumble about his thighs as she knelt in front of him.

Just a few minutes more of being inside the heat of Bella's mouth. Of her wicked little tongue moistly caressing the length of his shaft. Of her fingers about him as he instinctively began to move to that same mind-blowing rhythm.

Bella raised her lids to look at Gabriel, deliberately holding his gaze with hers as her tongue swirled provocatively about the head of his pulsing erection. Licking. Teasing. Tasting.

Gabriel's face was flushed with arousal, his eyes fevered, his jaw clenched, and the muscles standing out in his throat as he fought not to lose that control.

'No more!' he growled even as he reached down and pulled Bella away from him, grasping her arms to lift her up so that his mouth could capture hers. Bella straddled him as they kissed wildly, feverishly, Gabriel's hands hot against her back as his mouth made love to hers.

Gabriel stood up, their mouths still fused wildly

together. His hands cupped about Bella's bottom to lift her up with him before he lay her down on the carpeted floor, lifting his head to part her already ruined blouse and then feast on her naked breasts.

He kissed first one nipple and then the other, Bella whimpering softly when he finally raised his head to look down at the swollen fullness of her breasts. His gaze deliberately held hers as he moved to his knees beside her to brush the pads of his thumbs over those achingly sensitive nipples, watching the way Bella's eyes darkened and she groaned low in her throat even as she arched up into that caress.

Gabriel continued to hold that gaze as he unfastened her jeans and peeled them down her thighs to remove them completely, parting her legs so that he could move in between them. His hands were big and dark against her abdomen as he caressed her in slow swirling movements in a deliberate path to the soft, dark curls that were visible to him through the cream lace of her panties.

Bella was breathing hard as she watched Gabriel touching her, his fingers warm and gentle. A low moan escaped her as he swept one of those fingers against the lacy material that covered the cleft between her legs, her hips moving up to meet that tantalising caress.

That finger moved against her again.

Again Bella moved up to meet that caress.

And again.

Teasing her. Pleasuring her. Torturing her.

'Yes, Gabriel…!' Bella finally pleaded as she moved against him in frustration.

He peeled her panties down her thighs and legs to discard them completely, his eyes intense as he looked down at her before slowly lowering his head. First his hands touched her, then his lips, softly, tenderly as he kissed the scar that hadn't been there five years ago.

But Bella had no time to dwell on that as his fingers parted the dark curls beneath and his mouth moved lower…

Dear God!

Pleasure unlike anything she had ever known before radiated out to every part of her body as the sweep of Gabriel's tongue against that pulsing nub brought her to the edge of release and then took her crashing over it in wave after wave of such intensity it was almost pain.

Bella was mindless with pleasure, her breath releasing in a sob as she felt Gabriel part her sensitive folds and enter her, first with one finger, and then with two. As his tongue continued to caress that aching nub her head moved wildly from side to side and her hands clenched as Gabriel took her to a climax that was even more intense than the first.

It wasn't enough.

It would never be enough!

Bella surged up to push Gabriel down onto the carpet and pull off his remaining clothes before moving up and over him, her hands resting against his shoulders as the heat between her thighs became a hot caress against the hardness of his shaft, her breasts a temptation just beyond his reach as she bent slightly towards him.

'No, Bella—' Gabriel broke off with a groan as she opened herself to him and took him into her, inch by slow inch, until he was completely inside her. Her heat, her tightness wrapped around him. 'We must not do this—'

'*I* must,' she insisted.

Gabriel ceased breathing altogether as Bella began to move with an agonising slowness that sent the pleasure rocketing into his brain and down to his toes.

Gabriel felt himself grow even harder, bigger, no longer able to bear the torment of her breasts above him as he moved his head up and captured one of those rose-tipped breasts into his mouth.

Bella plunged down to take him deeper, before moving up so that only the very tip of him remained inside her. Before plunging down again and again. Gabriel was so big now, so long that it felt as if he touched the very centre of her.

His hands moved to grasp her hips and guide her movements as he felt his imminent release, hearing Bella's cry as she reached a climax at the same time as he did.

CHAPTER ELEVEN

'WE SHOULD not have done that!'

Bella had collapsed weakly against the dampness of Gabriel's chest as the last of the pleasure rippled through her body, but she raised her head now to look down at him incredulously. '*What* did you just say?'

Gabriel's expression was grim as he returned her gaze. 'I should not have done this, Bella—'

She gasped in shock, moving abruptly back and then away from him, clasping her ruined blouse about her nakedness as she disengaged their bodies before standing up. 'Get out, Gabriel,' she choked.

'Bella—'

'Just *get out*!' she repeated shakily, turning away to find her panties, her legs trembling slightly as she tried to balance before pulling them on over her nakedness.

How could Gabriel do this to her? How could he?

What she had thought of as being something beautiful, utterly unique, had now become nothing more than something she wished to forget.

To wish had never happened!

'Would you just put some clothes on and leave, Gabriel?'

He rose slowly to his feet, magnificent in his nakedness, his hair tousled about his shoulders, his chest
broad and muscled, thighs powerful still, his legs long
and elegant.

Bella turned away from looking at all that raw, male
beauty. 'I don't want you to say anything, Gabriel. I
don't want you to do anything. I just want you to get
dressed and leave. Now,' she insisted.

'Bella—'

'*Now!*'

'You misunderstood my reasoning just now, Bella—'

'Don't touch me!' She moved sharply away from the
hands he placed on her shoulders, shying away from
even that physical contact.

Gabriel frowned fiercely as he saw her expression.
'You did not seem to find my touch so distasteful a few
minutes ago,' he rasped.

'Any more than you did mine,' she retaliated. 'I guess
we both just got so carried away with the moment we
forgot to look at the broader picture!'

Gabriel's eyes narrowed. 'And what might that be?'
he asked softly.

'Will you just get some clothes on?' she repeated impatiently. 'I find it a little disconcerting talking to a man
when he's completely naked.'

'I'm not just any man, Isabella, I am your husband,'
he pointed out harshly as he swiftly pulled his jeans
back on and fastened them.

'I know exactly who and what you are, Gabriel,' she
said. 'What I meant, Gabriel, is that the only reason you
married me was because of Toby—'

'Isabella—'

'Would you have even thought of offering me marriage if not for Toby?' she challenged.

'Neither of us will ever know now what would have happened after we met again in San Francisco—'

'*I* know,' Bella said scornfully. 'I very much doubt we would ever have seen each other again after San Francisco if you hadn't learnt of Toby's existence!'

Gabriel drew in a deep, controlling breath. 'This is perhaps not the time to talk about this. You are distraught—'

'I'm *angry*, Gabriel, not distraught. With myself,' she added. 'For falling—yet again!—for your seduction routine!'

'My seduction routine?' he echoed incredulously.

Bella nodded. 'No doubt honed over years spent on the Formula One racing circuit! And don't bother trying to deny it,' she warned. 'I still remember the practised way you seduced me five years ago!'

He scowled. 'That was five years ago, Isabella—'

'Then you must be pleased to know that you haven't lost any of your seductive skills!' she snapped.

Gabriel studied her closely, wanting to take her in his arms, to explain his fears for her—

'Insulting me is only making this situation worse, Bella,' he told her softly instead.

'Worse? Could it be any worse?' she cried. 'We've just ripped each other's clothes off in a sexual frenzy— in my case, literally.' She looked down at her gaping blouse, the buttons scattered on the carpet at their feet. 'I don't want to talk about this any more, Gabriel,' she told him flatly, her expression bleak. 'All I want is for you to leave.'

Gabriel's mouth firmed. 'I will return tomorrow—'

'Don't hurry back on my account!' she exclaimed.

'We need to talk.'

'I very much doubt that there's anything you have to say that I will want to hear,' she told him wearily.

A nerve pulsed in Gabriel's clenched jaw. Bella looked so beautiful with the darkness of her hair tangled about her shoulders, and her lips still swollen from the heat of their kisses, so utterly desirable, that all Gabriel wanted was to take her in his arms and make love with her again. And again.

'Nevertheless, I will return later tomorrow,' he bit out with grim determination.

She raised mocking brows as he made no effort to leave. 'I hope you aren't waiting for me to tell you I'll be looking forward to it!'

'No, I am not expecting you to say that.' Gabriel gave a humourless smile. 'Your honesty is one of the things I like most about you, Bella.'

'One of the few things, I'm sure,' she said knowingly. 'If you'll excuse me, now?' She turned away. 'I would like to take a shower and then go to bed.'

Alone, Bella could have added, but didn't. What was the point in stating the obvious?

She raised her chin defensively. 'Goodbye, Gabriel.'

'It will never be goodbye between the two of us, Isabella,' he stated calmly.

No, it never would be, Bella accepted heavily once Gabriel had finally gone. They would continue with this sham of a marriage for as long as it took. For as long as Toby needed them to do so.

For Toby…

Her small, happily contented son had absolutely no idea that his very existence had condemned his parents to a marriage that was completely devoid of love.

Except Bella's love for Gabriel.

A love she would never—could never, reveal to him…

'Where have you been?'

'Where does it look as if I've been?' Bella answered Gabriel sarcastically as she carried on taking the bags of shopping from the boot of her car. 'I wasn't expecting you back just yet,' she added as Gabriel took some of those bags out of her hands.

She had seen the powerful black sports car parked outside the cottage as soon as she turned her own car down the lane, a heaviness settling in her chest as she easily recognised Gabriel sitting behind the wheel.

Despite her exhaustion Bella had lain awake in bed for hours the previous night, unable to stop thinking about Gabriel. About the wild ecstasy of their lovemaking. And then of his declaration that they shouldn't have made love at all…!

Consequently it had been almost dawn before she had finally fallen asleep. Almost midday before she'd woke up again, feeling as if she hadn't slept at all. Several hours, and half a dozen cups of black coffee later, before she'd summoned up the energy to dress and go out to shop for food.

Which was where she had obviously been when Gabriel had arrived at the cottage. Much earlier than she had expected—it was only a little after five o'clock— and looking much too rakishly handsome for Bella's comfort in a black polo shirt and faded jeans.

'Thanks,' Bella accepted coolly as he carried half a dozen of the bags through to the kitchen for her. 'Can I get you a coffee or anything?' she said offhandedly, her face averted as she began to unpack the bags.

But—as usual!—she was still very much aware of Gabriel as he stood only a couple of feet away from her as she put the groceries away in the cupboards. Silently. Watchfully.

'Better yet,' she added brightly, 'why don't you make yourself useful and prepare the coffee while I finish putting these things away? Gabriel...?' she said uncertainly when he didn't answer her. In fact, Bella realised with a frown, he hadn't said a word since asking where she had been...

Gabriel looked at her quizzically, easily noting the dark shadows beneath her eyes, and the hollows of her cheeks, the pallor of her face thrown into stark relief by the fact that her hair was drawn back and secured at her crown with a toothed clasp.

Dressed in a deep pink T-shirt that clung to the fullness of her breasts, and jeans that emphasised the slenderness of her hips and legs, and with her face completely bare of make-up, Bella looked ten years younger than the twenty-six years she had only yesterday evening assured him she actually was.

Gabriel's mouth tightened as he thought of yesterday evening. 'I will make the coffee. Then I wish for the two of us to talk.'

She stiffened. 'Not about last night, I hope?'

He gave a stiff inclination of his head. 'Amongst other things.'

Bella made a movement of denial. 'There's nothing left for us to say about last night—'

'There is *everything* for us to say about last night!' Gabriel contradicted her furiously before visibly controlling himself. 'I will not let you put even more barriers between us, Bella. If you prefer, I will talk, and you need only listen...?'

Bella eyed him warily, having no idea what he could have to say that she would want to listen to. He had said far too much last night!

'And if I don't like what you have to say?' she challenged.

'Then I will have to respect that,' he said curtly.

Bella continued to look at him wordlessly for several long seconds before giving an abrupt nod of her head. 'Fine,' she said. 'Just make the coffee first, hmm?'

What should have been a relaxed domestic scene, with Bella putting the groceries away and Gabriel making the pot of coffee, was anything but! Bella was far too aware of Gabriel—on every level—to feel in the least relaxed.

How could she possibly relax when Gabriel was just too vibrantly male? Too ruggedly handsome. Too physically overpowering. Too—too everything!

But, having finally put all the shopping away, two mugs of hot coffee poured and Gabriel already seated at the kitchen table, there was nothing else Bella could do to delay sitting down and listening while Gabriel talked.

'Well?' she prompted sharply after several seconds, the silence between them so absolute that Bella could hear every tick of the clock hanging on the wall above the dresser.

Gabriel's expression was pained. 'I realise you are still angry with me, Bella, but I do not believe I have done anything to deserve your contempt.'

Not recently, Bella acknowledged self-derisively, having accepted during her deliberations last night that she was just as responsible for what had happened between them the previous evening as Gabriel was. That she had wanted him as much as he had appeared to want her.

She sighed heavily. 'I'm not angry, Gabriel,' she admitted ruefully. 'At least, not with you.'

He gave her a searching glance. 'You are angry with yourself because we made love last night?'

'We had *sex* last night, Gabriel—'

'We *made love*—'

'You can call it what you like, but we both know what it really was!' Her eyes glittered angrily.

Gabriel drew in another controlling breath. 'I thought I was going to talk and you were going to listen?'

'Not if you're going to say things I don't agree with!' she snapped.

Gabriel didn't know whether to shake Bella or kiss her! Although he very much doubted that Bella would welcome either action in her present mood.

'I will endeavour not to do so,' he teased.

'You just can't guarantee it,' Bella acknowledged dryly.

Gabriel shrugged. 'It is not always possible to know what is or is not going to anger you.'

'Well, as long as you steer clear of last night or anything that happened five years ago, you should be on pretty safe ground!'

Gabriel grimaced. 'Ah.'

Her eyes widened. 'You *are* going to tell me about five years ago…?'

'It was my intention to do so, yes.'

'But—you've never wanted to talk about it!'

'The situation has changed— Bella…?' he questioned as she stood up abruptly and moved to stand with her back to the room as she stared out of the kitchen window.

Bella's neck was so delicately vulnerable, her back slender, her shoulders narrow—far too narrow, Gabriel acknowledged heavily, for her to have carried alone the burden of her pregnancy and then the bringing up of their son for the last four and a half years.

'Please, Bella…?' he asked again softly.

It felt as if Bella's heart were actually being squeezed in her chest as she heard the gentleness in Gabriel's tone.

When they were on the island she had asked Gabriel to tell her what really happened five years ago. At the time she had genuinely wanted to know the answer. But now—now when Bella already felt so vulnerable and exposed by her realised love for him, by the wildness of their lovemaking the previous evening—she really wasn't sure she could bear to hear Gabriel talk about his feelings for another woman.

Especially if he were to tell her he still had those feelings for Janine Childe…!

Coward, a little voice inside her head taunted mockingly. Bella had always known that Gabriel hadn't, didn't, and never would love her, so what difference did it make if he was now willing to talk about five years ago?

It shouldn't matter at all!

But it did…

Bella stiffened her shoulders, her expression deliberately unreadable as she turned back to face Gabriel. A defensive stance that almost crumbled as the gentleness she had heard in Gabriel's tone was echoed in the darkness of his eyes as he looked across the kitchen at her.

Damn it, she didn't want his pity!

She wanted his love. She had wanted that five years ago, and she wanted it even more now. But if she couldn't have that then she certainly didn't want his pity!

Her shoulders straightened and her chin raised in challenge. 'Go ahead,' she finally invited tightly.

Gabriel continued to look at her silently for several seconds, and then he gave a decisive inclination of his head. 'First I need to tell you where I have been since we parted yesterday evening—'

'You said we were going to talk about what happened five years ago!' Bella cut in impatiently. Having built herself up, having placed a shield about her shaky emotions, Bella now needed to get this conversation over with before that barrier crumbled into dust!

Gabriel sighed at the interruption. 'My actions since we parted yesterday are relevant to that past. Sit with me, Bella?' Gabriel encouraged huskily as he saw that her face was paler than ever, those dark shadows beneath her eyes emphasised further by that pallor.

The fact that Bella actually did as he asked told Gabriel how much his presence, this conversation, had unsettled her. The last thing he wanted to do was hurt Bella any more than he already had, and yet it seemed his mere presence had managed do that.

He rubbed his eyes wearily. 'I will leave any time you ask me to do so, Bella.'

She gave a humourless smile. 'Is that a promise?'

'If you wish it, yes,' Gabriel assured her wryly.

Her eyed widened at his compliance. 'Are you sure you haven't received a blow to the head while you've been away?'

'Very funny, Bella,' he drawled.

'One tries,' she teased lightly.

Gabriel wasn't fooled for a moment by Bella's attempt at levity, knew by the wariness in her eyes and the tension beside her mouth that it was only a façade.

As his own calm was only a façade.

A nerve pulsed beside the livid scar on Gabriel's cheek. 'Bella, when we were on the island you asked me what really happened five years ago, when three Formula One cars crashed and two other men were killed as a consequence. Do you still want to know the answer to that question?'

'Yes, of course!'

'And you will believe me if I tell you the truth?'

'Of course I'll believe you, Gabriel.' She looked irritated that he should doubt it.

He smiled briefly. 'As was stated at the time, the findings of the official enquiry were that it was a complete accident, but I knew—I have always known—that it was Paulo Descari, and not I, who was responsible for our three cars colliding.'

'But—' Bella gasped. 'It was deliberate?'

Gabriel's jaw clenched. 'I believe so, yes.'

Bella stared at him, her expression once again blank. Why on earth would Paulo Descari have done such a thing? Unless…

'Because Janine Childe had decided she had made a mistake? That she returned your love, after all?' Bella realised heavily. 'Had she told Paulo Descari she was ending their relationship in order to come back to you?'

Gabriel's expression was grim as he stood up abruptly. 'Neither of those things was possible, I am afraid, Bella,' he rasped. 'The first for the simple reason that there was no love on my side for Janine Childe to return. The second because it was I who had ended our brief relationship, and not the other way around as Janine so publicly claimed only hours after the accident. But I do believe Janine may have taunted Paulo with our relationship,' he continued. 'He tried to provoke an argument with me that morning, was so blind with jealousy that he would not believe me when I told him I had no feelings for Janine.' He sighed heavily. 'I was not physically responsible for the accident, Bella, but I have nevertheless always felt a certain guilt, not only because of my complete indifference to Janine, but because I survived and two other men did not.'

'But that's— You have no reason to feel guilty, Gabriel.' Bella gasped. 'You could so easily have died, too!'

'And instead I am here. With you,' Gabriel murmured huskily.

How long would it take for Bella to realise, to question, after the things he had just told her, the night the two of them had spent together five years ago?

Gabriel watched as the blankness left Bella's face to be replaced with a frown, that frown disappearing, too, seconds later as she looked across at him questioningly.

Gabriel drew in a controlling breath. 'I was unconscious for several days after the accident, and so was unable at the time to deny or confirm Janine's claim that I had caused the accident because I was still in love with her.' His top lip turned back contemptuously. 'By the time I was well enough to deny her accusations I simply did not care to do so,' he added flatly.

'Why didn't you?' Bella demanded incredulously.

'Surely you must have realised that Janine Childe's claims gave people reason to continue to have doubts despite the findings of the official enquiry?'

His eyes narrowed. 'Did you have reason to continue to doubt them, too, Bella?'

She shook her head vehemently. 'Not over your innocence, no.'

Gabriel had thought, had hoped this would be easier than it was. But it wasn't. Baring his soul in this way, with no idea of the outcome, was excruciating.

'I don't understand why you didn't speak out, Gabriel,' Bella said. 'From what you've said, you were supposed to be the one who died that day!'

He turned away. 'Jason was dead. As was Paulo. When people die, Bella, all that is left is the memories people who loved them have of them. What good did it do anyone, but especially Paulo and Jason's families, for me to claim that one man had possibly been deliberately responsible for the death of the other?'

Bella could see the logic behind Gabriel's words— she just couldn't make any sense of it!

'That was…very self-sacrificing, of you,' she murmured gently.

'More so than even I realised,' he acknowledged harshly.

She looked up sharply as a realisation hit her. 'You really didn't make love to me that night because you were upset at losing Janine Childe to another man, did you?'

His smile was rueful. 'No, I did not.'

'Then—that morning you—' She moistened dry lips. 'You said you would call me. Did you really mean it?'

'Yes.'

'You did?' The beat of Bella's heart sounded very loud in her ears as her thoughts—her hopes, rose wildly.

'I did,' Gabriel confirmed heavily. 'Our night together had been—surprising.'

'Really?'

'Yes.' Gabriel took a deep breath. 'Unfortunately that altercation with Paulo meant I did not have chance to ring you before the practice session, and obviously I was unable to do so afterwards. Then, once I recovered and there had been no word from you, I believed you did not want to know.'

Bella's hands were clenched so tightly that she could feel her nails piercing the skin of her palms. Gabriel hadn't been in love with Janine Childe, not then and certainly not now. Gabriel had meant it that morning five years ago when he had said he would call her.

Tears blurred Bella's vision, Gabriel just a hazy outline as he stood so still and silent across the kitchen. 'I thought—I didn't believe I would ever see you again after that night.'

'A belief that became fact,' Gabriel rasped.

'But not because you wanted it that way!' Bella protested achingly.

'No.'

'Gabriel, I—I don't know what to say!' She stood up restlessly. 'I was sitting at home that night when the announcement of the crash came on the evening news. Saw the two bodies lying on the ground. You being carried away on a stretcher before they placed you in the ambulance and rushed you off to hospital. It was the worst moment of my life.' She gave a disbelieving shake of her head. 'Or, at least, I thought it was, until Janine

Childe appeared on the television immediately afterwards claiming that you were still in love with her.'

'It never occurred to me—I never realised that her lies would have convinced anyone, but I suppose I knew the real Janine, and you didn't." Gabriel frowned.

'It was the one about your being in love with her that I thought to be true,' Bella admitted. 'I didn't know you well, Gabriel, but I certainly never believed you capable of deliberately harming another man.'

'Bella, what would you have done that day if you had not believed I was in love with Janine?'

'I would have come to you, of course!' she exclaimed. 'I wouldn't have cared who had tried to stop me. I would have made them let me see you!'

'Why?'

Bella raised wary eyes to his. 'Why…?'

'Why, Bella?' Gabriel repeated gruffly.

Because she had fallen in love with him that night, that was why! Because she was still in love with him!

Gabriel's eyes narrowed as he saw the uncertainty flicker across Bella's face. The wariness. The desire not to be hurt again.

Gabriel felt that same desire, both five years ago and again now.

He drew in a deep breath, accepting that one of them had to break the deadlock between them. 'Perhaps if I were to tell you why it was that I had no interest in what people believed happened that day…?'

Bella blinked, her throat moving convulsively as she swallowed hard before speaking. 'Why didn't you, Gabriel?'

His mouth twisted. 'For the same reason that nothing

mattered to me when I regained consciousness two days after the accident.' He shrugged. 'Because you were not there, Bella,' he admitted bluntly. 'You were not there. Had never been there. And no matter how much I wished for it during those three months I spent in hospital, you still did not come.'

Bella looked totally stunned now. 'I don't understand...'

'No, I do not suppose that you do,' he accepted ruefully as he was the one to take the two steps that separated them before raising one of his hands to curve it about the coolness of her cheek. 'My beautiful Bella. My brave beautiful Bella.' He smiled emotionally. 'After all this time, all you have suffered, you deserve to know the truth.'

'The truth...?'

'That I fell in love with you that night five years ago—'

'No...!' Her cry was agonised and Gabriel only just managed to prevent her from falling as her knees gave way beneath her.

'Yes, Bella.' Gabriel's arms moved about her, his cheek resting against the darkness of her hair as he gathered her close against his chest. 'Impossible as it must seem, I fell in love with you that night. I have loved you always, Bella. You and only you. So much so that there has been no other woman in my life, or my bed, these last five years,' he added gruffly.

Bella clung to him as his words washed over and then into her. She had been stunned by what he had told her about the accident and by Janine Childe's duplicity, but this was even more shocking.

Gabriel loved her. He had always loved her.

The tears fell hotly down Bella's cheeks as she clung to him.

As she cried for all the pain and disillusionment they had unwittingly caused each other through misunderstandings. For all the time they had wasted…

She pulled away from him slightly before looking up into his face, her heart aching as she still saw the uncertainty in his face. 'Gabriel, impossible as it must seem, I fell in love with you that night five years ago, too.' Bella held his gaze with hers as she deliberately repeated his words. 'I have loved you always, Gabriel. You and only you. So much so that there has been no other man in my life, or my bed, these last five years.'

His expression didn't change. He didn't blink. He didn't speak. He didn't even seem to be breathing as he continued to stare down at her.

'Gabriel?' Bella's gaze searched his face worriedly. 'Gabriel, I love you. I love you!' she repeated desperately as she reached up to clasp his arms and shake him slightly. 'I never meant to let you down after the accident, I just thought I had been a one-night stand to you. Gabriel, please—'

'You did not let me down, Bella,' he cut in harshly. 'You have never let me down. *I* was the one who let *you* down when it did not even occur to me that you might believe I was in love with Janine. *I* was the one who let *you* down by not even thinking you might become pregnant from our night together. How can you love me after what you have suffered because my pride would not let me be the one to seek you out again? How can you love me when my arrogance, my intolerance, meant you had to go through your pregnancy, Toby's birth, the first four and a half years of his life, completely alone?'

'Gabriel, I'd really rather you didn't continue to insult the man I love,' Bella interrupted shakily. 'And I wasn't alone,' she reassured him. 'I had my parents. My sister and brother.'

'I should have been there for you, too,' Gabriel growled in self-disgust. 'Instead of which, when we did finally meet up again, I only made matters worse by forcing you into marrying me.' He shook his head. 'I should not have done that, Bella.'

'You're Toby's father—'

'He was not the reason I forced our marriage upon you, Bella. It was—' He stopped and then sighed. 'Having met you again, having realised that I still love you, I could not bear the thought of having to let you go again!'

Gabriel hadn't married her just for Toby, after all?

Bella looked puzzled. 'But if you felt that way—if you do still love me—'

'I love you now more than ever, Bella,' he assured her fiercely.

'Then why did we leave the island so abruptly?'

'We left the island so suddenly for the same reason I should not have allowed our lovemaking last night to go as far as it did,' Gabriel cut in grimly. 'You almost died giving birth to Toby, Bella. I would not—I did not want to put your life at risk by another unplanned pregnancy, and so I decided we had to leave the island before I gave in to the temptation being alone there with you represented. That we needed to consult an obstetrician before we made love again. Instead of which, as soon as we were back here, I allowed—!' He shook his head.

'I had an appointment to see a specialist in Harley Street today, needed to know that a second pregnancy would not endanger your life. He was most unhelpful,' Gabriel said, patently annoyed, 'and said he could not pass comment before first examining you.'

'You spoke to an obstetrician about me...?' Bella echoed dazedly.

Gabriel frowned darkly. 'What if you are pregnant right now, Bella?' His face had gone pale at the mere thought of it. 'What if our time together last night results in another child?'

A slow, beatific smile curved Bella's lips as she realised their sudden flight from the island, Gabriel's grimness after they made love last night, had all been for one reason and one reason only.

'Then I, for one, would be absolutely thrilled,' she assured him breathlessly. 'I thought you wanted lots of brothers and sisters for Toby?' she cajoled as Gabriel still looked haunted.

'Not at the risk of losing you,' he stated definitely.

'We don't know for sure that there is any risk,' Bella teased him, no longer daunted by the fierceness of Gabriel's moods. He loved her. They loved each other. Together they could overcome any obstacles that might come their way.

'Until you have seen this obstetrician we do not know for sure that there is not, either,' Gabriel persisted.

'Have a little faith, Gabriel. Remember you're a Danti!'

Some of the tension started to leave Gabriel's body as Bella's eyes laughed up into his. 'Are you mocking me, Bella?'

'Just a little.' Her throaty chuckle gave lie to the

claim. 'I'm all for taking risks, Gabriel. In fact, I think a little more risk-taking right now might be good for both of us...' she added huskily, taking his hand in hers to begin walking towards the stairs, shooting him a provocative smile over her shoulder as she did so.

Gabriel followed Bella like a man in a daze, totally unable to deny her anything. Knowing that he never would be able to deny her anything. That, having found her again, knowing she loved him as much as he loved her, that she always had, he intended spending the rest of his life loving as well as protecting Bella.

Their daughter, Clara Louisa, was born safely and without complications exactly a year later, followed two years later by the equally safe birth of their twin sons, Simon Henry and Peter Cristo...

* * * * *

Pregnant by the Millionaire

CAROLE MORTIMER

CHAPTER ONE

NICK woke up alone.

Which was strange, because he was pretty sure he hadn't been alone when he'd fallen into a satiated asleep several hours ago.

Something about a goddess...?

Ah, yes—Hebe, the goddess of youth.

Tall, slender, with a long, straight curtain of silver-blonde hair and eyes of so pale a brown they were gold. Strange magnetic eyes, that gleamed with a multitude of secrets.

Not that he was interested in learning those secrets. Hebe had merely been a distraction, a way of putting the past and all the pain and the significance of the day behind him. He had wanted to forget, be diverted, and the presence of Hebe Johnson had certainly provided that. For a few hours, at least.

So where was she? It was still dark outside, and the tangled sheets beside him were still warm, so she couldn't have been gone long.

He frowned slightly at the thought of her having just disappeared into the night. That was usually *his* privilege! Wine, dine and bed a woman, but never ever become involved—least of all allow them into the inner privacy of his life.

Of course that was slightly more difficult when it was his bed they had shared!

Because she didn't live alone, he remembered now. Something about a flatmate. So after dinner he had brought her back to his apartment over the gallery for a drink instead—and other things!—breaking his cardinal rule in the bargain.

Two rules, in fact, he acknowledged with a grimace as he remembered that Hebe actually worked for him, two floors down, in the Cavendish Gallery on the ground floor.

But desperate times called for desperate measures, and so he had brought Hebe back here, needing to lose himself in the lithe beauty of her perfect, long-limbed body. And he had. He'd found himself dazzled, bewitched—the fact that she wasn't one of the sophisticated women who usually had a brief place in his life, adding to the excitement of the evening. To the point that his pain had been anaesthetised, if not completely erased.

Nick gave a groan as he remembered what yesterday signified, moving to sit up in the bed, needing to get away from the scene of that heated lovemaking now, and standing up to turn his back on those tumbled sheets before walking out of the bedroom.

Only to come to an abrupt halt as he saw he wasn't alone after all.

Hebe, the goddess, was just switching the light off as she came out of the kitchen with a glass of water in her hand, her nakedness only shielded by the fine silver-blonde hair that reached almost to her waist.

Nick instantly felt a stirring of renewed arousal as he looked at that golden body—legs long and silky, hips and waist slenderly curvaceous, breasts firm and uptilting, the nipples rosily pouting.

As if begging to be kissed. Again.

He had noticed her at the gallery several months ago, her beauty such that it was impossible for her not to stand out. But he hadn't so much as spoken to her until yesterday.

And now he wanted her. Again.

'What are you doing?' he prompted huskily as he padded softly across the room to join her, with only a small table-light for illumination.

Hebe's breath caught in her throat just at the sight of him. She was still not quite sure how she had ended up in Nick Cavendish's apartment. In his bed. In his arms.

She had been captivated by him since the moment she'd first seen him. In love, or more probably in lust, she acknowledged ruefully as she easily remembered each kiss and caress of the previous night, having been totally lost from the first moment Nick had held her in his arms and touched her.

Or perhaps she had been lost before that…

An American, the charismatic Nick Cavendish owned the London art gallery where she worked, as well as others in Paris and New York. His time was equally divided between the three, with apartments on the top floor of each building always ready for his use.

Hebe had been working at the gallery for several weeks before she'd first caught a glimpse of the elusive owner.

When he'd walked forcefully into the west room of the gallery four months ago, seemingly filled with boundless energy as he fired instructions one of the managers, Hebe had felt as if all the air had been knocked out of her lungs.

Over six feet tall, his body lithe and muscular, with overlong dark hair swept back from his olive-skinned face, and eyes a deep, deep blue, there was a wild ruggedness about him that spoke of the energy of a caged tiger. With the same threat of danger!

But she had never in her wildest dreams imagined he would notice her, a lowly junior employee. She had been leaving the gallery the evening before when she'd accidentally walked straight into him, but instead of getting a scornful look, as she had expected, they had both laughed and apologized. Still, she'd been totally stunned when he'd asked if she would join him for dinner, on the basis that she had worked at the gallery for some months now and it was time the two of them became acquainted.

Became acquainted!

They had become a lot more than that last night. Hebe was sure that not an inch of her body hadn't known the intimate touch of his hands or lips.

Her cheeks were flushed now with the memory of that intimacy.

And at the naked perfection of his body now. A body, as she had discovered the previous evening, that had that olive tan all over, a light covering of dark hair on the muscular width of his chest, and down over powerful hips and thighs.

As she saw the renewed state of his arousal, she felt a liquid melting between her own thighs as heat coursed through her already languorous body.

'I hope you don't mind—I was thirsty,' she answered him huskily, holding up the glass of water she had been drinking from.

Nick was thirsty too—but not for water. Taking the glass out of her hand, he placed it on a table, his eyes darkening as his head lowered to kiss one enticing nipple. He looked up into Hebe's face as he stroked his tongue moistly over that sensitive tip, feeling the increasing hardness of his own body as she groaned low in her throat, eyes gleaming like molten gold as her body arched against him, dark lashes sweeping low over her flushed cheeks.

She was beautiful, this goddess of youth, and he wanted to lose himself in her once again. Not to blot out the painful memories of yesterday this time, but because he wanted her with a fierceness that told him he wouldn't be gentle with her. That he couldn't be. He needed to drive his body into hers, but knew she would meet that desire with a heat of her own. As she had before.

He straightened to swing her up into his arms, capturing her mouth with his, tongue plundering, as her arms moved up about his neck, her fingers becoming entangled in the darkness of his hair.

Hebe was trembling as he laid her down amidst the twisted sheets, his mouth deepening its possession of hers as one of his hands caressed the burning tip of her breast, the nipple already hard and aroused, sending sensations of heat and liquid fire through the rest of her body.

She restlessly caressed the broad width of his back, before trailing a path to the firmness of his thighs, touching him there, loving the feel of his hardness against her hand. The groan low in his throat assured her that he approved too.

Nick fell back against the pillows as Hebe began to kiss his chest, down to the hollow of his flat stomach, and even lower over the hardness of his thighs. His breath caught in his throat as he felt the sensuous flick of her tongue against his heated flesh, and at the same time he knew that he wouldn't be able to take too much of this, that he wanted to be between the engulfing warmth of her thighs, inside her, stroking them both to that shuddering climax that he remembered so clearly—twice—from the night before.

He moved above her, looking down into her aroused face as he slowly entered her, her hips moving up to meet his, taking him deep inside her as she began to move slowly against him.

Hebe gasped minutes—hours?—later, as she felt the pleasure pulsing hotly through her, her body shuddering and quivering as that pleasure erupted out of control, taking her with it.

Taking Nick with it too, pulsating deep and deliciously inside her as he surrendered to the sensations of his body.

Hebe lay with her head resting against his chest in the aftermath, his arm about her waist, holding her loosely at his side.

She had never experienced anything like this. Their bodies seemed completely in tune, their lovemaking almost balletic in its intensity of emotion.

She smiled to herself as she realised how happy she felt, how totally relaxed and fulfilled. She really could so easily fall completely, mindlessly, in love with this man. If she wasn't already!

Which, considering her uninhibited response to him, she had a feeling she just might be.

Whatever, she felt closer to him than she ever had to anyone before, and wondered what the future held for them. Would they spend the day together? It was Sunday, so neither of them had to be at work today. Maybe they would make breakfast together? Before making love. Then perhaps they would go for a walk in the nearby park. Before making love. And then they could…

Hebe, exhausted and happy, drifted off to sleep.

Nick lay sleepless beside her, his body filled with satiation but his mind suddenly crystal clear.

Hebe Johnson was beautiful and desirable, and responded to him in a completely uninhibited way that he found irresistible. But it was her lack of control that warned him he *had* to resist her. Not for him the silken shackles of any woman, the cosy togetherness that tightened those ties until no thought or action could be called his own. Never again. That way lay all the pain and despair he had tried so hard to blot out the night before.

And she was still his employee. Untouchable, in fact. Though he had already done a hell of a lot more than touch her!

Creating a situation he had always avoided in the past.

Since his divorce two years ago he had known lots of women, had wined and dined them, bedded them, and moved on without any regrets. None of those relationships had lasted long enough to forge any sort of bond, least of all an emotional one. But an employee, as he had always known and therefore avoided, was going to be a little more difficult to walk away from.

But he was going to do it anyway. Walk away and not look back.

Quite what he'd do about the fact that Hebe worked for him he wasn't sure yet. The easiest way would be to dispense with her services at the gallery. But it didn't seem quite fair that she should lose her job because she had gone to bed with him. In fact, most women would assume their job was *more* secure after going to bed with the boss!

He turned slightly to look at her as she slept in his arms. Was that the reason Hebe had come so willingly with him the night before? The reason she had come back here and made love with him?

If it was, she was in for a nasty surprise!

No one, and nothing, held Nick Cavendish any more—least of all a silver-haired siren with golden eyes.

Hebe felt almost shy as she came into the ultra-modern kitchen several hours later.

Having woken up alone in Nick Cavendish's huge four-poster bed, with the disarray of the bedclothes a stark reminder of the heated lovemaking that had taken place there both last night and earlier this morning—as if she needed any reminder—she had collected up her scattered clothes and gone through to the luxury of the adjoining bathroom to shower and dress before going in search of Nick.

He was here, in the spacious kitchen, his back towards her as he made coffee, having pulled on faded denims and a black tee shirt over his nakedness.

Hebe looked at him, watching the muscles rippling in the broadness of his back as he moved, his shoulder-length dark hair brushed back to curl loosely against the nape of his neck.

Aged thirty-eight—twelve years older than her own twenty-six—he was without doubt the most gorgeous man she had ever seen. All over, she remembered with a plea-surable flush. Not an ounce of superfluous flesh on his body, and his hands—those hands that had caressed her so thoroughly—were long and tapered. And he made love with an artistry that spoke of an experience she came nowhere near matching.

Of course he had been married. For five years, according to Kate, another assistant at the gallery. Hebe had learnt this after Nick's second whirlwind visit three months ago, when he had snapped and snarled at them all before disappearing again on his way to terrorise the staff at his Paris gallery.

Kate had explained that he could be like that sometimes—that there had been a son from the marriage, a little boy who had died when he was only four. His death had precipitated the break-up and divorce of his parents two years ago, and still sometimes sent Nick Cavendish spiralling into a inferno of dark emotions that seemed to find no outlet.

Not surprising, really. Hebe could imagine nothing more traumatic than the death of your young child. But these intriguing snatches of information about her employer had only increased her interest in this enigmatically charismatic man.

She had watched him covertly during his lightning visits to the gallery. She had seen him dark and brooding as on that second visit, and smiling occasionally, but once laughing outright, which had softened and smoothed the lines of experience from his face, making him look almost boyish. Except for the deep well of pain never far from those intense blue eyes.

So he swept sporadically into the gallery, bringing his life and vitality with him, inspiring the people around him with his intensity, fascinating and intriguing Hebe—before once again disappearing and taking all that vitality with him.

But never in Hebe's wildest dreams had she ever imagined he would invite her out to dinner in the way that he had, that she would spend the night here with him in his apartment.

Nick sensed rather than heard Hebe's entrance into the kitchen, and he was aware of her silence as she stood in the doorway behind him whilst he continued to prepare the coffee, to delay the moment when they would have to make conversation. Conversation, he found, served very little purpose after spending the night with a woman.

To him, the following morning had always been the worst part of the brief, unfocused relationships he had indulged in before and since his divorce. What were you supposed to talk about, for God's sake? The weather? Who was going to win the tennis championship this year? The big U.S. golf tournament? Hardly post-lovemaking conversation topics, any of them!

But the alternative was discussing when they would see each other again—and that was just as unacceptable to Nick. Especially in this case. He knew now that he had made a terrible mistake in getting involved with Hebe Johnson, and certainly didn't intend compounding the situation by pretending this relationship—one-night-stand?—had any future.

Oh, well—time to face the music, Nick decided impatiently, and he turned to face her. The quicker he got this over with, the sooner he would be able to get on with his life.

She was once again dressed in the black silk blouse and fitted black trousers she had worn the day before, her hair falling silkily about her shoulders, her make-up attempting, and not quite succeeding, to hide the slight redness to her chin, where his late-night stubble and the intensity of their kisses had scratched that delicate creamy skin.

He wasn't even going to go there! No more thoughts of how wild and willing this woman had been in his arms. Otherwise he would just end up taking her back to bed again.

'Ready to leave?' he questioned dismissively as he took in her appearance. 'Or would you like a cup of coffee before you go?' He held up the coffeepot.

Hebe frowned at his abruptness. He couldn't wait to get rid of her, could he? So much for her imaginings of them spending the day together, talking together, laughing together, making love again…!

'I—don't think so, thank you,' she refused uncertainly, wondering if he really just expected her to leave now that the night was over.

An awkward silence followed.

What was she waiting for? Nick wondered impatiently. He had offered her coffee, she had refused, now it would be better for both of them if she just—

'I—perhaps I had better be going.' She spoke awkwardly as she seemed to sense his unspoken urging. Questioningly. As if she expected him to ask her to stay.

For what reason? They'd had dinner. They'd made love. They'd both enjoyed it. And now it was over. What else did she want from him? Because he had nothing else to give!

'My flatmate will probably be wondering where I've got to,' she added with a frown.

Nick hadn't bothered to ask last night whether that flatmate was male or female. He had been too caught up in smothering, numbing, his own inner pain, to care.

But he felt curious now, and wondered if Hebe Johnson were engaged, or at least had a steady boyfriend. She didn't come over as the sort of woman who indulged in extra-relationship affairs. But then, she hadn't exactly come over as the sort of woman who would go to bed with him last night either—and look how wrong he had been about that!

This was extremely awkward, Hebe decided uncomfortably as she continued to stand in the doorway, having no idea how she was supposed to behave the-morning-after-the-night-before. Probably because it was a long time since there had *been* a morning-after-the-night-before for her!

Not that she was a complete innocent—she had been in a relationship years ago, when she was at university. But she had never stayed in a man's apartment all night before, and as this man was Nick Cavendish, her employer for the last six months, it was doubly awkward.

He merely looked relieved at her suggestion that she leave. 'If you're sure you don't want coffee?' he prompted dismissively, as he poured some coffee into a mug for himself—black, with no sugar.

The repeat of the offer was made more out of politeness than anything else, Hebe realised with a sinking of her heart, as Nick sat down at the breakfast bar to take a sip of the steaming brew, no longer even looking at her.

She had been completely overwhelmed by the attention of this ruggedly handsome, gorgeously seductive man the night before, and hadn't been able to believe her luck when he had seemed to return her interest. But it looked as if she might have plenty of time to repent at leisure if his distant behaviour now was anything to go by.

Her cue not to make this any more embarrassing than it already was…

'I'll go, then,' she announced brightly. 'I—thank you for dinner last night,' she added awkwardly.

And everything else, she could have added, but didn't. After the intimacies they had shared the night before, this really was too embarrassingly awful. Something she didn't intend ever to repeat if this was what it felt like the following morning.

She looked a little bewildered by his abruptness, Nick acknowledged with a certain guilty irritation after glancing at her. Those amazing gold-coloured eyes were wide with wariness, and her cheeks had gone slightly pale at his obvious lack of enthusiasm.

What had she expected, for goodness' sake? That he would make declarations of undying love for her this morning? Assure her he couldn't live without her and invite her to come along with him to New York when he left later this morning?

Damn it, this was real life—not some fairy story. And they were adults, not romantic children!

They had both had a good time, but that was all it had been.

'I'm going back to New York later on today,' he told her dismissively. 'But I'll give you a call, okay?' he added—knowing he had no intention of doing any such thing.

He should never have become personally involved with an employee in the first place, so he certainly didn't intend to arrange to see Hebe Johnson on a social level again.

For one thing, he knew that if he met up with Hebe again, away from the gallery, then they would end up in bed together again too. Even now, looking at the soft pout of her mouth, that quicksilver hair, the willowy curves of her body in the silky blouse and fitted black trousers, he felt the stirring of desire for her—an ache he was absolutely determined to do nothing about.

She was definitely being given the brush-off, Hebe realised painfully. She wasn't so naïve that she didn't know that when a man said *I'll call you* after spending the night, without so much as asking for your telephone number, it meant that he had no intention of ever contacting you again!

Of course Nick was slightly different, in that he could, if he wanted, get her telephone number from Personnel at the Cavendish Gallery. She just didn't think, from his dismissive attitude this morning, that he was ever going to want to.

The excitement of having dinner with him last night, and the hours they had spent making love, and now being summararily dismissed this morning had ultimately to be the most humiliating experience of her entire life.

She couldn't get out of here fast enough!

She looked as if she were going to make a mad dash out of here without so much as a goodbye, Nick realised. Well, that was what he wanted, wasn't it? He frowned unwittingly, acknowledging that he didn't enjoy being on the receiving end of a casual dismissal. *He* was always the one to bid farewell, not the other way round.

He stood up, smiling slightly as he crossed the kitchen to put his arms about Hebe's waist and pull her into the hardness of his body. 'Goodbye, Hebe!' he murmured, his arousal undeniable.

She looked up at him, five or six inches shorter than his own six feet two inches in height, her eyes golden globes of uncertainty.

Hell, she had beautiful eyes, Nick thought with an inward groan. Beautiful everything, if his memory didn't deceive him. And he knew that it didn't.

Maybe they could meet again after all—

No! Don't be an idiot, Nick, he rebuked himself impatiently. Much better to just leave it like this.

Leave it, and hope that with time they would both forget last night had ever happened…

He certainly intended doing exactly that!

CHAPTER TWO

SIX weeks later Hebe was still waiting for the promised telephone call from Nick Cavendish.

She had been a fool ever to expect that he would phone, of course, and several conversations with Kate over the last few weeks had confirmed that Nick Cavendish did not get seriously involved with any of the women he went out with. The number of women he had been involved with since the end of his marriage, also according to Kate, had been legion, and none of them, Kate had told her wistfully—as if she'd guessed Hebe's interest was more than casual—had ever been employees of the Cavendish Galleries.

Or if they had they very quickly hadn't been, Hebe had decided.

In fact, she had lived most of the last six weeks half expecting to be told her employment at the Cavendish Gallery had been terminated. Of course it wasn't as easy as that to get rid of people nowadays, but she didn't doubt that if he wanted her out of here, Nick Cavendish would find a way.

The fact that he was—at last!—due back at the London gallery next week, in time for the opening of an exhibition they were giving was not conducive to helping Hebe concentrate on her work.

In fact, she felt decidedly clumsy today, and had been dropping things most of the morning, not seeming to be co-ordinated at all. Of course she knew the reason for her steadily increasing nervousness. Nick's arrival next week was approaching with a speed that made her head spin.

Maybe she should have called in sick for a few days. She was certainly feeling more than a little green round the edges, and hadn't even been able to eat at all today. Her anxiety at the prospect of seeing Nick again seemed to be increasing daily.

Although why *she* should be the one to feel so nervously on edge was beyond her. After all, Nick Cavendish had been the one to invite her out, not the other way round. And she hadn't invited herself back to his apartment either. In fact—

'Hebe?' rasped an all too familiar voice after six weeks' silence close to her ear.

She spun round sharply, at the same time dropping the name cards she had been preparing for next week's exhibition.

'Sorry!' she muttered, and she bent to pick them up with shaking fingers, taking the few seconds to bring some composure back to her demeanour.

Nick wasn't expected until *next week!*

'What are you doing here?' she prompted slowly as she straightened, eyes deeply golden in the paleness of her face.

He returned her gaze mockingly. 'It may have escaped your memory, Hebe, but I happen to own this gallery and have an apartment on the top floor of the building; I can come here any time I damn well please!'

Well…yes… But if she had had prior notice of his earlier than expected arrival she might not have overreacted in the way she just had. As it was, she felt completely wrong-footed.

She had made her mind up, during Nick's six weeks of silence, that she was going to be cool and composed when he did come back and would make no reference, if he didn't, to the fact that they had spent the night together in his apartment on the top floor of the building...

'Let's go up to my office,' Nick added with barely concealed impatience. 'I want to talk to you.'

He looked just the same, she acknowledged achingly. His olive skin was just as healthily tanned, his blue eyes as sharply intelligent, and his dark hair, though looking as if it had been trimmed slightly, was still long enough to rest silkily on broad shoulders. Dressed formally in a dark grey suit and snowy white shirt, with a silver-grey silk tie knotted neatly at his throat, he looked like a man who was firmly in control.

He looked exactly what he was, in fact—the confident multimillionaire owner of three prestigious art galleries.

Looking at him now, Hebe wondered how she could ever have thought he was seriously interested in her!

'Hebe!' he prompted, frowning at her continued silence.

She was behaving like an idiot, she realised, just standing here staring at him, completely tongue-tied by his unexpected appearance in the gallery.

She drew in a deep breath, willing herself to behave naturally. Well, as naturally as it was possible to be when confronted by the man who had haunted her days and filled her dreams for last six weeks!

'What can I do for you, Mr Cavendish?' she prompted with calm efficiency.

'You can come upstairs to my office with me,' he repeated firmly. 'Now!' he added, not even waiting for her answer this time, but turning abruptly on his heel and striding forcefully out of the room.

Kate, who was working nearby, shot Hebe a questioning look as she trailed out of the gallery behind Nick, and Hebe gave her a how-should-I-know? shrug in reply.

Because she really *didn't* know what this was about. They had had dinner together, spent a night together, but she hadn't told anyone about either of those things, let alone tried to contact Nick himself. So what was his problem?

The more she thought about it, acknowledging his brooding silence as he lithely climbed the stairs ahead of her to his office on the second floor, the angrier she became.

Had he expected, on the basis that she had spent the night with the boss, that she would have left her job here before he returned? Was that the reason he was so angry? Because he hadn't expected to see her still here at all?

Well, that was being more than a little unfair, wasn't it?

She loved her job here, liked the people she worked with too. Besides, none of the awkwardness of this situation was *her* fault, damn it!

Nick eyed her irritably as he closed his office door behind them. Unless he was mistaken, from her flushed cheeks and glowing golden eyes, he would take a guess at her being one very indignant young lady.

He perched on the edge of his cool Italian marble desk, which more than one customer at the gallery had tried to buy from him. He had always refused to sell it, though, liking the way it complemented the rest of the room, which was wood-panelled and slightly austere, although it did have a huge picture window that looked out over the river.

'So, what are you so angry about, Hebe?' he drawled ruefully, dark brows raised over mocking blue eyes. 'The fact that I was less than polite just now? Or the fact that I haven't called you for two months?' He met her gaze challengingly.

'Six weeks,' she came back sharply, her cheeks flushing with colour seconds later.

'Whatever.' He shrugged, knowing exactly how long it was since he had last seen her, but having no intention of letting Hebe know that he did.

He had been so sure that Hebe Johnson would be just like all the other women he had known over the last two years—taken and then forgotten. But for some inexplicable reason he hadn't quite succeeded in doing that where she was concerned. Memories of those golden eyes, that lithe silken body, came flashing into his mind at the most inconvenient of times. Irritating him intensely.

The flash of anger now in the depths of her warm eyes, and the way the fullness of those sensuous lips had tightened slightly, told him his careless attitude had only succeeded in increasing her anger. Which didn't particularly affect him.

Not on a business level, anyway.

On a personal level, he found both things sexy as hell!

She looked good today too, dressed in a cream blouse tucked into the tiny waistband of a knee-length fitted black skirt, her legs long and silky.

So much for his absence from the London gallery these last six weeks, his deliberate lack of the promised telephone call, his self-assurances that when he came back he would have forgotten all about Hebe Johnson!

Even before he'd seen the painting he had known he hadn't managed to do that.

His own mouth tightened as he glanced over to where he had placed the painting, on a stand to one side of his wide office, with a cover over it to protect it. But also so that Hebe Johnson shouldn't see it until he was ready for her to do so...

Hebe eyed Nick scathingly as he stood looking at her, and, even though inside was shaking, she gripped her hands tightly together to prevent Nick from seeing they were trembling.

'I'm sorry—were you supposed to call me?' she came back, with all the coolness she could muster.

Which was quite considerable, if the way his mouth thinned and his eyes narrowed to glittering blue slits was anything to go by!

'Okay, Hebe, forget that for the moment,' he dismissed briskly. 'And tell me what you know about Andrew Southern?'

She frowned as she dredged her memory for the relevant facts about the artist, having no idea why Nick was asking the question—unless it was an effort on his part to prove that she didn't know her job, so giving him an excuse to fire her?

She swallowed hard. 'English. Born 1953. Started painting in his early twenties, mainly portraits, but later moved on to landscapes—more recently the Alaskan wilderness—'

'I'm not asking for a bio on the guy, Hebe!' Nick cut in tersely, standing up restlessly. 'I asked what *you* know about him?'

'Me?' She blinked, stepping back slightly in the face of his leashed vitality. 'I've just told you what I know about him—'

'Don't be so coy, Hebe,' he cut her off again abruptly, blue eyes mocking. 'I'm not asking for details, just a confirmation that you know him. And if you can contact him personally.'

She was totally bewildered now. This conversation didn't appear to have anything to do with that night six weeks ago at all, nor with an effort to prove her incompetent, but everything, it seemed, to do with the artist Andrew Southern. Of whom she was an admirer, but had certainly never met him, let alone knew him personally.

She wasn't going to acknowledge the relationship, Nick realized frustratedly. Well, the guy was old enough to be her father, so maybe that explained her reluctance to talk about him. Whatever, Nick had been trying to arrange a meeting with Andrew Southern for years. For once neither the name Nick Cavendish nor the Cavendish Galleries themselves had opened that particular door. And now it seemed that Hebe, of all people, might be the key to that meeting.

From deciding that he had to stay as far away from Hebe as possible in future, or else take her to his bed again, he had now discovered that if he wanted to get anywhere near Andrew Southern with the idea of an exhibition of his work, then Hebe was the person he had to talk to.

'Look, Hebe, let's start this conversation again, shall we?' he reasoned pleasantly. 'I accept that I overstepped the employer/employee line with you six weeks ago, but by the same token you have to accept that it wasn't all one sided, huh?'

Hebe eyed him derisively. If that was his attempt at an apology for the night they had spent together, or for his non-existent telephone call since, then it was pretty lame. Besides which, an apology for the former was insulting, to say the least, just as an off-hand apology for the latter was totally inadequate.

She had been so miserable these last six weeks, wondering where she had gone wrong, what she had done to make Nick Cavendish not even want to call her again, let alone see her.

And now he had turned up unexpectedly, dismissing their night together as the satisfying of a brief, mutual attraction, before going on to talk about Andrew Southern—an artist of phenomenal reputation, and known as a complete recluse, who had been so for almost thirty years.

Making her realise just how little she understood Nick Cavendish.

She eyed him coolly now. 'Is that all?'

'No, of course—!' He broke off to draw in a deeply controlling breath. 'Are you deliberately trying to annoy me?' He looked at her with narrowed eyes.

She gave a mocking lift of her eyebrows. 'I seem to be doing that without trying!'

He relaxed slightly, an amused smile slightly curving those sculptured lips. 'I see now why I found you so intriguing that night,' he murmured softly.

It wasn't what she wanted to hear. Not here. Not now.

She had spent the first week after his departure back to New York in a frenzy of self-recrimination, with a deep-felt need for Nick to call her to nullify all those negative thoughts.

She was in love with him, totally physically enthralled with him—and this was the twenty-first century, for goodness' sake, not the Dark Ages, where a woman's wants and needs weren't considered as important as a man's, she had chided herself.

She had done nothing wrong by spending the night with a man she found so attractive and who had wanted her too!

But as the days and weeks had passed those assurances hadn't meant a whole lot.

And now standing here looking at Nick, they meant absolutely nothing.

She grimaced. 'I think it might be better if we both just forgot about that, don't you?'

It was a statement rather than a question, and Nick found himself deeply irritated by her easy dismissal.

Okay, so he hadn't been able to wait to get her out of his apartment that morning six weeks ago, and he hadn't called her as he said he would, but it was a bit of knock to his ego to realise that she was willing to dismiss the memories of him as easily as he had tried to dismiss her.

Or was she...?

He took a step towards her, lids lowered as he looked down at her with dark blue eyes, trailing one caressing finger down the smooth curve of her cheek. 'Am I so easy to forget, Hebe?' he murmured seductively, knowing that this was probably another mistake, but finding her coolness infuriating as hell. 'Was our lovemaking easy to forget too? Or has it kept you awake nights, thinking of all the ways we touched and aroused each other?'

She gave him a startled look even as the colour entered her cheeks, her lips parting slightly as her body swayed towards his.

'I thought so...' He murmured his satisfaction with her response, his wandering fingers parting her lips slightly, caressing that softness, before trailing the length of her throat down to the deep vee of her blouse and the creamy swell of her breasts. All the time his challenging gaze continued to hold hers.

How could this be happening? Hebe inwardly protested, even as she felt herself responding to his touch. The arousal of her breasts was instant, the nipples hard and sensitive, as she reached out instinctively to cling tightly to the broad width of his shoulders, her legs seeming in danger of melting beneath her.

But as suddenly as he had touched her she found herself thrust away from him, and Nick was stepping back, that devilishly handsome face now set in scathing dismissal.

'You really are a sexy little thing, aren't you?' he mused as he leant back against his desk, his blue gaze considering now, as he looked at the firm thrust of her breasts against her cream blouse.

'Mr Cavendish—'

'Oh, come on, Hebe,' he drawled tauntingly, shaking his head slightly, those blue eyes alight with mocking laughter. 'You can hardly go back to calling me *that* after sharing your body with me,' he reminded her, with a challenging rise of that square, uncompromising chin.

Hebe felt the colour warm her cheeks at his deliberate taunting. Why was he doing this to her? What perverse pleasure did he get out of humiliating her in this way?

She straightened defensively, glaring at him. 'At the same time as *you* shared your body with *me*!' she came back, with all the fury of her humiliation, uncaring now if this was just his way of trying to get her to resign from her job at the gallery.

Fine. Let him sack her. She was quickly reaching the point where she didn't care.

His smile was derisive. 'I'm flattered that amongst all your other lovers you've even remembered me.'

All her other—! What was he talking about? She had had one relationship before him, and that had been five years ago; ancient history rather than recent.

'Let's stop playing this game, shall we?' Nick said impatiently as he stood up.

'Gladly!' she agreed tautly. 'Can I go back to work now?' If she didn't get out of here soon she was very much afraid the humiliating tears that blurred her vision would escape and begin to fall hotly down her cheeks!

'No, you damn well—' Nick broke off abruptly, drawing in controlling breaths as he realised she had to be deliberately baiting him.

Because he knew of her relationship with Andrew Southern?

Probably, he accepted scathingly. Okay, so as an artist the man was a legend in his own lifetime, but he was still a man aged in his fifties, and Hebe was only in her midtwenties. And Nick had wondered if *he* was too old for her!

'Okay, Hebe,' he began reasoningly. 'I accept that your affair with Andrew Southern is none of my business—'

'My *what*?' she gasped incredulously, gold eyes wide with disbelief.

'It's past history, I realise that—'

'Past—!' Hebe gave a dazed shake of her head. 'But I told you. I don't even *know* Andrew Southern!' she protested indignantly.

'Evidence proves the contrary—'

'Evidence?' she repeated disgustedly. 'Look, Nick, I have no idea what you're talking about.' She shook her head, that amazing silver-blonde hair moving silkily against her creamy cheeks. 'Maybe you have jet-lag, and it's affecting your judgement. I don't know, but—'

'I came back from New York last week, Hebe,' he told her softly, his gaze narrowing as she looked at him sharply. 'I'd received information that there was a possibility of a hitherto unseen Andrew Southern coming up for sale in the north of England.' His mouth twisted. 'As you can imagine, I had no intention of letting anyone but Cavendish Galleries own that painting.'

'For Cavendish Galleries read Nick Cavendish!' she came back scathingly.

'Exactly.' He smiled in acknowledgement of her derision. 'Imagine my surprise when I saw the subject of the painting!'

Hebe gave a dazed shake of her head. She had no idea what this conversation was about, or where it could possibly be going. But Nick, it seemed, had been back in England a week already. A week during which he had neither telephoned her nor tried to see her again.

Until today. When he had done nothing but humiliate and embarrass her.

But he had taken her in his arms too…

To prove a point. Nothing else. And he *had* proved it too, hadn't he? She responded to him even when she didn't want to.

Sometimes she wasn't sure if she didn't hate him rather than love him!

'The subject of the painting…?' she prompted frowningly.

'Yes.' Nick was looking at her with narrowed eyes now. 'A portrait. A woman. A very beautiful woman, in fact.' He shrugged his broad shoulders as if that point was indisputable.

'It's one of his earlier paintings then—?'

'No,' Nick cut in with certainty. 'I can categorically say this work is recent. The last five years or so, I would say,' he added consideringly.

'But I thought he didn't paint portraits any more—'

'Obviously this woman inspired him to do so,' Nick cut in dryly.

Hebe didn't like the way he was looking at her now, as if critically dissecting every part of her body.

A body he had come to know intimately six weeks ago...

Except he hadn't seemed to find anything to critisise about it then, had he?

She shrugged. 'As far as I'm aware, Andrew Southern hasn't painted a portrait for over twenty years.'

'Are you doubting my expertise, Hebe?' Nick snapped tautly.

No, she wasn't doing that. Not in any way! She knew only too well what an masterful lover he was. And he hadn't built up the prestigious worldwide reputation of the Cavendish Galleries by not being extremely knowledgable about art. He knew his subject equally as well as he knew how to be a lover!

Nick was growing tired of Hebe's prevarication. He strode forcefully across his office to flick the covering from the painting displayed there, his piercing gaze never leaving Hebe's face as he did so. He wanted to see her reaction to the portrait.

Her eyes widened as she stared blankly at the portrait, her body tensing rigidly.

Not surprising, really, Nick thought with hard amusement.

The painting was of her. Sitting sideways on a chair, wearing a clinging dress of midnight-blue, her hair a glorious curtain of silver down the long length of her spine.

And that was where the formality of the portrait began and ended!

Because her expression could only be called sultry, with a knowing smile curving those pouting, kissable lips, and her eyes, those wonderful golden eyes, half closed as if in arousal. Her breasts were thrust slightly forward beneath the blue dress, the material clinging so closely to those long silken limbs that it was impossible to believe she wore anything beneath it.

That *Hebe* wore anything beneath it.

Because the woman was most certainly her.

Nick had kissed those same lips six weeks ago. Seen that arousal in her eyes. Caressed the proud tilt of those breasts. Suckled on those rosy nipples. And those long silken limbs had been wrapped around him more than once that night too.

'Who is she…?'

Nick turned sharply back to look at Hebe as she spoke in a whisper, his frown deepening as he saw how pale she was, her eyes like golden orbs in that pallor.

But they both knew her question was totally unnecessary. 'Oh, come on, Hebe.' He sighed his impatience as he moved to stand beside her. 'It's *you,* damn it!' He would have reached out and shaken her, except that she looked as if she might disintegrate at the slightest touch.

No doubt she had never thought this portrait—a portrait painted by a man who had obviously put the love he felt for its subject into every brushstroke—would ever be seen by the general public. That was the reason for her obvious shock. In fact, it was pure luck that it hadn't gone into a local auction with a lot of other things from a house cleared out by relatives after the death of its owner, consequently disappearing back into the realms of obscurity.

Luckily enough, the autioneer had been experienced enough to know the Andrew Southern signature—a swan with the single letter S beside it—and had called a friend of his in London to see if any of the big dealers were interested in coming to look at it. Nick most certainly had been, getting the man's promise that he would let no one else view it until he had flown in from New York to see it.

One look at the painting, at the almost luminous style that marked it as Southern's work and not some pale imitation, and Nick had known he had to have the painting. At any price.

It had taken some time and considerable skill to negotiate that price with the new owner and the auctioneer before bringing his prize back to London this morning, and his first priority had been to talk to Hebe Johnson.

Undoubtedly the woman in the portrait.

And, at the time of the painting, Andrew Southern's lover.

Something she seemed to be denying most strongly!

Hebe moved forward as if in a dream, her hand moving up to touch the painting, her fingers stopping only centimetres away from the canvas, trembling slightly. Her breathing was shallow.

'Who is she?' she repeated emotionally.

Nick stepped forward. 'For God's sake, Hebe, it's *you*—'

'It *isn't* me!' She turned to look at him, able to feel the rapid beat of her pulse in her throat. 'Look at it again, Nick,' she told him shakily, pleadingly, turning to look at the painting, a gut-wrenching pain in her chest as she did so.

'Of course it's you—'

'No,' she cut in quietly again. 'She has a birthmark, Nick. Look. There.' She pointed to the rose-shaped birthmark on the swell of one creamy breast, visible above the low neckline of the deep blue dress. 'And look here.' She pulled aside the open neck of her cream blouse, revealing her own creamy breast.

Completely bare of that rose-shaped birthmark...

Whoever the woman in the portrait was it most certainly wasn't Hebe.

She knew it wasn't.

But if it wasn't her, who—?

No, it couldn't be!

Could it…?

And that was when everything went dark…

CHAPTER THREE

NICK inwardly cursed as he leapt forward to catch Hebe before she hit the carpeted floor, swinging her up in his arms to carry her over to the leather sofa at the back of the room.

He had been expecting some sort of reaction to the portrait, but it certainly hadn't been this!

Embarassment, perhaps—because it was obvious that Andrew Southern had been Hebe's lover. And surprise that Nick actually had possession of the portrait had also been a possibility.

But he certainly hadn't expected Hebe to faint as she denied she was the woman in the portrait!

That birthmark apart—a pretty rose-shaped mark—there was no one else it could be but her.

He laid her down on the sofa, and Hebe started to groan slightly as she came back to consciousness, finally opening her eyes to look up at him as he bent over him.

And instantly closing them again, as if even the sight of him was too much for her.

'Hey, come on, Hebe. I realise *I'm* no oil painting, but I'm not that bad either!' he mocked as he moved back slightly.

The painting, Hebe remembered with a pained wince,

trying to collect herself. But to come to terms with the enormity of what she had seen, and what she was thinking, was going to take longer than the few seconds she'd had so far.

She swallowed hard, not sure how she felt about any of this. If that portrait really was who she thought it was, then—

'Here.'

She opened her eyes to find Nick holding out a glass of water.

She was freaking him out with this 'dying swan' routine, Nick decided impatiently as he put the rest of the bottle of water back in the fridge neatly disguised as an oak filing cabinet.

Who really fainted nowadays? People who were ill, hungry or had been hit over the head! He could rule out the former, because Hebe certainly wasn't ill. Nor had she been hit over the head. Except maybe metaphorically. That just left hungry.

'Have you had any lunch today?' he prompted suspiciously.

'Actually—' she swung her legs to the floor to sit up and take a sip of the chilled water '—no.'

He gave a shake of his head as he moved back to the fridge. 'Why haven't you?' he demanded as he took a chocolate bar out and handed it to her. 'Eat it,' he instructed, when she just looked at it. 'You'll feel better if you do.'

Hebe somehow doubted that, but the chocolate certainly couldn't do any harm. She had heard it was good for shock too. And she was certainly in shock.

She glanced at the portrait again as she slowly ate two squares of the chocolate.

The woman in the portrait was beautiful, much more so

than her. Couldn't Nick see that? And that woman had a sultry air about her, a sensuality, those golden eyes half closed with a secret that only she possessed.

Hebe felt herself begin to shake again as she took an educated guess at what that secret was.

She ate another two squares of chocolate before speaking huskily. 'Where did you get it?'

'I told you—the north of England.' Nick moved restlessly about the confines of the office.

Hebe gave him an impatient glance. 'Can't you be more specific? Who did you buy it from? Where did *they* get it?' It was suddenly imperative she knew these things.

Nick raised dark brows at her intensity. 'I bought it from a young couple who had just inherited an old house from the guy's great-uncle, or something like that. They had never seen the painting before he died, because the old man had the portrait hung in his bedroom, of all things,' he revealed, with a certain amount of distaste.

He couldn't say he felt exactly comfortable with some old man drooling over a portrait of a woman—Hebe!— who was certainly young enough to be his daughter, if not his granddaughter.

But the couple hadn't known anything about the woman in the portrait—who she was or how the great-uncle had come to have her portrait. Nick had known who she was— he just didn't have any idea what her portrait was doing in some old guy's bedroom and not in the possession of the man who had painted it with such love.

Hebe didn't look as if she were about to answer that question for him now, either!

She moistened dry lips. 'What was the man's name?'

'Hell, Hebe, what difference does it make what his name

was?' Nick snapped his impatience. 'He had your portrait, isn't that enough?'

'No.' She shook her head slowly, turning to look at him with dark gold eyes. 'Because, no matter what you might think to the contrary, Nick, the woman in the portrait isn't me.' She gave a humourless smile at his obvious scepticism. 'No, Nick, it isn't,' she insisted. 'Andrew Southern couldn't possibly have painted my portrait because I've never met him! But it looks as if my mother may have done,' she added, so softly Nick had trouble hearing her.

Her mother?

Hebe was trying to say the woman in the portrait was her *mother*?

How stupid did she think he was? Of *course* the portrait was of Hebe. It couldn't be anyone else.

Could it…?

Nick gave her a dark frown. 'You're telling me that you look exactly like your mother did at that age?'

'Ah.' She gave a grimace. 'Now, *that* is a very difficult question for me to answer—'

'Why is it, damn it?' he interrupted irritably. 'How difficult can it be to know whether you do or do not look like your mother?'

Hebe eyed him ruefully, understanding his incredulity at the situation, sympathising with it, even, but at the same time knowing she didn't have the answers that he wanted.

Except for one…

She raised silver-blonde brows. 'How about if you're adopted?'

Nick stopped pacing the room, looking down at her with disbelieving eyes. Was she seriously trying to tell him, expecting him to believe—?

But why not?

Hundreds of kids were adopted every year.

He moved to stand in front of the portrait, studying it closely. He had quickly seen the mirror-like similarities, but now he looked for the differences.

There was that birthmark, of course. But that didn't prove anything. It was a pretty birthmark, and perhaps Andrew Southern had used a little poetic licence—a lover's rose-coloured glasses—when he'd painted it there above the woman's breast?

There was that air of sensuality, too, he supposed. But, God knew, he knew just how sensual and sexual Hebe was. He'd seen her look just like that the night they'd spent making love together. No, that proved nothing.

Neither did the lean length of her body, those thrusting breasts and delicately arched throat.

The ring!

There was an emerald and diamond ring on the third finger of the woman's left hand. Nick assumed that it wasn't Andrew Southern Hebe had been engaged to, but the now deceased owner of the painting. Why else would someone have kept a piece of art worth so much? Especially if keeping it had been to spite his future wife and her lover. Hebe didn't wear a ring like that anymore. But if Hebe's fiancé had realised that she was having an affair with Andrew Southern—and how could he not, with the evidence of the portrait in front of him?—then he would have had every right to break off the engagement; apart from the fact that she was wearing such a revealing dress, Hebe looked as if she had just come from her lover's arms. And Nick, better than most, knew exactly how she looked at *that* moment!

No, there was nothing about this portrait that said Hebe was telling him the truth.

But what reason would she have to lie?

Because she had been found out?

Because, having already let two wealthy men slip through her grasp, she still hoped the two of *them* might have some sort of relationship?

His mouth twisted derisively as he turned back to her. 'It's an interesting idea, Hebe, but not very plausible, is it?' he dismissed.

She straightened defensively. 'Why isn't it?'

Damn it, why couldn't she just let it go? Admit she was the woman in the portrait and tell him where the hell he could find and speak to Andrew Southern?

He shook his head. 'Because it's too damned convenient, that's why,' he snapped.

'For whom?' she challenged shakily. Because it certainly wasn't convenient for her.

Her parents had told her long ago that she was adopted, of course. They were such wonderful parents, and because of this, and the fact that she never, ever wanted to hurt them, she had never even attempted to find out who her real parents were.

What would have been the point? Obviously they hadn't wanted her when she was born, so why should they want to know about her as an adult...?

'Look, Hebe, I don't give a damn if you've posed nude for the guy. I just want a way in to Andrew Southern, past his guard-dog of an agent!' Nick told her with brutal honesty.

Hebe flinched slightly at his callousness. 'Well, when you find it,' she said evenly, 'please let me know—because after this I would like to talk to him too!'

Nick's mouth twisted derisively. 'You're right; talking isn't something you do too much of when you're in bed, is it?'

'Insults are going to get us nowhere, Nick,' she told him shakily, the chocolate seeming to have done very little to allay her shock. In fact, she felt decidedly sick now.

But then, it wasn't every day you were confronted with a painting possibly of the mother you had never known. A painting, moreover, that was everything Nick said it was.

Whoever the woman was, Andrew Southern had been in love with her when he'd painted her portrait. It was there in every brushstroke, every soft nuance of the woman's sensual beauty.

Did that mean that the artist was Hebe's father...?

Or had that been the man who had owned the portrait all these years and kept it hidden from view?

They were questions that Hebe certainly wanted answers to.

But for the moment she had to deal with Nick's disbelief...

She drew in a deep breath. 'You can think what you like about the portrait, Nick. Your opinion is really of little interest to me. *I* know that woman isn't me, and that's what's important.'

He looked at her frustratedly for several seconds. 'You're seriously expecting me to believe, if that portrait is of your mother, that it's—what?—twenty-six, twenty-seven years old?'

She shrugged at his sceptisism. 'That timescale would certainly fit in with the period when Andrew Southern was still painting portraits, yes. And for the record, Nick,' she added ruefully, 'I'm not *expecting* you to believe anything. I told you, it's what *I* think that's important.'

And what she thought was that she had to see Andrew Southern herself, and ask him about the woman in the portrait…

But if a man like Nick Cavendish, with all of the prestige of the Cavendish Galleries behind him, couldn't get past the reclusive artist's agent, then how did *she* expect to do so?

She would find a way.

She had to!

There was no way she could just leave here and pretend she had never seen that portrait. The portrait of the woman who surely had to be her mother…

She would need to speak to her parents too, of course. She couldn't just go off in search of her real parents without telling them about it first. She owed them that, and they would understand, she was sure. They had brought her up with a sure sense of how important she was to them, of how much she was loved, but at the same time had taught her independence of spirit and mind. They couldn't fail to support her in her search for the woman in the portrait.

'Well, if that's all, Nick, I think I'll go now.' Hebe put the glass of water down on the low table in front of her before standing up.

And instantly swayed dizzily again.

In fact, she felt as if she really were going to be sick!

'What the hell is wrong with you?' Nick stepped forward to grasp her arm, his expression dark and brooding.

She looked up at him with slightly unfocusing eyes. 'I told you—I haven't had any lunch today.' She tried to move away from him. Even that light touch on her arm was enough to send a thrill of awareness coursing through her veins.

So much for hating him!

Reasonably she might do so; he had been nothing but

insulting today, with none of that exciting lover of six weeks ago about him. But emotionally her body still responded to his slightest touch.

'You're coming upstairs with me,' he announced grimly.

'Upstairs?' She stared at him with startled eyes.

His mouth twisted derisively. 'Don't look so worried, Hebe; I'm not so filled with lust for you that I'm dragging you upstairs to have my wicked way with you!'

'Again!' she came back tartly, stung by his mockery.

'Again,' he acknowledged tauntingly, keeping a firm hold of her arm as he walked her over to the door. 'You're dizzy from not having eaten any lunch, and I have food upstairs in my apartment; the logical thing to do is take you up there and feed you,' he explained dryly.

Logic? When had *logic* had anything to do with their relationship so far?

'If you're happy to let me go for the day, I can easily go home and get myself something to eat.' She firmly stood her ground.

She did not want to go upstairs to his apartment. Today had been humiliating enough without returning to the scene of her naïve stupidity in thinking this man seriously liked her!

Nick's mouth tightened. 'No, I'm not happy to do that, Hebe. For one thing, you don't look as if you could make it downstairs, let alone home,' he derided. 'And, for another, I haven't finished talking to you yet.'

That sounded ominous…

'I've told you—I don't know anything about Andrew Southern,' she insisted stubbornly. 'Not where he is or how you might get to meet him. I wish I did!'

Nick eyed her frowningly. Did she seriously expect him to believe that?

Yes, he acknowledged impatiently after a glance at her guileless expression, that was exactly what she expected.

It was up to him to ensure that she knew she hadn't succeeded in convincing him of anything. Not for a moment!

'We'll talk again after you've eaten,' he told her firmly, taking her with him out into the carpeted hallway.

Hebe glared at him. 'Do you never take no for an answer?'

Nick gave a wolfish grin. 'You, of all people, should know that I don't!'

That had certainly silenced her, he noted with satisfaction. That poutingly kissable mouth was set firmly as the two of them got into the private lift to go up one floor to his apartment.

Meaning that Hebe would enter his completely private domain for a second time!

'Is an omelette okay with you?' he rasped tersely, releasing her arm to stride through to the open-plan kitchen with its white and chrome fixtures.

Hebe took her time following him, obviously no more comfortable being back here than he was to have her here.

He would feed her the omelette, get some straight answers out of her, and then she could leave—

Where the hell was she?

He strode back out into the sitting room, coming to an abrupt halt as he saw her holding and looking at one of the photographs that usually stood on the coffee table in front of the window. 'What do you think you're doing?' he bit out coldly, his face devoid of all expression.

Hebe almost dropped the photograph she had picked up to have a better look at, grasping it with both hands against her chest, knowing from the furious look on Nick's face that his question didn't require an answer—that he knew exactly what she had been doing.

The photograph was of a little boy about three or four years old. A gorgeous little boy grinning happily into the camera lens. A little boy, with Nick's dark hair and blue eyes...

Nick moved forcefully across the room to snatch the photograph out of her hands, those blue eyes glacially cold as he glared at her through narrowed lids.

She swallowed hard. 'I'm sorry. I—he's very beautiful.'

A nerve pulsed in his tightly clenched jaw. 'Yes, he was,' he ground out harshly.

Was. It was his son, then.

Hebe felt a tightening of her chest at the thought of all that life and boyish happiness no longer existing.

How much worse was that realisation for Nick...!

'I'm sorry,' she said again.

Nick put the photograph carefully back on the table before giving her a sharp glance. 'You know who he is?'

'I—yes,' she admitted reluctantly. 'One of the other girls told me that you had a son.'

'Luke,' he bit out harshly. 'His name was Luke.'

Luke... Four years old. His death simply too much for his parents to deal with together, driving them irrevocably apart.

'I really am sorry,' Hebe repeated huskily. 'I shouldn't have— Please believe me when I tell you I never meant to—'

'To what?' he challenged with a lift of that arrogant jaw. 'Pry? Stick your nose in where it doesn't belong?' He gave a disgusted shake of his head, his face set in grim lines.

Hebe flinched at his obvious fury. 'It wasn't like that,' she protested softly. 'I just saw his photograph, and—' And what? Hadn't she been prying, after all? Well...yes. But not with any intention of annoying or upsetting Nick. She had just been curious, that was all.

And in being so she had turned Nick's undoubted anger on her once again.

So what was new?

But surely he knew she hadn't *deliberately* set out to cause him pain in this way? Even though it seemed that was exactly what she had done.

'I really am sorry,' she said again firmly, before moving past him to walk into the kitchen, feeling it best to give him a few minutes' privacy.

It seemed to be an afternoon for upsets. Nick where his son was concerned and her own puzzlement and curiosity about the woman in the portrait and the man who had painted it.

But *she* would possibly be able to find answers to her own questions, whereas Nick would probably never understand why his son, a little boy of four, had had to die.

It probably all came down to a matter of faith. And the death of a four year old child certainly tested that to the limits!

She looked up nervously a few minutes later as Nick came back into the kitchen, thankfully with some of the colour back in his cheeks, his expression less grim.

'I got eggs and milk out of the fridge.' She shrugged, pointing to where she had placed them on the worktop. 'I wasn't sure what else you needed.'

Nick slipped off the jacket of his suit and hung it on the back of one of the bar stools before taking down one of the frying pans from a display of them hanging from a rack above the work table in the middle of the kitchen. 'Cheese or mushrooms?' he bit out economically as he cracked the eggs into a bowl.

Hebe had to swallow down the nausea at the thought of either filling. 'Plain, if that's okay?' It still felt decidedly strange to be up here in Nick's apartment again, let alone having him cook for her.

Kate, having witnessed their departure, was going to be more than a little curious when Hebe finally returned downstairs to the gallery!

Nick's impatience was all inward as he warmed the oil in the pan while beating the eggs, before adding the milk. He was regretting now that he had made the offer to cook for Hebe in the first place.

He never talked to anyone about Luke. He couldn't. Still, three years later, he found his son's death too painful to discuss with any degree of emotional normality. It was because the subject had been too painful that he and his now ex-wife Sally had stopped talking to each other— neither of them able to think of anything else when they were together, but unable to put those thoughts into words, the whole thing being just too painful.

So he certainly didn't intend discussing Luke with Hebe, a woman he had spent a single night of passion with!

He dropped the egg mixture into the frying pan and let it cook before turning to speak to Hebe. 'You'll find a knife and fork— What the hell—!' he rasped, as a white-faced Hebe ran past him out of the kitchen, her hand pressed tightly to her mouth.

She barely made it to the bathroom that adjoined the master bedroom—ironically, the only bathroom she knew the location of—before she was well and truly sick.

It had been the smell of the eggs cooking in the frying pan that had done it, tipping her sensitive stomach over the edge, the nausea just too much to control any longer.

'Here you go,' Nick murmured behind her seconds later, and he placed a damp cloth on her forehead.

This was so humiliating!

Not quite as bad as that morning six weeks ago when, the night over, Nick hadn't been able to wait for her to leave, but pretty close.

She sat back on her heels, holding the cloth to her forehead herself now, the nausea seeming to have passed. Although quite what she had found to be sick with, considering she hadn't eaten anything today except the chocolate Nick had insisted on giving her a short time ago, was a mystery!

'Feeling better now?' Nick prompted abruptly.

'A little—thank you.' She nodded, not quite able to look at him.

She had caused nothing but trouble this morning— trouble she was sure Nick couldn't wait to be rid of.

'I'll just give my face a wash, and then I think I would like to leave, after all.' She could probably quite happily eat the omelette now that she had got rid of whatever had upset her stomach, but in the circumstances it was probably better if she didn't stay.

'I don't think so, Hebe.'

She looked up at him sharply. Only to find him staring at her with cold, glittering blue eyes, his hands clenched into fists at his sides.

'What do you mean?' she prompted warily.

'I mean I don't think that you're going to be leaving here any time soon,' Nick bit out tautly.

Hebe's eyes widened. 'But I can assure you that I feel absolutely fine now.'

'Yes, I'm sure you do,' he ground out harshly. 'It's a

curious fact, but women in your condition usually *do* feel better once they've actually been sick,' he added forcefully.

She blinked frowningly. 'My condition?'

Nick drew in a harsh breath, looking at her as if he would dearly like to put his hands around her throat and strangle her. 'Hebe, unless I'm very much mistaken—and Lord knows I hope I am!' he muttered grimly, 'the fact that you fainted a short time ago for no reason—'

'I had just seen a portrait of the mother I've never known!' she defended incredulously.

Nick shook his head, so tense Hebe almost felt as if she could reach out and touch it. 'The fact that you fainted, coupled with your earlier dizziness and your nausea just now, when I started cooking the eggs, all point to one conclusion as far as I can see.'

Hebe blinked, her hand on the side of the sink as she slowly stood up to face him. 'They do...?'

The glittering gaze moved down the length of her body, coming to rest on her stomach. 'You're pregnant, Hebe,' he bit out abruptly. 'About six weeks, I would say!' he added with barely suppressed fury.

Pregnant!

But she couldn't be!

Could she...?

CHAPTER FOUR

HE had completely forgotten, Nick realised self-disgust-edly, the *fourth* reason that women at least sometimes fainted.

Sally, when she'd been expecting Luke, had fainted several times during the early months of her pregnancy. She had woken up feeling sick every morning for the first three months, too—usually making a miraculous recovery once she had actually been sick, and so able to enjoy the rest of the day.

Hebe Johnson, Nick was pretty sure, was pregnant with his baby.

'I assumed you were on the Pill, for God's sake!' he muttered impatiently. But assumption, he knew, was the mother of all—

'What?' Hebe returned vaguely, appearing to be completely dazed, her face once again deathly pale, her eyes huge luminous golden globes.

'Look, let's get out of this bathroom, at least,' he suggested impatiently, sure that it couldn't be helping her nausea to still be in the room where she had actually been sick. Taking a firm hold of her arm, he led her through to his bedroom when she made no effort to move herself. He sat her firmly down in the bedroom chair. 'Now,' he muttered sharply. 'I asked if you're on the Pill?'

She blinked up at him, really looking as if she were in shock this time. 'Why would I be?' she finally answered distractedly.

'For God's sake, pull yourself together, Hebe,' he snapped, and he moved away impatiently, sure that his looming over her couldn't be helping the situation.

Although if she really was pregnant he couldn't see that there was any help for either of them!

'It's quite simple, Hebe. Were you, or were you not using any contraception when we went to bed together six weeks ago?' He bit the words out as succinctly as he could in the circumstances, knowing that one of them, at least, had to try and make sense of all this.

Even if he didn't *feel* very sensible!

He had needed to be with someone that night six weeks ago—had needed to lose himself in her, to blot out the painful memories and then move on. But if Hebe really was pregnant from that night then moving on wasn't an option. For either of them…

Hebe drew in a deep breath, at last managing to fight down the panic his announcement had caused. Of course she wasn't pregnant. No matter what people said, all those dire warnings parents gave to pubescent offspring about it 'only taking once', she could not be pregnant from that single night she had spent in Nick's arms.

But it hadn't just been 'once', a little voice inside her head reminded her. She and Nick had made love three times that night. Not once.

She was *not* pregnant!

It was ridiculous to even suggest that she was.

She straightened in the chair, determined to take some control of this situation. 'No, I wasn't. But that doesn't mean—'

'Why weren't you?' Nick rounded on her impatiently. 'You're what? Twenty-five, twenty-six years old—?'

'Twenty-six,' she confirmed, her own impatience rising to meet his as she glared at him. 'But I'm not in a relationship. And I certainly don't take contraceptive pills just on the off-chance I might meet a man I want to go to bed with!'

'But that's exactly what you did!' he came back exasperatedly.

She paled even more. 'But it wasn't planned—'

'Wasn't it?' he challenged coldly. 'I seem to remember it was *you* who bumped into me that evening…'

Hebe became very still, her breathing shallow as she stared at him, her blood seeming to have turned to ice in her veins. 'And just what is *that* supposed to mean?' she prompted slowly.

He shook his head. 'You wouldn't be the first woman to set this sort of trap for a man. What were you hoping for, Hebe? That I would pay you off—'

'How dare you?' she finally managed to gasp disbelievingly.

He couldn't really think—believe— He did, she acknowledged dazedly as she saw the glittering anger in his eyes.

'Give it up, Hebe,' he bit out disgustedly. 'The outraged virgin act doesn't suit you at all!'

No, she hadn't been a virgin when they went to bed together. She had had one previous relationship before Nick. But that had been five years ago, with a fellow student at university and the experience had not been repeated until that impetuous night with Nick. Nor since, either!

She really had been totally besotted with him, had found his attention flattering, his obvious desire for her to spend the night with him too tempting to resist.

She looked at him coldly. 'Why are you turning all this round on me? I didn't notice *you* using any protection that night either!' she challenged.

He eyed her scornfully. He knew she had a point, but he was in no mood to admit that right now. 'Because no one told me I needed to!'

'Because I didn't even *think* about getting pregnant!' she snapped, standing up impatiently. 'And I'm not! This conversation is acedemic,' she dismissed. 'I'm not pregnant. I've obviously just eaten something that's disagreed with me—'

'You haven't eaten anything at all since yesterday,' Nick reminded her impatiently.

Well, that was true. But it still didn't mean— She could not be pregnant!

'There's one quick and easy way to settle all this,' Nick decided brusquely, marching out of the bedroom.

Hebe quickly followed him, wondering what he was going to do. He was in the kitchen, putting his jacket back on when she got found him. 'Where are you going?' She frowned her confusion; *she* was the one who was leaving, not him!

He gave her a scathing glance. 'To a chemist. To buy a pregnancy test. I don't see any point in continuing our present conversation until we know one way or the other whether you actually *are* pregnant,' he added grimly, picking up what appeared to be his car keys.

Hebe gave a firm shake of her head. 'I won't be here when you get back.'

Nick halted in the doorway, his face set into grimly determined lines as he turned back to her. 'You had damn well better be,' he warned angrily.

Hebe's chin rose challengingly. 'Aren't you afraid of what else I might "pry" into while you're gone?' she taunted.

Nick gave a humourless smile. 'Touch anything and I promise you you'll regret it,' he warned softly.

She believed him!

She believed his threat about her leaving too. But that didn't stop her, as soon as she knew he had definitely gone, from quietly letting herself out of the apartment and making her way back downstairs, pausing only long enough to pick up her jacket and bag from the staffroom before leaving the gallery.

Nick really could just go ahead and sack her if he liked!

He might be used to issuing orders and expecting them to be obeyed, but after his insults she had no intention of obeying anyone who spoke to her in that autocratic tone.

And she refused even to *think* about his assertion that she was pregnant. Of course she wasn't. The whole idea was ridiculous.

Besides, she had some telephone calls she needed to make before the close of business for the day—telephone calls she couldn't make from Nick's apartment.

She had a lot of friends from university working in the art world who, like her, had decided to work in galleries or agencies instead of painting professionally themselves. One of them, she was sure, would give her some sort of lead on Andrew Southern's agent.

She was determined to track the artist down, no matter how impossible Nick seemed to think it was. Nothing was impossible if you had the right motivation. And she most certainly had that!

Where was her mother now?

Living in England somewhere? With a husband and possibly other children?

Maybe. Hebe had no intention of disrupting her life, but now that she had seen that portrait she just needed to know.

Was Andrew Southern her father?

Why, if he had loved her mother, hadn't he married her when he knew she was expecting his child? If Hebe *was* his child…!

Why had she, Hebe, been given up for adoption?

None of those things had been of interest to her before she saw that portrait—and, whether he realised it or not, she had Nick Cavendish to thank for that!

It took half a dozen telephone calls once she got home to even track down Andrew Southern's agent, and then a call to the agency only resulted in the receptionist telling her that she could make an appointment to speak to Mr Gillespie, and he would be happy to pass along any commission she might care to make, but she very much doubted he would be able to help Hebe in regard to meeting or talking to Andrew Southern personally.

Hebe made an appointment for the following day, anyway. If nothing else she could give the agent a letter, possibly a photograph of herself, to forward on to the reclusive artist. If her mother had meant anything to Andrew Southern at all—and that portrait seemed to say that she had—then the photograph of Hebe alone would surely be enough to pique his interest!

It was what she was hoping for, at least…

* * *

Nick banged forcefully on the apartment door, his anger not having diminished in the least on the drive over here after discovering that Hebe had indeed gone from his own apartment before he'd returned.

What did she think she was playing at?

He had told her to stay put.

She hadn't.

He had told her they would talk further when he got back.

She hadn't been there to talk to.

And he was furious. With her. With himself. With the fact that he had become more and more convinced since leaving her earlier that she *was* pregnant.

If Hebe was to be believed about having had no other relationships in her life—and her anger at the suggestion had seemed fairly convincing—then he was going to have baby...

A little girl who would look like Hebe. Or a little boy who looked like him. And Luke...

He banged on the door again, his fist raised a third time when the it suddenly opened. Hebe eyed him coldly from just inside her apartment.

'There's no need to break the door down, Nick,' she snapped. 'I was just eating a sandwich when I heard your—knock,' she drawled pointedly.

He drew in an impatient breath. 'What sort of sandwich?' he demanded to know. 'You do realise that there are certain things you can't eat when you're pregnant?' he added impatiently as he walked past her into the apartment, to look around him curiously.

The apartment took up the second floor of one of the old Victorian buildings London was so famous for, with huge bay windows that looked out on a tree-lined avenue.

The sitting room was bright and sunny, the walls painted yellow, multicoloured scatter rugs on the polished wood floor, the brown sofa and chairs festooned with an assortment of cushions in autumn colours.

He turned to look at Hebe. She certainly looked a lot better than she had when he'd left her earlier. The colour was back in her cheeks, the sparkle—anger—was back in those gold-coloured eyes. She was looking very slim too, in the faded denims and fitted black tee shirt she had changed into since returning home.

Well, the slimness was soon going to change, if his assumption proved correct!

Although he had a feeling Hebe was going to be one of those women who put hardly any weight on while pregnant, and that despite the growing baby she would retain that air of delicacy that so appealed to him.

He took a crushed paper bag out of his jacket pocket. 'For you,' he told her dryly.

Hebe made no effort to take the bag from him, and in fact put both her hands behind her back instead. She knew exactly what was in the bag, and had no intention of satisfying his curiosity. 'I don't remember inviting you inside,' she said irritably.

'You didn't,' he confirmed, strolling over to where her plate, with its half-eaten sandwich, still sat on the table. He lifted one corner of the bread to look at the filling. 'Cheese.' He nodded approvingly. 'You'll need to keep up your calcium intake.'

'Nick—'

'Hebe?' he came back challengingly.

'Don't you think you've taken this far enough?' She sighed wearily, sitting down on the chair at the table.

'Insulted me enough? I told you—I was faint and dizzy from hunger earlier, and for no other reason,' she said firmly.

He put the bag down on the table next to her sandwich. 'We'll know in a few minutes, won't we?' he said grimly. 'You can do this test any time of the day and get a correct result,' he assured her determinedly.

'A negative one, you mean?' She nodded.

'Hebe.' Nick moved down on his haunches beside the chair. 'You weren't on the Pill. I didn't use any precautions, either. Did you go to the doctor for a morning-after pill?'

'Certainly not!' She was horrified at the suggestion.

'No, I thought not,' he accepted flatly. 'Have you had a period since we were together?'

Her cheeks suffused with embarrassed colour. 'Now, look—'

'Have you?' he persisted.

Had she? Her periods had never been particularly regular, anyway—sporadic at best—so she tended not to take too much notice of dates, just dealing with them when they arrived. But, no, she didn't think she had—

She grabbed the bag containing the pregnancy test, got up and strode determinedly from the room. She would do his test, prove to Nick once and for all that she was not pregnant, and then hopefully he would just go away and leave her alone.

Blue.

The little line in the middle of the window was blue.

Blue for *positive*.

Hebe sat on the side of the bath, her head bent down between her knees as she breathed in short, controlling gasps, trying not to faint again.

She hadn't believed the result the first time, had been sure it was faulty, so had taken out the second tube in the double pack—trust Nick to want to make doubly sure!— and done it again.

That one had a positive blue line through the middle of it too.

She was definitely, positively pregnant.

With Nick Cavendish's baby.

A baby *he* certainly didn't want.

Did *she*?

She had never given much thought to having a baby of her own. Or, at least, if she had, it had been as part of and a progression of a loving marriage.

Not the result of a single night spent in Nick Cavendish's arms!

Now what did she do?

She was pregnant. She had the spark of a tiny new life growing inside her. Her very own son or daughter. But it wasn't just hers. It was Nick's son or daughter, too!

And therein lay the problem. It was obvious from what Nick had said earlier that he believed she had deliberately got herself pregnant in order to trap him in some way.

What—?

'Hebe? Are you okay?' A soft knock on the bathroom door accompanied Nick's pressing query.

She straightened and looked apprehensively at the door, wondering how she was supposed to go out there and tell Nick that she was expecting his baby after all.

She could lie, of course. That was always an option. She could tell him that the result was negative—

But he wouldn't believe her, and would no doubt insist on being present when he made her do yet another test!

Because he *knew,* somehow he already knew, that she was pregnant.

'Hebe?' he prompted more urgently.

She drew in a deep breath, chewing her top lip before answering him. 'Go away,' she finally managed to groan.

There was silence on the other side of the door for several seconds, and then Nick rattled the door handle impatiently. 'Open the door, Hebe,' he ordered steadily.

'I said go away!' she muttered.

'No way,' he answered determinedly. 'Either you open the damned door, Hebe, or you stand back out of the way while I kick it down,' he instructed evenly.

He was going to kick the bathroom door down? She moved out of the way, just in case.

'That's harassment, Nick,' she told him frowningly.

'Your choice.' The shrug could be heard in his voice.

'I'm pregnant—okay!' she shouted through the locked door. 'You were right all the time and I was wrong. Because I'm pregnant!' Her voice broke slightly as saying the words brought alive the enormity of what was happening to her.

No matter what Nick might choose to think, she was not going to ask him for help. Accepting any assistance from him after the things he had implied earlier was not an option. Although she had no idea how she was going to manage to support herself and the baby, either. Even if Nick let her keep her job at the gallery, she would only be able to work until the seventh month or so. Her parents would want to help, she felt sure. But was it fair to ask them? After all, they had adopted her and given her so much—how could she now ask them to help her in single-motherhood? That would just—

She didn't have any time for further thought or worry

as the bathroom door crashed back on its hinges, the lock having splintered away from the frame as Nick kicked it.

She stared up at him dazedly as he stood in the doorway. 'You actually broke the door down,' she murmured incredulously as she stood up to examine the damage.

He shrugged, his expression grim. 'I told you that I would if you didn't unlock it.'

Yes, but— He couldn't just go around breaking up her apartment! What was her flatmate Gina going to say, when she came home from work later and saw the damage Nick had done to the door?

'You had no right to do that.' She gasped her indignation. 'No need—'

'I had *every* need, damn it,' he grated harshly. 'You wouldn't open the door.' He shrugged unapologetically. 'I couldn't tell what you were doing in here.'

She gave a dazed shake of her head. 'It's a bathroom, Nick; what could I possibly have been doing?'

'I had no way of knowing, did I? With that door between us,' he came back hardly. 'So a word of warning, Hebe,' he added tautly. 'Don't ever put a locked door between us again!'

Hebe just continued to stare at him. Had the whole world gone mad? *Her* world, at least!

Hebe didn't want to listen to him any more. She couldn't think with him glaring at her like that. His eyes were no longer filled with the shadowy pain of the past but full of accusation now instead. And that accusation was directed at her. Because he believed she had deliberately set out to get pregnant that night they'd spent together!

She didn't even look at him as she brushed past him to go back into the sitting room. It all looked so normal, exactly as she had left it this morning, with the bright autumn colours that she and Gina had had so much fun decorating with, her pot plants in the window, the early-evening sun shining through the almost floor to ceiling windows.

Only she had changed then, for she wasn't the same person who had left the apartment early this morning to go to work as usual.

She was pregnant. With Nick Cavendish's child. And that meant her life would never be back to what she thought of as normal ever again.

'Well?' She turned back to him challengingly. 'When are you going to start accusing me again of being a gold-digger? Of deliberately getting myself pregnant so that I can get my hands on all that lovely Cavendish money? Because you *do* think that's what I've done, don't you, Nick?' she scorned disgustedly.

Nick continued to look at her through narrowed lids. Yes, as he had driven to the chemist, bought the pregnancy test and driven back to his apartment only to find her gone, that was exactly what he had thought Hebe had done.

And he still did. Nothing had changed his belief about that.

It just didn't matter any more. No, damn it, it mattered—but not to the ultimate outcome. Because Hebe was having his baby. *His* baby. And, whatever she might have thought would result from this, this child was going to be his as well as hers.

'Don't bother to answer that,' she dismissed disgustedly. 'I know that's what you think. Well, do you want to know what *I* think?' Her eyes flashed like molten gold.

Nick felt some of his own anger draining out of him as he took in all her outraged indignation. She really was a beautiful young woman. A woman who would be even more beautiful as her pregnancy developed. Nick knew from when Sally had been expecting Luke that pregnant women seemed to take on a beauty all their own, glowing from the inside rather than out.

A glowingly pregnant Hebe was going to be a sight to behold.

'Yes,' he answered briskly, moving to one of the armchairs to sit down and look up at her. 'I would be very interested to hear what you think.'

'I'll bet!' Hebe scorned. 'You don't seem to have taken too much notice of what I've had to say so far!' She looked pointedly at the shattered bathroom door.

Couldn't she see that was because he had been in shock himself? Because he couldn't believe—hadn't dared to hope—despite what he had said to the contrary, that Hebe really could be pregnant with their child.

He had loved being a father to Luke, and had been devastated when his son had died so tragically, so suddenly. He had felt totally bereft. Now, it seemed, he was to be given a second chance at fatherhood. With Hebe. He had never thought about having another child after Luke, but now the opportunity had presented itself he found he wanted this baby more than anything else in the world.

It was just going to take a little getting used to...

'I'm listening now, Hebe,' he assured her gruffly.

She would just bet he was. Waiting to hear her make demands, no doubt. To try and blackmail him out of some of the Cavendish fortune!

Well he was going to be disappointed.

She drew in a deep breath. 'This is *my* baby, Nick—'

'And mine,' he put in quietly.

'But you can't be sure of that, can you?' she taunted, pacing the room restlessly as she looked at him. 'How do you know, how can you be *sure,* I haven't been with another man in the last six weeks?' she challenged.

He didn't move, but a nerve began to pulse just below his jaw. 'Have you?'

'No, I haven't, damn you!' she denied furiously. 'But there's no way you can be sure—absolutely sure—is there?' she taunted.

He continued to look at her for several long, breathless seconds, and then he nodded. 'A doctor will be able to confirm just how pregnant you are.'

Hebe looked at him, frowning, but his expression was so inscrutable it was impossible to read any emotion behind those blue eyes. 'And you will accept that?'

His eyes narrowed on her probingly. 'If you insist we can have tests done too,' he finally murmured softly.

'If *I* insist...?' she prompted suspiciously.

'Hebe, once this baby is established as mine, that's exactly what it will be!' he grated harshly.

She gave a disbelieving shake of her head. 'Are you saying you would take this baby away from me?'

'I'm not saying that at all.' He shrugged. 'Although, obviously that will ultimately be your decision.'

'I don't understand you!' she muttered emotionally.

'It's quite simple, Hebe. If you want to get your hands on "all that lovely Cavendish money" then you will also have to accept that I come along with it,' he bit out decisively.

Hebe stopped her pacing to stare at him incredulously. 'But I don't *want* your money,' she finally burst out forcefully. 'I'm not interested in it. Or you!'

'Methinks you doth protest too much,' he taunted.

'I'm not protesting at all,' she snapped, stung by his mockery. 'I'm stating a fact.'

'A fact, Hebe, the bottom line, is I now have a responsibility to you and the baby,' he shrugged.

A responsibility? Was that what she had become?

After years of independence, of paying her own way, was that was she was going to be reduced to?

No, she wouldn't become that! No matter how difficult going it alone was going to be, she wouldn't become that...

She gave a firm shake of her head. 'I don't need or want your help, thank you,' she told him stiffly.

'Haven't you understood yet, Hebe?' Nick ground out fiercely. 'I'm not asking, I'm *telling* you how it's going to be!'

Hebe raised her head to look at him numbly. 'What do you mean?'

'Simply that I am going to marry you, Hebe,' he told her grimly. 'Just as quickly as the arrangements can be made!'

Nick was going to *marry* her?

He couldn't be serious!

CHAPTER FIVE

NICK watched Hebe's face suffuse with a look of horror as the full realisation of what he had just said hit her.

Not exactly a flattering response to a proposal of marriage!

Certainly not the response he had been expecting.

Most women he knew, in Hebe's position, would have jumped at the idea of marrying him.

Hebe just looked as if he had dealt her another insult!

Unless he was just meant to *think* she was horrified at the suggestion?

He tried to force this idea from his mind. If the two of them were to be married and have a child together, there had to be some sort of common ground for them other than the baby. It would be a disaster otherwise—their marriage just a battleground. Even if they were going to be marrying for reasons other than love.

'Oh, come on, Hebe,' he chided tauntingly. 'It won't be so bad. You won't have to work any more. You can spend as much of that Cavendish money as you like redecorating my apartments, if they don't suit.' Looking round at this apartment at its warmth and homeliness, he had a feeling that the chrome and leather décor in his own homes wouldn't be what Hebe would choose at all. 'Or we could buy a house,' he suggested, as the thought occurred to him. 'It would probably be better for the baby if it had a garden to play in—'

'Stop, Nick!' she cut in forcefully. 'Just stop! I am *not* going to marry you—'

'Oh yes, you are,' Nick assured her softly.

'No. I'm. Not,' she said firmly.

'Oh-yes-you-are,' he repeated, with restrained anger.

'No!' She shook her head decisively. 'I don't want to marry you. I don't know you! You don't know me, either!' she reasoned frustratedly. 'And what you do know you don't like!'

Nick gave a lazy smile as his gaze moved slowly over the slim contours of her body. Whether she realised it or not, her nipples were taut with tension beneath that fitted tee shirt. 'Oh, I think you'll find I like my side of the bargain just fine,' he said mockingly.

Hebe eyed him with frustration, knowing he was deliberately misunderstanding her. What he was talking about was purely physical. The two of them had undoubtedly found a compatability that single night they'd spent together, but that had nothing to do with the commitment of marrying someone, living with them every day. He was thinking only of the nights—not the days, weeks and years of living together.

'I think you'll like it just fine, too, Hebe,' he murmured throatily as he stood up to move purposefully towards her. 'Would you like me to demonstrate how much you'll like it?'

'No…' Hebe took a step back, her eyes wide as she easily guessed his intention.

She already knew that she *did* like—only too well!

Nick paid absolutely no attention to her half-hearted

protest, taking her in his arms as his head lowered and his lips claimed hers.

Oh, God…!

Hebe simply melted against him, having no defences against his marauding mouth and hands as she felt the flood of warmth between her thighs, her breasts highly sensitised against the hardness of his chest.

His mouth moved hungrily against hers, sipping and tasting, the moist warmth of his tongue moving erotically against her lips before dipping deep into the hot cavern beneath.

Burning desire ripped through her, tearing her defences apart in a single assault, and her hands clung to the strength of his shoulders as she gave in to that engulfing fire.

His mouth broke away from hers, his lips and tongue trailing heatedly down the creamy column of her throat, his hands pushing her tee shirt impatiently aside. Taking one fiery nipple into the heat of his mouth, tongue caressing, teeth gently biting, he let his hand move down between her legs, cupping her there, just that touch through denim and silk making her quiver with pleasure.

She wanted— She needed—

Nick gave her what she needed, his palm pressing against the hardened nub between her legs, pressing more firmly as his mouth moved to her other breast, drawing the nipple into his mouth, sucking deeply as his tongue moved moistly, teeth biting with the same rhythm as his hand stroked, seeming to find that hardened nub unerringly as he touched and caressed her to fever pitch.

She couldn't take any more. She felt as thought she was about to explode. She could feel the pleasure building until it couldn't be contained, finally finding her release in long, convulsing waves of pleasure so deeply felt it was almost pain.

She collapsed weakly against him as he kissed her breasts gently in the aftermath of her release, realising her hands had become entangled in the dark thickness of his hair as she held him against her.

What had she done?

Stupid question—she *knew* what she had done. She just had no idea how to continue fighting Nick after responding to him so wantonly.

Nick straightened slowly, pulling Hebe's tee shirt down as he raised his head to look at her flushed face and pleasure-dazed eyes. His own body was still hard with desire—a desire he had no intention of satisfying. It was Hebe's pleasure that was important right now, to show her what they could find together any time she wanted once they were married.

She looked at him frowningly. 'But you haven't—'

'I don't need to, Hebe,' he assured her huskily. 'That was for you. Sex may not have been part of your plan, but I dare you to deny wanting me after that,' he murmured throatily.

Wrong thing to say, Nick. So very wrong, he realized, as she tensed before moving abruptly away from him.

But he had needed to make her see just what they could have together besides the baby now growing inside her.

His baby, he acknowledged again fiercely. *His.*

And he would do anything—anything at all—to ensure that Hebe realised she was going to marry him rather than be paid off.

Even take advantage of Hebe's response to him?

Yes, if that was what it took!

Damn it, he would keep Hebe naked in bed for a month if that was what he had to do to make her see sense!

Because she *would* marry him. *Would* become his wife. The mother of his child.

Hebe shook her head, trying to clear it of the cottonwool her brain had become as Nick kissed and caressed her.

She had to think, damn it. Had to make Nick understand that no matter how she responded to him she couldn't marry him.

Which, after her arousal just now, and the way she still trembled in the aftermath of that shattering release, wasn't going to be easy to do!

She raised her chin determinedly. 'That's just sex, Nick,' she dismissed firmly.

He shrugged. 'It's a start.'

'No, it isn't.' Her voice rose heatedly. 'Marriage is for people who love each other, who want to be together for the rest of their lives—'

'Or for people who have already made a baby together,' he put in pointedly.

Hebe closed her eyes, wishing she could shut out the truth of his words as easily. They *had* made a baby together. And did she have the right to deny that child both its parents?

Yes—if they didn't love each other!

But she *did* love Nick...

It was impossible to try and tell herself differently. Her fascination for him all those months ago had blossomed into love during that night they'd spent together six weeks ago.

The same time as their child had found a place and nestled inside her body...!

If Nick had loved her in return she knew that she wouldn't have hesitated in agreeing to marry him. She would be the happiest woman in the world right now if that were true.

But it wasn't. He thought she was after his money, not his love.

And surely love on one side was just as bad as no love between them at all?

'Why does it have to be marriage?' She frowned.

He raised dark brows. 'You would rather just live with me?'

'No! I mean, of course I wouldn't,' she admitted irritably. 'I simply don't understand why you feel you have to marry me.'

His mouth quirked with black humour. 'Perhaps I make it a point of honour to marry the mothers of my children? It's certainly something I've done so far in my life!' he added derisively.

Hebe looked at him searchingly. He couldn't think this child would be a replacement for the one he had lost? Luke had been Luke. This child, whether boy or girl, could only ever be itself and no one else.

She moistened her lips with the tip of her tongue. 'I realise that losing Luke must have been devastating—'

'Do you?' Even that dark humour had gone now, and grim lines were etched beside his nose and mouth. 'Yes, it was—devastating,' he conceded slowly. 'It was also three years ago. And nothing and no one can ever change that.'

'Exactly.' She breathed her relief that he had quite literally taken the words out of her mouth. 'This baby—' *Oh, God...!* 'This baby,' she began again, 'can't replace him—'

'You think that's what I want? To *replace* him?' Nick suddenly seemed bigger and more ominous in his obvious anger.

Hebe eyed him warily, knowing she had stepped onto dangerous ground. 'Well, I—'

'You can't replace people any more than you can bring them back to life!' he ground out harshly, blue eyes glittering with emotion. 'Hebe, do you have *any* idea of the significance of that night we spent together six weeks ago?'

She grimaced. 'Well, I'm pregnant, if that's what you mean—'

'No, that *isn't* what I mean!' Nick swung away from her, his hands clenched at his sides, fury emanating from every muscle and sinew of his body. 'That day, six weeks ago, was the anniversary of Luke's death,' he told her flatly. 'Three years to the day since some maniac got in his car after consuming too much wine with his business lunch and drove straight through a crowd of afternoon shoppers on the busy streets of New York. Sally and Luke were amongst them. Sally was seriously injured and Luke—Luke was dead before the medics even got there!'

Hebe could still hear the pain and horror of that day in his voice.

Not just to lose a child, but to lose him in such an awful way.

To receive a telephone call, probably from some unknown person, telling him that his wife had been seriously injured and his son was dead.

And this baby—Hebe's baby—had been conceived on the night of the anniversary of that little boy's death…

How eerie was that? Almost as if—

No, she wouldn't think of it in that way. It was just coincidence. Or perhaps a little more than that, she conceded. Nick had probably needed a woman in his bed that night to help anaesthetize him, to keep the pain of that anniversary at bay.

And because of that need Hebe was now pregnant with his child.

She shook her head. 'Please believe me when I say I really am sorry about that. It must have been awful for you. And Sally,' she added quietly.

She had known of her own baby's existence for only minutes—had no idea if it was a boy or a girl, even—but even so she knew she would be devastated if it were taken away from her now.

'But I can't marry you, Nick.' She groaned. 'People don't marry each other any more just because the woman's pregnant—'

'Judging by the fact that you were adopted, that certainly seems to have been the case in *your* family so far, I agree!' he cut in scathingly.

Hebe gasped, staring at him disbelievingly. 'That—that was—unforgivable!'

'Yes, it was,' he acknowledged, giving a self-disgusted shake of his head. 'I apologise. But I do mean to marry you, Hebe. This child will know its mother and its father. And don't tell me we don't have to get married for that, either,' he warned grimly. 'I don't want to be some part-time father with weekend and vacation access to my own kid! I mean this child to have parents who live together—two people he or she will call Mommy and Daddy.'

'And what about what *I* want?' Hebe protested emotionally.

Nick gave her a considering look. 'You were brought up by two people who loved you, weren't you? Parents who gave you the nurturing and security that your real mother, whoever she was, obviously thought she couldn't provide?'

'Yes…' Hebe eyed him uncertainly, not quite sure where he was going with this.

'Meaning you weren't left to live alone with your

mother, possibly brought up in daycare once you were old enough to be left, so that your mother could go back to work in order to support you both, not too much money coming in on that single wage. Or alternatively with a father in the background who maybe had access to you but only took it up sporadically, breaking your heart some- where along the way—'

'It wouldn't be like that!' Hebe could quite clearly see where he was going with this now.

'Not if I agree to keep you and the child in the lifestyle to which you wish to become accustomed, no,' he acknowl- edged sarcastically. 'But I'm not going to do that, Hebe. The only way in which you will have that is by marrying me,' he told her implacably. 'I intend being in this child's life every single day, Hebe,' he assured her determinedly. 'There in the morning when it wakes up, to love and care for it each and every single day. There at night to read it a bedtime story, to care for it when it's sick or upset.'

'And its mother?' she demanded. 'Once you've married me to get what you want, what are you going to *do* with me?'

His expression became less intense. 'I've already shown you what we can have together, Hebe,' he drawled mock- ingly. 'It's all I have to give.'

She couldn't deny her response to him. Couldn't deny his response to her—had felt his need pressed against her, as throbbingly heated as her own desire.

But would that last? More to the point, was it enough to base a marriage on?

'Has it occurred to you, Nick,' she said slowly, 'that perhaps now I know your conditions I may not even *want* this baby?'

His hands clenched at his sides, his expression grimly

forbidding. 'I hope you're not talking about what I think you are!'

Hebe sighed, knowing abortion wasn't even a possibility as far as she was concerned. That it wasn't as far as Nick was concerned either, if his sudden fury was anything to go by.

'No,' she conceded heavily. 'I couldn't do that.'

'I should damn well hope not,' he rasped uncompromisingly.

She shook her head. 'It was just an idea. Not one I meant to be taken seriously, I might add,' she said, as she saw his anger hadn't abated in the least at her explanation.

'If I thought for a moment that it was—'

'I've said that it wasn't!' she defended firmly. 'I can't even think straight at the moment, Nick.' She sighed. 'This is all just too much on top of everything else. I don't even know who I really am!' she explained shakily.

'Then we'll find out together,' he said quietly. 'In fact, I insist on it,' he added hardly.

Frowning, she looked at him. 'What do you mean?'

'Isn't it obvious, Hebe?' he rasped impatiently. 'You're expecting a baby, but you don't know for certain who your real parents were—not their medical history, anything. For the baby's sake, at least, I think we need to know those things, don't you?'

For the baby's sake...

Of course. How could she have thought Nick would offer to help her for any other reason? After all, he believed the woman in the portrait was her! And that she had deliberately got pregnant!

It was as if she had had a bucket of ice water thrown over her. The trembling of her body was for quite another reason now.

'Yes,' she acknowledged hollowly, having no intention of telling him that she had already made an appointment to speak to Andrew Southern's agent tomorrow. She would keep that appointment alone and find out what she could about the woman she thought was her mother, and her relationship with Andrew Southern.

He nodded briskly. 'The first thing we need to do concerning that is talk to your parents—see if they know anything, anything at all, about your real parents.'

'But of course they don't.' Hebe frowned. 'They would have told me if they did.'

'Would they?' Nick prompted softly.

'Of course,' she answered impatiently. 'What possible reason could they have for not telling me?'

He shrugged. 'Perhaps the fact that they wanted you to have a settled, loving childhood, and not have your life ripped in two, as some adopted children's lives seem to be once they've located their real parents.' He shook his head. 'I don't know, Hebe. But I do think we at least have to ask them, don't you?'

'I suppose so,' she agreed reluctantly. 'I'll go and see them at the weekend—'

'*We'll* go and see them at the weekend,' Nick corrected firmly. 'It's going to be *we* in everything from now on, Hebe,' he told her firmly, and she looked at him with a frown.

We.

Hebe and Nick.

Hebe and Nick Cavendish.

How unlikely was that?

Completely unlikely! There was no way she could agree to marry this man just because he said she must. Absolutely no way!

'Tomorrow I'll see what I can do about arranging for the two of us to get married as quickly as possible.' Nick nodded distractedly, obviously having taken absolutely no notice whatsoever of her refusal. 'Today is Thursday, so I think it might be better if you took the rest of the week off. Saturday we'll go and see your parents, and Sunday we'll move your things into my apartment—*our* apartment,' he corrected ruefully.

'I'm not moving into your apartment on Sunday or at any other time!' Hebe protested incredulously. 'And I'm not marrying you either!'

'Of course you are,' he answered mildly.

'No—'

'Yes, Hebe, you are,' he repeated patiently.

'Is what I want to be of absolutely no consideration at all?' she gasped.

Nick eyed her critically. 'But you *are* getting what you want, Hebe. More than you want, in fact,' he added sarcastically. 'You really hadn't planned on getting me as your husband into the bargain, had you?' he mused grimly.

If Nick had loved her, if he had wanted to marry her, then she wouldn't have hesitated to say yes to his proposal. But he had made his feelings for her all too plain: he thought she was an opportunist and a gold-digger.

'You can't force me—'

'Calm down, Hebe,' he soothed. 'All this upset isn't good for the baby.'

The baby. That was all he cared about. All he would *ever* care about...

'I will marry you, Hebe. I insist on it. Do you really think you have the right to deny our child all the things I can give it? Or do you want this to deteriorate into a battle?' he added softly. 'A battle I would have every intention of winning?'

She blinked, a sinking feeling in the base of her stomach. 'What do you mean?'

He wasn't being fair, threatening her in this way. He knew he wasn't. But marriage between them was non-negotiable as far as he was concerned. Hebe could have anything and everything she wanted as his wife—but only as his wife.

'I would fight you for custody, Hebe,' he told her flatly. 'In fact, if you persist in fighting me on this I'll go to my lawyers right now and draw up papers to set the custody battle in motion.'

She was looking at him as if he were some sort of monster now. And maybe he was. But he wouldn't back down on this. He couldn't. There was too much at stake. He couldn't let this second chance at being a father pass him by.

She swallowed hard. 'You would really do that…?'

'If I'm forced to, yes,' he bit out tautly.

'Even if it meant I'd end up hating you?' she said emotionally.

Having Hebe hate him from the onset was not a good idea, he knew, but what choice was she giving him…?

'Even then,' he said grimly.

Hebe was looking at him now as if she had never seen him before—or as if she wished she never seen him in the first place!

She shook her head, turning away. 'I think I would like to be alone now for a while, if you don't mind,' she said abruptly.

Nick did mind—was reluctant to leave her. Even for a moment. He wasn't sure, now that she knew he was insisting on marriage rather than the settlement she had hoped for, that she wouldn't attempt to run away from him and hide if he left her on her own. Unless he could convince her beforehand that there was nowhere she could go that he wouldn't find her!

'We are getting married, Hebe,' he told her softly. 'You are going to move into my apartment. And we are going to see your parents on Saturday. And don't think I wouldn't find you if you tried to run away from me,' he added challengingly, knowing by the way her cheeks paled that she had at least been thinking about doing exactly that.

Hebe looked at him with dull eyes. 'You're really serious about this?'

'Most assuredly,' he bit out.

She nodded. 'I'll call my parents and tell them to expect us some time in the afternoon,' she said.

'And you'll move into my apartment on Sunday?'

She sighed. 'Let's just take one step at a time, hmm?'

They didn't have time for 'one step at a time', damn it!

But one look at her pale and drawn face told him that she really had had enough for one day.

Maybe he shouldn't have said those things to her in her condition. They were the truth, but maybe he shouldn't have been so harsh.

Or told her about Luke…!

But he hadn't felt he could do anything else in the circumstances. He had been fighting for his life—and his baby—and if that meant he had to fight dirty, then he was willing to do it.

Maybe he shouldn't have made love to her in that way, either. She was pregnant, after all. But he hadn't, as she chose to think, just wanted to prove a point to her. He had needed to hold her, to make love to her, and he knew he had been needing to do so ever since he'd seen her again in the gallery earlier this afternoon, his body responding uncontrollably just at the sight of her.

Even before that...!

He had tried to put her from his mind these last six weeks, in the same way he had every other woman he had been involved with since he and Sally parted, but Hebe had persisted in popping into his mind at the most inconvenient of times.

Because she had been so delicious to make love to, he had told himself. Because she had made love to him so deliciously too.

But neither of those things explained why he had still been able to imagine the delicate curve of her cheek, the beauty of those unusual gold-coloured eyes, the way a dimple appeared in her left cheek when she smiled, the husky sound of her laugh.

And then he had seen the portrait.

A portrait he had been convinced on sight was Hebe, the woman who had been haunting his days—and nights—for the last five weeks.

He had been filled with a mindless fury the first time he'd looked at the portrait, his imagination running riot and his mind going into overdrive thinking of the scenario that might have preceded the painting of it. Hebe's face and body were exactly as they had looked that night five weeks before, when *he* had made love to her.

He had known then and there that he had to have the portrait—and that, despite it being an almost priceless Andrew Southern, once he had it no one else would be allowed to look at it but him.

He had also known in that moment that he didn't want

anyone else but him to see the real Hebe like that again, either—that he wanted to take her back to his bed and keep her there.

He hadn't expected it to happen quite in this way, but the ultimate result was the same. And this way he didn't have to admit to any of these feelings. He could take Hebe as his wife whether she wanted it or not.

For better or for worse...!

'Okay,' he conceded huskily. 'I'll call round tomorrow evening and let you know what I've managed to sort out about the wedding.' No matter what Hebe said he wasn't letting go of that; she *would* marry him. And soon. 'Maybe the two of us could go out to dinner?'

Hebe gave him a rueful smile. 'I think it's a little late for us to start dating, don't you?'

'You said it yourself, Hebe. We need to start getting to know each other,' he insisted. 'By my reckoning, we have precisely seven and a half months in which to do that!'

By her reckoning too, Hebe mused dully, feeling as if a trapdoor were closing behind her. She had no doubts whatsoever that Nick meant it when he said she wouldn't be able to hide from him and that he would find her.

He meant what he said about marrying her too.

Just as he meant his threat regarding a fight for custody of the baby she carried deep inside her if she didn't agree to marriage.

It was obvious why he felt so strongly about it too. Luke's death meant that he had no intention of losing this second child.

But by this time tomorrow she would have been to see David Gillespie, Andrew Southern's agent, and would have at least set that situation in motion.

Once she had the answers she needed she would take great delight in telling Nick just exactly how wrong about her he had been!

In regard to the portrait, at any rate…

This pregnancy she couldn't, and wouldn't, do anything about.

Which meant she either had to marry Nick or fight him.

With all the Cavendish millions behind him, it was a fight she already knew Nick was sure to win!

That trapdoor closed with a resounding bang!

CHAPTER SIX

HEBE knew she was no closer to accepting her fate, when she opened the door to Nick's knock the following evening, than she had been the previous day.

But she had taken the day off as he'd suggested—it had fitted in with her appointment to see David Gillespie, anyway. An appointment that had been as frustratingly unsatisfactory as the secretary had warned her on the telephone that it would be.

No, David Gillspie had told her. He couldn't possibly reveal Andrew Southern's address. No, he certainly couldn't give her the artist's telephone number either. No, it didn't matter that her mother was an old friend of the artist. He still couldn't give her the address or telephone number.

Hebe had even tried mentioning the portrait—also to no avail. It wasn't catalogued in the artist's work, so it was probably a fake, the elderly man had claimed regretfully.

The best that Hebe had been able to get was a promise that yes, he would forward a letter on to the artist. But with the added warning that she probably wouldn't receive a reply!

Hebe didn't agree with him, and she had taken a great

deal of time and care over the wording of that letter, including a recent photograph of herself, too.

Of course it was Friday today, so Andrew Southern wouldn't receive the letter until tomorrow at the earliest. But surely once the weekend was over the letter and photograph would elicit some sort of a response?

If it didn't, then Andrew Southern wasn't the man she'd thought he was!

'You look beautiful,' Nick told her huskily as he took in her appearance in a fitted black knee-length dress, before stepping forward to plant a light kiss on her mouth.

A kiss that took her totally by surprise!

So much so that she felt herself respond instinctively, before common sense took over and she moved abruptly away; this man was forcing her to marry him! 'There's no need for any sort of play-acting when we're alone, Nick,' she told him curtly.

'Who's play-acting?' He raised dark brows over mocking blue eyes, looking wonderfully handsome in a black silk shirt and a gunmetal grey jacket, his black fitted trousers sitting low down on narrow waist and thighs. 'I happen to enjoy kissing you. I had the distinct impression you enjoyed being kissed by me too...' he added scathingly. 'And I would have thought that when we're alone—considering what our kisses usually lead to—would be exactly the right time!'

Hebe felt a delicate blush highlight her cheeks. As he'd said, she enjoyed a lot more than being kissed by him.

'I'm merely pointing out that my flatmate has already gone out for the evening, so there's no one to impress!' she bit out dismissively.

His brows rose even higher. 'I'm beginning to wonder

if this elusive flatmate exists!' he taunted, obviously deciding to ignore her jibe.

Hebe's mouth tightened . 'Oh, she exists,' she assured him tersely. 'Are we going straight out to dinner?' She wasn't even sure she was going to be able to eat; nothing else she had eaten today seemed to have wanted to stay down.

Being pregnant, she was quickly discovering, was a very uncomfortable state to be in. In fact, at the moment it felt a little like the seasickness she had suffered as a child on a day trip to Calais with her parents!

But this was only in the early stages of pregnancy, so the magazine she had bought when she went out earlier had informed her. Perfectly normal. The sickness usually disappeared by about the fourth month.

Only another seven or eight weeks to go, then!

By which time, if she didn't manage to keep any food down at all, she would have lost weight rather than gained any!

'Yes, straight out, I think,' Nick decided lightly. 'Hopefully there will be less chance of us having an argument if we're in the middle of a crowded restaurant!' he added derisively.

Hebe arched a blonde brow. 'Do you think so?'

Nick chuckled. 'Not really, no.' His gaze sharpened. 'How are you feeling today?'

'In what way?' She avoided his question as she collected her cream silk jacket from the back of the chair where she had put it earlier, having no intention of going anywhere near her bedroom once Nick arrived.

They might never leave the apartment at all if she did that—and, no matter what Nick might think to the contrary, Gina really did exist, and was expected back later this evening!

Nick's mouth twisted wryly. 'In any way!'

'Well, I haven't changed my mind about marrying you, if that's what you mean,' she muttered, as she slipped her arms into the jacket he held out for her.

His mouth tightened now. 'Hebe, could we at least start the evening without fighting?'

She shrugged. 'You were the one who asked!'

'And we both know I was referring to your nausea,' he came back impatiently.

'Then why didn't you just say so?' She grimaced. 'I've only been sick four times today so far. Not bad, considering I haven't been able to eat or drink anything all day!'

Nick frowned at this information, not at all happy with the fact that she was being quite so sick. He had noted the paleness of her cheeks when he'd arrived, but had hoped that was just due to the tension of the situation.

'Sally—my ex-wife,' he explained shortly, 'saw a guy over here when she was pregnant with Luke. I think it might be advisable for me to make an appointment for you to go and see him—'

'No!' Hebe cut in vehemently, her expression fierce. 'I don't want to go and see some specialist your wife saw when she was expecting Luke!' He looked surprised by her forcefulness.

Nick frowned darkly. 'Why the hell not? This guy's the best that there is.'

'I'm sure he is.' She grimaced. 'But Sally was your wife, and I'm just—just—'

'The woman who is shortly going to be my wife,' he cut in grimly.

Was everything going to be this much of a battle with Hebe? Probably, he acknowledged heavily.

But he wasn't going to give up. Making sure his baby was all right and having Hebe in his bed was going to be worth every battle scar...

'Hebe, you may as well get used to the idea,' he told her firmly. 'You and I, and the baby you're expecting, are going to be a family. End of story.'

She gave him a pitying look. 'If you really think it's going to be that simple then I feel sorry for you!'

Of course he didn't think it was going to be that simple. He already knew just how determined Hebe could be, how with her it was the irresistible force meeting the immovable object; he just happened to believe that the sooner she accepted they were going to be married the better it would be for both of them!

And the baby...

The thought of Hebe pregnant with his child was still strange to him. It was a wonder, a miracle, and even if he was not at all happy with Hebe's methods he knew he had spent most of the day walking around with a ridiculous smile on his face. More than one of his exployees had done a double-take at it.

About the same amount of time Hebe had spent being thoroughly sick, by the sound of it.

'Come on.' He took a firm hold of her arm. 'We'll simply go through the menu until we find something that *does* stay down!'

Bruschetta and olives, Hebe eventually found, after a false start with soup and asparagus; the latter she hadn't even got as far as her mouth, the smell having been enough to put her off.

'Better?' Nick murmured, with obvious relief.

Obviously he wasn't used to taking out such a fastidious eater, and normally she wouldn't have been—had always been able to eat anything in the past.

But the *maître'd* at this exclusive restaurant was most attentive, seeming completely unconcerned that the waiter had had to bring three starters before they found something Hebe could eat, simply whisking away the plates that had offended.

Obviously there were some benefits to being out with Nick Cavendish, after all!

'Would you like me to order some more?' he offered, once she had eaten all the bread and succulent olives with obvious enjoyment.

Embarassingly so, if she thought about it. But she had been hungry.

She grimaced. 'Let's just wait and see if this stays down, shall we?' She frowned across at him questioningly. 'I hope that isn't a smile I see on your face?'

Nick instantly sobered. 'Not at all. I'm just pleased you've found something you can eat.'

Hebe continued to eye him suspiciously for several seconds, but as he continued to blandly meet her gaze she finally gave up. 'Believe me, pregnancy isn't all it's cracked up to be,' she muttered, disgruntled.

'Not many things are,' Nick drawled.

She stiffened defensively. 'I hope that wasn't yet another snipe at me?'

'Not at all,' he came back smoothly. 'In fact, I've left all my sniper bullets at home this evening! Did you telephone your parents today?' he prompted briskly, before she could come back with another sharp comment.

She had. And a very difficult call it had been, too. She couldn't just tell her parents over the telephone that she was pregnant, for goodness' sake; she owed them more than that.

But as soon as she had mentioned bringing a male friend home with her, her mother had gone into hyperdrive. No doubt she had the colour of the bridesmaids' dresses and the flowers picked out for the wedding already!

Which posed yet another problem for Hebe.

If, as Nick insisted, she really *did* have marry him, or risk him trying to take the baby from her, then she didn't want her parents to realise why they were getting married. She knew she wouldn't be able to keep the baby secret for long, and she didn't mind them finding out about that so much, but she couldn't let them see that Nick didn't love her.

Her parents, she was sure, had always dreamt of a romantic wedding for their only daughter—with a white flowing dress, and orange blossom, and confetti by the bucketful.

The quick wedding that Nick had talked about would no doubt be a visit to a register office with none of those things!

But even that wouldn't have been so bad if the main ingredient had been in evidence.

Love.

Like her parents, Hebe had always assumed she would marry someone she loved, who loved her in return. Fifty per cent of that—her own feelings for Nick—just wouldn't do!

'Hebe?' Nick prompted guardedly at her continued silence.

She drew in a ragged breath. 'Yes, I called them. I told them I was bringing you to meet them on Saturday. They jumped to the obvious conclusion,' she added flatly.

That she was bringing home the man she intended marrying, Nick hoped. He wondered why Hebe didn't look a little happier about it.

It was what she wanted, after all. The Cavendish money at her disposal. The fact that he came along with the money might have come as something of a shock to her, but, as he had just told her, not too many things turned out quite as you planned them!

Including the way he felt about Hebe…

When his marriage to Sally, his college sweetheart, had broken down, he had vowed never to fall in love or marry again. But inwardly he had known after that one night he and Hebe had spent together—and tried to dismiss!—that Hebe was different. He'd known and been all the crueller in dismissing her the following morning.

But he hadn't forgotten her in all the weeks he had been away. In fact he hadn't so much as looked at another woman during that time—had known then that he would have to see Hebe again when he got back to London.

Of course he hadn't expected the portrait!

Or to come back to London and find that Hebe was pregnant!

Deliberately so?

He couldn't be absolutely sure about that. That was the problem…

But at least he was willing to make a go of this marriage. Why didn't Hebe just accept that if he had decided just to go for custody of the baby when it was born she wouldn't have found herself in half such an advantageous position?

'Never mind, Hebe,' he advised hardly, reaching into his jacket pocket to take out a small velvet box and place it on the table in front of her. 'Maybe this will help cheer you up.' He sat back to watch her reaction.

Which wasn't at all what he had imagined it would be.

Hebe was staring down at the ring box as if it were about to leap up and bite her!

Or maybe it was just that she had thought she would get

to choose her engagement ring herself, he realised harshly. A nice big rock of a diamond, no doubt.

Remembering the ring inside the box, Nick didn't think she was going to be disappointed!

He was.

What idiotic part of his brain had tried to convince him to give Hebe a chance? That perhaps he had been mistaken about her motives and maybe she hadn't got herself pregnant deliberately at all?

Whichever part it was, it needed shooting!

'For God's sake open it, Hebe,' he rasped, and sat forward slightly. 'I'm pretty sure you're going to like it,' he said impatiently. 'And if you don't we can change it for something bigger and better,' he added mockingly.

He was a fool, a blind, stupid fool, for wanting to believe that maybe Hebe's physical reaction to him meant she felt something more for him, after all, than just an appreciation of his bank balance.

But she was right. It was just sex.

Well, she could have as much of that as she liked. He would keep his emotions for the baby when it was born!

Hebe swallowed hard, reaching out for the box tentatively, sure she already knew what was inside. She felt stunned by the gesture. Nick had said they were getting married. Just that. But if her hunch was right this box contained an engagement ring. It was so totally unexpected.

She looked up at him uncertainly before opening the box, searching those hard, uncompromising features for some sign that this ring meant any more than a shackle of ownership.

The narrowed coldness of his eyes, that mocking twist to his lips, told her it didn't.

She lifted the lid to the box, not quite gasping as she

gazed down at the ring inside, but her breath definitely arrested in her lungs, and her eyes were wide.

It was the hugest diamond she had ever seen—several carats at least—surrounded by half a dozen slightly smaller diamonds, and the name on the lid of the box alone told her it must have cost a small fortune. A very minute part of the Cavendish millions, but still a fortune.

She closed the lid with a resounding snap. 'Why are you giving me this?' she challenged.

'Why do you think?' he snapped impatiently.

'Are you deliberately trying to insult me?' She frowned agitatedly, pushing the box back across the table at him before putting both her hands firmly under the table, as if to stop him making her accept something she didn't want. Or need.

An engagement ring between them was a farce. And that ring—that ring with its gaudy diamonds—was nothing but an insult.

Nick made no effort to take the box. 'You would have preferred a sapphire instead, maybe? Or possibly another emerald? We can go back to the store tomorrow—'

'I don't remember saying I wanted an engagement ring from you at all,' she told him forcefully. 'But that—*that*— You *are* deliberately trying to insult me, aren't you?' She glared at him, two bright spots of angry colour in her cheeks.

His eyes glittered with a similar anger. 'What's wrong with it? Not big enough? I'm sure they have others—'

'Not big enough!' she repeated incredulously. 'If the diamonds had been any bigger they would have blinded everyone in the restaurant.'

She would *not* walk around with that thing on her finger—a deliberately ostentatious sign of ownership. She might as well walk around with a neon sign over her head saying *This woman has just been bought!*

Because that was obviously what Nick thought he had done!

'Will you keep your voice down, Hebe?' he muttered, as several other diners looked their way curiously. 'Tell me what's wrong with the ring, and we'll change it.'

She glared at him. 'If that had been a diamond an eighth, even a quarter of the size, it might—just might—have been acceptable. But that—that isn't a ring. It's a ball and chain!' She was breathing deeply in her agitation. 'I think I would like to leave now, if you don't mind.' She placed her napkin firmly back on the table.

'Fine—if that's what you want!' He threw his own napkin on the table, signalling for the bill, needing to get out of here himself.

He knew she'd said she didn't want to get married, but she didn't have to throw it back in his face quite so vehemently! Why didn't she just accept that there was no way she was going to get any of his money unless she became his wife? What *was* it about this woman?

A woman who made his pulse sing and his body rouse with desire every time he looked at her!

Hebe could feel the displeasure emanating from Nick as the two of them left the restaurant.

But what else had he expected—presenting her with that gaudily over-the-top ring?

That she would gather it up with greedy hands, no doubt, she recognised heavily.

But she had hated that ring, and all that it represented, on sight.

Couldn't Nick see that…?

'Will you be able to return the ring and get your money back?' she prompted abruptly as they approached Nick's car.

'Don't worry about it,' he dismissed tersely, opening the car door for her.

It was a beautiful, low red sports-car—the sort of car that Hebe had only ever seen in glossy magazines. The sort of car you would expect a man like Nick to drive. And this was only the car he owned and drove while in London. Goodness knew what other cars he had in Paris and New York!

'This is a nice car,' she offered placatingly once they were both safely seated inside, aware of the impending visit to her parents tomorrow, and that she hadn't spoken to Nick about it yet.

She still had to ask for his help in convincing her parents this was a love-match rather than a marriage of convenience. *Nick's* convenience!

He nodded curty. 'I'll buy you one like it, if you like.'

She drew in a sharp breath. 'And why would you want to do that?'

'Oh, cut the act, Hebe,' he told her uninterestedly. 'I'm really not convinced.'

That she wasn't after his money or the expensive gifts he was deliberately offering her...

'Fine—buy me the car,' she accepted heavily, knowing that nothing she said or did would convince this cynical man she wasn't just after his money. 'As long as you accept that in another six months you'll have to pry me out of it with a tin opener!' she muttered sarcastically.

When she was nearly eight months pregnant with their baby...

The baby that had become so real to her during her hours alone at the flat today.

Everywhere had been so quiet and peaceful, so much so that Hebe had been able to hear her own heartbeat, had imagined the tiny heartbeat inside her. She had laid her hands protectively on the flatness of her stomach and mentally tried to reach inside and talk to that flickering life.

And she had been sure she received the echoing answer—*I'm here...*

She glanced at Nick, wishing she could share that with him but knowing she couldn't—that he wouldn't understand the wonder she felt at the life growing inside her. Without being sexist, she supposed no man could completely understand the miracle of it all.

Especially when that man believed the pregnancy was only a means to an end as far as she was concerned.

'I'm sure you'll cope,' Nick dismissed impatiently, weary of every damned thing turning into an argument.

This wasn't just a battle, it was a minefield!

And Hebe obviously sensed that too, staying silent on the drive back to her apartment—a still empty apartment as they had only been gone an hour or so. She removed her jacket before eyeing him warily.

'What?' he prompted tersely, the tension finally getting to him.

She moistened her lips with the tip of her tongue before answering him.

Something Nick dearly wished she hadn't done as he found himself fascinated by the sensuality of the movement, his gaze locked on the pink edge of her tongue as it moved softly over those highly kissable lips.

Lips he desperately wanted to kiss!

At least on that level he could reach her, could understand her, and give her something they both got satisfaction from.

The type of satisfaction he had craved since he had parted from her twenty-four hours ago. Just thinking about her caused a stirring in his body, and the cold shower he had taken before coming over here earlier had done nothing to alleviate his discomfort.

But before he could take the step needed to pull her into his arms and make love to her, Hebe, unaware of his rising desire, began to answer him.

'I need to talk to you about this visit to my parents tomorrow,' she began awkwardly.

Ah. Yes. Nick could see how this was going to be a problem for her.

'No need,' he dismissed dryly. 'I take it your parents wouldn't be too happy if they knew the real reason we're getting married? That it would be—preferable if they believe we're actually in love with each other?'

Colour heightened her cheeks. 'They—they wouldn't understand this situation at all.' She grimaced.

No, he didn't for a moment think that they would understand their daughter's calculating machinations. Any more than his own parents would. Although he had no doubt that they would welcome Hebe into their family. The fact that she was expecting their grandchild would be enough to ensure that.

They would probably like Hebe for herself too, though, he admitted grudgingly. She was a warm and likeable woman apart from the fact that he didn't trust her motives at all—she might have refused the ring, but surely that was just because she didn't want to have to marry him to get her hands on his money. She certainly hadn't created such a fuss about his offer to buy her a sports-car. And once they were safely married she would no doubt be willing to accept a damn sight more than that!

Hebe was a mercenary little gold-digger, and the sooner he accepted that the better off he would be!

He shrugged. 'That isn't a problem for me, Hebe. But how do you think you'll cope with pretending to be in love with me?' he added tauntingly.

Hebe kept her lashes lowered over her eyes, her expressive golden eyes that she knew would show him at that moment that no pretence was necessary where she was concerned. In spite of everything, she *did* love Nick. To the point of distraction.

She already loved the baby growing inside her too.

And maybe, maybe after they were married, with time, Nick might even come to love her?

Or was she just living in fantasy land?

Probably, she acknowledged self-derisively. But that fantasy was all she had to cling to at this moment.

Because she was going to marry him. She now saw it as the only chance she had of showing him she wasn't the woman he thought she was.

Starting with drawing the line, a very firm line, at what gifts she would accept from him and what she wouldn't. Their baby wasn't for sale, and neither was she—and the sooner Nick realised that the better!

Her face was deliberately expressionless as she looked at him. 'I'm sure I'll cope too,' she derided. 'After all, we both know how charming you can be when you choose!' she added cuttingly, remembering exactly how charming he had been that evening six weeks ago.

Charming enough for her to believe he really was interested in her.

How naïve she had been…and she was certainly paying for that naïveté now!

'I'm very tired, Nick,' she sighed. 'If you wouldn't mind going now, I think I would like to go to bed…?' she added warily as he stared at her broodingly from across the room.

He wasn't staying here tonight, if that was what he thought. Her bedroom door was remaining shut against him until after they were married! Hopefully by then she would have convinced him of her innocence, at least.

'I don't mind at all,' he finally answered with hard dismissal. 'I didn't get to finish my dinner earlier, so I think I'll go and get myself something else to eat,' he added dryly.

Hebe gave him a sharp look, stung by his easy acquiescence to her request that he leave. 'You're going out again?'

Nick gave her a mocking look. 'Does that bother you?'

Yes! Came the instant answer. It bothered her very much.

After all, she was probably just one of several women Nick had been involved with during his visits to England. No doubt one of those other women would be quite happy to join him for a late supper. And whatever else was on offer…

Hebe realised that fidelity in their marriage was something else they hadn't discussed. The thought of Nick in bed with some other woman was totally unacceptable to her, but if she told him that he would probably laugh in her face!

'Not in the least,' she assured him dismissively.

His expression darkened ominously. 'That's what I thought,' he rasped. 'But once we're married, Hebe, get used to the idea that I will be the *only* man in your life. In your bed. Is that understood?' he prompted hardly.

She eyed him challengingly. Nick had unwittingly played right into her hands. 'And does the same apply to you?'

'Oh, yes, Hebe,' he murmured throatily as he took a step towards her, easily taking her in his arms and moulding her body to his. 'Keep me happy in your bed, and I promise I'll stay there,' he assured her throatily before his mouth claimed hers.

This wasn't quite the answer Hebe wanted to hear, but now Nick was kissing her she could no longer think straight.

She didn't have a single lucid thought in her head but her desire for him as his tongue moved tantalisingly over her lips to part them and deepen the kiss.

His hands moved up to cradle each side of her face, holding her mouth up to his as he explored with his tongue, sucking the moist warmth of her own tongue into his mouth and gently biting, arousing emotions in her that caused a pulsing warmth between her legs. Her whole body was trembling with need when he finally lifted his head to look down at her desire-drugged eyes and full, still-parted lips.

'Yes.' He murmured his satisfaction as he released her. 'I don't think pretending to be in love with you is going to be any hardship at all! Sure you still want me to leave, Hebe?' he added tauntingly.

Yes!

No...!

Of course she didn't want him to leave; she would much rather have just melted in his arms.

But the relevant word in his statement was 'pretending', and that was all being in love with her would ever be to Nick—a pretence.

'I'm sure,' she murmured huskily.

He gave a dismissive shrug. 'Your loss.'

Oh, yes, she knew that, Hebe acknowledged heavily as she watched him go, waiting until the apartment door had closed softly behind him before dropping weakly down into an armchair.

How was she going to be able to bear being married to a man she loved but who felt nothing but contempt for her?

A man who only had to touch her to melt her to the core of her being…!

CHAPTER SEVEN

'STOP looking so worried, Hebe,' Nick told her derisively as she sat beside him on the drive to her parents' home. 'Didn't I already prove last night that my performance in front of your parents will be faultless? As yours had better be when you meet *my* parents,' he added grimly.

Hebe eyed him sharply. 'I'm going to meet your parents…?' She simply hadn't given Nick's family a thought, and realised she had no idea what it consisted of, besides his ex-wife Sally and Luke.

'Well, of course you're going to meet my parents,' Nick came back impatiently. 'And the rest of the Cavendish clan eventually too, no doubt.' He gave her a brief glance. 'I thought you understood, Hebe, my main home is in New York.'

'You're expecting me to move to New York with you?' She gasped in dismay.

She had assumed England would be their main home, had never even imagined that Nick would expect her to—

But *why* hadn't she? Her wants and wishes hadn't been of too much importance so far in this relationship.

In fact, Nick seemed to be of the opinion that if he kept her 'barefoot and pregnant', and satisfied in his bed, she should just be happy with the fact that he was keeping her at all!

She didn't want to move to New York, Nick realized irritably. Yet another mistake he had made where Hebe was concerned!

'I'd have thought most women would love living in New York. But if you prefer we'll buy a house in England.' He sighed. 'It ultimately makes no difference to me where we live, I suppose.' In fact, the more he thought about it, a house out in the London suburbs, with a big garden for their child to play in as it grew up, didn't sound like such a bad idea.

She was eyeing him uncertainly. 'You would really do that…?'

'Why not?' He shrugged. 'I can travel to Paris and New York from here as easily as I can travel to London and Paris from New York.'

Of course he could, Hebe acknowledged frowningly. And if he had become bored with her in his bed by then he could also see whatever women he chose when visiting those other cities!

'Fine,' she accepted abruptly, turning to look sightlessly out of the window.

This visit to her parents was a nightmare as far as Hebe was concerned. How could she possibly manage to convince them that she was marrying Nick because she loved him when every conversation they had seemed to end like this? When it was only on a physical level that the two of them seemed to find any compatibility at all?

'Here.'

She turned to find Nick holding out the ring box from last night.

Her expression darkened as she looked at it. 'I told

you—I don't want it,' she said forcefully. Not even to convince her parents of their relationship could she wear that—that insult of a ring!

Nick sighed heavily. 'Will you just take the damned box, Hebe? So that I can use both hands to drive?' He rasped his impatience with her stubbornness.

She took the box gingerly from his fingers.

'Don't just look at it—open it!' Nick bit out irritably.

She gave him another frowning glance before opening it. Inside was a thin gold band supporting a medium-sized yellow stone surrounded by six smaller diamonds...

'It's a yellow sapphire,' Nick told her abruptly. 'The colour reminded me of your eyes.'

Tears instantly stung those eyes. Something else she had discovered about pregnancy was that tears came all too easily. In fact, emotions altogether came all too easily.

This ring was delicately beautiful—exactly the sort of ring she would have picked herself, given the choice.

And Nick had chosen a yellow sapphire because it matched the colour of her eyes.

'It's beautiful,' she told him breathlessly.

'Then put it on,' he encouraged.

She took the ring from the box and slid it onto the third finger of her left hand. It was a perfect fit.

She looked up at him shyly. 'Did you manage to get your money back on the other one?'

'I didn't even try,' he drawled ruefully. 'I'm keeping it for our tenth wedding anniversary. Or the birth of our fourth child—whichever comes first!'

Fourth child...?

Nick spoke about this marriage as if it would be a permanency rather than an expediency.

Something until this moment Hebe hadn't thought he meant it to be at all.

'It really is a lovely ring, Nick. Thank you,' she told him softly.

'You're actually going to accept this one?' He frowned.

'Of course.' Her voice was huskier than ever.

'Hey, you aren't crying, are you…?' he prompted uncertainly a couple of seconds later, when he obviously heard the sob she had tried so hard to suppress.

She *was* crying. The threatening tears had finally cascaded hotly down her cheeks. They were impossible to control, it seemed.

Nick was going to think she was an idiot, an emotional fool—crying over a ring.

But it wasn't just about the ring.

It was everything. The enormity of her pregnancy. Nick's insistence that she marry him. The uncertainty of what their future together might bring.

Apart from the four children Nick seemed to have planned!

Nick took another hard glance at her before pulling the car over to the side of the country road they were travelling along, putting it in neutral before turning fully in his seat to look at her. 'I guess we can make it three children if the idea of four scares you this much!' he chided, and he took her in his arms.

His teasing just seemed to make her cry all the harder.

Was he ever going to do or say something that *didn't* reduce this woman to anger or tears? When she was like this, she looked so vulnerable, and all he could think about was protecting her.

He didn't remember Sally being this emotional—not even when she had been expecting Luke…

'You aren't going to convince your parents of anything except that I beat you, if we turn up at their place with you looking all red and blotchy from crying,' he drawled.

He was rewarded by a choked laugh as Hebe raised her face to look at him.

Looking decidedly unred and unblotchy, her face was still beautiful in spite of her tears. Nick felt as if he could drown in those misty golden eyes.

But drowning in her beautiful eyes would do him no damned good at all, he told himself firmly, before releasing her to move back behind the wheel and restart the engine, his expression grimly set as he began the last ten miles or so of their journey.

Keep your eye on the ball, Nick, he taunted himself.

Hebe wasn't marrying him because she loved him. This wasn't a love-match at all. She was expecting his baby, and in return she would want certain things from him. That was it.

Fifteen minutes later, when he met Hebe's parents he learnt exactly why she had been so concerned about their reaction to the two of them.

Henry Johnson was a tall, thin, slightly stooped figure— a retired history professor at Cambridge University, no less—and his wife Jean was the sort of round, homely woman whose husband and child were her whole world, who had made a home for them that was as warm and welcoming as she was herself.

There was no way this couple would ever understand the sort of marriage that he and Hebe were going to have!

'Oh, darling Hebe, how wonderful!' her mother said tearfully when Hebe showed her the engagement ring.

Her father gave her a bear hug. 'You might have

brought Nick home to meet us earlier than this,' he chided, but affectionately rather than in genuine rebuke. 'The owner of the Cavendish Gallery, no less,' he added, slightly dazed.

'My fault, sir,' Nick assured him as the two men shook hands. 'It's all happened so quickly. Hebe just knocked me off my feet the first time I saw her!' Literally, as he remembered it!

Henry nodded, as if he perfectly understood how that could happen to a man where his beautiful daughter was concerned.

They were a little older than Nick had expected—both of them in their sixties, he would guess. That meant Henry and Jean must have been in their late thirties when they'd adopted Hebe. Nick wondered why they had left it so late to decide that was what they were going to do.

The ubiquitous English answer to any occasion, a cup of tea, soon appeared—though Henry was profusely apologetic that they didn't have any champagne to toast the happy couple with.

Nick saw Hebe flinch at the description. So much for his assurances that *he* would behave as if they *were* a happy couple; Hebe looked as if she was about to burst out with the truth at any moment, and damn the consequences...

'Tea is fine, sir,' he assured the older man as he took his cup and saucer. 'Hebe can't drink champagne in her condition anyhow,' he added determinedly. 'Not until after the baby is born, in another seven and a half months or so,' he added for good measure.

Let her try to talk her way out of *that!*

Hebe gave Nick an incredulous look as she saw her parents' stunned reaction to his announcement, but met only glittering challenge in his gaze. His hard, uncompromising gaze.

He was leaving her no way out. That cold blue stare told her so only too clearly. She was his. The baby was his.

She had been wavering, it was true. She had looked at her parents and wondered if perhaps they would understand if she confided her pregnancy to them and asked them to help her. But the relaxed way Nick had made his announcement, the possessiveness in his tone, gave her no opening to do that.

As he had known it wouldn't...

Damn him!

'Mum, Dad.' She turned anxiously to her parents. 'I didn't mean to tell you quite as abruptly as that.' She shot Nick a censorious glance before crossing the room to take her mother's hands in hers. 'But Nick and I *are* expecting a baby, early next year.'

'Which means the wedding is going to be very soon,' Nick put in firmly, though his conversation with Hebe the night before had not got that far. 'My lawyers are working on the paperwork at the moment.'

His *lawyers...!*

Why on earth were his lawyers working on their wedding arrangements? Unless Nick intended making her sign one of those pre-nuptial agreements, or something equally cold and calculated?

Well, she wasn't signing anything like that. Not now. Not ever.

But this wasn't the time to argue that point with him. She was too concerned with calming her parents' shock at the rapidity of everything to have time to worry about Nick and his Machiavellian plans.

'Perhaps a small sherry might be a good idea,' her father said weakly, moving to the cabinet to pour three glasses.

One for himself. One for her mother. And one for Nick.

Who wasn't in shock at all. Instead he looked as if he were enjoying every second of this.

'Well, I suppose it's about time I was a grandmother!' Her mother was the first to recover from the shock, squeezing Hebe's hand supportively.

'You don't intend taking our little girl away to America, do you, Nick?' Her father was more practical.

'No, sir,' he assured him easily. 'Hebe has expressed a wish to live in England, and I'm happy to go along with that. Whatever Hebe wants,' he added, with a challenging raise of his brows across the room at her.

Her father gave him a beaming smile, as if he was quite happy with any man who wanted to want to spoil and look after his 'little girl' in the way Nick seemed to want to.

Except that Hebe knew he didn't.

He wanted the baby she carried. And if he had to concede certain things to the baby's mother to achieve that, then he would do so. On his own terms, of course.

But she couldn't let any of her trepidation show in front of her parents. She knew that she had to make them believe she was as happy with the situation as Nick implied he was.

'We'll want you and Daddy to come up to London for the wedding, of course,' she told her mother warmly. 'In fact, you'll probably be our only guests!' She had no idea what arrangements Nick had discussed with his lawyers, but she very much doubted they would involve a big wedding.

'Not at all, Hebe,' Nick put in smoothly. 'Your flatmate will want to come, of course. And any of your friends you can think of. And I've decided to close the gallery for the day, so that all the staff there can attend too. My own parents will be there, naturally. Along with my younger sister and her family.' He met her gaze confrontationally.

She couldn't believe this. She had expected their wedding to be almost a clandestine affair, with as few people as possible knowing it was taking place, and now Nick had announced he was inviting half of London and all of his close family, as well as her own parents.

'I was keeping it as a surprise, honey,' he murmured indulgently, and as he moved to kiss her lightly on the lips, his arm moving about the slenderness of her waist.

For her parents' sake, of course.

As these elaborate wedding plans probably were too.

'We'll be having a reception at one of the leading hotels,' he told her parents, his arm like a steel band around Hebe as he held her tightly—shackled!—to his side. 'I think it might be better if I were to book you a suite there for a couple of nights too. I'm sure Hebe will want her mother to help her get ready on the day—won't you, honey?' Blue eyes glittered down at her with mocking amusement.

Where was all this coming from? Hebe wondered, feeling dazed.

Of course Nick had been married before, so he was probably more cognizant with wedding arrangements than she was, but even so...!

'We do just have one tiny concern.' Nick turned back to her parents. 'Obviously Hebe has told me that she's adopted. I'm sure she was irresistible as a baby,' he added favourably, as Hebe's father frowned slightly. 'We were just wondering if you had any information on Hebe's real parents?' He looked at them enquiringly. 'Obviously with Hebe expecting a baby the medical history of her birth parents would be real helpful,' he added, with country-boy charm.

Which Hebe, knowing him only too well, didn't fall for at all.

She wasn't sure her parents did either. Glancing at her father, she saw he was still frowning and her mother was looking up at him a little anxiously.

'What sort of thing do you want to know?' her father prompted guardedly.

Nick shrugged. 'As I said, just medical history—stuff like that,' he dismissed easily.

He could feel the sudden tension in the room, and wondered if Hebe had noticed it too.

It was a perfectly legitimate question in the circumstances, surely...?

'Perhaps you know the name of Hebe's birth mother?' he continued lightly. 'Or her father, perhaps.'

'No,' Henry answered slowly. 'I don't believe that was ever mentioned to us.'

Was it just his imagination, Nick wondered, or was the other man's reply just a little ambiguous?

'I told you that Mum and Dad wouldn't know, Nick,' Hebe cut in tensely, at the same time smiling reassuringly at her parents. 'Nick is such a fusspot where this baby is concerned.' She attempted to dismiss him. 'I've assured him that I'm perfectly healthy, and that everything with the baby is going to be just fine, too.'

She hadn't assured him of any such thing. And even if she did, he would want a second opinion. A medical opinion. He had yet to tell her, wanting to avoid having another argument and so cause tension before they met her parents, that he had made that particular appointment for Monday afternoon...

Right now, though, he was far from satisfied with the answers he had received from the Johnsons about Hebe's real parents.

'Sometimes when people adopt children, things like medical histories are discussed, aren't they?' he persisted lightly.

'Sometimes I'm sure that they are.' Henry's reply seemed a little guarded.

'But not in this case?'

'No.' There was definite challenge in the other man's expression now.

The atmosphere had changed from warmly congenial to tensely suspicious.

Why?

What did this couple have to hide?

Because they *were* hiding something. Nick was sure of it.

'Oh, well—I just thought it worth asking. But I'm sure that the doctor will be able to check everything out,' he dismissed, with a lightness he was far from feeling.

'I must tell you about the interesting painting Nick came across a week or so ago.' Hebe cut smoothly into the conversation, obviously changing the subject. 'An Andrew Southern portrait. Have you heard of him?' she prompted her parents lightly.

Nick tensed, having no idea where Hebe was going with this conversation. Surely she didn't want her parents to know about that portrait of her? It wasn't exactly the sort of thing you could bring home to show your family—the raw sensuality of the subject—Hebe—was all too obvious!

'Of course we've heard of him, darling,' Henry confirmed mildly. 'One of his paintings is worth a small fortune, surely?' He addressed this remark to Nick.

'Oh, Nick has a very large fortune—don't you, darling?' Hebe prompted challengingly.

Nick had used her parents shamefully to manipulate her, and now she intended doing the same where he was concerned.

She couldn't be sure that Andrew Southern would respond to her letter and the photograph, and if he didn't she needed more information than Nick had given her to be able to continue her own search for the origins of that portrait. To do that she needed a piece of information Nick hadn't yet revealed.

'Not as large as it once was,' Nick muttered tersely, the warning glitter in his eyes more than meeting her challenge.

Hebe turned unconcernedly back to her parents, knowing Nick was furious with her for bringing up the subject of the portrait. Well she couldn't help that. He had asked the questions he wanted answering, without consulting her or warning her, and now she was going to do the same. Whether he liked it or not.

Because she *knew* that portrait wasn't of her, even if he wouldn't accept that it wasn't.

'It's an unseen portrait the artist painted over twenty years ago,' she confided to her parents. 'Nick is so pleased with it—aren't you, darling?' she prompted, with an insincere sweetness she knew he would recognise as such even if her parents didn't.

'Oh, very,' he confirmed tightly.

'How on earth did you find it?' Hebe's mother smiled with interest.

'Hidden away in a house in the north of England,' Nick answered abruptly, obviously not wanting to pursue this subject at all.

Too bad—because Hebe did!

'Yes. What did you say was the name of the original owner, Nick?' Hebe prompted readily, completely putting him on the spot. The increased glitter in his eyes told her how incensed he was.

Well, so what? she thought. At the moment she was more interested in knowing who had been the original owner of her mother's portrait than she was concerned with Nick obvious displeasure.

'I didn't,' Nick came back stiffly, wondering why Hebe was asking this now. 'And I'm sure Henry and Jean aren't interested in this—'

'On the contrary,' Hebe's father interrupted. 'It all sounds fascinating,' the historian in him prompted inquisitively.

Hebe gave Nick another one of those over-sweet smiles, her smile turning to genuine amusement as she saw how annoyed he was.

But, no matter what he might otherwise wish, he couldn't have things all his own way.

As he seemed used to having!

So far today he had bought her an engagement ring it would have been churlish to refuse, tricked her into what sounded like a full-scale wedding rather than the quiet affair she had been expecting, and questioned her adoptive parents about her real parents.

It was time he told her some of the things *she* wanted to know!

'Not really,' he dismissed easily now. 'The man died, his relatives found and then sold the portrait. End of story.'

'And are you going to put it into one of your galleries?' her mother questioned brightly.

'No!' Nick came back harshly.

Hebe turned to look at him frowningly. If he wasn't going to put the portrait in one of his galleries, then what was he going to do with it...?

'No,' he repeated less violently, seeming to force himself to relax, even while he frowned darkly in Hebe's direction. 'I happen to like this portrait and I intend keeping it for myself.'

'But how wonderful!' her mother came back innocently. 'You'll have to let us see it when we come down to London.'

Much to Nick's discomfort and Hebe's amusement!

She had stood all the abuse from Nick she was going to with regard to that portrait. It wasn't a portrait of her, no matter what Nick believed.

She was slightly surprised at his decision not to show the portrait, after going to all that trouble to purchase it, but perhaps he had decided he didn't want his future wife on public display like that?

Or that it would be yet another thing to torment her with when they were alone!

Yes, that sounded more like the Nick she knew and—

She broke off those thoughts abruptly. What was the point of thinking about her love for Nick when she was obviously just another possession to him? A *prize* possession, because she carried his child.

Besides, she still didn't have the answers she was looking for!

'What makes this portrait so interesting, though,' she continued cheerfully, 'is that it isn't listed anywhere as one of the artist's works.'

Nick's gaze narrowed searchingly on Hebe's face. How did she know that? Unless she had been checking up on the portrait herself? Which made no sense to him whatsoever. She *knew* Andrew Southern had painted that portrait of her, whether it was listed or not, so why persist in pushing the subject?

'Perhaps it's a forgery?' Jean mused.

'Oh, no, Jean,' Nick answered the older woman assuredly. 'It's most definitely authentic.'

'Kept hidden away in some man's attic for the last twenty-odd years,' Hebe put in teasingly.

She wasn't going to leave this alone, was she? Nick brooded. She obviously still wanted something from him. But what? And more to the point, why?

'Actually, Jacob Gardner kept it in his— Are you okay there, Jean?' He moved forward quickly to catch her cup and saucer as they seemed to leap out of her hand of their own volition.

'Oh, how silly of me.' Jean got up agitatedly to take the cup and saucer away from him. 'I'll take these things out to the kitchen so that there are no more accidents,' she added swiftly, before picking up the laden tray and bustling from the room, her husband following her a few seconds later.

Nick was left not just with a suspicion, but with the certainty that these two elderly people were hiding something...

He just had no idea what.

A searching look at Hebe showed him that she had seen it too, and was just as puzzled. Her baiting of him to get information had somehow backfired on her in a way she hadn't expected...

CHAPTER EIGHT

'YOUR parents are hiding something.'

Hebe gave Nick a frowning glance as he drove them back to London later that evening.

He was right, of course, though she was loath to admit it. Her parents *were* hiding something. Her mother's accident with her cup and saucer after hearing Jacob Gardner's name mentioned had to be indicative of something.

Hebe just had no idea what it was!

Her father had changed the subject once her parents had returned to the sitting room a few minutes later, going back to talking of the forthcoming wedding—a subject guaranteed to put Hebe herself on edge.

'Of course they aren't,' she defended now, having already decided she would talk to her parents in private about this—probably when they came down to London. No concrete plans had been made on that suggestion, though, and wouldn't be until they all knew the date and time of the wedding. 'You're just imagining things, Nick,' she said airily, not wanting him to pursue this particular subject. 'Now, tell me exactly what paper-work it is that your lawyers are working on?' she added scathingly.

She hadn't forgotten that remark, even if he had hoped she had!

'It wouldn't happen to be a pre-nuptial agreement, would it?' she prompted angrily.

Nick raised dark brows. 'Would you sign it if it were?'

'Absolutely not!' she snapped.

'I didn't think so,' he mused.

'They're an insult to everyone involved,' Hebe told him caustically.

'Most of them aren't worth the paper they're written on, either,' he drawled.

'Oh, I have no doubt that any pre-nuptial agreement *your* lawyers prepared would be watertight!' she replied with disgust.

'Probably,' Nick conceded dryly. 'But that isn't what they're doing, and you wouldn't sign it if they were. The paperwork they're dealing with has to do with the fact that I'm an American getting married in England, so this conversation is rather pointless, wouldn't you say?'

Completely, it seemed, and Hebe turned so Nick couldn't see the embarrassment flooding her cheeks. But she felt happier knowing it was only the legal details of their marriage that Nick's lawyers were dealing with, but now she had nothing to distract her thoughts from slipping back to her parents' odd reaction earlier.

That conversation at her parents' house hadn't gone at all as she had expected. She had thought to get Jacob Gardner's name from Nick, but not the response she had from her parents.

'I guess that was probably the intention,' Nick drawled knowingly.

'I have no idea what you're talking about,' she snapped

resentfully. He was far too astute for comfort, this man she was marrying...

'No?' He quirked dark, sceptical brows over questioning blue eyes. 'Your parents obviously know of your involvement with Jacob Gardner, and they would rather I didn't know about it too—is that what all the mystery is about?'

'I have never been involved with a man called Jacob Gardner!' she protested heatedly. 'I had never even heard his name until you mentioned it!'

'Oh, please, Hebe—your parents had,' he said quietly. 'So you must have told them!'

She'd realized her parents knew the name, but she had no idea how.

Neither did she understand how Nick had jumped to the conclusion that she had known Jacob Gardner in that way. A man who Nick himself said had been quite old when he died.

She shook her head. 'I have no idea why you should think I was ever involved with him!'

'It's quite simple—logical, really, if you think about it.' Nick shrugged, his expression grim. 'Andrew Southern painted that portrait. A portrait that was in Jacob Gardner's possession when he died. In the portrait you're wearing an engagement ring. Emeralds and diamonds, as I recall,' he added hardly. 'Which is why you didn't get emeralds and diamonds from me!'

Hebe had noticed the ring, of course. She just hadn't realised that Nick had...

'I'm not asking you for emeralds and diamonds!' she came back tartly.

'Just as well,' Nick rasped dismissively, knowing that

the thought of Hebe wearing any man's ring but his filled him with jealous fury. She was his, damn it. *His!*

But that ring on her finger in the portrait, the fact that Jacob Gardner had owned the portrait, and Hebe's mother's reaction to the man's name—it was enough to convince him that what he had suspected all along was, in fact, true. Hebe had to have been engaged to Jacob Gardner when she'd had an affair with Andrew Southern!

And the thought of her involved with either man was enough to fill him with a blinding rage!

'You were engaged to Jacob Gardner and you had an affair with Andrew Southern. Just admit it, and then get past it,' he rasped furiously, his hands tight on the steering wheel.

'Let me see if I've got this right?' Hebe turned to him, frowning. 'I was engaged to Jacob Gardner—an obviously wealthy man if he could commission an Andrew Southern portrait of me—and then when I met Andrew Southern I changed my allegiance to him—probably because I discovered he was the wealthier of the two men?' she prompted. 'And when my relationship with both men didn't work out I obviously set out to entrap the owner of the Cavendish Galleries instead! Tell me if I've got any of that wrong, Nick?' she prompted with impatient anger.

No, that sounded about right to him!

He was so angry he wanted to hate her, and yet all he could think about was making love to her instead.

'Where are we going?' Hebe prompted frowningly, as she realised they weren't heading in the direction of her flat.

'My apartment.' Nick tersely confirmed her suspicions.

She swallowed hard, not liking his mood at all. It was

too dark and dangerous for her to feel in the least comfortable with him in the privacy of his apartment. This conversation about Andrew Southern and Jacob Gardner had made him seem almost a stranger.

Which, she accepted resignedly, was precisely what he still was!

'Why?' she prompted softly.

Nick shot her a brief, sardonic sideways glance. 'Maybe I just want to be alone with my fiancée for a while?'

Hebe drew in a ragged breath, knowing exactly what that meant; and Nick making love to her in anger was not something she wanted. 'I don't think so, Nick.'

'Why the hell not?' he bit out roughly.

'You don't need me to tell you that,' she said quietly.

He inhaled and exhaled noisily before answering her. 'I'm not going to hurt you, Hebe,' he finally murmured, self-derisively.

Maybe not physically—after all, he had the baby's welfare to think of!—but emotionally this man would rip her to shreds.

But he didn't need to be in the privacy of his apartment to do that. He could do it with just a glance!

'The opposite, in fact,' he added huskily. 'I'm going to make love to you until you cry out for mercy!'

Hebe knew he could do it too, and there was a melting warmth inside her just at the thought of making love with him again. 'I would rather just go straight home, Nick,' she told him determinedly.

His mouth thinned. 'Am I not to get to spend *any* time alone with you today?'

'We're alone now,' she pointed out ruefully. 'We just don't seem to be communicating too well!'

'We communicate better when we're in bed together, I agree!' he rasped.

Which was exactly where Nick wanted to be right now—in bed with Hebe, breathing in her perfume, touching her, caressing her, feeling her response to him as he buried himself deep in the engulfing warmth of her body.

He ached with wanting her!

In fact, he couldn't ever remember wanting any woman as much as he wanted Hebe. All the time. Able to think of nothing but her when they were apart. Just wanting to kiss and caress her when they were together.

It was like a heated madness, one from which he could find no respite even in sleep. Lying awake most of the previous night as he thought only of the time when he would be with Hebe again.

He had fallen in love with her, he had finally admitted that to himself some time around dawn this morning.

Fallen in love with a woman whose motives he still couldn't trust.

Madness.

But it was a madness that he knew he could do nothing about. He loved Hebe. And even if she hadn't been expecting his baby he knew that he would still have had to make her his own—that he couldn't bear the thought of any other man near her, let alone sharing the intimacies that they had together.

Although he was still unsure why, even though Hebe might have wanted to confirm that Jacob Gardner had still owned the portrait when he died, she had done so in front of her parents.

Despite the explanation he had just given for the other men being in Hebe's life, and the fact that she must have talked to her parents about Jacob Gardner, at least in the past, it just didn't add up for her to involve her parents in that way…

Oh, to hell with it! He was giving himself a headache just thinking about it. Obviously Hebe *had* been involved with both men, and that was an end to it.

'Hebe…?' he prompted tersely at her continued silence.

'What do you want me to say?' she came back wearily, her head resting back on her seat.

'I don't want—' He broke off, drawing in a deep, controlling breath. 'Oh, just forget it. I'm not going to beg!' he assured her hardly; he would rather take another cold shower followed by a restless night than do that!

Hebe eyed him frowningly. She didn't understand him at all. How could he still want to make love to her when he believed she had been involved with one man who had been old enough to be her father and another surely old enough to be her grandfather?

But he obviously did. And he just thought she was being difficult by refusing.

She didn't want Nick making love to her when he was angry, as if to prove a point of ownership. Even in her inexperience, she knew that wasn't how two people making love should be.

She sighed. 'We'll be married soon, Nick. Can't you wait until then?'

His jaw clenched tensely. 'Why the hell should I?'

She gasped. 'I'm not just an object for you to pick up and put down when you please, Nick!'

His jaw clenched grimly. 'I have *never* used you as an object, damn it!'

'That's exactly what you're proposing to do now,' she came back heatedly.

His eyes glittered dangerously as he gave her a brief scathing glance. 'I wouldn't touch you now if you begged me to!' he snapped.

'And that isn't going to happen,' she assured him, just as angrily. If Nick's plans worked out—which she was sure they would—the two of them would be married in a few weeks, and then she would be sharing Nick's bed on a permanent basis.

Oh, God...!

'This way,' Nick instructed her abruptly the following evening, as Hebe began to take her things through to his bedroom. Instead, he lead her into the bedroom next to his, also overlooking the river, and put her suitcase down on the bed before turning to look at her.

If anything, she looked in worse shape than he did!

Which was precisely why, on the journey from her apartment, he had actually decided to put her in the bedroom adjoining his, rather than sharing a bedroom with him.

It had been a tough few days for both of them, he had acknowledged last night, after dropping Hebe off at her apartment and returning home alone, to call his parents and then his younger sister to tell them about the wedding. Natalie had been absolutely agog at the speed with which he was contemplating remarrying.

Explaining about the baby—something that had made his mother cry with happiness and his sister exclaim with joy—had helped, of course, but their curiosity about his future bride, the questions he hadn't been able to answer about Hebe, had made him realise that he and Hebe really did need to take a little time, a step back, in order to get to know each other better before they were married.

Out of bed, that was.

Hebe looked surprised at being put into the spare room.

'After what you said yesterday, I decided it would be better for both of us if you had your own room until after the wedding,' he explained quickly as he easily interpreted her questioning look.

Hebe wasn't sure how she felt about it, she didn't seem to be able to think straight at all today. She had slept badly after the strain of their parting last night, with Nick driving away as soon as she had stepped out of the car.

It had been no good telling herself it was what she wanted. Of course it was—but at the same time she longed for the closeness of making love with Nick, knowing they could reach each other on that level if no other.

To add to her misery, she was still totally bewildered as to what to do about her parents.

They had obviously recognised Jacob Gardner's name when Nick had mentioned it, but she couldn't imagine under what circumstances. The more she thought about it, the more puzzled she became.

She knew what conclusion Nick had come to, but as she knew that certainly wasn't the correct one, she was left to try and work out for herself what it was. Not wanting to talk about an obviously sensitive subject in a telephone conversation with her parents, she would have to wait to talk to them when they came to London for the wedding.

But that hadn't stopped her thinking. And wondering.

Jacob Gardner had lived in the north of England, and to her knowledge her parents had never lived anywhere but Cambridgeshire, their lives completely wrapped up in the university there.

Her parents had never, in the twenty-six years Hebe had been alive, mentioned knowing or befriending a man called Jacob Gardner.

Yet their reaction was undeniable. They had heard the man's name before, if nothing else.

How?

And if they *had* known him why hadn't they exclaimed over the coincidence, rather than behaving as they had, with her mother dropping her cup and saucer, and her father going very quiet?

Round and round her thoughts had gone the night before. And her highly-charged feelings about Nick hadn't helped her relax, either.

Their relationship, precarious at the best of times, looked like standing even less chance of survival if he was going to continue believing she had been intimately involved with two wealthy men she had actually never even met.

'It's lovely—thank you,' she said now, forcing her attention back to her new home.

And it really was a beautiful bedroom, dominated by yet another four-poster bed, with red and gold coverings and drapes. The furniture looked like Louis IV—very ornate, and very different from the more austere furnishings in Nick's adjoining room.

Had this once been Sally's room?

She wasn't sure she could bear it if it had—

'I didn't buy and open the London gallery until two years ago, Hebe,' Nick drawled, in answer to her unasked question, his gaze quizzically mocking as she gave him a sharp look. 'I'm sure you remember the bathroom from your previous— visits,' he added derisively, as he opened the door that went through to the bathroom, separating the two bedrooms.

Of course she remembered the bathroom. She had showered in it the morning after their first night together. And she had been ill in it six weeks later.

It was a room almost as large as the bedrooms, with a huge glass-doored shower in one corner, a large mirrored vanity and two sinks along the back wall, whilst the other wall was taken up by the hugest cream-coloured bath she had ever seen—Jacuzzi bath that looked as if it could seat four comfortably and six rather more—intimately.

'Go ahead and take a bath if you want to,' Nick invited nonchalantly, as he obviously saw her gaze on it and misunderstood the reason for it. 'I have some papers I need to read anyway.'

Consider yourself dismissed, Hebe, she thought with contempt, when she found herself alone in the bathroom a few seconds later.

But it wasn't such a bad idea. She hadn't slept well, and Nick seemed more remote today than he had ever been. She'd also had an emotional parting from Gina an hour or so ago, the two of them having shared the flat for almost a year now, and a nice warm bath would certainly help her to relax.

Wow, she thought admiringly a few minutes later, as she let herself down into the scented, bubbled water, her head resting back against one of the soft waterproof pillows along the edge. Luxury indeed after the cramped bathroom she had shared with Gina. She would fall asleep in here if she wasn't careful!

Hebe looked asleep to Nick as he quietly opened the bathroom door almost an hour later. He hoped she wouldn't think he was intruding on her privacy, but he had been genuinely worried that she had been gone so long—although he had to admit that the thought of Hebe lying naked in the bath had been a constant distraction from his papers...

He might be denied her bed, but that didn't mean he couldn't kiss her, did it?

Hebe felt the nuzzle of lips against her throat first, tensing in surprise, and then relaxing again as she felt the caress of Nick's hands as they travelled down the slope of her breasts to cup and hold them. She felt the instant melting of her body as she looked down to watch the touch of his thumbtips against the pouting nipples.

There was something very erotic about watching those long, tanned, almost disembodied hands as they gently stroked and kneaded her breasts, the fingers first flicking against her sensitised nipples and then squeezing gently, those dual sensations sending a warm melting between her thighs. Her legs parted instinctively, the rhythmic movement of Nick's hands and the added warmth of the water against her sensitivity almost sending her over the edge.

What was Nick doing to her?

One of his hands left her breast to move down the slope of her stomach to the vee between her thighs, unerringly finding the aching nub, caressing her lightly there, all the time with his other hand paying homage to her breast.

Hebe's neck arched and her head fell back as she felt the excitement building inside her, her eyes wide as she found herself looking up into Nick's desire-flushed face.

'Ask me, Hebe,' he prompted fiercely. 'Ask me to keep touching you. *Ask me,* damn it!' he groaned throatily.

At that moment, Hebe knew she would have begged

if Nick had asked her to, so desperately did she feel the
need for the touch of his hands and the release only he
could give her.

'Please, Nick!' she murmured urgently. 'Please!'

His head swooped down and his lips captured hers
fiercely and possessively. He was seemingly pushed beyond
the limit of his control. He raised his head to look down at
her again, holding her gaze with his as his head moved
lower. Hebe's back arched, allowing full access for his lips
to capture the breast his hand had forsaken to move between
her thighs, and his caress there increase its rhythm as
pleasure seemed to rip through every particle of her body.

Hebe collapsed back limply against the side of the bath,
satiated beyond belief, beyond possibility.

Nick continued to lick and gently suck the rosy nipple
between his lips, enjoying Hebe too much to stop yet,
wanting to take her over that edge again and again, until
he knew she was utterly, completely his.

She reached her second climax quickly, her whole body
shaking with the intensity of her release.

'No more, Nick,' she gasped weakly. 'I can't. Not again!'

'Oh, yes,' he murmured gruffly, sliding into the bath
fully clothed. 'You can…!'

And she could, Hebe found, seeing, feeling and
knowing nothing but Nick as he took possession of her
mouth, his tongue seeking and finding hers, all the time his
hands caressing the swell of her breasts and the nipples that
were hard and sensitive to the touch.

'I want you, Nick,' she finally gasped, when his mouth
released hers to travel down to her breast and draw the tip
once more inside, his tongue licking slowly across it. 'I
want you inside me. Now!' she murmured achingly, as the

pleasure became unbearable, her hips moving rhythmically against his caressing hand.

It was too late. The power of her release this time completely robbed her of breath, a sob of ecstasy catching in her throat.

'I need you inside me, Nick,' she urged, when she finally found breath again to speak. 'Please!' The heated ache inside her cried out for his full possession.

God, she looked wonderful like this, Nick acknowledged heatedly as he stood up with her in his arms and carried her through to the bedroom. He just wanted to make love to her all day long. All week long! Damn it, he never wanted to stop!

But Hebe had her own ideas about that, he quickly learnt. She was kneeling up on the bed to slowly divest him of his wet clothes, her lips leaving a trail of fire over his chilled skin as she slipped the wet shirt from his shoulders, kissing across his shoulders and down his chest, looking up at him with smouldering gold-coloured eyes as she ran her tongue across his own hardened nipple before moving lower to dip erotically into his navel.

God…!

Nick had never experienced anything like this before. The throb of his thighs was becoming unbearable as he strained against the wet denim.

Wet denim that Hebe peeled quickly from his body, releasing him, her hands caressing him lightly there, like butterfly wings, as she kissed the inside of his thighs, her mouth hot and moist. A groan low in Nick's throat escaped as he ached for those lips about him.

'What do you want, Nick?' Hebe prompted huskily as she continued to kiss him, her tongue trailing the length of him now, driving him quietly, madly insane. 'Tell me what you want?'

'For God's sake…' he gasped achingly.

'Tell me, Nick,' she urged softly.

'Take me, Hebe,' he groaned. 'For God's sake—ah…!' Barely had her lips touched him when he realised he had almost reached the point of his own release, knew he was going over the edge, too aroused to stop himself. 'What—?' he cried, as she released him to move above and over him.

Hebe moved slowly, holding Nick's heated gaze as she gradually took the pulsing length of him inside her, breasts thrust forward for his mouth to reach as she began to move above him. His lips found and took one rosy nipple deep inside his mouth as he moved in the same rhythm beneath her.

They reached their climax together, hot, pulsing and explosive, looking into each other's eyes as Hebe arched ecstatically above him before collapsing weakly on his chest.

Amazing.

Incredible.

Unbelievable.

Making love with Nick had to be the most erotic experience of her life!

Nick's arms were wrapped around Hebe, and the silver-gold of her hair draped across his chest as he held her against him, their breathing steadying, the fierce beat of his heart slowly returning to normal.

But deep inside him Nick knew his life would never be normal again.

He had been married for five years, had known women before and since his marriage, but never before had he ever been with anyone like Hebe.

She was magnificent.

An enchantress.

He had thought to possess and bind her to him with the force of their lovemaking, and instead he found himself possessed and bound to Hebe.

For ever.

His arms tightened about her as he dismissed, expelled, any thought that he might ever lose her. That would never happen. He wanted Hebe. And no matter what her reasons for marrying him, he vowed she would stay with him always.

He could no longer contemplate a life without her!

'So much for waiting until after we're married,' she murmured self-derisively.

'You said you wanted me. And I can't keep my hands off you,' he admitted gruffly. 'Not that I tried too hard,' he acknowledged. 'Hebe— Damn!' he muttered impatiently as the telephone on the bedside table began to ring.

Hebe raised her head to look at him, deeply resentful of this interruption to their closeness. 'Leave it, Nick,' she encouraged throatily.

The longer they stayed here, in their own world, without outside influences, the more she hoped that they would come to know and understand each other. They had to if their marriage was to stand any chance at all.

And physically, she knew, they were perfectly attuned. It was a start.

The telephone kept ringing, and by the tenth ring Hebe could see that Nick was becoming restless.

She moved off his chest, smiling slightly. 'Go ahead and answer it,' She nodded. 'It must be something important to keep ringing like that.'

His expression darkened. 'If it isn't, I'm going to wring someone's neck!'

'As long as it isn't mine,' she teased.

He kissed her lingeringly on the lips to dispel that idea, before turning to pick up the receiver. 'Yes? What—?' He sat up in bed, his expression suddenly strained. 'Could you just hold on a minute?' he asked the caller gruffly, even as he swung his legs off the bed. 'I'll put the call on hold and take it in the other room,' he told Hebe abruptly.

Hebe watched him go with languid eyes, admiring the hard nakedness of his body as he strolled across the bedroom, feeling too lazy, too satiated to move.

When Nick came back they would talk. Or rather *she* would talk and Nick would listen. And this time he would believe her. He *had* to!

When Nick came back...

Ten minutes later he still hadn't returned to the bedroom, and the bedcovers were feeling slightly damp and uncomfortable beneath Hebe. She smiled as she realised they had been so desperate for each other that they had lain on the bed together still dripping wet from the bath.

Hebe smiled again dreamily as she got up to go in search of dry bedsheets. There had to be some in the apartment somewhere. And if they were to sleep in that bed tonight the covers would have to be changed first. It—

'That's wonderful, Sally,' she heard Nick murmur huskily in the sitting-room, and came to an abrupt halt as she realised the call had to be from his ex-wife.

A call Nick had deliberately chosen not to take in front of Hebe...

But why would his ex-wife, a woman he had been divorced from for two years, be calling him?

'Yes, of course I'll come and see you when I get back to New York.' Nick spoke gruffly. 'I agree, it's been too long. It's past time we put the past behind us and talked. I'm so glad to give it another try. And, Sally...' Nick paused slightly. 'I can't tell you how pleased I am that you called me like this,' he added warmly.

Hebe beat a hasty retreat—not back to Nick's bedroom, but to her own, tears blurring her vision as she shut the door firmly behind her.

So much for their lovemaking...!

From the brief part of the conversation Hebe had overheard, Sally obviously wanted the two of them to meet and talk about a reconciliation. At least! And it was a sentiment Nick obviously echoed.

What did that make of their own impending marriage?

And the baby she carried?

CHAPTER NINE

SHE was no nearer answering those questions the next morning, as she and Nick sat silently at the breakfast bar, neither of them eating, but both having drunk copious cups of coffee since they'd got up just after seven o'clock.

Hebe had been lying in bed pretending she was asleep by the time Nick got off the phone the previous evening, forcing herself not to move or change the even tenor of her breathing as he came into the room and looked down at her, calling her name softly, sounding puzzled rather than annoyed when she didn't respond.

She hadn't been asleep, of course. How could she possibly have slept when she had no idea what was going to happen next?

Surely the fact that Sally had telephoned Nick now, when he was on the eve of marrying someone else, had to be significant?

If nothing else, it was a case of dog-in-a-manger: Sally couldn't live with Nick herself, but she didn't want anyone else to have him either!

And, if that were true, the other question was how had Sally known Nick was going to remarry? Logically it had to be either Nick himself who had told her—although that was unlikely, in view of his initial surprise at Sally's call. It must have been a member of Nick's family who had chosen to impart that information to his first wife.

Anyway, it didn't matter how the other woman had found out. Her motive for calling Nick had been obvious and the closeness Hebe and Nick had shared had been totally shattered by her call.

In fact, Hebe had ended up crying herself to sleep. She was angry with Nick. But she was angry with herself too! Angry because a part of her had still wanted to get up out of her bed and go to him, to lose herself in his arms once again.

She stood up abruptly. 'I had better be getting to work—'

'Don't be silly, Hebe.' Nick turned to her impatiently. He looked as if he hadn't slept too well the previous night, either, and his temper was on a very short fuse. 'I spoke to Jane and told her you won't be working at the gallery any more.'

Hebe eyes flashed deeply gold. 'Then you had better just go and tell her differently, hadn't you?'

Nick scowled. 'And why would I do that?'

'Because until Gina finds someone else to share the flat with her I intend paying my half of the rent, and I need a job to be able to do that. Besides,' she added irritably, '*I'll* decide when and if I leave my job!'

Nick eyed her impatiently. 'Not if I decide to sack you first,' he bit out tersely.

'You can try,' Hebe challenged. 'That should look quite interesting in the newspapers—Wife Sues Husband for Unfair Dismissal!'

Nick drew in a long, controlling breath in an effort to hold on to his already tightly stretched temper. 'Hebe, as my wife you will have no need to work. Ever again.'

Angry colour flared in the pallor of her cheeks. 'I'm not your wife yet—'

'Semantics—'

'Sense,' she came back forcefully. 'I do have rent to pay.'

'I'll pay your damned rent until Gina finds someone else,' he snarled, impatient with her stubbornness.

Just impatient, really. He hadn't been able to believe it when he'd got back to his bedroom last night and found Hebe gone.

She hadn't been in the bathroom or the kitchen when he'd looked, leaving only the spare room. And that was where he'd found her, curled up in the bed there, fast asleep!

She hadn't responded to the soft prompting of calling her name, either, and other than actually shaking her awake Nick had had no choice but to leave her there and go back to his own bedroom.

To a soaking wet bed!

By the time he had completely changed the bedclothes and got into bed himself he had been wide awake, staring at the portrait he had brought up from his office the previous day.

Hebe...

He could just see himself in the years to come, Nick brooded, staring at a portrait of the woman he loved because the reality still eluded him. Just like Jacob Gardner, damn it!

Another night without sleep certainly hadn't calmed his annoyance.

As Hebe was learning only too well!

She stiffened resentfully at his dictatorial tone. 'I don't need you to pay my rent or anything else! If something should go wrong with this pregnancy—'

'What do you mean, go wrong?' Nick pounced harshly, his frown fierce.

'No, Nick—I wouldn't do anything to harm this baby,' she sighed wearily as she saw the accusation in his eyes. 'According to your theory of my being a gold-digger that wouldn't serve my purpose at all, now, would it?' She gave a derisive shake of her head. 'But if anything should go wrong you won't want me as your wife any more, will you? Which means I'll need a job!' she scorned.

Though she somehow couldn't see herself continuing to work for Nick—or him letting her do so—if the two of them divorced.

Nick glowered at her for several long seconds. 'That won't happen,' he finally growled. 'And if it should I'll just get you pregnant again!'

Her eyes widened. 'Why on earth would you want to repeat the same mistake with a little gold-digger like me?'

His mouth twisted scornfully. 'For exactly that reason,' he told her coldly. 'There is no way I am ever going to let you divorce me, Hebe!'

Hebe realized that was because Nick believed a divorce would result in a divorce settlement—the handing over to her of lots of Cavendish money—and he had no intention of that ever happening!

'Fine,' she snapped. 'But even as your wife I'll decide what I'm going to do, not you!'

He closed his lids briefly, his eyes deeply blue when he opened them to look at her once again. 'You're just spoiling for a fight this morning, aren't you?'

She stiffened. 'Not that I'm aware of, no.'

'Liar,' he muttered disgustedly, his gaze probing now.

'And I'm not exactly in a good mood myself,' he warned her unnecessarily. 'Why the hell had you disappeared when I came back to bed last night?'

Hebe avoided that searching gaze, not wanting him to so much as guess that she had overheard some of his conversation with his ex-wife. That would be just too embarrassing. Besides, with the opinion Nick already had of her as a schemer, he would probably think she had listened to his telephone call on purpose.

She shrugged dismissively. 'I was tired, so I went to bed.'

Nick breathed deeply through his nose as he continued to look at her. 'You were already *in* bed—'

'But not my own bed,' she insisted.

He shook his head frustratedly. 'You don't seriously think I'm going to let you continue to sleep in another room after last night?'

'That's exactly what I think,' she dismissed, turning away, wondering when—or if—he was ever going to tell her that it had been Sally who'd telephoned him yesterday evening.

Probably never, she decided heavily.

After all, he had loved Sally, and their child had been born into a marriage of love. This child would be born into a marriage of convenience. If their marriage still went ahead, that was.

'As I said, I'm going to work now,' she told him stiffly.

Going down two floors to work was going to be convenient, at least. It was about the only convenience for her that she could think of in connection with this marriage.

'Only until lunchtime,' Nick informed her flatly. 'You have an appointment with an obstetrician at two o'clock this afternoon,' he explained at her questioning look.

Hebe's eyes widened as she turned back to look at him. 'I thought I told you—'

'Hebe, in view of your negative comments, I had the other guy's secretary recommend another obstetrician.' He scorned her objection.

'You did?' She eyed him uncertainly.

His mouth twisted ruefully. 'I did.'

'I bet you were popular!' she mused.

Nick shrugged. 'I'm not out to win any popularity contests—as I'm sure you know only too well!' he added hardly.

Hebe's humour instantly disappeared. What was she smiling about when she was still so angry and upset with him over that telephone call from Sally last night? She was so confused by her own feelings for him, that she could cheerfully have hit him over the head with his own coffee mug!

'Oh, yes,' she agreed derisively. 'I'm well aware of that!'

'Good.' Nick stood up abruptly. 'I'm going down to my office this morning, to deal with paperwork. We'll meet up here for lunch at about twelve-thirty—'

'You're expecting me to start cooking for you already?'

His eyes glittered deeply blue. 'I usually have a sandwich for lunch. Which I'm quite capable of getting for myself. And you too, if necessary. I intend making sure that you eat properly in future,' he added.

'Like a brood mare!' she flung back scathingly.

Nick took a step towards her, his face dark with fury now, hands tightly clenched at his sides.

Totally intimidating, Hebe acknowledged warily.

Nick's eyes narrowed as he sensed her apprehension, and he forced himself to relax, his expression noncommittal, hands loose at his sides. 'I think it might be better if you don't bait me like that again, Hebe,' he warned softly.

Her chin rose defiantly. 'And if I do?'

Nick gave a humourless smile. 'Then you're going to get just what you're asking for!'

She swallowed hard, and moistened her kissable lips with the tip of her tongue.

Instantly shooting Nick's temperature sky-high and creating an ache in his body.

He could visualise only too easily where those lips and tongue had been last night, and he burned to make love to her again.

She raised dark blonde brows. 'And what's that?'

He forced a mocking smile, inwardly fighting his need to take her in his arms and forget everything but the two of them. Which, from their uncontrollable response to each other, he knew he could do. It was only that Hebe was likely to hate him for it. Hate him more, that was…

'Exactly the same as you got last night,' he drawled in answer to her challenge. 'Probably with a few variations— I wouldn't want you to get bored with sharing my bed!'

Her eyes widened. 'You're blaming *me* for last night?'

He shook his head, his smile humourless. 'I don't think you can attach blame to something so mutually satisfying—do you?'

Hebe's cheeks felt fiery red, and she was unable to deny her response to him. Her only consolation was that Nick seemed to want her as much as she wanted him.

'I'm going to work,' she repeated abruptly.

'We'll make a move from here at about one-thirty—'

'*We'll* make a move?' she echoed, turning slowly.

Nick eyed her scornfully. After losing Luke, there was

no way he was going to miss out on any part of his new baby's life. 'You don't seriously think I'm going to let you go to the doctor's alone, do you?'

She simply hadn't given it any thought at all. She wasn't used to being a couple, to having someone else around all the time.

And after Nick's obvious warmth to Sally on the telephone last night, and the fact that the two of them were obviously going to see each other the next time Nick was in New York, it might be as well if she didn't get used to it, either!

'I'm not a child, Nick,' she snapped. 'I am capable of getting myself wherever I want to go!'

'But why take the tube or a cab when I'm offering to drive you? Besides,' he added grimly, 'I want to hear what the doctor has to say.'

Hebe tensed. 'Why?'

'Because it's my baby too!' he came back with controlled force. 'And the sooner you get used to that idea, the easier things are going to be!'

Yes, it *was* Nick's baby too, she accepted heavily. No matter what the reason for Sally Cavendish's call the previous evening, or whether she and Nick became reconciled emotionally Hebe knew that Nick took the responsibility of his child seriously. It was the only reason she was here in his life at all...

And she mustn't ever lose sight of that fact.

As she almost had last night.

She just had no defences, no way of resisting, when Nick touched her. And it was no good pretending that she did.

Nick watched their motions flickering across her expressive face—the uncertainty, the apprehension.

Damn it, he didn't want this woman to be frightened

of him! He wanted the impossible— this marriage somehow to work, for the two of them to reach some sort of understanding.

Quite how he went about achieving that, when all they did when they weren't in bed together was argue, he had no idea.

Maybe if they tried to stop arguing it might be a start…

'Look, Hebe, let's call a truce, shall we?' he prompted gently. 'This constant bickering isn't doing a damn thing for me, and I doubt it is for you either.'

She eyed him mockingly. 'Don't try and pretend it's *me* you're concerned about, Nick—'

'Will you just stop?' he ground out frustratedly, grasping her shoulders to shake her slightly, her hair a silken tumble about her shoulders. 'I don't want to argue with you any more—okay?'

She grimaced, golden eyes troubled. 'Your moods are so unpredictable…'

He gave a hard laugh. 'Is there anywhere that says an expectant father has to be predictable?'

'I suppose not,' Hebe allowed with a sigh. 'But I might be able to understand you better if you were.'

Nick raised dark brows, his gaze searching on the pale beauty of her face. 'Do you *want* to understand me?'

A shutter seemed to come down over those expressive eyes, her expression once more defensive. 'Not particularly,' she dismissed scathingly.

Well, *he* wanted to understand her!

Last night, with Hebe, had been the closest thing to perfection he had ever known in his life. No, it hadn't been just close—it had been perfection.

He refused to believe Hebe could have been with him

like that, given of herself like that, without feeling something more for him than appreciation for his millions!

Unless he was just deluding himself...?

He released her abruptly, turning away. 'You're right.
It's past time we were both getting to work.'

'Yes, sir!' Hebe came back tauntingly.

Nick closed his eyes briefly before walking away. He
had to walk away, otherwise he really might do something
he would regret.

Hebe watched Nick leave, her heart heavy, knowing
that the closeness they had reached last night before Sally's
call really had been a myth—that they had no common
ground but the baby she carried.

The next seven and a half months, until her body became
her own once more, loomed over her like a dark shadow.

Work—that was the answer. She had always loved her
job at the gallery, and even knowing of Nick's brooding
presence up in his office on the second floor wouldn't rob
her of that pleasure today. She quickly lost herself in her
work once she had explained to Jane, the manager, that
Nick had been mistaken, and she intended working for
several more months yet.

Her colleagues were agog with curiosity, of course, and
eyed her ring enviously, which made things a little
awkward. But once they realised Hebe was just her normal
self, even if she was shortly going to marry the owner of
the gallery, they all settled down to the easy friendship they
had always enjoyed.

Well, more or less, Hebe acknowledged ruefully.

There were no more comments in her hearing about
their gorgeous boss, or any wondering about what Nick
looked like naked, but if that was the only change in their

behaviour, Hebe could certainly cope with that. In fact, talking about Nick like that wasn't something she wanted to do right now, anyway!

It was her hormones that caused this weakness in her legs and the ache in her body whenever she thought of him, she tried to convince herself. They were all haywire because she was expecting a baby, that was all.

She repeated that to herself when Nick walked into the gallery later that morning, and she felt the heat course through her body just looking at him.

He really was as gorgeous as her work colleagues said he was—and she had very good reason to know exactly how Nick looked naked!

She tensed as he strode forcefully down the gallery towards her with his usual vitality, remembering how she had run her fingers through that overlong dark hair last night, how muscled that body was beneath the tailored grey suit he wore.

'Yes?' She faced him defensively.

'We have an audience, Hebe,' Nick murmured softly with a pointed look at Kate, working further down the cavernous gallery. 'Is that all the greeting you have for your fiancé?'

She shot him an irritated glance. 'So you want us to maintain a certain—discretion in front of the rest of your employees, don't you?'

No, not really, he thought. Discretion was the last thing that came to mind in connection with his thoughts about Hebe! And she wasn't just an employee, for God's sake, she was his fiancée.

'I thought that would be what you'd want,' he drawled dryly. 'I also thought you might like to know that my lawyers have telephoned, and the wedding has been arranged—two weeks on Friday, two-thirty in the afternoon,' he informed her with satisfaction—and watched as her face paled in response to the news that she was marrying him in eighteen days' time.

Damn it, why did she always act as if marrying him was almost as bad as being marched to the gallows, instead of a wedding to a man who had more money than she could spend in a lifetime?

'I thought you might like to call your parents and let them know now that we have a definite date and time,' he rasped.

'I tried calling them earlier, but there was no answer,' she revealed with a slight frown.

Nick tensed, wondering why, when she had only seen them on Saturday, she should have tried to call them this morning. 'Oh?'

Hebe grimaced. 'They're usually at home on a Monday morning.'

He shrugged. 'Perhaps this Monday morning they decided to do something different.'

'Maybe.' She nodded, obviously not satisfied.

Nick frowned. 'I'm sure it's nothing to worry about, Hebe.'

She had tried *not* to, but the more she had thought about it the more convinced she had become that her parents had behaved very strangely on Saturday after Jacob Gardner's name had been mentioned. Her call to them this morning had been an effort to reassure herself that they hadn't— only to have the phone ringing and ringing their end, remaining unanswered.

'I'll call them back later,' she dismissed now, not wanting Nick to realise how troubled she was.

'Maybe—'

'Nick—Hebe. I'm sorry to interrupt.' A slightly breathless Jane approached them. 'But you have visitors.'

'Just put them in a room somewhere and I'll be out shortly,' Nick said, with obvious impatience.

'Actually, it's Hebe who has visitors,' Jane corrected awkwardly.

'I do...?' Hebe's eyes widened in surprise.

Jane nodded. 'They say they're your parents—'

Hebe didn't wait for the other woman to finish, and turned sharply on her heel to hurry from the room, not knowing whether Nick followed her or not—although she thought he probably would.

She had no idea what her parents were doing here, of all places, but at least she now had an answer as to where they had been this morning...!

CHAPTER TEN

NICK'S long strides easily caught up with Hebe's shorter ones as she left the gallery, and he was at her side when they reached the huge marble entrance hall where Jean and Henry stood waiting.

He felt glad that he was there when he saw the strain on the older couple's faces, more sure than ever that the disquiet he had felt on Saturday had been justified.

'I hope you don't mind, Nick?' Jean said anxiously, even as she clasped both Hebe's hands in hers. 'We need to talk to Hebe. To both of you,' she added softly.

'If we could go somewhere—less public?' Henry prompted quietly, as half a dozen people passed them on their way into the gallery.

'Mum? Dad?' Hebe frowned her concern as she looked at them both. 'What's wrong? Has something happened?'

'We just need to talk to you, darling.' Her mother squeezed her hands reassuringly. 'We—have some things to explain.' She looked pained at the admission.

'We'll go upstairs to my apartment,' Nick decided briskly. 'Hebe?' he prompted pointedly, as she made no effort to move, her face pale as she looked searchingly at her mother.

Jean, he could easily see, was under extreme emotional pressure. Her eyes looked red and tearful; her face was as white as Hebe's.

Whatever was going on here, Nick intended being at Hebe's side when it happened. Whatever it was!

Hebe could feel her tension rising with the lift as it ascended, wondering if what her parents needed to talk to her so urgently about had something to do with Jacob Gardner.

She knew that Andrew Southern must have received her letter and photograph by now, and that even though she had given him the address of her flat, and the number of her mobile if he should want to contact her, there had been no response from him.

She was disappointed—deeply so. But if her parents could tell her something about Jacob Gardner that would at least be something.

Although she wasn't at all happy at the stress her parents appeared to be under…

'Here we go.' Nick led the way into his apartment.

Their apartment now, Hebe supposed, wondering if her parents had tried to contact her at her old flat before coming here, and been surprised when Gina told them she had moved out. She had thought to save that little piece of information until her parents came to London for the wedding, deciding there was no point in their knowing before then.

Little had she known they were going to surprise her with a visit.

'You look as if you could do with something to drink, Jean?' Nick frowned. 'Henry?'

'Perhaps a small glass of brandy,' her father accepted gruffly.

To Hebe's knowledge her father only ever drank brandy when he was sick or worried about something; looking at him, at both her parents, it was easy to see that this time it was the latter.

'What's wrong?' she prompted again, once the drinks had been poured and they were all seated in the sitting room.

Her mother gave a shaky sigh. 'We should have told you at the weekend,' she said, flustered. 'Your father wanted to tell you then.' She gave him a rueful smile. 'But I begged him not to. I see now that he was right all along— that we should have told you years ago.' She shook her head sadly.

'Told me what?' Hebe pressed anxiously, her tension increasing by the second.

Nick moved to stand behind Hebe's chair, quietly supportive—whether she wanted his support or not.

Which she probably didn't, he accepted heavily—but she was going to get it anyway!

'About your mother,' Henry said, taking charge of the conversation.

'My—mother…?' Hebe repeated slowly.

Hebe's mother? Nick repeated too, inwardly, having been sure that this conversation was going to be about Jacob Gardner after Jean's reaction to his name at the weekend.

What did Hebe's *mother* have to do with Jacob Gardner?

Besides which, hadn't Jean and Henry assured him on Saturday that they had no knowledge of Hebe's mother?

No…he suddenly realised. What Henry had actually said was that the name of Hebe's father had never been mentioned…

Nick had thought the other man's reply ambiguous at the time. Now he realised why!

'What do you know about Hebe's mother?' he prompted harshly.

'Please, Nick.' Hebe turned to him pleadingly. 'Let them—let them tell this in their own time.'

She had a feeling she knew at least part of what her parents were going to say, as she was sure now that they had known of her mother's connection to Jacob Gardner all along—if not to Andrew Southern. They probably knew her name too.

Hebe had no idea why they would have kept such a thing from her, as they had always been so open about everything else, and had brought her up to be the same way. They must have had a good reason for not telling her about her mother. And, having seen the portrait, with its overt sensuality, she could perhaps guess what that reason was.

'You asked about the medical history of Hebe's real parents on Saturday, Nick,' her father reminded the younger man ruefully. 'I told you then that we had no idea. I wasn't exactly truthful. We really don't know anything about Hebe's real father.' His voice hardened slightly. 'But now we know of Hebe's pregnancy, we—'

'Your mother died in childbirth, Hebe,' her mother told her emotionally. 'She was so tiny, so delicate, and they left it too late to do anything about it. The birth went terribly wrong, and—and she died and the baby lived. *You* lived.' Tears glistened, and then fell from pained brown eyes.

It was all too much for Hebe to take in. Her mother was *dead*.

It was a possibility she had never even thought of.

When she had first learnt of her adoption, before dismissing the whole thing as unimportant, she had imagined lots of reasons why her mother had given her up. Perhaps she had been very young, a single mother, or even a married woman who hadn't been able to support another child in the family. But death—death had never been an option…

The woman in the portrait, so young and alive, had *died* giving birth to her?

It didn't seem possible. It was a cruelty that shouldn't have been allowed.

Like the death of Nick's son Luke…

She turned to him as his hand came down firmly on her shoulder. 'I can't—' She shook her head. 'I can't believe it, Nick—can you?'

Oh, he could believe it, all right. It wasn't the believing of it that was the problem!

He fixed his glittering gaze on her parents. 'Are you saying—are you telling us that Hebe may have a similar medical problem when she gives birth to our baby?' He had caught the relevance of Jean's statement even if Hebe hadn't.

'It's a possibility.' Henry was the one to answer him. 'Can you see why we had to tell you?'

'I can see why you should have told us on Saturday, not waited until now—'

'Nick!' Hebe cautioned emotionally.

He shook his head impatiently. 'I'm sorry, Hebe, but your parents knew all the time that your mother had died in childbirth, knew the risk of the same thing happening to you, and yet only now—' He broke off abruptly, turning sharply to look searchingly at the older couple.

There was something else significant in what Jean had just said about Hebe's mother…

'How do you *know* that Hebe's mother was, to quote you, Jean, "so tiny, so delicate"?' he prompted shrewdly.

'You're an intelligent man, Nick,' Henry complimented

him gruffly. 'The reason we know those things is because Claudia, Hebe's mother, was our daughter.'

It was Nick's turn to be left speechless.

And if *he* was stunned by this revelation, how much more shocked must Hebe feel?

Except she didn't appear shocked when he glanced down at her. Instead there was an excited glow in her golden eyes as she turned to him, a look of anticipation on her face.

'Would you go and get the portrait, Nick?' The animation was audible in her voice.

'Portrait?' He frowned his confusion.

'*The* portrait, Nick,' she said, very firmly.

What the hell did she want her portrait for now? Why show *that* to her adoptive parents—her grandparents?—at all? They were talking about her mother, for God's sake—

Nick froze. 'Hebe…?' he questioned slowly.

She nodded. 'Please.'

Nick moved to his bedroom as if in a dream, a truth—a startling truth—hitting him right between the eyes.

A truth he had scorned.

A truth he had accused Hebe of lying about.

The woman in the portrait *was* her mother!

'Are you okay, darling?' Hebe's mother prompted anxiously once they were alone. 'We shouldn't have deceived you, I know…'

'I'm okay,' Hebe assured her warmly. 'I'm not too sure about Nick, though,' she added ruefully, having seen the stunned look on his arrogantly handsome face as he went into his bedroom.

'You're not upset or angry, or feeling we've let you down, because all this time we've never told you we're your grandparents and not your adoptive parents?' her mother probed emotionally.

It was a little strange, Hebe had to admit, but at the same time it all made perfect sense. Her mother—Claudia—had died giving birth to her, and so Claudia's parents had taken Hebe in as their own.

She stood up, moving to hug the people who had been the only parents she knew. Kind, giving people, who had loved her and cared for her all her life. How could she possibly be angry with them? Whatever they had done, she was sure they had done it out of love and nothing else.

She smiled tearfully as she stood back. 'How could I possibly be angry with you? You did what you thought was best, I'm sure.'

'We still should have told you,' her father admitted heavily. 'But we had lost Claudia, and you—you were so like she was as a baby.' His voice grew husky with emotion. 'A tiny little thing, with a mop of blonde hair. We loved you on sight. And we had made so many mistakes with Claudia, it seemed. We so wanted a second chance with you.'

'A second chance...?' Hebe had time to ask curiously, before Nick came back into the room with the portrait.

She crossed the room to his side. 'Just stand it on the sofa, would you, please, Nick?' she requested softly, knowing by the grim expression on his face that he was still far from satisfied with the explanation they had been given.

Well, maybe once her parents had seen Claudia's portrait he would be given an explanation he could accept!

Nick heard Jean give a pained gasp as he stood the portrait up against the back of the sofa, turning to see Henry walking dazedly across the room for a closer look, the lines of strain on his face making him look every one of his sixty-odd years.

Henry reached out a hand, just as Hebe had the first time she'd seen the portrait, not quite touching the canvas, but almost tracing a hand lovingly over the creamy contours of the beautiful face.

'Tell me, Dad,' Hebe said softly as she stood beside him in front of the portrait. 'Did Claudia have a birthmark?'

'She did.' Jean was the one to answer as she moved to join her husband and granddaughter. 'A tiny red rose-shape, just—there…!' She gasped as she saw the portrait fully. 'Claudia…!' she cried brokenly, her tears falling in earnest now as she gazed in awe at the portrait. 'But how…?'

'It's the portrait I told you about on Saturday—the one that Nick found hidden away in a man's house after he died,' Hebe explained happily.

'Jacob Gardner's house,' Nick put in harshly, wishing he felt as happy as she did about all of this.

This portrait obviously *was* of Claudia Johnson, as Hebe had always claimed it was. Henry and Jean's reactions to seeing it were too genuine for it to be otherwise. But if that was true then it made a complete nonsense of the things Nick had accused Hebe of doing. Accusations she had vehemently denied. He had called her a liar. A liar and a gold-digger…!

Henry turned to look at him questioningly. '*This* is the Andrew Southern portrait you told us about?'

'Yes,' Nick bit out tautly.

'Twenty-seven years ago, Claudia was engaged to a man called Jacob Gardner.' Jean sighed. 'He was much older than her, thirty years or so, but he was very wealthy, and when he asked her to marry him she accepted.'

'And then she met Andrew Southern and fell in love with him instead,' Nick grated grimly.

Everything he had accused Hebe of doing, in fact.

Accused and punished her for. His jealousy of the other men such that he had wanted to make Hebe his over and over again, in order to banish them from her mind and heart.

Dear God, how she must hate him!

He couldn't even look at her at this moment. He needed time in which to re-evaluate this whole situation.

And time, it seemed, was something he didn't have.

'We don't know that for certain,' Hebe spoke quietly. 'Although admittedly this portrait looks as if it was painted by a man who—*knew* his subject more intimately than an artist and his model.'

She couldn't quite look at her parents. Claudia might have been her biological mother, but she was a woman Hebe had never known. Whereas she had been Henry and Jean's daughter—someone Jean had given birth to, that the two of them had brought up and loved.

'We don't really know what their relationship was,' she added firmly.

'I can't believe this is our Claudia.' Her mother still gazed tearfully down at the portrait. 'She was so beautiful, wasn't she? She was absolutely adorable as a child, too. It was only when she got to about sixteen that—well—' She broke off, looking to her husband for assistance.

'She became a little wild.' Hebe's father spoke sadly, shaking his head. 'We don't know where we went wrong. She started going out all the time, sometimes staying out all night. And when we tried to talk to her she just shrugged it off as fussing and carried on exactly the same as before. And then finally—finally she ran away from home, when she was seventeen.' He sat down abruptly in one of the armchairs.

'She had such a love of life,' Jean added chokingly. 'But we didn't know what to do with her any more—couldn't seem to reach her. She ran off, didn't contact us for months, and then it was only the one letter. We didn't even know she was pregnant until we received an urgent telephone call from the hospital. We were too late. When we got there Claudia had already died,' she sobbed. 'But there was Hebe,' she said, smiling through her tears. 'And we believed we had been given a second chance, that with Hebe we would not make the same mistakes.' Tears began to fill her eyes once more.

'You didn't make any mistakes,' Hebe hastened to assure her, holding tightly on to her mother's hand. 'Not with Claudia or with me. You're the best parents anyone could ever have,' she said with certainty. 'And if she had been given the time Claudia would probably have calmed down, settled down, maybe even married and provided you with lots more grandchildren.'

'As it was, it broke our hearts when she ran off like that,' Henry continued heavily. 'Not knowing where she was, what she was doing. Then, as Jean said, after six months of silence she wrote to us, without giving us an address to write back, to say she had a job singing in a hotel in the north of England somewhere—'

'Leeds,' Nick put in quickly.

'Yes, that's right.' Hebe's father nodded. 'She met Jacob Gardner there one evening when he went in to have dinner with friends. Apparently he fell in love with her on sight. She was so excited about her engagement. She wrote that she would bring him down to meet us before the wedding.'

He sighed heavily. 'It all seemed so incredible, so—' He shook his head. 'She was only eighteen years old.'

Hebe looked at the portrait, at her mother, eighteen years old, with all her life ahead of her. Within a year she had been dead.

Nick looked at the portrait too, at those differences Hebe had insisted existed. Apart from the birthmark, the woman in the portrait still looked like a slightly younger version of Hebe to him, if a more knowing, more feral version of her.

But it *wasn't* Hebe.

No wonder she had been so angry with him for not believing her when she'd claimed it wasn't her. When she had denied ever having been engaged to Jacob Gardner or having an affair with Andrew Southern either.

Which meant her innocence completely undermined his other accusation—that she was a gold-digger...

He looked at Hebe now, at those beautiful eyes that entranced him, the sensual fluidity of her body that enraptured him, her intelligence that enthralled him.

And he knew that she didn't want his money at all—that *he* was the one who had assumed that rather than Hebe ever having said that was what she wanted. Now he realised that she had only agreed to marry him because he had threatened her—threatened to take her baby away from her if she didn't.

Thinking of Luke, of his own pain when he'd died, of how Sally's heart had been broken when she'd lost her child, he knew Hebe must hate him for threatening to do the same to her if she didn't marry him.

Had he expected, had he *seriously* expected them to make a marriage based on his threats and Hebe's fear that he might take her baby from her if she didn't stay with him?

The signs had all been there if only he hadn't been blinded by his own unforgiving attitude: the fact that Hebe wouldn't accept that huge diamond engagement ring, her disgust over the expensive car, her refusal to leave her job and be kept by him. But he had chosen to think she was just acting as if she wasn't interested in those things, that the demands would begin once they were married.

What sort of hardened cynic had he become?

More to the point, how could he ever hope to have Hebe fall in love with him after the way he had treated her?

'You don't think that Jacob Gardner was your father?' Jean was the one to prompt Hebe softly.

Hebe gave a rueful smile. 'Look at the portrait, Mum. What do *you* think?'

'Hmm.' Her mother grimaced. 'I think Andrew Southern was in love with Claudia.'

'But was Claudia in love with him? That's the question.' Hebe shrugged.

'I think so,' her father answered consideringly. 'Look at Claudia's face—that glow. It's the glow of a woman who has just been thoroughly loved,' he acknowledged with a wince. 'What do you think, Nick?'

'I think it's not the sort of portrait you would hang over the family fireplace,' Nick acknowledged stiffly.

'Only in a man's bedroom, hmm?' Hebe turned to mock him, only to find herself frowning when she saw the grim expression on his face, felt the restless anger emanating from him.

What was wrong with him?

She had tried to tell him all these things when he'd first showed her the portrait, that it wasn't her but her mother, so why—?

That was what was wrong with him. The fact that she had been right. And he had been wrong. About her, most of all.

Hebe gave him a searching look, and Nick, becoming aware of that look, turned to her with glittering blue eyes so fierce and angry that she only just stopped herself taking a step back from him.

Obviously Nick didn't like to be wrong!

'I also think,' Nick bit out forcefully, 'that with Claudia and Jacob Gardner both dead, there is only one person left in this triangle who can tell us the truth. It's Andrew Southern we need to talk to next.'

'I've already tried to contact him—with no luck,' Hebe revealed with a disappointed shrug.

'You have?' Nick frowned darkly.

'Yes, I have,' she confirmed defensively. 'I gave his agent a letter and a photograph to forward on to him last Friday. No response, I'm afraid,' she confided to her parents.

'A photograph?' Nick prompted suspiciously.

'Of me,' Hebe told him dryly. 'You said it yourself, Nick. My likeness to the woman in the portrait, to Claudia, is too much of a coincidence for it to be accidental. I was hoping that Andrew Southern would think so too, would realise that I have to be Claudia's daughter, and possibly his too. But he hasn't responded, so I guess that theory was wrong.'

And she had been so hopeful too—had hoped to be able to throw the truth in Nick's face once she had it, to prove that the things he believed about her were completely untrue.

Of course Jean and Henry had done that for her by explaining exactly who Claudia was, but she was still disappointed that Andrew Southern hadn't even bothered to so much as acknowledge her letter.

'Not necessarily,' Nick muttered grimly. 'It's only

Monday now, Hebe,' he said. 'We have no idea when his agent forwarded the letter; Andrew Southern may not even have received it yet.'

She supposed that could be a possibility…

'So you think I could still hear from him?' she asked slowly.

'I believe it's a possibility, yes.' Nick nodded tersely. 'And if you don't, I'll go and see his agent myself. You need to get to the bottom of this.'

She did?

Or Nick did?

'In the meantime,' Nick added briskly. 'Hebe has an appointment with a specialist this afternoon; we'll talk to him about Claudia's medical history, and ask him to check whether or not Hebe could have a smiliar problem.'

Hebe had forgotten all about her doctor's appointment this afternoon in the excitement of this conversation.

But Nick obviously hadn't…

He couldn't seriously think that just because her mother had died in childbirth she might too, could he?

Even if he did, hadn't he realised yet that it would solve all his problems for him—that he would be able to have his baby and get rid of his gold-digging wife in one fell swoop!

At the moment he looked like that saying—'found a penny but lost a pound'.

Although quite what the 'penny' and the 'pound' were in all of this Hebe had no idea…!

CHAPTER ELEVEN

'CHEER up, Nick,' Hebe told him lightly, as they drove away from the doctor's consulting rooms two hours later. 'It might never happen!'

It already had, as far as he was concerned.

Neil Adams's prognosis had been excellent, assuring them that Hebe probably would not have the same problem during childbirth as her mother had, and that even if she did, now that he was aware of it, he was sure they could deal with it when the time came. He had told them to just go away until next month, when he would examine Hebe again, and enjoy the pregnancy.

Something Nick hadn't let Hebe do too much of so far!

Admittedly, they had only known about it for a few days, but Nick was all too aware that he had made those days pretty miserable for Hebe.

Even if she *did* seem bright and bubbly now!

He was still slightly in shock over discovering that the portrait *had* been of another woman, after all. Claudia—Hebe's mother.

How stunned Hebe must have been when he'd produced that portrait, knowing it wasn't her even as Nick accused her of all manner of indiscretions.

God, it made him cringe to remember the awful things he had said to her!

Accusations he certainly owed her an apology for.

But he owed her more than that, he acknowledged heavily. He owed Hebe the offer of her freedom, along with his support, emotionally and financially, during her pregnancy and after...

She had been so adamant on Thursday that she wasn't pregnant, so convinced that she couldn't be, and she must have been totally shellshocked when the tests had shown that she was.

And what had *he* done? Armed with the knowledge—so he'd thought—that Hebe had once been engaged to Jacob Gardner and then had had an unsuccessful affair with Andrew Southern, he had accused her of getting pregnant on purpose in order to trap herself a millionaire husband, that was what he had done!

When what he should have been doing was assuring her that everything would work out fine, that he would look after her during her pregnancy, telling her that she would have no worries after the baby was born either, because he would care for both of them.

He should have made all those offers without conditions, without even thinking she might want to marry him, let alone forcing her into doing so!

He glanced at her briefly now, appreciative of just how beautiful she was. It was odd, but she appeared even more so since the doctor had confirmed her pregnancy. She seemed to have taken on that inner glow, her eyes deeply golden, her face creamy and flushed.

She was everything and more that he could ever want in a wife, he realised. She had shown herself to be loyal and loving where her parents were concerned, understanding of the youthful mother who had died giving her life, and, most of all, she had put up with his boorish behaviour when inside she must have felt like screaming her innocence at him.

Yes, Hebe was just too good for him, and he had to let her go.

Nick didn't look too happy, Hebe had to acknowledge, wondering what he could possibly be scowling about so darkly.

'I do believe that Claudia was just a rebellious teenager who got into a situation way over her head...' she began tentatively.

'Could we leave this for now, Hebe?' Nick rasped curtly. 'Obviously we need to talk, but I would rather wait until we get back ho—to the apartment,' he corrected harshly.

She grimaced at this noticeable change of word. 'I was only trying to explain to you that I'm well past the rebellious teenager stage. So you needn't fear a repeat of my mother's behaviour.'

Nick shot her a narrow-eyed glance. 'Claudia was just a kid.'

'Exactly.' Hebe nodded. 'I just thought I would mention it, in case you think that sort of behaviour is hereditary too.'

If it were possible, Nick now looked even more unapproachable.

Personally, she was relieved to have the truth out in the open.

Her parents had returned home to Cambridgeshire soon after the four of them had sat down for a snack lunch Hebe had prepared—with Hebe's promise that she would call them later, to let them know how she had got on at the doctor's.

Strangely, Hebe felt closer to her parents than ever now that she knew they were actually her grandparents, and her mother had promised to get out all the old photographs of Claudia the next time Hebe went home. Hebe felt more as if Claudia had been a sister rather than her mother—the age difference between them was really not that great.

And the child she was expecting would help to bridge any lingering awkwardness there might be at the truth at last being told, binding them all together as a family.

Although Hebe wasn't sure, after a sideways glance at Nick's uncompromising face, that he still wanted to be a part of that family...

She wasn't in the least reassured once they got back to the apartment. Instead of sitting down, Nick paced up and down the room like a caged tiger.

'What is it, Nick?' she finally prompted with a sigh. 'Do you want to call the wedding off? Is that it?'

He stopped his pacing to look at her. 'Is that what you want?'

Her heart sank. She had only asked the question half-heartedly, sure that Nick would still want to marry her, if only to gain complete access to his child.

Then she remembered Sally's telephone call the previous evening and her spirits sank.

She stiffened defensively. 'I asked you first.'

He gave a humourless smile. 'Let's not play that particular game, shall we?' He looked down at her grimly. 'What do you want, Hebe?'

She wanted him!

But she wanted *all* of him, heart and soul, not just the small part of himself he was willing to give her.

And she knew he didn't have it to give. She knew that part of him still belonged to Sally…

He was more remote than he had ever seemed before—the expression on his rakishly handsome face arrogantly distant, not even the denims and casual blue polo-neck he had changed into before they went out making him seem accessible.

Something had changed since last night, and she didn't believe it was only what they now knew about Claudia. Nick's mood had been dark before they had discovered that, which only left Sally's telephone call.

Why didn't she answer him, damn it? Nick brooded impatiently. Why didn't she tell him exactly what she thought of him, and the way he had treated her, and then just walk out of here? It was what he deserved, after all.

He forced his expression to relax. 'I'm willing to go along with whatever it is you want, Hebe,' he assured her quietly.

She continued to look at him for several long seconds, drawing in a ragged breath before answering him. 'Do you believe me when I tell you that I didn't intentionally get pregnant, that it was as much of a surprise to me as it was to you?'

'I believe you.' He nodded. 'I'm sorry that I ever accused you of behaving any differently. I apologise. Most sincerely. There's simply no excuse for the things I've said, the things I've done.' He ran a hand over his eyes. 'You have every reason to hate me.'

'I don't hate you, Nick,' she mused ruefully. 'You're the father of my baby, after all.'

Yes, he was. He was most certainly that. And even if he couldn't hold on to Hebe, he could still continue to see her through their child.

It wouldn't be enough. It would never be enough. But if it was all she was willing to give him he knew he would have to accept that.

It was too late, far too late, for him to try to woo this woman, he had hurt her and wounded her too much for that ever to be possible.

'I *am* sorry, Hebe,' he breathed shakily.

She was very pale now. 'Don't be,' she assured him gently. 'I—I'll go now, then?' she prompted softly.

Nick wanted to get down on his knees, to beg her not to go, and convince her that it would all be so different if she would only stay with him. But that wouldn't be fair of him. He had already messed up her life enough by giving her a child she had neither expected nor wanted, without adding to her misery.

'Will you ever be able to forgive me?' He couldn't stop himself from groaning.

'We can't choose where we love, Nick,' she said flatly. 'It's either there or it isn't.'

And Nick could see that it most certainly wasn't there for Hebe where he was concerned!

Maybe this was his punishment for treating her the way he had. To love a woman who would never, ever love him in return.

Hebe just wanted to get this conversation over with. She couldn't stand it any more. She was sure now that Nick was going back to New York to be with Sally. He would make himself financially responsible for their child, but that was it.

Maybe it was better that it had happened now, before the two of them had made the mistake of getting married—but she just didn't know how she was going to bear it.

Nick would pop in and out of her life and the baby's, a virtual stranger to both of them, his life and his love elsewhere.

Was this how it had been for Claudia? In love with Andrew Southern but rejected by him, and discarded by Jacob Gardner, too, when he'd discovered her relationship with the other man?

But Claudia had only been eighteen years of age, whereas *she* was twenty-six and, as she had told Nick on more than one occasion, more than capable of taking care of herself.

She certainly wasn't going to ask for the love of a man who couldn't be with her because he still loved his first wife!

She stood up abruptly. 'I really think I should go now, Nick. I'll just go and pack my things. Thank goodness Gina hasn't had time yet to find another flatmate,' she added as an attempt at a joke. But her smile and the rest of her face felt as if they were rigidly set.

'I'll drive you back to your apartment—'

'That really isn't necessary—'

'Necessary or not, I intend doing it,' Nick insisted determinedly. 'It's the least I can do,' he added.

'Okay, then. Thank you,' she accepted softly.

They both looked as if they had been through a war— and lost, Hebe decided as she went through to the spare bedroom to collect her things. She hadn't really had time to unpack yet. Five minutes to throw her things back in the case, and she would be out of here.

Out of Nick's life for good.

She only hoped she'd manage to hold back the tears until she was safely back at the flat. It would be just too humiliating if she were to start crying in front of him.

She didn't belong here anyway, she decided with a last look around the beautiful bedroom with its four-poster bed. Neither she nor the baby belonged here.

'Let me take that for you,' Nick said, and he took the suitcase out of Hebe's hand when she came back from the bedroom. 'I—I have the portrait ready for you to take, too,' he added calmly, indicating it wrapped on the sofa and ready to go.

He hadn't been sure what to do about Claudia's portrait. He had thought of offering it to the Johnsons before they left, but it hadn't seemed quite appropriate somehow. But for Hebe, for the moment, it was the only picture she had of her mother, and it surely belonged with her.

He didn't need the portrait to be reminded of Hebe, anyway. He knew he would have the image of her inside his head every day for the rest of his life.

Hebe looked startled by the offer. 'Oh, I couldn't,' she refused stiltedly. 'I—it's an original Andrew Southern, worth a lot of money. Show it in your gallery or some-thing—' she added awkwardly.

'It belongs to you, Hebe,' Nick cut in firmly. 'Not in a public gallery.'

She had taken just about all she could take from him today. She was holding on to her emotions by a very thin thread, and now she knew that he didn't want even Claudia's portrait in his apartment as a reminder of the mistake he had almost made.

'Frightened you might get all the men panting over a portrait of the grandmother of your son or daughter, Nick?' she taunted.

He deserved that, Nick decided heavily. And more.

'I just want you to have it, Hebe,' he answered abruptly. 'It belongs to you and your family.'

But as Nick had said, it was hardly the sort of portrait she could hang over the fireplace in the family sitting room!

'Fine,' she accepted tersely. 'I suppose I can always sell it one day, and put the money into trust for our son or daughter.'

Nick winced slightly. 'I will provide for our child, Hebe. As I will provide for you.'

Hebe shook her head. 'Only until I can go back to work again, and earn my own living. No need to pay for the mistake twice,' she added derisively.

'Our baby is not a mistake!' he snapped impatiently, his handsome face livid with anger.

Hebe eyed him ruefully. 'I was talking about me, Nick, not the baby.'

His dark brows were low over his narrowed blue eyes. 'You weren't a mistake either, Hebe,' he muttered gruffly.

Hebe knew she was something he was going to have to explain to Sally when he returned to New York and the two of them had that 'talk'. She only hoped the other woman would understand, would accept that he hadn't compounded his mistake by actually marrying Hebe.

Which reminded her... 'I'll leave it up to you to see that the wedding arrangements are cancelled.' After all, except for the day and time, she didn't really know what those arrangements were, anyway.

'I'll see to that—yes.' He nodded tersely. 'Now, can we get the hell out of here?' he rasped impatiently. 'I've never liked goodbyes, and this one is— Let's just go, huh?' He ran a hand through the long thickness of his hair.

'You'll be wanting this back, too.' Hebe started to take the yellow sapphire and diamond ring off her finger.

'Will you please stop adding insult to injury?' Nick snapped forcefully, glaring down at her. 'The ring is yours. The portrait is yours. And anything else I can get you to accept from me will be yours, too.'

But not his heart.

Not his love.

Which was all she really wanted...

But pride could only take her so far, and she knew that in the months ahead she was going to need Nick's financial help, at least. She wished she were in a position to turn away that offer of help, but she wasn't—not without becoming a burden to her parents. It was no good even pretending she was.

'Fine,' she accepted tersely. 'I'm ready to go if you are.' She nodded.

Nick wasn't sure he would ever be ready to help Hebe leave his life in this way. But he also knew he didn't have a choice. Because he had done this to himself.

If only he hadn't seen that portrait and assumed it was Hebe. If only he had listened to her when she'd told him it wasn't her. If only he hadn't acted on the assumption that she had already tried to entrap two wealthy men and failed. He'd believed that he was just the third in line, with the added inducement of pregnancy before the marriage this time. If he hadn't, maybe he would have been able to ask Hebe to give him a second chance.

But he *had* done all of those things.

And Hebe walking out of his life was exactly what he deserved!

Hebe could quite easily have broken down and cried on the journey to her flat, staring out through the side window of the car as she blinked back those ready tears, determined she had to hold on until after Nick had left her—because she couldn't let him see how much this parting from him was hurting her.

She didn't even know when she was going to see him again.

Or if.

Nick might just decide to handle all the financial details through his lawyers, and eventual access to the baby would be handled in the same way.

Even being forced into marrying Nick would be better than never knowing when or if she would ever see him again!

She turned to him after unlocking the door to her flat. 'Can I continue to work at the gallery until—until—'

'Work at the gallery as long as you want to—or not. Whatever you decide to do,' he came back curtly. 'I'll instruct Jane as such when I get back.'

'I just—'

'Hebe, can we go inside? This portrait weighs a ton!' He grimaced, resting the painting against his knee. 'I've probably given myself a hernia carrying it up the stairs as it is!'

She smiled. 'You—'

'Excuse me,' a voice behind them interrupted. 'I'm looking for Flat—' The voice broke of abruptly.

Hebe had turned at the first query, her gaze becoming quizzical as the man stopped speaking, his face slowly draining of colour as he just stood and stared at her.

'Claudia…?' the man gasped disbelievingly.

There was only one man Hebe could think of who might mistake her for her mother.

But it couldn't be—!

CHAPTER TWELVE

'ANDREW SOUTHERN?' Nick enquired, as neither Hebe nor the man staring at her with a dazed look seemed able to speak.

'Yes,' the artist confirmed in a strangulated voice, not taking his gaze from Hebe for a moment.

Nick knew how the other man felt—he didn't want to stop looking at Hebe either!

But he knew the other man's fascination with Hebe was for quite another reason than his own...

He recognised Andrew Southern from photographs he had seen, although he was older now, of course, the dark hair heavily peppered with grey, his handsome face weathered and lined, his eyes a deep, piercing grey.

Hebe's father. Or not.

It didn't really matter at that moment; the other man had cared enough, after receiving Hebe's letter, to come to London in person rather than just writing back or telephoning.

Hebe couldn't be unaware of the relevance of that either.

Hebe swallowed hard, unable to move or stop looking at the man who might be her real father. The two of them simply stared at each other.

Andrew Southern was the first to recover, shaking his

head ruefully. 'Of course you aren't Claudia,' he murmured gruffly. 'You're far too young to be her. But the likeness... the likeness—' He stopped as his voice broke emotionally.

'Uncanny, isn't it?' Nick said bitterly.

Hebe knew it was this likeness that had resulted in him making such a mistake where she was concerned—and Nick wasn't a man who liked to make mistakes.

'My name is Hebe,' she told the older man huskily. 'You received my letter?'

'Yes,' he breathed, and Hebe looked at him again. He was a man aged in his early fifties, tall and handsome, with grey eyes that seemed to see into the soul.

An artist's eyes, Hebe decided. Eyes that saw beyond the outer shell of a person into the very heart of them. As he had once seen beyond Claudia's youthful recklessness...?

'Would you like to come inside?' she invited shyly as she pushed the flat door open, aware of Nick standing back until the older man had entered, and then following behind carrying the portrait.

The portrait...!

Nick anticipated Hebe's request, placing the portrait on the table before removing the covering, then turning to look at the older man as he propped the portrait against the wall.

Andrew Southern went even paler, seemingly possessed by the same stupor as first Hebe and then her parents had been on seeing the portrait.

The difference was that this man had actually painted the picture, already knew every loving brushstroke, every soft nuance and shading of Claudia's beautiful face and body.

'I never thought I would see this portrait again,' Andrew

Southern murmured as he gazed at it in wonder. 'How did you get it?' he breathed raggedly.

Nick was the one to answer him. 'I bought it from Jacob Gardner's great-nephew after he died.'

'Claudia!' Andrew's voice broke emotionally. 'I tried to buy it back from Jacob Gardner myself after—after Claudia left. But he refused to sell it to me.'

'He never married,' Nick told him quietly.

'No.' Andrew sighed. 'How could any man after Claudia? My darling Claudia…!' He buried his face in his hands and began to sob.

This man, Nick knew with startling clarity, had loved Claudia with the same depth, the same deep need, with which *he* now loved Hebe.

But for some as yet unexplained reason Andrew had lost his Claudia.

Was Nick really going to allow the same thing to happen to him where Hebe was concerned?

'I'm so sorry,' Hebe murmured, and she moved forward to put a hand on Andrew Southern's shaking shoulders.

The artist looked up with a tear-ravaged face. '*You're* sorry?' he choked self-derisively. 'I let this wonderful creature slip through my fingers like molten gold, and you're sorry?' He gave a self-disgusted shake of his head. 'I should have acted sooner than I did. Should never—' He broke off. 'I've spent the last twenty-six years aching for just another glimpse of her, just to see her smile in that mischievous way of hers, to be able to hold her one more time!'

No! Nick cried inwardly. He was not going to live his own life in that way—give Hebe up without even telling her how he felt about her. And if he tried hard enough he just might—might!—be able to convince her into caring for him with even a little of the deep love he felt for her.

'Claudia is the reason you stopped appearing in public?' Hebe prompted softly. 'The reason you stopped painting portraits, too?' she realized, with sudden insight.

'Losing Claudia is the reason I gave up those things, yes,' Andrew Southern confirmed gruffly. 'I changed my life completely after what I had done!'

Hebe looked at him quizzically. 'What did you do?'

He shook his head. 'Claudia was engaged to marry Jacob Gardner when he commissioned me to paint her portrait, and I was married—if not happily—but it made no difference. We—we took one look at each other and neither Jacob nor my wife seemed to matter any more.'

At last Hebe had a possible explanation as to why Claudia, after breaking off her engagement to Jacob Gardner, had left alone rather than with Andrew Southern. Because he'd already had a wife…

'But why, if you loved each other, did you let her go off alone like that to have her baby?' She frowned. 'Or didn't you love her enough to leave your wife, is that it?'

All of this was starting to have a familiar ring to it as far as Hebe was concerned. History repeating itself. Well, not quite, she corrected herself. Nick didn't love her, but he was leaving her to have her baby alone and going back to his ex-wife.

'Of course I loved her enough to leave my wife!' His eyes glittered emotionally. 'But we argued. Claudia—she didn't believe me when I said I would end my marriage to be with her. But I did end it. And I went to see her the same day to tell her I had, that I only wanted to be with her, wanted her to come and live with me. She didn't tell me she was pregnant!' Andrew groaned fiercely. 'She had been there the day before, but when I went back the next day to tell her I couldn't live without her, that I loved her, she—she had gone. I never saw her again.' He closed his eyes as if to shut out the pain.

Except Nick knew that the older man couldn't do that, and he couldn't either. The image of Andrew's Claudia, and Hebe for him, couldn't be shut out. It was etched into the brain for all time.

Claudia and Hebe were women the men in their lives loved for a lifetime.

Jacob Gardner had continued to love Claudia even after she had betrayed and then left him. The portrait in his bedroom after all those years was evidence of that. And Andrew Southern's pain at losing his Claudia was unmistakable. Nick knew without doubt that he loved Hebe in that same all-consuming way.

'I—' Hebe paused, moistening suddenly dry lips. 'You realise I'm Claudia's baby?' she asked Andrew Southern warily.

He gave a choked laugh as he looked at her. 'You couldn't be anyone else!' He reached up a shaking hand to touch her cheek lightly. 'You are so like her,' he breathed softly. 'So very, very like her.'

Hebe shot Nick a rueful glance. 'Yes.'

A glance he returned with a glittering determination she didn't understand. But then, she never had understood Nick, so why should that change now, when he was shortly going to go out of her life for good?

She turned back to Andrew Southern. 'The question is—' she grimaced '—am I your daughter or Jacob Gardner's?'

'Mine, of course!' the artist claimed frowningly. 'Claudia—your mother—didn't have that sort of relationship with Jacob Gardner. In fact she had never had that sort of relationship with anyone before me,' he admitted gruffly.

Hebe blinked. 'But—'

'There was no one else before me, Hebe,' he told her firmly. 'Claudia liked to give the impression that she was wild and untamed, that she was worldly-wise, even. But in reality she was a sweet, enchanting young woman who had never been with a man before me. I felt a complete heel when I realised that the first time we made love.' He gave a shaky sigh. 'I wasn't happily married, but that was no excuse for seducing an innocent!'

Hebe didn't really care about that. She just felt happier knowing that her parents' love and care for Claudia hadn't been misplaced at all, and that she really had just been the rebellious teenager Hebe had told Nick she'd been.

Andrew Southern's gaze was pained. 'I tried to find her. I really tried, Hebe.' He looked at her earnestly. 'But she had just disappeared.'

Hebe gave a tearful smile. 'I don't think she intended you to find her—or anyone else, in fact.' She drew in a deep breath. 'I didn't know when I wrote to you on Friday, but—but Claudia's parents only learnt of her whereabouts when the hospital called them as next of kin. She died giving birth to me,' she explained as gently as she could. 'They brought me up, and have been the only parents I've never known.'

Andrew gave another choked sob. 'All these years... I never knew what had happened to her, Hebe. Why she left so suddenly,' he explained as she looked puzzled. 'Until I received your letter this morning and saw that photograph of you I never knew that she was expecting my child. And it never—it never even occurred to me that she might have been dead all these years.' He gave a disbelieving shake of his head, as if he still couldn't take it all in.

Nick looked at the other man admiringly, not sure he would be staying even this much together if he had just learnt that Hebe was dead.

'Or that you had a daughter?' Hebe put in softly.

Andrew Southern's face lit up as he looked at her, but the sorrow remained etched beside his eyes and mouth. 'Or that I have the gift of a daughter. A very beautiful daughter,' he added gruffly.

'Who, in seven months' time, is going to make you a grandfather,' Nick added gently, and he stepped forward to place his arm possessively about Hebe's shoulders.

She gave him a surprised look. What was Nick doing? Andrew Southern—her father—didn't need to know about the baby she was expecting. It served no purpose at this moment, and would surely make it more difficult for Nick to just walk away, as he intended doing.

Andrew Southern looked at the younger man with sharply assessing eyes. 'And am I going to have to get my shotgun oiled and ready…?' he finally murmured derisively.

'No,' Nick answered firmly. 'Hebe and I are getting married. If she'll have me…?' He turned to look down at her uncertainly.

She swallowed hard, shaking her head, not understanding this at all.

'Looks like you have some persuading to do there, Nick.' Andrew had misinterpreted that dazed shake of her head as a refusal. 'Feel free to take her off somewhere private. I'm quite happy sitting here looking at Claudia's portrait for an hour or six—or a lifetime,' he added, and he sat down in the armchair beside the painting, already seeming to have forgotten their existence as his eyes misted tearfully and the tears began to fall for the woman he had loved and would never see again.

Hebe took Nick into the room that had used to be her bedroom, bare now of everything that marked it as being hers, not understanding what was going on at all.

'Do you think he's going to be all right?' She frowned with concern.

'I think that he's probably had twenty-six years to come to terms with losing Claudia, so her death makes it no more final,' Nick answered carefully. 'With your agreement, I would like to give him the portrait of Claudia? It belongs with him, don't you think?'

'Yes,' she answered, slightly breathlessly, appreciating his understanding. 'Oh, yes! But I—I thought we had agreed to cancel the wedding.' She looked up at him, puzzled. 'I told you, I'm not going to be difficult—'

'I am,' he cut in grimly, his dark blue gaze fixed firmly on hers. 'Hebe, I don't intend ending up like Andrew—in love with a woman for the rest of my life but not *with* her.'

'I realise that,' she acknowledged softly. 'That's why I agreed to end the engagement, and forget our marriage. I know you and Sally want to be reconciled—'

'Sally?' Nick cut in sharply. 'What the hell does *Sally* have to do with any of this?'

Hebe looked confused. 'I didn't mean to, but I overheard you talking to her on the telephone yesterday evening.' She swallowed hard. 'I know she's the reason you no longer want a marriage of convenience with me—that the two of you want to be together and that you're going to talk things over when you go back to New York.'

Nick looked at her incredulously. *That* was why, after the two of them had made love so beautifully, so thoroughly, Hebe had gone to the spare room to sleep last night! The reason she had been so ready to call off the engagement and cancel the wedding. Because she thought he was still in love with Sally!

'Hebe.' He breathed deeply. 'Sally remarried a year ago, very happily. Last night she called to tell me—she was so happy she had to share it with me—that she had just given birth to a little girl.' He watched Hebe closely for her reaction. 'I probably should have told you about it, but you had gone from my bedroom when I got back, and in the morning— Well, you know what it was like between us this morning.'

Hebe stared at him incredulously. 'Sally's had a *baby*…?'

'Yes.' He nodded, hope starting to blossom and grow.

'Hebe, I know you might find this hard to believe after the way I've behaved—' he shook his head self-disgustedly '—but the only woman I want to be with, the only woman I love, will *ever* love, is you!'

Hebe's incredulity turned to wonder. 'You do…?'

'I do,' he assured her grimly. 'I think I fell in love with you six weeks ago. These last two years, when I've been—involved with a woman, I've just forgotten about her once I've walked away,' he admitted ruefully. 'But you—you were different. I thought about nothing but you for five weeks—six if you count the week after I bought the portrait. I knew even then that I would have to see you again once I returned to London, that somehow you had got under my skin.'

Hebe moistened her dry lips, hardly able to believe Nick was saying these things to her. 'But the portrait changed all that…?'

He nodded, sighing. 'Because I'm an idiot. Because I didn't believe you when you told me you weren't the woman in the portrait. It looked like you!' he groaned. 'The you I had seen the night we spent together. The you who had been like a living flame in my arms. The you who had been haunting my days and invading my nights.' He shook his head. 'Seeing that portrait, imagining the man who had painted it looking at you and seeing exactly what I had seen, touching you in the way I had touched you— I was so angry I think I was blind with rage the next time we met,' he admitted.

Nick *was* saying these things to her!

'And now?' she prompted breathlessly. 'Now that you know the truth? You released me from our engagement and agreed to cancel the wedding,' she reminded him huskily.

He gave a humourless smile. 'I was trying to do the honourable thing. I realised that I had bullied you into both those things because of my mistaken belief that you were trying to trap me into marriage by getting pregnant on purpose. And I *was* mistaken, Hebe. I know now that you were just as surprised by your pregnancy as I was. Worse, you were probably terrified. And I've behaved like a complete bastard to you,' he murmured self-disgustedly.

'But now?' she prompted again.

'Now, after listening to Andrew, hearing him describe how much he loved Claudia and the hell his life has been for him since he lost her, I've decided—unless I want to go quietly insane—that I have to forget being honourable,' he said determinedly. 'I don't want to be another Jacob or Andrew, my life barren and loveless because I've let the woman I love walk away from me without even trying to show her how much I love her and want to be with her. If it takes me months, or even years, I'm going to woo you, Hebe Johnson.' He reached out to grasp her arms. 'I'm going to woo you and win you. I love you too much, need you too much, to ever be able to let you just walk away from me. Will you allow me to do that, Hebe?' he pressed fiercely. 'Will you give me a chance to court you, care for you, love you?'

Hebe almost laughed at the ridiculousness of that question—she already loved him so much that parting from him today had been like a nightmare she couldn't awaken from!

'No, I don't think so, Nick,' she told him emotionally. 'No, I don't mean it like that!' she hastened to assure him as he went deathly pale. 'You see, I already love you.' She smiled. 'I've loved you for months—before you even spoke to me the first time,' she admitted joyously. 'And if it's all right with you, I would like to go ahead with our wedding!'

'Hebe…?' He looked at her in disbelief..

'I love you, Nick!' It felt so good to be able to say those words at last—to let her love for this man shine in her eyes and light up her face. 'I love you, and I want to spend the rest of my life with you!'

Nick stared down at her as he drew in a shaky breath. 'For eternity.' He spoke forcefully. 'I'm not willing to settle for anything less!'

'Eternity,' she echoed with a happy laugh. 'I'm not willing to settle for anything less either!'

'I swear to you that we're going to be happy together, Hebe,' Nick assured her firmly. 'So very, very happy.'

She believed him.

And when their son and daughter, Andrew Henry and Claudia Luka, were born seven months later, mother and babies all healthy, Hebe knew she had been right to trust and believe in Nick—that their love for each other just grew stronger each and every day they were together.

As it would for eternity.

Liam's Secret Son

CAROLE MORTIMER

For Peter

CHAPTER ONE

'DID you know there's a contact lens in your cup of tea?'

Laura's only outward show that she was in the least affected by the lilting Irish drawl she now heard behind her was a slight—barely perceptible, she hoped!—tremble of her hand as she continued to raise the cup to her lips.

Déjà vu...

Except she didn't just have a feeling that this had happened before—it *had* happened before!

Where had he come from? She was sitting in the lounge of a luxurious hotel, was seated so that she could see both the main entrance and smaller back entrance, and yet somehow Liam had managed to enter without her being aware of it. He now stood behind her.

She carefully placed the cup and saucer back down on the tray on the table in front of her, her movements deliberate and slow. 'In the first place, this is coffee; I don't drink tea,' she returned huskily, delaying the moment when she would have to turn around and face him. 'And in the second—I don't wear contact lenses!'

'In that case...' he was very close now, his warm breath stirring the dark tendrils of hair that curled at her nape '...you have the most incredibly beautiful eyes I've ever seen.'

'How can you possibly tell that from where you're standing?' she replied dryly, her face still averted.

'Ah, Laura, now you've gone and broken the spell,' Liam teased lightly, the Irish lilt in his voice stronger than

5

ever. 'Your next line in the script should have been something else entirely!'

Eight years ago, perhaps it had been. But this was another lifetime. A different Laura. She was no longer an impressionable English Literature student, in the third and final year of her degree.

And Liam was no longer a world-famous author come to give the students a lecture of whom she had been slightly in awe.

She drew in a deeply controlling breath before sitting forward and turning to face him, glad of that control as she found herself looking up into his handsome, laughing face.

He hadn't changed a bit!

The thing that struck one most when first faced with Liam O'Reilly was his sheer size: six foot four inches tall, with a lithely muscular body that exuded vitality. He was dressed today, as always, with a complete disregard for his surroundings, in faded blue denims, blue tee shirt and black jacket. Second came recognition of the blue-black sheen to the overlong hair that brushed his shoulders, the intelligence in those intense blue eyes, the handsome face that looked as if it were carved out of hard, rugged stone.

But none of her inner dismay at the apparent lack of any change in his appearance showed as Laura continued to look at him with her 'incredibly beautiful eyes', one a clear shining blue, the other emerald-green. Which was the reason for his assumption, eight years ago, that she must have lost one of her tinted contact lenses.

She had been teased unmercifully about her different coloured eyes when she was at her all-girls, boarding-school, but as she'd grown older it had ceased to bother her as she'd come to realise that men actually found the strangeness of her eyes intriguing. As Liam once had...

She gave a cool smile. 'I suppose I should feel flattered

that you still remember that particular conversation,' she dismissed with a shrug of her slender shoulders, aware even as she did so that the noise and bustle of the busy hotel had faded into the background.

Those deep blue eyes, surrounded by long dark lashes that should have looked ridiculous on such an otherwise muscularly attractive man—but somehow didn't—narrowed speculatively. 'But you aren't, are you?' he finally said slowly.

Flattered that he should still remember, after all these years, the first real conversation they had ever had? No, she wasn't flattered. After what had followed, why on earth should she be?

No! She quickly brought her resentful thoughts under control. Anger was not an option. Better to make no reply at all than one that sounded in the least emotional.

Liam tilted his head thoughtfully to one side at her continued silence. 'You've had all that beautiful long dark hair cut off,' he murmured frowningly.

'It's easier to manage,' she bit out abruptly, knowing that the short, dark cap of almost black hair made a perfect oval for her gamine features—those different-coloured eyes, the small pointed nose, the wide mouth and determined chin. The softening tendrils of hair at her temples and nape took away the severity of the short style.

'I like it.' He nodded approvingly.

Her earlier resentment returned. She didn't care whether he liked her hair in this style or not. In fact, if she were completely honest, she didn't care what Liam O'Reilly felt about anything!

She determinedly swallowed down those angry feelings. 'Would you care to join me?' She indicated the tray containing her pot of coffee. 'I can ask for another cup.'

Liam gave a glance down at the serviceable watch he

wore on his right wrist. He was left-handed, Laura remembered all too clearly. As were a lot of artistic people.

'Or perhaps you're already meeting someone here?' she suggested lightly as she noted that glance.

'As a matter of fact, I am,' he admitted. 'But not for a few more minutes yet,' he added with satisfaction, moving around the chair she sat in to sprawl his long length into the chair opposite.

Laura would have never actually said that Liam *sat* in a chair; his exceptional height meant that chairs were either usually too low or too lacking in depth for him.

At five feet eight inches tall in her stockinged feet, Laura was quite tall herself, an image she deliberately nurtured nowadays by wearing tailored suits and blouses. Her suit was dark charcoal today, her blouse emerald-green. It was an image she was more than grateful for at this moment, Liam always having had the effect in the past of making her feel tiny. And very feminine.

'Would you like coffee?' she offered, her hands calmly clasped on her skirt-covered thighs as she coolly faced him.

'No, thanks,' he refused. 'I find it almost as addictive as the cigarettes I once smoked.' His mouth twisted with distaste.

Laura's eyes widened. 'You've given up smoking?' When she had known him eight years ago he had smoked at least thirty a day. More so when he was working. When...?

Liam grinned at her surprise. 'Hard to believe, isn't it? Liam O'Reilly, the hard drinker, hard smoker is a reformed character.'

'I doubt it's quite as serious as that,' she replied mockingly.

He gave a low laugh, those dark blue eyes gleaming as

he looked across at her. 'You've grown up, little Laura,' he pronounced admiringly.

'At twenty-nine, I should hope that I have!'

Which made him now thirty-nine, Laura realised, also noting, now that she could see him more clearly, that her first impression of his not having changed wasn't quite correct. The last eight years had definitely left their mark. There were lines now beside his eyes and mouth that owed nothing to laughter, a sprinkling of grey in the blue-black hair at his temples.

'Twenty-nine,' Liam repeated thoughtfully, blue eyes narrowed. 'And what have you been doing with yourself the last eight years, Laura?' he prompted hardly, his gaze moving—subconsciously, it seemed—to the ring finger on her left hand.

A finger that, although completely bare, nevertheless showed the mark of her having once worn a ring there...

'This and that,' she dismissed unhelpfully, having no intention of telling him anything about herself. 'And what about you? What have you been doing the last eight years?'

His mouth twisted. 'Obviously not writing,' he observed harshly.

'No?' Laura didn't give away, by word or facial expression, the fact that she was well aware that no new Liam O'Reilly book had appeared on the bookshelves for over eight years. 'But then, you probably didn't need to write again after the amazing success you had with *Time Bomb*,' she went on lightly.

'"Didn't need to write again!"' Liam repeated accusingly, no longer lounging back in his chair but sitting tensely forward, eyes gleaming like twin jewels, his face intensely alight with emotion.

'I meant from a monetary angle, of course,' Laura continued, still meeting the fierceness of his gaze unflinchingly.

That she had hit upon a raw nerve she didn't doubt. But she had a need to see his response to that direct hit. 'You must have made millions out of *Time Bomb*. The film rights alone—'

'And what good has all that money been to me when I haven't written a word since?' he rasped.

She shrugged. 'Presumably it's kept you in relative comfort over the last eight years—even without the drink and cigarettes!' she teased. 'You certainly seemed to be enjoying your life the last time I saw you,' she couldn't resist adding.

Which had to be an understatement! Liam had achieved a certain amount of success with the four books he'd published before the political thriller *Time Bomb*. But nothing like the explosion—and she excused the pun!—that had followed the publication of his fifth book.

Three weeks after the release of the hardback edition, *Time Bomb* had been number one in the bestseller lists. Liam had appeared on numerous television programmes, the film rights had been bought, and Liam had been whisked off to Hollywood to write the screenplay and help with the casting.

The last Laura had seen of Liam had been a photograph in the newspapers, when he'd married the beautiful blonde-haired actress who had been about to play the female lead in the film of his book.

And Laura Carter, the student Liam had been seeing before he'd left England, had been left behind and forgotten.

At first she had been bewildered by Liam's abandonment, disbelieving that she could mean so little to him when she had been slavishly devoted to him. But as the days and then weeks had passed, with no word from him, she had become angry. This had been followed by bitterness when she'd seen the photograph in the newspapers of him with his bride, and finally had come acceptance that Liam no longer considered her a part—even remotely—of his new life in America. With that acceptance had come her desire to move on, to make a success of her own life.

Her poise now, the expensive cut of her clothes, the large diamond solitaire ring she wore on her right hand, all bore testimony to the fact that she had done exactly that.

Liam's expression was bleak. 'That must have been a long time ago,' he answered her last remark sarcastically.

'Maybe it was.' Another lifetime again, she acknowledged inwardly. 'So, what's important enough now to bring you back from sunny California to a cold English winter?' she prompted with a casual change of subject.

Liam forced himself to relax with obvious effort, once again leaning back in the chair, although his eyes still gleamed fiercely blue. 'I didn't come from California,' he corrected. 'I moved back to Ireland five years ago.'

Which was probably the reason his Irish brogue sounded slightly stronger than it had eight years ago, Laura decided. She hadn't known of the move, of course, had deliberately not interested herself in any of Liam's movements after learning of his marriage.

'That must have been something of a cultural shock to your American wife,' she remarked.

'I wouldn't know,' he drawled scathingly. 'Diana divorced me seven years ago. The marriage only lasted six months, Laura,' he explained as she raised her brows questioningly. 'Because of work commitments we only spent about six weeks of that time together,' he added bitterly. 'Not my idea of a marriage!'

Liam had only been married for six months! Six months! If she had only known—

What would she have done differently if she had known? Nothing, came the flat answer. Liam had made his choices, as she had made hers. Nothing, and no one, could ever change that.

Liam gave another glance at his wristwatch. 'Look, I really do have to meet someone in a few minutes. In fact…' He glanced around the crowded lounge with narrowed eyes. 'I have to go now,' he murmured as a man who had just entered the lounge caught and held his eye. 'But I would like to see you again, Laura—

'I don't think that's a good idea,' she cut in briskly, also glancing across the room at the man who had just entered, returning the polite inclination of his head with one of her own. 'It's been—interesting seeing you again, Liam,' she said without any trace of sincerity. 'But I have to be going myself now.' She stood up, slim and elegant in her fitted suit and blouse, the strap of her patent black leather bag thrown over her shoulder.

'Laura!' Liam grasped her arm as she would have moved smoothly past him. 'I want to see you again,' he told her determinedly.

She looked at him. 'To talk about old times, Liam?' she taunted, shaking her head. 'I don't think so, thank you.' She gave a humourless smile.

Liam's eyes narrowed to blue slits. 'I'm booked in here for another couple of days, Laura. Call me. If you don't,' he continued softly as she was about to refuse, 'I'll stay in London until I find you again,' he assured her.

At least now she knew the reason she hadn't seen him arrive at the hotel; he was actually a guest here and had probably come downstairs in the lift, which she couldn't see from here in the lounge.

But that didn't change the fact that there was an underlying threat to his words. Or that she had her own reasons for not wanting him to find her. Not yet, anyway.

'How melodramatic you've become, Liam,' she responded. 'If it's that important to you, I'll give you a ring later.' When she would make it plain to him that she had no intention of meeting him on a social level while he was in London!

He gave her an intense look before slowly releasing her arm. 'It's that important to me,' he said, with a terse nod of his head.

She raised dark, sceptical brows at the admission. 'Now, if you'll excuse me, I really do have to go.' She spoke coolly, aware of Liam's gaze on her as she walked across the lounge and out into the reception area, collecting her outdoor coat from the attendant there before stepping outside into the bitingly cold November wind.

Not that she felt the ice of that wind; the shock of seeing Liam again had completely numbed her now. Face to face with him, remembering all that had happened between them in the past, it hadn't been too difficult to keep up a veneer of cool self-possession. But now she was alone, away from the hotel, reaction had begun to set in.

Eight years ago she had dreamt of meeting Liam again, just once, if only for a few minutes. Part of her had longed to see him again; another part of her had been angry at his cruel desertion.

'Mrs Shipley.' Paul, her driver, stood by the car parked beside the pavement, the back door held open invitingly.

'Thank you,' she accepted distractedly, grateful for the warmth and privacy of the back seat of the limousine as the driver closed the door behind her.

'Back to the office, Mrs Shipley?' Paul prompted politely once he was seated behind the wheel.

'No. Yes! I—'

Get a grip, Laura, she ordered herself firmly. Okay, so she had seen Liam again. So what? No doubt he was still the charming rogue he had been eight years ago, but that didn't make her the same impressionable Laura Carter. She was Laura Shipley now; she ran her own business, owned a house in London, a villa in Majorca, travelled in chauffeur-driven cars wherever she chose to go. A single meeting with Liam O'Reilly was not going to take any of that away from her.

'Yes, Paul, back to the office.' She spoke more firmly now, relaxing back in her seat as the car moved slowly out into the flow of traffic.

There was no hurry for her to return home; Bobby wouldn't be back for another hour and a half yet. Besides, she had told Perry that she would wait at the office for his report.

She wondered how his own conversation with Liam was progressing...!

CHAPTER TWO

'AMAZING,' Perry enthused, pacing up and down the room excitedly an hour later. 'I still can't believe the way you just knew, three weeks ago, that despite the fact the author was claiming to be one Reilly O'Shea, the manuscript that landed on my desk was really by Liam O'Reilly!'

Laura sat behind her own wide, imposing desk watching her senior editor. The jacket to her suit had been discarded in the warmth of the office, her emerald silk blouse a perfect foil for her dark colouring.

The way she had just known...!

She'd read that last Liam O'Reilly novel from cover to cover. She knew every twist and turn of the writer's mind; knew every phrase and nuance, how he dotted every 'i' and crossed every 't'—of course she had recognised the manuscript that had been submitted to Shipley Publishing three weeks ago. Its sheer brilliance—brought to her attention by Perry—had been created by the same person!

She hadn't quite been able to believe it, though, had found it incredible to believe that Liam might actually be writing again. Even more astounding was that the manuscript had been submitted under a different name, even if the name Reilly O'Shea wasn't so far from Liam's own. It was because of the uncertainty surrounding that name that she had felt today's charade at the hotel necessary. It had been eight years since she last saw Liam, and he might have changed in that time—she certainly had! But if anyone could recognise Liam O'Reilly, no matter what the changes, she knew she could.

15

So she had deliberately arranged to be at the hotel today, strategically placed so that she might alert Perry when he arrived for his arranged meeting as to whether or not she had been correct in her assertion that the author was actually Liam O'Reilly.

It had not been part of the plan, however, for Liam to actually spot and recognise her! As it hadn't been her intention to agree to telephone him later at his hotel...!

Laura still came over hot and then cold at the memory of that unexpected meeting between the two of them. Eight years. And apart from those added tell-tale lines, a little grey in the darkness of his hair, Liam looked exactly the same. The fact that he had recognised her too—despite her own changed hairstyle and the denims and tee shirts she'd used to wear having been replaced by the classically elegant suit and blouse—had momentarily stunned her.

But only momentarily, she was relieved to recall. The self-assurance she had acquired over the last eight years had stood her in good stead, even down to the acknowledging nod of her head she had given Perry when he'd arrived in the hotel lounge.

That Perry was pleased at the way his meeting with the author had gone was obvious. He was bubbling over with excitement at the prospect of Shipley Publishing being in possession of the long-awaited new Liam O'Reilly novel. Except that Laura knew it wasn't going to be as easy as that...

She calmly brought her senior editor back to earth. 'What actually happened at the meeting, Perry?'

Perry dropped down into the chair opposite hers. Comfortably so, Laura noted abstractedly, unlike Liam earlier when he had tried to bend his long length into the chair at the hotel—Oh, bother Liam—and how he did or did not fit himself into chairs!

'Well, I covered a lot of ground with him, but we still have a long way to go, of course.' Some of Perry's excitement faded as he frowned slightly. 'The biggest obstacle we're going to face is that, despite several promptings from me about previous books and other even broader hints, the man stuck like glue to the identity of Reilly O'Shea.'

Laura nodded. 'Do you have any idea why?'

'Oh, that's easy,' Perry replied. 'It's how we're going to deal with it that's the problem. We have our hands on a Liam O'Reilly manuscript, and—'

'Can we just go back a couple of steps, Perry?' Laura interrupted slowly. 'You know why the man is determined not to admit to being Liam O'Reilly?'

Since reading the manuscript three weeks ago Laura had racked her brains as to a possible explanation for the use of a pseudonym. All to no avail. As Liam O'Reilly he could ask for, and receive, an exorbitant advance payment and subsequent royalty percentages. As a first-time author, a possible risk for any publishing house, he would receive much less. Also, a Liam O'Reilly novel was sure to receive much more publicity than that of an unknown author. And surely readership, after months, possibly years of work, was what every author wanted…?

'Of course,' the boyishly handsome Perry agreed; a little under six feet tall, blond-haired, blue-eyed, he exuded an energy that totally belied his thirty-five years.

'Then I wish you would explain it to me,' Laura encouraged lightly. 'Because I have no idea why such a successful author would want to keep his identity secret!'

'For exactly that reason.' Perry grinned. 'Years ago, with the publication of his fifth book, the man became a phenomenon. Top of the bestseller lists, both hardback and then paperback, for almost a year, the darling of the literary world, a huge feather in the cap of any society hostess.

Then the book was made into a film that carried off most of the Oscars for that year. The man was the star to outshine all stars!'

'Yes?' So far this explanation had done little other than tell her things she already knew.

'I've started with an astronomical explanation so I may as well continue.' Perry grimaced. 'You see, he wasn't a star, Laura, he was a comet. He came into our orbit, shone brightly for what was, after all, a very brief period in a single lifetime, and then disappeared again. Without trace, apparently.'

'But—'

'I have a feeling he wants to do things differently the second time around,' Perry said quietly.

'But as soon as it becomes public knowledge exactly who Reilly O'Shea is—'

'It may not come to that,' her senior editor interrupted firmly. 'Despite the fact I accept I was actually talking to Liam O'Reilly today, I had to carry out the meeting as if I were talking to Reilly O'Shea. We obviously discussed the possibility of a contract to publish the manuscript...' Perry hesitated. 'He had some quite interesting clauses of his own that he would like in any such agreement.'

Laura raised dark brows at the arrogance of the man. 'Such as?'

'No personal publicity. No public appearances. In fact his privacy completely guaranteed, or it was no deal.' Perry shrugged at her incredulous expression. 'Strange requests from a first-time author, I agree,' he commented dryly. 'But not so strange coming from a man who has already had a taste of all those things—and hated every moment of it!'

As an interested bystander in that blaze of publicity, of those personal appearances, Laura couldn't agree with

Perry's conclusion; eight years ago Liam had given the appearance of enjoying every moment of his success!

She sighed. 'As you say, we obviously have a long way to go yet. How did you leave the meeting?' she prompted interestedly.

'He's staying in London another couple of days, I said I would call him before he left. To be honest, it was one of the most difficult meetings I've ever had to attend. I loved *Time Bomb* eight years ago, but I have to say that I think *Josie's World* is even better—and all the time I was talking to Reilly—Liam—I just wanted to tell him that!' He shook his head.

'I'm glad that you didn't give in to the temptation,' Laura remarked dryly, looking at the slender gold watch on her wrist before shuffling some papers together on her desk. 'I have to go now, Perry, but we'll talk about this again first thing in the morning.' She paused. 'Although, I have to admit, I'm not sure exactly how we proceed from here.'

What troubled her the most, she had to admit, was keeping her own identity out of any future negotiations with the author. For reasons of her own, she did not want Liam to know that *she* was Shipley Publishing...!

The dark blue telephone that stood on her bedside table seemed to be glowering at her, even when she didn't actually look at it, silently reproaching her for not picking up the receiver and punching out the number of Liam's hotel.

As was her custom for the last two years, she had retired to her bedroom once dinner was over, taking a pile of work with her. She was sitting up in bed now, her narrow silk-clad shoulders surrounded by sumptuous satin cream-coloured pillows, glasses perched on the end of her nose, as she read through the latest manuscript of Shipley's most successful author.

So far, came that disquieting little voice in her head. Because she had no doubt, if they really could secure Liam's novel, that he would instantly eclipse Elizabeth Starling as Shipley's top author!

Elizabeth's latest manuscript was good, in fact it was more than good, but it didn't stand a chance of holding Laura's attention tonight.

She lay back with a sigh, removing her gold-framed glasses. She really didn't wear contact lenses, coloured or otherwise, but she did wear glasses for reading nowadays. Possibly because she did so much of it.

Not that she was complaining about her lot in life. Her marriage to Robert had been as fulfilling as it had been successful. It was because of him that she was now head of Shipley Publishing. If that position of power could also make things a little lonely at times, then it was by far outweighed by its compensations: financial security, this beautiful house in London, her villa in Majorca, the servants that ran both those homes so efficiently.

No, the reason for her restlessness tonight had nothing to do with any lack of material comfort in her own life.

Liam was expecting her to call him at his hotel. Part of her said, Forget what he expected; after the way he had treated her eight years ago he had no right to expect anything from her! But another part of her remembered his threat that if she didn't call him then he would do everything in his power to find her. And that she most certainly did not want.

Besides, she had information that Liam certainly didn't have—knew exactly the reason he was in London at the moment. Whereas he knew absolutely nothing about her life now. She wished it to remain that way.

'Mr O'Reilly's room, please,' she requested briskly, once her call was answered at the hotel.

'The line in Mr O'Reilly's suite is ringing for you now,' came back the competent reply.

A suite... Expensive in a prestigious hotel like that one. So Liam did still possess some of the wealth that had come to him years ago. She had wondered. It had never been easy to tell what his financial position might be from Liam's outward appearance; he very rarely wore anything other than denims, casual shirt and a jacket. Exactly as he had today. He—

'Yes?' came the terse reply as the receiver was picked up the other end.

'Liam,' Laura returned, forcing her tone to sound casually light. 'You asked me to call you,' she reminded him. Unnecessarily, she was sure. There had been a determination about Liam earlier today that had brooked no argument against his request.

'So I did, Laura,' he returned in that lilting voice, his initial terseness having disappeared on recognition of her voice. 'I wanted to ask you to have dinner with me.'

'I've already eaten,' she answered with inward satisfaction.

'It's only nine o'clock,' Liam protested.

'When I'm at home I always dine at seven-thirty,' she said firmly.

'And where's home, Laura?' he enquired huskily.

'Nice try, Liam.' She gave a softly confident laugh. Although her hand tightly gripping the receiver was slightly damp with tension...

'I thought so,' he came back mockingly. 'You were a little less than enthusiastic about my calling you when I mentioned it at the hotel earlier today, too,' he continued thoughtfully. 'Why the secrecy, Laura? Could it be that you don't live alone?' There was a sharp edge to his voice now.

'How clever of you to guess, Liam,' she teased. 'Although it couldn't have been that difficult. After all, it's been eight years.' And this man had been married and divorced in that time—wasn't it logical that she might have done at least one of those things too?

'You aren't wearing a wedding ring,' he bit out.

She hadn't been mistaken earlier about the reason for that glance at her left hand! 'Not all women do nowadays,' Laura rejoined.

'You would if you were my wife,' Liam rasped.

'If I were *your* wife I would also carry a certificate of insanity!' she snapped.

Then wished she hadn't. The silence that followed her outburst was icy cold, the only sound their joint breathing down the respective receivers.

Why had she said that? It was no good telling herself she had been goaded into it by Liam's arrogance. Her intention had been to keep this call as short and impersonal as possible; two minutes into the conversation she had let Liam break through her reserve.

But once again it was that cool control that came to rescue the situation, allowing her to remain silent after her outburst.

'You know, Laura—' Liam was finally the one to break that silence, speaking slowly '—you and I should have met years ago.'

'Strange, but I thought we did,' she said acidly. 'There must be something wrong with your memory, Liam,' she added with barely contained sarcasm.

'Nothing at all,' Liam drawled. 'But if you had been this Laura Carter eight years ago, perhaps things would have worked out differently between us.'

'Oh, please, Liam.' She sighed her disgust. 'It has been eight years—and in that time I've probably heard every chat-up line there is. That one ranks right down there at the bottom!' she assured him.

'It isn't a chat-up line! I'm not sure I even know any of them any more,' he said self-disgustedly. 'Unlike you, it seems, I've lived a very quiet life the last five years. Come and have a drink with me, Laura,' he pressed.

'I thought you said you didn't drink any more,' she reminded him dryly.

'I occasionally indulge in a social glass of white wine,' he corrected.

'I'm afraid I'm booked up for the next two evenings,' she refused.

It was just like Liam to assume that she could drop whatever arrangements she might have made in her social life just so that she could go and have a drink with him!

Probably because eight years ago she would have done exactly that. She had been head over heels in love with Liam then, had taken any opportunity she could to spend time with him, even to the point of letting down other friends if he'd asked to see her.

But that had been then. This was now. The two situations were completely different.

'I meant now, Laura,' Liam cut softly into her indignant thoughts.

'Now?' she repeated incredulously.

'Why not?' he pressed huskily.

'Because I'm already in bed!' she protested astoundedly.

And then wished that she hadn't. It was, after all, only ten minutes past nine!

'Alone?' Liam prompted harshly.

What on earth—! 'I would hardly be calling you if I weren't!' she answered with cold disdain.

'You might be surprised at what some women are capable of,' he rasped scathingly.

'Not this woman,' she assured him indignantly.

'So you're in bed. But alone. What's to stop you joining me for that drink?'

Having to get up. To dress. To put on make-up she had already removed. Drive over to the hotel. All just to spend time with someone she didn't want to be with!

'I don't think so, thanks,' she refused distantly. 'I did as you asked and called you. I don't think I owe our past—friendship any more than that.'

'I disagree,' Liam refuted. 'Aren't you in the least bit curious about the last eight years, Laura? I know I am.'

Laura was suddenly very tense. 'Curious about what, Liam?' she enquired guardedly.

'What's happened to you during that time,' he came back instantly. 'Because you certainly aren't the impressionable university student I knew back then!'

'Thank goodness!' she said with some relief. 'Look, Liam, I only called you at all against my better judgement—'

'Why against your better judgement, Laura? Am I so awful, so morally depraved, that you want nothing more to do with me?'

'Don't be ridiculous, Liam,' she cried. 'I don't even know you any more—'

'My point exactly,' he pounced with satisfaction.

'And I don't want to know you, either!' she concluded firmly.

'That isn't very kind, Laura.'

Kind! Had it been kind eight years ago when he'd left for Hollywood and just walked out of her life? When he hadn't even called, sent so much as a postcard? Had never even troubled himself to find out if she were okay after he'd left?

This man didn't even know the meaning of the word *kind*!

Thankfully she had found other people in her life who did...

'We have nothing to talk about, Liam,' she assured him flatly. 'Absolutely nothing in common.'

If you took away the fact that she owned a publishing house, he was an author, and it would be mutually beneficial to both of them if Shipley Publishing were to acquire Liam's latest novel...!

'We have the past—'

'It's been my experience that to indulge in reminiscences is a complete waste of time, Liam,' she told him bluntly. 'People very rarely remember the same experience in exactly the same way!'

'I remember our relationship eight years ago as something sweet and rather beautiful—'

'Oh, please spare me that, Liam,' she cut in disgustedly.

'—in *my* life,' he finished.

Maybe in retrospect that was how it now appeared to him. It was a pity he hadn't felt the same way eight years ago!

'Which just bears out my earlier statement about people acquiring differing impressions. Of the past or anything else,' she said briskly. 'I remember myself as a rather stupid twenty-one-year-old, totally infatuated with a world-famous author—an author who probably found me a complete pain in the—'

'Now you're being unkind again, Laura,' Liam cut in. 'To yourself, I mean.'

'No, just realistic,' she drawled. 'No wonder you couldn't wait to get away—from me as well as England!'

'It wasn't like that—'

'It was exactly like that, Liam,' she assured him laughingly. 'I must have been such a nuisance, following you around all those months like some faithful little lap-dog, hanging on your every word, there every time you turned around—'

'I said it wasn't like that, Laura,' he told her angrily. 'The fact that you remember it as such is a good enough reason for us to meet up for that drink!'

'You're very persistent, Liam,' she said wearily. 'Or is it just a question of my being something of a challenge now that I'm obviously not as malleable as I used to be?'

'I never thought of you as malleable!' he barked.

She sighed, wondering exactly what she should do for the best.

As Laura, there was no doubt in her mind that she didn't want to meet Liam; she still remembered all too vividly the pain she had felt after knowing him in the past. But as the owner of Shipley Publishing she knew that at some stage in the negotiations she was going to have to deal with him. Perhaps it was better to get any personal awkwardness between them out of the way before that became necessary? Although that didn't include, at this stage, telling him that she was now Laura *Shipley*...

'Or perhaps it's just that you think your husband might object to your meeting me for a drink?' Liam put in softly.

Laura stiffened resentfully. 'Let's leave my husband out of this,' she retorted. Robert, and her marriage to him, were not things she ever intended to talk about to Liam. They might have a business relationship ahead of them, but that certainly didn't involve confidences about her personal life.

'Gladly,' Liam returned shortly. 'So what's it to be, Laura? Meet me for a drink tonight? Or I come looking for you tomorrow?'

'That sounds decidedly like a threat, Liam.' It didn't just *sound* like a threat—it *was* one!

'If that's the way you care to take it,' he conceded with exasperation.

'I think I should warn you—I don't respond too well to threats,' she told him stiffly.

'Then don't take it as one,' he replied impatiently. 'My goodness, Laura, you didn't used to be this difficult!'

She had used not to be a lot of things. But it was those changes, in herself as well as her life, that now gave her the inner strength and security to accept his invitation. Liam couldn't touch her emotionally. Not any more.

'Okay, Liam, I'll meet you for that drink,' she accepted graciously.

'Why ever couldn't you have just agreed to do that ten minutes ago?' he demanded.

'I didn't want to make it that easy for you,' she told him with blunt honesty.

He sighed. 'I would take a guess that you don't intend making anything easy for me!'

She laughed softly. 'You would guess correctly. Give me forty minutes or so to dress and get over to you,' she continued briskly, throwing back the satin sheets to get out of bed.

'I'll have the champagne waiting on ice for you,' he came back huskily.

Laura stiffened. 'Let me make it clear from the onset, Liam—we do not have anything to celebrate,' she told him flatly.

'Maybe you don't—but I do.' He sounded completely unperturbed by her outburst. 'I'll tell you about it when you get here,' he promised.

Laura dressed, frowning at her reflection in the mirror as she put on her make-up. Exactly what did Liam have to celebrate? What did he intend telling her about when she got to the hotel? She couldn't believe, after the secrecy he had maintained concerning his manuscript, *Josie's World*, that he intended telling her about that.

And if he did how she would actually respond?

In the circumstances, how *could* she respond...?

CHAPTER THREE

A QUICK look around the bar and lounge area on her arrival at the hotel a short time later showed her that Liam wasn't in any of them. Which could mean only one thing...

Laura marched determinedly over to the reception desk, her eyes, with their different colours, sparkling angrily. 'Could you call Mr O'Reilly's suite, please, and tell him that Laura is waiting for him downstairs?'

'Certainly, madam.' The receptionist smiled at her before doing exactly that, putting her hand over the receiver after a minute or so's conversation with Liam. 'Mr O'Reilly would like you to join him in his suite on the third floor—'

'Could you tell Mr O'Reilly that I am waiting for him downstairs in Reception—with or without the champagne!' Laura was so angry her voice shook slightly, and her hands clenched into fists at her sides.

How dared he? How dared he assume she would go up to his suite for the agreed drink? Exactly who did he think he was? More to the point, *what* did he think she was?

The receptionist related the message, ending the call a few seconds later before smiling at Laura with vacuous politeness. 'Mr O'Reilly says he will join you here in a few minutes.'

'Thank you,' Laura accepted stiffly, before marching over to sit in one of the sumptuous armchairs that filled the reception area, glaring across at the four lifts as she waited for Liam to appear from one of them, not even sure now that she was going to stay for the proposed drink!

She sat and fumed as she waited. Liam had a nerve, just

assuming— The arrogance of him! The absolute, unmitigating gall of the man!

'I would tell you how beautiful you look when you're angry,' an amused voice remarked behind her, very close to her ear, 'but I very much doubt, in your present frame of mind, that you would appreciate the hackneyed compliment!'

Laura, having spun round angrily at the first sound of Liam's voice, found herself with her face only inches away from his own.

For the second time today, exactly where had he come from?

She had seated herself facing towards the lifts this time, and still she had missed his arrival. The man was more elusive than a taxi in the theatre district of London on a Saturday evening!

'I walked down,' he drawled as he seemed to guess some of her thoughts.

'Three floors?' she gasped disbelievingly. The Liam she'd used to know had sometimes found walking from the bedroom to the kitchen too much effort!

He grinned at her obvious scepticism. 'I've taken up hiking in the countryside since I moved back to Ireland.' His expression darkened. 'For a while it became my salvation!'

'How nice,' Laura returned insincerely, not wanting to hear the reasons why he had needed salvation. 'You decided not to bring down the champagne, I see.' She looked pointedly at his empty hands.

'It's waiting for us in the bar.' He gave a sweep of his hand in that direction.

Meaning what? Laura wondered as she stood up. That he had intended the two of them drinking in the bar the whole time? Or that he had made a hasty call down to the barman and asked him to put a second bottle of champagne on ice? Somehow Laura had an idea it was the second option!

'You think too much,' Liam teased, moving to lightly clasp her arm as they strolled through to the bar. 'You also look gorgeous,' he added admiringly.

She frowned at the compliment. She had dressed in black trousers and a fitted black leather shirt deliberately, considering them to be smart but unalluring. The last thing she wanted was for Liam to think she was out to appear attractive to him. She had obviously failed!

Laura studied him as they sipped the champagne that had been poured for them, having unemotionally noted the female interest engendered in the bar by his dark Irish good looks. Some things never changed, she acknowledged dryly; Liam always had been able to attract every woman within a ten-yard-radius, no matter what her age!

'So, Laura.' Liam looked across at her with laughing blue eyes. 'What's your conclusion?'

She inwardly stiffened at his perception, while outwardly giving every impression she was completely relaxed sitting in the armchair placed next to his. 'Concerning what?' She was deliberately unhelpful.

'Concerning any physical changes you might see in me after all these years,' he drawled unconcernedly.

Unconcernedly, Laura guessed, because he knew that none of those changes had detracted from his rugged good looks.

She shrugged. 'We're both eight years older, Liam.'

He chuckled softly. 'Very tactfully said, Laura—but in no way does it answer my question.'

She raised dark brows. 'Because, quite honestly, I don't see the point in the question, let alone the answer,' she replied tersely.

Blue eyes narrowed speculatively. 'What's he like?' he murmured slowly.

It took all of her inner control to maintain her composure. 'Who?' she finally asked stiffly.

'The man you married.'

Her gaze was cool now. 'Robert's the most kind, wonderful, considerate person I have ever known,' she answered without hesitation.

Liam looked less than pleased by her reply, scowling darkly. 'But what's he like in bed?' he probed.

Laura, in the process of sipping her champagne, almost choked over the bubbly liquid, glaring at him with icy eyes. 'How dare you?' she gasped once she could catch her breath, her hand shaking slightly as she slammed her champagne glass down on the table that stood in front of them. 'Just who do you think you are? You have absolutely no right—'

'That bad, hmm?' Liam put in consideringly, still studying her with narrowed eyes.

'What's that supposed to mean?' She glared at him, two bright red spots of angry colour in her cheeks.

'Too defensive, Laura. Too outraged. Just too everything, really,' he taunted. 'The next thing you're going to tell me is that the kindness, consideration and being wonderful far outweigh the fact that he doesn't satisfy you in bed.' He quirked mocking brows.

'You're completely wrong there, Liam,' she replied scathingly, bending to pick up her clutch bag. 'Because I have nothing further to say to you—about Robert or anything else!' She stood up, looking down at him contemptuously. 'You *have* changed in the last eight years, Liam—and certainly not for the better!'

'Oh, for goodness' sake sit down, Laura,' he said wearily. 'Okay, I was out of order making those remarks about your husband.' *Even if they are true*, his tone implied. 'I apologise, okay?' he prompted irritably as she still glared down at him.

'No, it's not okay,' she told him from between stiff lips, completely unyielding.

He sat forward, reaching out to clasp one of her hands in his. 'Did it ever occur to you that I might be feeling a little jealous?' he asked. 'After all, you used to think *I* was wonderful,' he added self-derisively.

She gave a scornful laugh. 'That was before I grew up enough to be able to pick the gold from the dross!'

Before he released her, Liam's fingers tightened briefly about hers—the only outward sign he gave that he was angered by her deliberate insult.

And it had been deliberate, she inwardly acknowledged, provoked by his insulting remarks about Robert. She wouldn't allow anyone to do that. Robert had been her salvation in a time of deep crisis.

She had also been thrown a little by Liam's suggestion that he might actually be jealous of her feelings for Robert. Until she'd realised Liam might just feel put out, the feelings of adoration she had once had for him having now passed on to Robert!

For a moment, a very brief moment, she had actually thought she might have been mistaken about how unfeeling he had been in the past. She obviously wasn't; Liam's feelings of jealousy were just as selfish as all his other emotions had always been!

She gave a humourless smile. 'I did try to warn you that this was a mistake, Liam,' she said. 'We have nothing in common now—if we ever did. Old friends meeting in this way—'

'Old lovers!' he corrected harshly, blue eyes alight with

emotion. 'Don't try to totally negate our past together, Laura.'

She felt frozen to the spot, actually able to feel the colour drain from her cheeks. Negate their past? She would like to wipe it from her memory bank altogether!

Lovers... Yes, they had been lovers. But she had been determined, these last eight years, never to think of that again. She didn't want to think about it!

'Please sit down, Laura,' Liam encouraged quietly. 'I promise I'll try not to be insulting again.'

'You'll *try*, Liam?' she repeated dryly, giving a shake of her head at his arrogance. 'You'll have to do better than that if you expect me to stay!'

He gave a rueful smile. 'You have to accept sometimes I can be insulting without meaning to be.'

Laura gave a pained wince. 'And that's the best excuse you can give for some of the things you've already said to me?'

'Without actually lying—yes!'

She sat down abruptly. 'You really are the most arrogant man I've ever had the misfortune to meet!'

He grinned, leaning forward to replenish their champagne glasses. 'Well, at least I have that distinction—the *most* arrogant man you've ever met.'

'Arrogance is not a virtue, Liam.'

'I'll try to remember that,' he said wryly. 'Now, let's drink a toast...' He held her full glass of champagne out to her before picking up his own glass.

He had hinted on the telephone that he had something to celebrate, and Laura had wondered if he might mean the prospect of publication for his new book. If it should turn out that *was* what it was, what was she going to do? To carry on pleading ignorance would be deceptive in the extreme. But to tell him the truth, after his bluntness already this evening, would be even more unacceptable...

She swallowed hard. 'A toast to what?'

'Old lovers and new friends?' he suggested.

She gave the ghost of a smile, relieved the toast hadn't been what she had expected—although the alternative hadn't been much better! 'The first I choose to forget—the second isn't very likely,' she told him honestly.

'Let's drink to us anyway,' he encouraged huskily.

'To 'us'...?

'Did you tell him about us?' Liam asked slowly, once the toast had been drunk.

She stiffened. 'Robert, you mean?' she said delaying.

'Of course I mean Robert,' he confirmed laughingly. 'Unless you've had any other husbands the last eight years? Just out of interest,' he continued lightly, 'how long ago did you marry him?'

'Robert and I were married seven and a half years ago,' she answered flatly.

'No time for any other husbands.' Liam answered his own question. 'And only a few months after I left for California,' he added pointedly.

'Nowhere near as hasty as your own marriage,' Laura returned harshly. 'You had barely arrived on the tarmac at Los Angeles airport before your own engagement, and subsequent marriage took place!'

She could still remember her feelings of absolute desolation when she had seen the speculation in the newspapers concerning his relationship with Diana Porter. That desolation had been complete when the photographs of his wedding had appeared a few weeks later. If it hadn't been for Robert—

'It looks as if neither of us were too heartbroken at our

separation,' Liam acknowledged. 'I suppose your beloved uncle approves of Robert too?'

Laura's movements were deliberate and calm as she placed her champagne glass back down on the low table in front of her. They had to be; her hand was shaking so much she was in danger of spilling the bubbly wine.

Her parents had been killed in a car crash when she was only sixteen, leaving her without any close family to speak of. It had been left to her godfather, her honorary 'uncle' and guardian, also the executor of her parents' will, to organise the continued payment of her boarding-school fees, so enabling her to stay on at school and sit her 'A' levels before going on to university.

Obviously when she'd met Liam, eight and a half a years ago she had told him about her beloved godfather in the course of their own relationship. But the two men had never met.

Obviously her godfather had expressed curiosity about this worldly-wise man in her life, and she had suggested to Liam several times that perhaps the two men should meet. It had been a suggestion he had chosen to ignore.

And the reason for his reticence had become obvious once he had gone to America and married someone else within a few months: the complication of meeting the guardian of the young student whom he had only been casually involved with for six months previously had not entered into any of his plans! That would have made everything just a little too serious—and Liam hadn't ever had any serious intentions where Laura was concerned!

She looked at him coldly now. 'I don't happen to think of any of this—any part of my life now, in fact—is your business, Liam,' she told him icily. 'Just as I have no interest in your personal life now,' she concluded contemptuously.

Liam looked completely unperturbed by her coldness. 'How about my professional one?' he teased. 'Wouldn't you like to know what—?'

'No!' she sharply cut him off before he could say something that might put her in a compromising position. Telling her that Shipley Publishing was interested in publishing his latest novel would certainly do that! 'No, Liam, I don't want to know anything about your professional life either.' She spoke more calmly. 'In fact—' she gave a glance at her wristwatch '—I really should be going now.'

'Cinderella turns into a pumpkin at the stroke of eleven?' Liam suggested.

She smiled, shaking her head. 'You obviously don't know your fairy-tales very well, Liam. Cinderella turned back into a ragged drudge. But not until midnight.'

He shrugged. 'Put my ignorance down to my deprived childhood. My mother didn't have the time to read me fairy-tales; she was too busy going out to work to keep my three sisters and myself after my father died.'

He made the remark without any show of bitterness in his tone, and yet Laura knew that it couldn't have been easy for the four children, nor their mother. Their father had been killed when Liam, the eldest child, was only seven. She couldn't imagine how Mary O'Reilly had managed during those years at all. The fact that Liam had become a successful writer by the time he was in his mid-twenties had helped all his family financially. But it couldn't take away the struggle of the children's early years.

But she didn't want to think about the hardships of Liam's fatherless childhood. The last thing she wanted was to see Liam in any sort of vulnerable light!

'Are your mother and sisters all well?' she felt compelled to enquire politely.

He smiled at the thought of his family. 'Very much so. Mama lives very comfortably in a lovely cottage on the west coast of Ireland, and all three of my sisters are happily married with children of their own. Fourteen between them, at the last count.'

Laura smiled. 'Your mother must love that.'

He grimaced. 'My mother won't be completely happy until I've provided her with a male grandchild to carry on the family name.'

Laura raised dark brows. 'Surely there must be lots of O'Reillys in Ireland?'

'To be sure there are,' Liam answered with a deliberate Irish lilt to his voice. 'But there aren't any other male members of this particular O'Reilly branch,' he explained ruefully.

'So that puts the onus on you?' she responded. 'And is a little O'Reilly, male or female, a future possibility?'

'Not this side of the next millennium!' he bit out harshly.

'Your poor mother!' Laura rebuked, standing up in preparation for leaving. 'Thank you for the champagne, Liam; I enjoyed it.'

'If not the company, hmm?' He stood up too, standing only inches away from her.

Laura wished he weren't standing quite so close. She could smell the faint elusiveness of his aftershave, feel the heat that emanated from his body. But she didn't want to be aware of him in any way.

'The company was fine too,' she said firmly. 'Enjoy the rest of your stay in London, Liam. Perhaps the two of us will meet up accidentally again one day—in another eight years or so!' She turned to leave.

'I'll walk as far as the door with you.' Liam had moved to lightly grasp her elbow as he walked confidently beside her. 'It's the least I can do as I can't actually see you home,' he elaborated at her startled glance.

Laura didn't even qualify the remark with a reply. She just wanted to get away from there, as far away from Liam as quickly as possible. If that meant suffering a few more minutes of his company, then so be it!

'This is farther than the door,' she observed, looking up pointedly at the awning over their heads as they stood outside the entrance to the hotel.

'I didn't think you would be too happy about my doing this actually inside the hotel,' Liam murmured, before his head bent and his mouth claimed hers.

The kiss was so unexpected that for a moment Laura was totally stunned. But as she felt the heated waves of compliance sweeping over her, felt her body remembering the physical joy of this man even if she chose not to, she knew she had to break away. Now!

She wrenched her mouth away from Liam's, pushing at his arms as they curved about her waist. 'That was completely uncalled-for!' she gasped as she at last managed to escape those steely bands, her breathing erratic in her agitation, a flush to her cheeks as she glared at him.

'But necessary,' Liam rasped. 'For me.' He gave a rueful shake of his head. 'I know you're a married woman, and I apologise because of that. But—you can tell him from me he's a lucky man.'

Her blue and green eyes flashed. 'I intend forgetting any of—*this*, the moment I enter the taxi,' she told him forcefully. 'You're even more despicable than I remember!'

He looked unconcerned. 'Sticks and stones,' he replied.

She would have liked to do more than break a few bones—she felt like hitting him over the head with something heavy and painful!

She hadn't lost her temper like this in eight years. If ever!

Only hours into meeting Liam again and she was a mass of seething emotions. All of which she could quite happily do without.

'One day, Liam,' she ground out between gritted teeth, 'you're going to come up against someone—a situation— you have no control over. Let me know when that day comes—I would like to sit and watch!'

He quirked dark brows. 'You never used to be vindictive, Laura.'

There were so many things she had never used to be. She couldn't even think back now, to the light-hearted, carefree young girl she had once been, without feeling a deep sorrow for the fact that she was no more. She had grown up eight years ago—overnight, it seemed—never to return.

'I'm not vindictive now, either. Just a little jaded. Now I really must be going,' she said briskly. 'It's late, and some of us have to go to work in the morning.'

Liam accompanied her to the taxi, holding the back door open for her. 'What work do you do?' he asked interestedly.

Laura looked up at him for several moments. It was on the tip of her tongue to tell him she owned and ran the Shipley Publishing house. But she knew she would be doing it for the wrong reasons, that a part of her—the part of her that was still angry at the way he had kissed her—just wanted to see the look of stunned disbelief on his face when she told him!

'I'm a book editor,' she told him economically, still clinging on to the truth as far as she dared without revealing everything. After all, it was true that she read all manuscripts due for publication by Shipley Publishing. She would be doing less than her job if she weren't completely aware of what her own company was presenting to the public.

'Really?' Liam looked impressed. 'What—?'

'It's been—interesting, Liam,' she cut in dismissively. 'But I really do have to—'

'I want to see you again, Laura,' he told her grimly.

'Impossible,' she told him firmly. 'Goodnight,' she added abruptly, before pulling the door shut in his face and leaning forward to give the driver her address as he accelerated the taxi away from the hotel.

She didn't look back. Even though a part of her knew that Liam still stood on the pavement watching the car, and her, until they turned out of sight down a side road.

Which was when Laura finally felt able to sit back in her seat and let some of the tension flow out of her.

She had known it wasn't a good idea to meet up with Liam again—had only given in because at the time she had felt it was preferable to having him seek her out. But the fact of the matter was that at some time in the near future Liam would have to know exactly who and what she was. And after spending the last hour in his company she wished she had simply waited for that to happen.

Anything would have been preferable to the last hour. To that kiss...!

She tentatively ran the tip of her tongue over the sensitivity of her lips, still able to feel the pressure of Liam's mouth there, a slight tingling sensation that seemed almost to numb her lips.

How could he still affect her in that way? After all that had happened, all the pain, the disillusionment, how could she still feel this way?

What way did she feel?

Confused. Disorientated. Angry with herself. Angry with

Liam. All of which was completely unproductive, when she needed to be focused, controlled, sure of herself.

The next time she saw Liam, she promised herself as she saw her journey was almost at an end, she would be exactly that!

The lights were on in the house when she let herself in a few minutes later and went straight to the kitchen, where she knew Amy Faulkner, her housekeeper, would be sitting drinking tea and watching television while she waited for Laura to return home.

Short, plump and homely, aged in her mid-fifties, Amy had been Robert's housekeeper for almost twenty years when he and Laura were married. The older woman had welcomed Laura into the house as if she were the daughter she'd never had, and the two of them had got on from the beginning. Laura had been more than grateful for the other woman's presence this last couple of years.

The housekeeper smiled at her warmly now as she stood up to turn down the sound on the predicted television programme. 'Had a good evening, Mrs Shipley?'

Good? That wasn't quite the way Laura would have chosen to describe it!

'It was just business, Amy,' she responded. 'How's everything been here?'

The older woman smiled. 'Wonderful. He's been fast asleep since before you went out. Not a sound out of him.'

Laura nodded distractedly. 'I think I'll just pop upstairs and check on him before going to bed myself. Thanks for taking over at such short notice this evening, Amy.' She smiled her gratitude.

'Any time, Laura. You know that,' the other woman told her gently. 'I know it can't be easy for you. And he's absolutely fine with me, you know.'

'I do know.' She squeezed Amy's arm gratefully. 'But thank you anyway.'

She made sure she was as quiet as possible going up the stairs, not wanting to wake him, moving with sure steps to the bedroom that adjoined her own.

A nightlight gave a warm glow to the room, allowing Laura to find her way without bumping into or stepping on anything to the rocking-chair that stood beside the bed.

She sat down in the rocking-chair, tears of love welling up in her eyes as she looked down at the sleeping figure in the bed.

Only his head and shoulders were actually visible above the bedcovers, the shoulders narrow, the mouth slightly open in sleep. Dark lashes fanned out over cheeks that glowed pale in the half-light, the hair dark and softly curling against the pillow.

Robert Shipley.

Junior, she inwardly added warmly. He always insisted on the 'Junior.'

But to all who loved him he was Bobby.

Seven years old. Black-haired. Blue-eyed. Mischievous. With a bright enquiring mind.

He was the absolute love of Laura's life...

He was also the reason that her private life had to be kept strictly that, where Liam O'Reilly was concerned.

Because Mary O'Reilly, Liam's mother, although in complete ignorance of the fact, already had her much-wanted grandson.

Except his name wasn't O'Reilly. And it never would be.

Even though Bobby was undoubtedly Liam O'Reilly's son...

CHAPTER FOUR

'—SAYS he wants to come in for a meeting.'

Laura stared up at Perry with unseeing eyes. She hadn't heard anything more he said since he'd come into her office a few minutes ago and actually told her that Liam had rung him this morning.

She swallowed hard. 'Sorry, Perry, what did you say?' She frowned in an effort to concentrate.

She hadn't slept well at all last night, with thoughts going round and round in her head, but none of them really going anywhere.

For over seven years, since she had decided to marry Robert, she had lived in dread of Liam somehow walking back into her life, of his taking one look at Bobby and trying to claim him for his own. Something she would never, ever allow. Liam had given up any rights to his son when he had callously walked out of her life eight years ago.

Of course there was no way he could have known she was pregnant when he left; she hadn't known it herself then. But if Liam had bothered, just once, to contact her, she could have told him the two of them were expecting a child.

Instead, she had read in the newspapers of his marriage to another woman!

Pregnant, alone, terrified, she had hated him with a vengeance, never wanted to set eyes on him ever again.

Time had dulled those feelings, of course. Not least be-

44

cause Robert had been a wonderful husband and father. She owed him everything that she had become.

As time had passed Liam O'Reilly had become a thing of the past, an interlude in her life she could look back at with a certain amount of embarrassment. In retrospect, she could see she had thrown herself at him, had refused to read the signs that would have told her the feelings she'd had for him weren't reciprocated.

Which didn't mean she considered Liam completely blameless in what had ultimately happened; he had done nothing to stop their relationship becoming an intimate one. And being able to look at the situation with adult eyes didn't mean she had forgiven him, or that she ever wanted to see him again either!

But there had been no way she could just ignore that manuscript when Perry had first shown it to her three weeks ago. He was her senior editor and had been presented with a brilliant manuscript, even though he hadn't known the real identity of the author then. He had brought that manuscript to Laura for her immediate attention. There had been no way, without arousing Perry's extreme curiosity, that she could have just ignored it. Even though she had guessed from the first chapter just who the author was!

'Liam O'Reilly has decided to go back to Ireland later this evening,' Perry repeated patiently. 'He wants to come in and talk about a contract before he leaves.'

'Reilly O'Shea,' she corrected lightly, giving herself necessary time to think.

Liam wanted to come here. He might ask to meet the head of Shipley Publishing!

Her.

'What did you tell him?' she asked Perry cautiously.

'That I have a really busy schedule for today, but that I'll call him back.'

Liam had decided to go back to Ireland. Why? She didn't believe for a moment that it had anything to do with their unsatisfactory meeting—from Liam's point of view, that was!—the evening before.

His reasons for leaving London earlier than expected were actually irrelevant; what was important was that his change of plans meant he wanted to come here. Today.

She drew in a sharp breath, determinedly businesslike. 'Are you and David—' her rights manager '—ready to talk contracts with him?'

Perry hesitated. 'Depends who we're talking to, doesn't it?' He frowned, shaking his head. 'This is a really tricky situation, Laura. I'm not sure that you shouldn't deal with it personally.'

That was the very last thing she wanted!

She leant back in her leather chair, every inch the businesswoman in her black trouser suit and white silk blouse. 'Power dressing' Robert had called it, but at twenty-nine, she knew she was considered very young to be the head of a publishing house, and she needed every edge she could get.

'I'm sure you're more than capable of dealing with it yourself, Perry.' She smiled at him confidently as he sat across the desk from her, playing to his ego.

Perry was an ambitious man, who enjoyed his position as senior editor at this prestigious publisher; he would not like having his capabilities questioned.

'Ordinarily, yes,' he sighed. 'But in this case I don't have the first idea how to go about it. I want this manuscript very badly, want O'Reilly's signature on a contract before he has the chance to change his mind or go to another publisher. But how am I supposed to go about that without telling the man I know exactly who he is? Worse, that I want the book published with Liam O'Reilly's name on the cover? I don't want to frighten him off.'

Her smile lacked humour this time. 'He doesn't sound the type that scares easily!'

'Nevertheless, I still think personal input from you at any meeting with him would—'

'Would give him completely the wrong impression of his own importance,' she cut in sharply. 'Perhaps the best thing would be to tell him you're too busy to see him today, after all, Perry. It is very short notice, and—'

'Laura, he's asked to take the manuscript back to Ireland with him if we haven't made him a definite offer by the end of today,' Perry put in quietly, obviously reluctantly. And with very good reason.

Even as Reilly O'Shea—especially as Reilly O'Shea!— this author was behaving with extreme arrogance. New authors could often wait months to hear back from a publisher after submitting a manuscript: the fact that they had contacted Liam—through an impersonal post office box number of course!—after only a matter of weeks should have pleased him, not given him an over-inflated opinion of his own importance! But then, no matter what the author might claim to the contrary, this *was* Liam O'Reilly they were dealing with...

'I know, I know!' Perry stood up impatiently. 'Your first instinct, as mine was, is probably to tell him to go to hell.' He paced the room. 'But I can *feel* the success of this book, Laura. I don't want to lose it,' he added heavily.

'You're sure you aren't biting off a little more than you can chew?' Than Laura could swallow. Publishing Liam's book was one thing—as long as she had as little to do with it, and him, as possible!—but having him dictate terms at this early stage of things was too much. 'He sounds as if he's going to be a difficult man to deal with.'

As she knew only too well. Just that brief hour in his company yesterday evening had shown that, if anything, Liam's arrogance had grown over the years, not diminished.

Which was a little hard to take, in this particular instance, when the man hadn't had a book published for eight years.

Except that, like Perry, she knew *Josie's World*, the whimsical story of a girl growing to maturity in a small Irish village, was so beautifully written that it was going to outsell anything they had every published before.

The problem here was that Liam knew it too!

'Difficult or not,' Perry answered grimly, 'I want that book.'

Laura spoke quickly. 'Then I suggest you discuss terms with him.'

'And if I need to talk to you?'

'Call me,' she answered abruptly. Under no circumstances was he to bring Liam anywhere near her! She glanced at her watch. 'It's ten-thirty now. Ask him to come in and see you at four o'clock.' When she would already have left her office for the day in order to collect Bobby from school.

As Amy had said last night, it wasn't easy for her juggling motherhood with being head of Shipley Publishing. But with help from people like Amy, and a very loyal and reliable level of management at Shipley Publishing, she managed to keep all those balls in the air. If her own personal life seemed to suffer because of it, then it didn't really matter; she already had more than she could ever have hoped for.

'That way you aren't going to look too compliant,' she told Perry encouragingly. 'As for the problem of who you're dealing with; I think his arrogance this morning probably answers that question for you!'

'You're right,' Perry agreed. 'Sorry.' He grimaced. 'I was just thrown there for a few minutes.' He walked purposefully to the door, obviously no longer thrown. 'I'll call him and tell him I can spare him a few minutes at four o'clock.' He paused in the open doorway. 'Wish me luck.'

She nodded, smiling—knowing he was going to need it! Liam was a force to be reckoned with—she was just relieved she wasn't the one who would have to deal with it!

'—told you, Mrs Shipley is busy and— You really can't go in there!' Ruth, her secretary, could be heard protesting agitatedly even as the office door was forcefully opened.

'No?' A sceptical Liam O'Reilly stood arrogantly in that open doorway, dark brows raised as he looked challengingly across the room at Laura as she sat behind the imposing desk in front of the window.

Laura's first thought—stupidly!—was that it was only three o'clock! The man shouldn't have arrived at Shipley Publishing for another hour!

'I'm so sorry, Mrs Shipley.' Ruth, small, plump, red-haired, very efficient at her job, looked crossly indignant at the way Liam had just trampled over her! 'This—gentleman she announced sceptically, 'asked to see you. But as he doesn't have an appointment—'

'And as I told this young—lady,' Liam bit back with the same sarcasm, 'I don't need an appointment to see you.' Again he looked at Laura with those hard, challenging blue eyes.

He most certainly did need an appointment! And if he had asked for one he most certainly wouldn't have got one. Although, in the circumstances, it was a little late in the day to be worrying about that now!

Laura slowly put the pen she had been working with down on the desk-top, ignoring Liam to smile reassuringly at her secretary. 'It's all right, Ruth,' she lied. 'Mr O'Reilly and I are—acquainted.'

Ruth gave the intruder another indignant glare before turning back to Laura. 'If you're sure...?'

She nodded. 'It's fine.'

It was far from fine!

How dared Liam just push his way in here? More to the point, how had he known she was here at all?

'Nice office,' he drawled as Ruth closed the door behind him.

It was a beautiful office; there were oak-panelled book-shelves on three of the wall's supporting copies of past and recent books published by the company. Her own desk was of the same mellowed oak and a plush fitted blue carpet covered the floor.

But, at the same time as Laura acknowledged the luxurious appointments of her office, she knew Liam was no more interested in their surroundings at the moment than she was.

What was he *doing* here?

She eyed him warily as he strode further into the room, blue denims old and faded, grey shirt beneath a loose black jacket. No wonder Ruth had tried to block his path into Laura's office; he hardly looked the part of a successful author, let alone a millionaire!

'Mrs Shipley,' he murmured, almost to himself, it seemed.

Laura stiffened. It wasn't what he had said so much as the way he had said it. Insultingly. Deliberately so, she was sure.

'Mr O'Reilly,' she returned with equal deliberation. 'Or do I mean Mr O'Shea?'

After all, if he now knew who she was, there was absolutely no longer any point in any pretence on her part concerning his own attempt at subterfuge. At least she had only lied by omission—which was no lie at all; Liam had never asked her for her married name!

Blue eyes narrowed as Liam looked her over speculatively.

Which was a little like being studied under a microscope! Laura felt as if, just by looking at her in this way, Liam was trying to discover what else it was he didn't know about her.

'If it's not too stupid a question,' she began when she couldn't stand that cold scrutiny any longer, 'how did you know where to find me?'

'I asked downstairs and was directed to the top floor,' he returned satirically.

'Very funny, Liam,' she said wearily. 'You know very well that isn't what I meant at all!'

'Isn't it?' he replied sharply. 'Tell me, Laura, have you enjoyed the little game you've been playing with me the last two days?' he rasped harshly, blue eyes dark with anger.

'Game?' she echoed dazedly, in no way recovered yet from the shock of his being here, in her office. A place he had no right to be! 'I haven't been playing any games, Liam—'

'No?' he cut in scathingly. 'Yesterday afternoon at the hotel you and Perry Webster gave no indication that the two of you knew each other, and yet you're his employer. Last night, when we met for a drink, you deliberately didn't tell me that you know exactly what I'm doing in London at the moment—'

'Not deliberately,' she interrupted firmly. 'Never that. I simply didn't see the point in—'

'"Didn't see the point"!' Liam repeated with cold fury, moving across the room with deceptively light footsteps.

'I'll tell you what the point is, Laura.' He stood just across the other side of her desk now, leaning forward menacingly as he spoke to her. 'The point is that you deliberately made a fool of me.'

'I did not!' she gasped.

'Oh, yes, Mrs Shipley,' he insisted, 'you did.'

Laura shook her head. 'I told you I was married—'

'But not who you were married to,' Liam scorned.

'What difference does it make who I was married to?' she challenged heatedly. 'I didn't see it bothering you last night when you—'

'Yes?' he taunted softly, suddenly very still. 'When I what?'

'Oh, never mind, Liam,' she dismissed, heated colour in her cheeks now. 'As I see it, you are the one who has been hiding behind another identity, not me!'

'And as I see it,' he returned forcefully, 'you've known from the beginning that I was Reilly O'Shea—and you've used that knowledge to extract a little revenge.'

'A little—!' She was so angry now she couldn't even complete her sentence. 'If you think that's true, Liam, then you must have a very low opinion of me,' she said furiously. 'And an even more inflated opinion of the role you once played in my life!'

They glared at each other wordlessly across the width of the desk for several long minutes. Laura was determined not to be the first to look away, but Liam was equally determined, apparently.

And then the atmosphere between them shifted slightly, changed, no longer charged with anger but with something else entirely.

'Do I?' he finally said.

Laura's gaze was locked with his, her breathing low and shallow. 'Do you what?' she repeated softly.

'Have an over-inflated opinion of what we once meant to each other?' he encouraged huskily.

What they once meant to each other—!

His implication was enough to break the spell. For Laura, at least. She shook her head, her expression derisive. 'I think we covered that quite well last night, Liam—I was an infatuated young student; you were an older, more worldly-wise man, flattered by—'

'I'm well aware of the fact that I am some years older than you, Laura,' he interjected, straightening away from the desk. 'I certainly don't need to keep being reminded of it!'

She was relieved he had moved his overwhelming presence away from her desk, but at the same time she was determined to put their past relationship in perspective. The way that she'd had to do for herself eight years ago, when she had thought her world was falling apart!

'You—'

'But talking of older men,' he continued hardly, blue eyes narrowed again, 'I believe Robert Shipley—'

'I told you last night. I will not discuss Robert with you. Under any circumstances,' she added tautly as Liam would have spoken, her eyes flashing a warning.

'Robert Shipley was fifty-three when you married him,' Liam continued, undaunted.

Laura half rose from her chair. 'I—'

'And fifty-eight when he died two years ago and left you as his widow and sole heir,' Liam finished softly.

Laura dropped back into the leather chair, the colour draining from her cheeks.

Every thing that Liam said was true but one.

Robert *had* been fifty-three when they'd married seven and a half years ago. And he had only been fifty-eight when he'd died five years later. Leaving her his widow.

But Liam was wrong about her being Robert's sole heir; the houses and half his fortune were hers, yes. But the other half of the money, and Shipley Publishing, she only held in trust. Robert Shipley Junior—Bobby, Liam's own son— was actually heir to all of that...

CHAPTER FIVE

'YOU *have* been doing your homework, haven't you?' she said calmly, determined not to show any signs of the inner panic she felt at his disclosures.

He had been doing his homework; but not well enough if he didn't know about Robert Shipley Junior...

'You still haven't told me how you came to realise I'm now Laura Shipley,' she prompted, dark brows raised over curious eyes.

Liam shrugged. 'It wasn't that difficult. The taxi you took home last night is based at the hotel. I saw the driver this morning, told him you had left something behind when you left last night, and asked him the address at which he had dropped you so that I could return it.'

Laura drew in a harsh breath. 'As easy as that?' she bit out sharply, wishing she'd had the forethought to have Paul drive her to and from the hotel last night. Except she had already dismissed him for the day when Liam had telephoned and asked to meet her...

'As easy as that.' Liam nodded his satisfaction. 'After that it was a simple matter of making a few enquiries about the occupant of a certain house in Knightsbridge.'

It gave her an uneasy feeling to know that it really had been that easy. She had thought she was safe, protected, and now she felt more than a little vulnerable.

'You can imagine my surprise when the occupant turned out to be one Laura Shipley, owner of Shipley Publishing,' Liam explained hardly.

Surprise sounded the least of his emotions!

'And here you are,' she said brightly. 'I believe you have an appointment with Perry in forty minutes or so—'

'Forget Perry,' Liam rasped. 'It's you I came here to see—'

'I'm sorry, Liam, but I'm afraid I have another appointment in twenty minutes, and as I have to drive there—'

'Cancel it,' he grated harshly.

Her eyes widened incredulously at his arrogance. 'I most certainly will not,' she replied indignantly.

Laura was due to meet Bobby from school today. She usually took him to school in the mornings, and Amy collected him in the afternoons, but on Tuesdays, Amy's day off, Laura always collected Bobby too. There was no way she would ever be late in doing that, let alone just send Paul to collect him in the car.

Although she had no intention of sharing any of that information with Liam!

Liam moved to sit down in the chair facing her desk, his long length slouched against the leather, his eyes narrowed as he studied her thoughtfully. 'You take all of this quite seriously, don't you?' he finally said. 'Shipley Publishing,' he added as she looked at him blankly.

Laura's thoughts had all been on her son, and it took a moment for her to realise exactly what Liam had said. 'Of course I take it seriously,' she snapped. 'You obviously considered this publishing house good enough for your manuscript,' she pointed out.

He looked over at her with scornful eyes. 'That was before I realised you ran it.'

She bridled at his deliberate insult. 'And what difference does that make?' she challenged.

His mouth twisted. 'A lot!'

She drew in a sharp breath. 'You've signed nothing yet,

Liam, and are under no obligation—as we aren't—to take this any further. In view of that—'

'In view of nothing, Laura,' he cut in forcefully. 'What did you think of *Josie's World*?' He watched her with narrowed eyes. 'And don't tell me you haven't read it—because I won't believe you.'

'One thing about you hasn't changed in eight years, Liam—you're just as arrogant as you ever were!' she said disgustedly.

He remained unmoved by her outburst, his face expressionless as he continued to look at her. 'Well?'

Laura sighed. 'I'm sure you're aware that *Josie's World* is a brilliantly written, wonderfully emotional book.'

'Is it?'

She looked at him sharply. For the first time since they had met again yesterday she heard a note of uncertainty in Liam's voice...

Did he really not know how good his book was?

She could see anxiety in those deep blue eyes now, tension about those sculptured lips as he waited for her answer.

Could it be, that after an absence of eight years, Liam had actually lost confidence in his ability to judge the worth of his own writing? It wasn't an inconceivable idea. It was just totally unexpected from a man with Liam's arrogance!

But she could see from the stiff set of his shoulders, the tension that emanated from him, that her answer to his question was very important to him.

Part of her, she inwardly admitted, wanted to play down the brilliance of the manuscript he had presented to them, if only to wipe some of the remaining arrogance off that handsome face. It might also make Perry's job easier later if she played down how good *Josie's World* was...

But another part of her, the entirely truthful part, couldn't do that, not even if she did feel Liam needed to be taken down a peg or two. In the face of his obvious—to her!—professional uncertainty, to negate the brilliance of his manuscript would not only be cruel in the extreme, it would be dishonest.

Liam might bring out a lot of emotions in her, but dishonesty was certainly not one of them!

'It is,' she confirmed abruptly, shifting some papers on her desk so that she didn't actually have to look at him and see the look of triumph she was sure would be on his face now. 'There's a problem with the name of the author, of course—'

'How long did it take you to realise I had written it?' Liam interrupted interestedly.

The first chapter. The first page. The first *paragraph*.

'Not long,' she responded carefully. 'Perry believes the subterfuge is because of a desire on your part not to repeat what happened eight years ago...? The excess publicity, et cetera...' She looked at him questioningly.

Liam gave a slight inclination of his head. 'You have a very bright-senior editor there, Laura,' he drawled dryly.

'I like to think so,' she agreed. 'In view of your obvious satisfaction with his capabilities, I'm sure you will have no problem dealing together—'

'Only the one,' Liam cut in softly.

Laura eyed him warily now, not liking the gentleness of that tone at all. 'Which is?'

'I—' He broke off as the telephone rang on her desk. 'You had better take that,' he advised. 'It's probably your watch-dog, Ruth, checking that I haven't strangled you!'

Laura gave him a withering glance before picking up the receiver, colour entering her cheeks as she discovered that Ruth was indeed the caller. But not to check on whether Laura had been strangled by Liam!

'I'll be right out,' she told her secretary abruptly before

ringing off, looking across at Liam as she did so. 'My car is waiting downstairs,' she informed him, standing up. 'I'm sure Ruth will be happy to provide you with a cup of coffee while you wait for your appointment with Perry at four o'clock.'

Liam also stood up, instantly dwarfing Laura. 'And I'm sure that the only thing Ruth would be happy to provide me with is the door! Besides, I have no intention of seeing Perry at four o'clock—or any other time.'

Laura's wariness returned. 'You've decided to go to another publisher?''

From Shipley Publishing's point of view, she would be very sorry if that were the case. But from a personal point of view...? She could only feel relief at having the possibility of seeing Liam on a regular basis effectively removed!

'Not at all,' he dismissed. 'I've just decided I would prefer to have you as my editor rather than Perry Webster.'

Laura stared at him with one very green eye and one very blue one. '*You*—have—decided!' she finally managed to gasp, shaking her head dazedly. 'I hate to be the one to break this to you, Liam—'

'I have the feeling you don't hate it at all,' he drawled in reply. 'But whatever it is you hate, Laura, I suggest you save it for when we meet again in the morning; you have an appointment in—ten minutes.' He adjusted the time after a quick glance at the watch on his right wrist.

She was going to be late in getting to the school if she didn't leave now!

But Liam's statement of a few minutes ago was so—so unbelievable that she felt rooted to the spot. Just who did he think he was? The obvious answer to that was Liam O'Reilly, but his name, prestigious though it might be in the literary world, did not give him the right to dictate terms to her. Least of all who his editor was going to be! If he really didn't feel he could work with Perry, then there were plenty of other editors at Shipley he could choose from—though they did not include her!

'I thought you were returning to Ireland this evening?' she queried as she picked up her shoulder-bag.

'I was,' Liam confirmed, walking over to the door with her.

'What happened to change your plans?' As if she really needed to ask that!

Since his telephone call to Perry this morning Liam had found out that *she* was Shipley Publishing—and he was enjoying playing the cat-and-mouse game with her that he had initially accused her of playing with him. Well, that stopped right now!

'Never mind,' she said suddenly. 'I really do have to go now—'

'Could you drop me off somewhere?' Liam suggested sardonically.

'No, I couldn't!' Her face was red from anger now. 'Liam—'

'In that case, before I go I'll make an appointment with Watch-dog Ruth for the two of us to meet tomorrow morning,' he told her unconcernedly.

Laura paused with her hand on the door. 'Liam, I have no intention of having a meeting with you tomorrow morning, or indeed any other time,' she said frustratedly, all the while aware of the time ticking away. 'Perry is more than capable of dealing with any queries you may have—'

'Not the ones I want answers to,' Liam put in softly.

Laura gave him another sharp look, not liking the way this unexpected meeting had gone at all. But she really did not have the time to deal with this just now; she had Bobby to think of.

'Make what appointments you like, Liam,' she advised him impatiently. 'But I will have nothing to say to you in the morning that I haven't already said.'

Liam gave her a considering look. 'Is he important to you?' he finally asked consideringly.

She gave him a startled look. If it hadn't been for the fact that she had to leave immediately she would have made sure Liam was fully aware of exactly how this situation lay! As it was... 'Who?' she prompted irritably.

He folded his arms across the width of his chest. 'The man you're going off to meet—and don't say it isn't a man,' he stated, as she would have spoken. 'I recognise that flush in your cheeks, that glow in those incredibly beautiful eyes, only too well.'

'You do?' she said sceptically.

'I most certainly do,' Liam rasped. 'You always glowed like this when you were excited or pleased about something.'

She didn't want to hear how she looked when she was excited or pleased—or to remember the occasions when Liam must have seen her in that particular state.

'Goodbye, Liam,' she told him with blazing dismissal, wrenching open the door to hurry from the office without a backward glance, giving Ruth a brief wave before she hurried out to the lift and downstairs to the waiting car.

But she couldn't bring herself to relax as Paul drove in the direction of Bobby's school, aware that she was cutting things very fine for picking her son up on time. Secure and confident as Bobby was generally, he was still only seven, and he tended to become anxious if there was no one there to meet him when the school bell rang at the end of the day.

'With a minute to spare,' Paul told her with satisfaction as he pulled the car into the school car park.

'Thanks, Paul,' Laura told him with relief, before hurrying off to Bobby's classroom.

Liam had said she looked pleased and excited, but he had obviously mistaken the reason for those emotions. She was always pleased to be with Bobby, and in his case her excitement was actually maternal pride.

She smiled with that love and pride as she watched her son through the classroom window as he packed his books away for the day. The tallest in his class, he was a very handsome little boy, dark hair curling slightly, blue eyes bright and alert, his features still showing signs of babyhood.

Liam's son...

Laura frowned as she acknowledged the likeness between father and son. It wasn't just that their colouring was the same; Bobby had a certain proud bearing in his stance, and was obviously going to be as tall as his natural father.

For the first time, as she watched her son unobserved, she pondered the question of whether or not one day— when Bobby was old enough for Liam not to be able to even attempt to have a share in his son's childhood or teenage years!—she would have to tell him about his real father.

For her own sake, she answered a definite no; after the pain of the past she couldn't contemplate sharing even Bobby's adulthood with Liam! From Bobby's point of view she was less sure. He had loved Robert as his own father, been devastated at his 'daddy's' death two years ago. But the truth of the matter was Bobby's real father was still very much alive... Was she right to deny him all knowledge of that?

Why did Liam have to come back into their lives in this way and present her with this dilemma?

'Why are you frowning, Mummy?' Bobby asked curiously at her side, having joined her without her even noticing, and with his hand now nestling comfortably in hers as he looked up at her.

She determinedly pushed away her disquieting thoughts, smiling down at her son. 'Was I, darling?' she parried, taking his school bag from him. 'I was actually just wondering if you would like to go out and have a burger for tea?'

As she had expected—and hoped!—the thought of going out for tea instead of going straight home totally diverted Bobby from the fact that she had initially looked less than happy.

She pushed thoughts of Liam away into a locked compartment in her mind. She intended keeping it that way. If she knew Liam—and she was sure she did!—then he would have made that appointment to see her in the morning; she could think about him again then.

Easier said than done! She had managed to get through tea at the burger restaurant, had bathed Bobby at home, done his homework with him, read him a story after she'd put him to bed, all without allowing a single thought of Liam to interfere. She wasn't so lucky now she was alone in her own bedroom later that evening!

Eight years ago Liam, a lecturer when he wasn't actually writing, had come to her university to give a talk on modern literature. She remembered that the hall had been packed that day, all of the students, having read at least one Liam O'Reilly book, now curious to see and listen to the man himself.

Laura hadn't heard a word he'd said!

As soon as Liam had stepped on to the podium she had been mesmerised—by the way he looked, the way he moved, the soft, lilting seduction of his voice.

The lecture had passed in a daze for Laura, and she had

still been lost in daydreams of the handsome author when she'd gone to the refectory for her lunch, picking uninterestedly at the pasta salad she hadn't remembered choosing, sipping lukewarm coffee she had forgotten to put any sugar in.

'Did you know there's a contact-lens in your tea?'

Those words! Ill-fated, if she had but known it. But at the time all she had cared about was the fact that the man she'd been daydreaming about had just spoken to her, the lilting attraction of his voice unmistakable.

Her cheeks had been fiery red as she'd looked up to see Liam O'Reilly standing beside her table with his own laden luncheon tray, and her breath had caught in her throat as she'd gazed up into the rugged handsomeness of his face.

She'd moistened suddenly dry lips. 'I don't drink tea,' she returned shyly. 'And I don't wear contact lenses either,' she added, well aware that he had to be referring to the differing colours of her eyes.

He grinned down at her. 'I know. Oh, not that you don't drink tea,' he explained as he put his tray down next to hers on the table. 'I meant the contact lenses; I couldn't help but notice the incredibly unusual beauty of your eyes at the lecture earlier.'

Those eyes widened now, even as she swallowed hard. 'You—saw me there?'

He grinned. 'Second row, third seat in. Mind if I join you?' He indicated the otherwise empty seats around the table at which she sat.

'Er—no. I mean, yes. No, of course I don't mind if you join me,' she corrected self-consciously.

All the time at the lecture, when she had been gazing at him like some besotted idiot, he had actually noticed her too! Or maybe he had noticed her *because* she'd been gazing at him like a besotted idiot...?

'I enjoyed the lecture,' she told him nervously as he lowered his lean length into the chair beside hers.

He gave her a sideways glance, a smile still playing about those sculptured lips. 'Did you?' he drawled teasingly. As if he were well aware of the fact that she hadn't heard a word he said!

'Don't look so stricken,' he advised gently as the colour first came and then as quickly receded from her face, leaving her very pale, her eyes huge pools of colour in that paleness. 'You weren't the only one who looked ready to fall asleep,' he assured her humourously. 'I'm well aware that for most of you a degree is the only goal, that a lot of the work that precedes obtaining that degree can be boring in the extreme—'

'You weren't in the least boring!' she burst out protestingly as she realised he thought that was the reason for her inattentiveness. 'I—I was fascinated,' she told him truthfully—even if that fascination hadn't exactly been with what he was saying!

'Prove it,' he invited, taking a mouthful of the chicken sandwich he had chosen for his lunch.

She swallowed hard, eyeing him warily. If he intended going through a question-and-answer session on his talk that morning she might as well own up to the truth right now; until she had chance to look at a friend's notes she wouldn't have a clue what he had actually talked about!

'Have dinner with me this evening?' he asked lightly.

Dinner...? Liam O'Reilly wanted her to have dinner with him?

She stared at him, trying to tell from his expression exactly what he meant by such an invitation. He looked back at her with questioning blue eyes—eyes that told her nothing!

Laura moistened her lips again, frowning up at him, her uncertainty mirrored on her face.

Liam chuckled softly. 'Is it such a difficult thing to decide?' he teased.

'I—er—no,' she answered hesitantly. 'I just— Why on earth would you invite me out to dinner with you?' Her frown deepened.

Dark brows rose over deep blue eyes. 'Because I've never met anyone before with such incredible, beautiful, unusual eyes,' he confessed.

Laura grimaced. 'I think you're playing with me, Mr O'Reilly,' she said heavily.

'That's your prerogative,' he conceded huskily. 'But the dinner invitation stands. And the name's Liam.'

'Laura,' she returned shortly. 'Laura Carter.'

'Well, now that we've formally introduced ourselves— would you care to have dinner with me this evening, Laura?' He quirked dark brows once more.

'Yes,' she answered quickly—before she could give herself time to think too much about it and say no!

She had no idea why he had invited her out to dinner— but she knew exactly why she wanted to accept; he was just as mesmerising on a one-to-one basis as he had been on the podium earlier. In fact—more so!

He nodded. 'And make sure you bring your appetite with you this evening; I can't abide women who pick at their food.' He looked pointedly at her almost untouched salad.

By the end of that first evening together Laura was no nearer knowing the reason for Liam's invitation than she had been when he'd made it.

They had talked about any number of things—books, art, Ireland, what Laura intended doing with her degree—always supposing she got it!—when her course finished next summer—but not by word or deed had Liam made even the remotest romantic move on her.

He had, however, asked to see her again.

And again.

In fact, within a few very short weeks Laura found herself spending most of her spare time with him, helping to type out any lectures he might have to give, often accompanying him to those lectures too, immensely proud of the fact that she was obviously with him.

Over those next few months she was to learn a lot of things Liam 'couldn't abide' about women. They included women being clingingly possessive. Women who talked too much. Women who didn't have an opinion of their own. Women without a sense of humour. Women who giggled inanely. Extrovert women. Introvert women. Women who were too fat. Women who were too thin. The list seemed endless.

By the time she had listened to all the things Liam didn't like about women, and had desperately tried to make sure she was none of those things in order that he should continue to spend time with her, Laura had had no idea who or what she was any more!

And now, with his announcement earlier today that he intended her to be the editor of his new book, Liam was obviously still trying to call all the shots!

Well, this was eight years on. And she knew exactly who she was now. She was Laura Shipley. Widow of Robert. Mother of Bobby. Trustee owner of Shipley Publishing.

One thing she most assuredly was not, and never would be, was Liam O'Reilly's editor!

CHAPTER SIX

'WHAT on earth do you think you're doing?'

Liam glanced at her over the top of the business diary he had picked up from her desk and was now looking at. 'Making sure you don't have another prior engagement to escape to this morning,' he finally drawled in satisfaction, snapping the diary shut before dropping it down.

Laura glared at him frustratedly. As he had said he would, Liam had made his appointment to see her this morning; in fact, he was her first appointment for the day. Which didn't augur too well for the rest of it!

'Satisfied?' she snapped impatiently, placing the diary neatly back in its original place.

Liam raised mocking brows. 'Hardly,' he replied, dropping down into the chair that faced hers, wearing his usual denims, shirt and a black jacket. 'Now perhaps we can continue our conversation of yesterday,' he said, looking across at her with a smile.

Not exactly. As he had said, they had last spoken yesterday; she had had over eighteen hours to recover from the shock of having him invade her office in the way that he had. She had also spoken with Perry when she'd come in the first thing this morning, knew that Liam had cancelled his meeting with him yesterday afternoon...

'I believe we concluded that particular conversation, Liam,' she came back calmly. 'In the circumstances, it was very unwise of you not to keep your appointment with Perry yesterday,' she added coolly.

Liam arched dark brows. 'That sounds suspiciously like a threat to me, Mrs Shipley,' he returned softly.

She was not in the best of humour this morning, had slept very badly after those thoughts of her early relationship with Liam eight years ago had come flooding back with such clarity. She certainly wasn't in the mood to deal with any more of Liam's games.

'Take it as you like, Liam,' she sighed. 'I told you yesterday. I run this company; I no longer have the time to be an editor too—'

'Make me the exception,' he cut in.

She looked at him incredulously; he was the very last person she would make an exception for—in anything!

She sighed, shaking her head. 'No.'

'Why not?'

'*Why not?*' she spluttered. 'It must be obvious why not!' she said exasperatedly.

'Because we were once lovers?' he mused consideringly. 'But that was years ago, Laura. A lot has happened since then. We've both been married to other people, for one thing—happily or not so happily.' He grimaced with feeling. 'Surely you aren't afraid that history might repeat itself, are you, Laura?'

'Certainly not!' she gasped indignantly. The only thing she was afraid of was that he would discover she had a son—his son!

The only thing!

He shrugged broad shoulders. 'Then where's the problem?'

'Liam, are you learning-impaired? Why do I have to keep repeating myself? I—'

'No longer edit any of the books yourself,' he finished dryly. 'I did hear that the first time you said it. As I recall, I asked you to make me the exception. Laura,' he continued smoothly as she would have spoken, 'make no mistake. I *will* go to another publisher.'

She drew in a sharp breath, having given this alternative some thought last night too—when she hadn't been remembering what it had been like between them in the beginning, eight years ago!

To pass up the chance to publish the new Liam O'Reilly book would be madness from a purely business point of view, she knew, but not to the extreme where it would damage the company. After all, they already had a number of highly successful authors.

No, it wouldn't be the end of the world if Shipley Publishing were to lose this particular novel to another publisher—it just wouldn't make sense to anyone but herself! Not that she particularly cared about that either; she was well past the stage of explaining herself to anyone.

No, it was none of that that made her hesitate in telling Liam to go ahead and find himself another publisher...

It was the wrong construction Liam had already put on her actions—that she was in some way frightened of working with him—that caused her to balk at telling him to go, and take his manuscript with him. She already knew there was no way that history would repeat itself where the two of them were concerned!

'That sounds suspiciously like a threat to *me*, Liam.' She repeated his own words of a few minutes ago.

He shrugged. 'That's probably because it is one,' he acknowledged suavely. 'Laura—' He sat forward, his expression intense as he glared at her across the width of the desk. 'I would like the two of us to work together on this. Won't you at least give it a try?' he encouraged.

When all else fails, use the charm, Laura inwardly derided. The fact that that charm had once worked on her very effectively did not mean it would do so now!

'Or is it that you don't think you're up to the job?' he added tautingly.

Her lips curved into a humourless smile—the charm hadn't lasted long! 'Nice try, Liam,' she responded. 'But I believe I have already mentioned that after I left university I became a book editor...?'

'So you did.' He nodded. 'And would that editing job have been here at Shipley Publishing?'

Laura didn't like the mildness of his tone. 'And if it was?'

'Within a few months you ended up marrying the owner of the company.'

Laura stiffened resentfully. 'I don't think I care for the implication behind your words—'

'What implication would that be?' Liam prompted, again mildly.

Her mouth tightened. 'I'm sure you're well aware of what I'm referring to. But you know nothing about my life, Liam, either now or in the past; I suggest we leave it that way.'

'I'm interested, that's all.'

She gave a short laugh. 'That interest is doing nothing to solve the immediate problem.'

'Which is...?'

She had forgotten his habit of being deliberately obtuse when it suited him. It was just as annoying now as it had been eight years ago!

'Agreement on an editor for you,' she reminded him impatiently.

'I've already told you my preference—'

'And I've already told *you* it's completely out of the question!' she interrupted briskly.

'It's stalemate, then.'

She drew in a quick breath. 'Perhaps you should take your novel to another publisher, Liam—'

'You little coward! He stood up forcefully, glaring at her with glittering blue eyes, at once dominating the office with his sheer size.

Laura stood up too, tension in every inch of her slender body. 'How dare you?' She was breathing hard in her agitation.

'How dare I?' he repeated scathingly. 'I'll tell you how I dare—'

'Laura, I— Oops!' A confused Perry stood in the doorway, grimacing his awkwardness at having apparently interrupted a heated conversation, his brief knock obviously having passed unheard between the two adversaries.

Because that was what they were, Laura inwardly acknowledged angrily. She couldn't even be in the same room with Liam without her hackles rising!

'You asked me to join you at nine-thirty,' Perry reminded her uncomfortably.

She had asked her senior editor to join them at that time because she had thought—erroneously, as it turned out!— that she and Liam might have come to some agreement about his editor by then. She had forgotten how completely unreasonable Liam could be when he wanted to be!

'Do come in, Perry,' she invited, forcing some of the tension from her body as she smiled welcomingly across the room at him.

'Do *not* come in, Perry,' Liam told the other man grimly. 'I'm sure it was very nice of Laura to invite you to join us—' he rasped his displeasure '—but the two of us haven't finished talking yet,' he added with a challenging glance in her direction.

'Oh, I think we have, Mr O'Reilly,' she told him just as

determinedly. 'More than finished,' she concluded forcefully.

Liam continued to look at her for several long seconds, and then he gave a barely perceptible shrug before turning back to the younger man. 'It appears you had better come in, after all, Perry. Although I should warn you,' he continued softly as the younger man did exactly that, closing the door behind him, 'some of what you might hear in the next few minutes may come as something of a surprise to you.'

Laura didn't miss the warning in his voice—she would be being particularly stupid if she had! Well, two could play at that game!

'I think Liam is referring to the fact that he and I knew each other several years ago,' she told Perry smoothly, indicating that he should sit down in the chair next to the one Liam had occupied until a few minutes ago. 'Perry already knows that, Liam,' she said as she resumed her own seat behind the desk. 'It was the reason I was able to recognise you at the hotel two days ago,' she reminded him.

Liam's mouth tightened at the memory of that meeting, and the construction—with hindsight—he had put on her behaviour. 'Very Sherlock Holmes,' he grated.

She held up her palms. 'Why don't you sit down again, Liam?' she invited. 'I have just finished explaining to Liam that you will make him a wonderful editor.' She smiled warmly at Perry.

'And I have just finished explaining to Laura,' Liam said forcefully, making no move to resume his own seat, 'that, wonderful as you might be—' his mouth twisted derisively as he looked at the other man '—if I decide to sign a contract for Shipley Publishing to publish my book, I have already chosen my own editor.'

Laura looked at him frustratedly. He wasn't going to budge an inch!

'You have?' Perry looked completely puzzled.

'Liam is—' Laura broke off with a frown as the telephone began to ring on her desk. She had asked Ruth to hold all her calls until after Liam had gone. Which meant that this was a call Ruth had decided couldn't wait. 'Excuse me,' she murmured, and took the call, the colour draining from her cheeks as she listened.

Bobby! Oh, dear Heaven, Bobby!

'I'll be right there,' she managed to choke, before slamming down the receiver and standing up. 'I have to go,' she told the two men distractedly, picking up her bag and hurrying over to the door.

'Laura, whatever—?'

'I can't talk to you any more just now, Liam,' she told him impatiently. 'Don't you understand? I have to go!' Her beloved Bobby was hurt, needed her! He had fallen down some stairs at school, was on his way to the hospital right now.

Steely fingers gripped her upper arm, spinning her round. 'No, I don't understand,' Liam ground out. 'What on earth is wrong?' He groaned concernedly, as his narrowed gaze took in her white face and frantic expression.

Laura shook her head. 'I don't have the time for this, Liam,' she snapped. Bobby was all that was important to her now. 'Talk to Perry or don't talk to Perry,' she added with impatient dismissal as Liam seemed about to protest again. 'Take your manuscript to another publisher if that's what you want to do.'

Liam's hand dropped away from her arm. 'You don't care either way. Is that it?' he rasped.

She glared up at him with glittering eyes. 'No, I don't care either way,' she confirmed, before turning to almost run from the room, her only thought now to get to Bobby as quickly as possible.

It had been the headmaster of Bobby's school on the telephone. Her son had fallen down some stairs, seemed to be in considerable pain, and an ambulance had been called. Laura's only concern was to get to the hospital as quickly as she could.

She arrived at the hospital at the same time as Bobby did, the teacher who had accompanied him in the ambulance at his side as he was wheeled into the Accident and Emergency Department on a trolley.

A trolley that was far too big for such a little boy, making him look younger and more defenceless than usual...

Tears filled Laura's eyes as she hurried over to him, having to blink back those tears as she saw the look of relief on Bobby's face as he saw her there, his own tears immediately starting to fall. Laura knew it wouldn't help anyone to have the two of them in floods of tears!

'I bumped my head and my knee hurts, Mommy,' Bobby sobbed into her neck as she held him close to her.

'Have you thought that there's probably a dent or two in the stairs now, too?' she attempted to tease, and was rewarded for her attempt at levity with a teary smile from her son.

'I never thought of that,' Bobby giggled, obviously less distressed now that his mummy was here.

She ruffled the dark silkiness of his hair as she smiled down at him. Bobby was so precious to her that from the time he was a baby what she had really wanted to do was gather him up in her arms, wrap him in cotton-wool and never let any harm come to him.

Robert had been the one to show her she couldn't do that, that it wouldn't be fair to Bobby to deny him all the fun and games that all little boys enjoyed.

Robert had also been the one to encourage her to go back to work once Bobby was old enough for kindergarten, and by the time Bobby had begun 'big' school, with Robert only recently dead, she had been more than grateful to have Shipley Publishing to occupy her time and thoughts.

But she did wish that Robert were at her side now, if only to help guide her through the pain of seeing their son hurt. It was at times like this that she missed Robert the most...

To Laura's relief, an X-ray on Bobby's knee showed that he hadn't actually broken anything when he fell, just badly bruised it. Another X-ray showed that his skull had sustained no fracture either. Although the bump on the head necessitated him spending the night in hospital, just in case there were any signs of concussion.

'You can stay with him, of course,' the doctor told her smilingly.

She had never intended doing anything else. Bobby was seven years old, had never spent a night away from home in his life, let alone in the awesome surroundings of a hospital ward. Of course Laura would stay with him!

'I'm just going to pop home and get us some night things,' she explained to her son shortly after helping him to drink his tea.

Bobby was well settled into his private room on the children's ward by now, the nurse having obligingly put his favourite video on the overhead television attached to the wall. It seemed as good a time as any for Laura to leave for a short time to collect the things they were going to need for their overnight stay.

'And Teddy?' he prompted, his face still pale from the shock of his fall.

The teddy bear, Bobby's usual night companion, rather tattered now, had been a gift to Laura when Robert had first visited her in the hospital after Bobby was born. It had been in his cot as a baby and continued to share his bed now that he was growing up, had become even more precious to him since Robert's death two years ago.

'And Teddy, of course,' Laura assured Bobby with a choke, once again having to blink back the tears.

Although he liked to think he was the man of the house now that his daddy was gone, Bobby was still such a baby, Laura acknowledged tearfully on her drive back to the house. Never more so that when he was hurt and helpless, as he was now. Oh, how she wished Robert were here!

But sitting in the back of a taxi, crying her eyes out because of her son's pain and the loss of her husband, was not the Laura Shipley she thought she had become, she acknowledged sadly. In fact, these moments of weakness were not a good idea, she decided, even as the tears wouldn't seem to stop flowing.

'Here you are, love.' The middle-aged taxi-driver stuck his hand through the open window between the front and back of the vehicle, holding out a tissue to her. 'Have a good blow,' he advised gently. 'You'll feel much better.'

Laura took the tissue, noisily following his advice. Goodness knew what the poor man was thinking, having just picked her up from outside the hospital!

'Thank you,' she told him gratefully, this stranger's kindness making her feel tearful all over again.

Pull yourself together, Laura, she told herself firmly as she paid off the taxi-driver outside the house, having assured the poor man that everything was fine. Bobby had had an accident, yes, but he was going to be all right. A bit battered and bruised, perhaps, but all right.

'Oh, Mrs Shipley—Laura.' A rather breathless Amy came down the hallway to greet her as she let herself into the house. 'How's Master Bobby?' She frowned her concern as she took in Laura's tear-streaked face, Laura having telephoned her from the hospital earlier and explained the situation to her.

Laura smiled reassuringly. 'Asking for Teddy.'

'Thank goodness.' Amy sighed her relief. 'Er—there's a man waiting in the sitting room to see you,' she added anxiously, obviously extremely flustered by this strange turn of events. 'I told him you were out, and that I had no idea when you would be back, but he insisted on waiting for your return. He simply wouldn't leave.' She frowned her consternation.

There was only one man that Laura knew who had that sort of arrogance—Liam O'Reilly!

'You didn't tell him where I was, did you?' she prompted sharply. She didn't want Liam even to know of Bobby's existence, let alone have the chance to start adding two and two together and come up with the correct answer!

'Certainly not,' Amy assured her indignantly. 'He says his name is Liam O'Reilly.' She confirmed Laura's suspicion. 'I don't care what his name is; the man is altogether too fond of having his own way, if you ask me.'

Even though she was less than pleased at this interruption, Laura couldn't help but smile at her housekeeper's unflattering first impression of Liam. As Laura knew only too well, Amy's second impression of him was unlikely to be any more complimentary!

'How long has he been here?' Laura kept her voice deliberately low, not wanting to let Liam know she was home just yet; she needed to tidy herself and redo her make-up before she faced Liam.

'An hour or so,' Amy frowned. 'I took him in a tray of tea about half an hour ago.' She sniffed dismissively. 'After all, he could be pocketing all the family silver in there, for all I know!'

'Highly unlikely,' Laura assured her with an affectionate smile. 'I agree with you about his arrogance, but I don't think he's a thief! I'll just go upstairs and—'

'Laura...?'

She turned at the sound of Liam's husky drawl, instantly irritated at his intrusion into the home she had shared with her husband and now shared with only Bobby, as well as at the fact that she hadn't had time to tidy herself before confronting him.

'Thanks, Amy.' She gave the housekeeper's arm a reassuring squeeze before turning back to Liam. 'I believe you wanted to see me?' she acknowledged coolly, dark brows raised.

He gave an arrogant inclination of his head, still dressed—as she was!—as he had been during their meeting this morning.

Goodness, that seemed a long time ago, Laura inwardly acknowledged. So much had happened since that time. She felt emotionally drained after the upset of Bobby's accident and the time spent at the hospital with him, trying to be cheerful when she had really felt like crying. She couldn't have felt less like talking to Liam!

'Could you bring me some coffee?' she prompted Amy gently, before preceding Liam into the sitting room.

The soft click of the latch told her he had closed the door firmly behind them.

'You look terrible.'

Laura turned again at the harshly made criticism, glaring across at Liam as he stood beside the closed door. How dared he come here, invading her home, refusing to leave, and then insult her the moment he saw her?

If he wasn't so selfish, if he hadn't been eight years ago, then he would have been sharing her distress over their son today! Instead of that, all he could do was stand there and be rude and insulting!

'Thank you for those few kind words,' she returned caustically. 'Now, what do you want?' she demanded abruptly.

He didn't answer, didn't move, just stood there looking at her, his gaze narrowed, a contemptuous twist to his lips.

Laura, her nerves already frayed to breaking point, withstood his critical gaze as best she could, knowing that the tears were still dangerously close. The last thing she wanted was to cry in front of Liam. He had no right to be here, let alone—let alone—

'He must be really something,' Liam finally said.

She swallowed hard. 'He?'

'The man you rushed off to see this morning,' he bit out contemptuously. 'The man you've apparently spent the day with.' His gaze sharpened on the paleness of her face and he took several steps towards her. 'The man who's made you cry...' he added slowly, the evidence of her recent tears obviously unmistakable now that he was standing only a couple of feet away from her. 'Laura what on earth—?'

'Ah, the coffee.' She turned gratefully as the door opened and Amy entered carrying the coffee tray, with a plate of sandwiches beside the single cup; obviously her housekeeper did not intend Liam to have the mistaken impression he was in the least welcome here! 'Thank you, Amy.' Laura smiled with gratitude, sitting down to pour the rich brew into the cup, biting gratefully into one of the chicken sandwiches as she did so.

She had been drinking coffee from a vending machine all day, had had absolutely nothing to eat, so Amy's coffee and sandwiches tasted like nectar to her. They also, thankfully, helped to eliminate her tearfulness. Having even slightly battered defences when around Liam was not a good idea!

'Now.' Laura sat back after eating the sandwich and drinking half a cup of coffee. 'You were saying?' She eyed Liam challengingly.

He gave an inclination of his head. 'I was about to ask you why you bother with a man who can reduce you to this state?' His eyes swept over her tear-stained dishevelled appearance.

She looked back at him unflinchingly, refreshed, her self-confidence back in place. 'That's easy to explain, Liam.' She smiled as she thought of her beloved son. 'I love him.'

A nerve pulsed in the hard column of his throat, the blue gaze suddenly icy. 'You thought you loved me once,' he reminded her harshly.

Her smile widened. 'As I've already told you—'

'That was before you learnt to tell the gold from the dross,' Liam finished grimly.

Her brows rose mockingly. 'My, my, you do have a good memory,' she drawled, picking up another sandwich and biting into it hungrily.

'Where you're concerned, yes!' he barked.

Laura shook her head ruefully. 'I somehow find that difficult to believe, Liam. In fact, until our encounter in the hotel a couple of days ago, I doubt you had even given me a thought for the last eight years!'

His mouth tightened at her deliberate taunt. 'You—'

'How did you conclude your meeting with Perry this morning?' she interrupted in a brisk businesslike tone; she didn't want to know whether or not Liam had ever thought of her in those eight intervening years!

His lips twisted. 'You mean, is he my editor or not?' Liam paused. 'Not,' he replied tightly at her confirming nod.

Laura gave a heavy sigh. 'I'm sorry about that,' she said with genuine regret; *Josie's World* was a wonderful book.

'But I'm sure you will have no problem finding yourself another publisher.'

'Not so fast, Laura,' Liam cut in. 'I don't want another publisher.'

'You aren't still determined to have me as your editor?' she demanded, no longer relaxed in her chair as she sat forward tensely.

'"Determined" isn't quite the word I would use,' he replied. 'It's more a case of who I feel I can work with. The relationship between an author and an editor is a very delicate one. It requires—'

'I know what it requires, Liam,' she put in. 'And we simply do not have that sort of relationship.'

'We could have.'

'No,' she bit out decisively, 'We could not. Now, if you wouldn't mind, Liam?' She gave a hurried glance at her wristwatch. 'I have to go out again.' She had told Bobby she would only be an hour or so, and it was approaching that time already.

Liam's eyes narrowed to icy slits. 'To see the same man?'

Bobby, she knew, would absolutely love that description!

'To see the same man,' she confirmed, standing up. She probably just had enough time left to freshen up and change, collect their nightclothes, before driving herself back to the hospital.

Liam's hand reaching out to grasp her arm took her totally by surprise. 'Didn't you learn your lesson with me?' he rasped.

The more Laura tried to twist her arm out of his grasp, the tighter his hold became. She was breathing hard with agitation when she finally looked up at him. 'Which lesson would that be, Liam?' she challenged, head thrown back as she looked at him contemptuously. 'How to tell the bastards from the good guys?'

Blue eyes seemed to catch fire as he glared down at her, the fierceness of that gaze finally settling on her slightly parted lips. 'You'll never know how hard I tried to be a good guy with you, Laura,' he muttered.

Her mouth turned down scornfully. 'You didn't try hard enough! Now, let me go!' Once again she tired to wrench her arm out of his grasp.

'I let you go once before, and lived to regret it,' he murmured grimly, shaking his head. 'If you think I'm going to do it now, when there's nothing and no one standing between us, then you're out of your mind!'

Laura stopped struggling to stare up at him, hardly breathing, very aware of the close proximity of their two bodies, suddenly feeling incredibly hot.

He was so close now she could see every pore of his skin, the dark shadow of stubble on his chin that indicated he was in need of his second shave of the day, the grim lines beside his mouth and eyes, those eyes so deeply blue it was impossible to see where the iris ended and the pupil began.

She felt the wanton weakness of her body as Liam slowly, determinedly, began to draw her up against him, those firmly sculptured lips almost touching hers now, their breath intermingled.

'No!' She pulled back so sharply she took Liam completely by surprise, releasing herself from his grasp but knowing she would have bruises on her wrist later because of her abrupt action.

Bruises? They were nothing compared to the other damage Liam could wreak in her life if he got too close!

Because Liam was wrong when he said no one stood

between them. Bobby stood between them. And he always would.

But she acknowledged it wasn't only Bobby that had prevented her from giving in to that momentary weakness she had felt towards Liam. Her own pride wouldn't allow him to see that he could still affect her in this way!

Her eyes sparkled with anger as she glared across at him. 'I would like you to leave, Liam,' she bit out tautly. 'Now!' she added viciously, as he would have spoken. 'You weren't invited here, have no right to be here.' She shook her head. 'And now I would like you to leave!'

A nerve pulsed in his tightly clenched jaw as he continued to look at her for long, breathless seconds. Finally, he gave a harshly controlled sigh. 'All right, Laura, I'll go,' he told her. 'But I'm not leaving London.'

She drew in a sharp breath, reaction starting to set in as she began to tremble. 'That is completely—'

'Or you,' Liam added huskily.

Her head went back proudly, her smile scornful. 'That presupposes I want you to stay, Liam—and I'm sure I've made it more than obvious that's the last thing I want!'

His mouth twisted into a rueful smile. 'What you want and what you get are often two completely different things.'

'You already taught me that particular lesson eight years ago,' she flew back at him.

His expression softened. 'I never meant to hurt you, Laura—'

'Who knows—or cares—what you meant to do, Liam?' she cut in hotly. 'The result was the same! Now, will you please go?'

'I will.' He nodded. 'But you haven't seen the last of me,' he promised, his Irish brogue very much in evidence.

And he let himself out of the sitting-room and then out of the house...!

Laura sat down—before her legs gave way beneath her. She was shaking so badly by this time that it was a distinct possibility that was what would happen!

What was she going to do?

She knew from what he had said that Liam had no intention of disappearing from her life in the near future, obviously finding this more mature and self-confident Laura much more interesting than he had found the totally besotted Laura eight years ago.

Well, she had no intention of letting him anywhere near the life she had now. She would instruct Amy never to let him in the house again, would leave the same instructions with the reception at Shipley Publishing. The way her life was now, with very little other than Bobby and the office to occupy her time, that should at least make things a little more difficult for him to get to her again.

Although, knowing Liam as she did, she had a feeling he would find a way round that if he felt determined enough...

CHAPTER SEVEN

SHE spent a very restless night at the hospital with Bobby. The unfamiliar surroundings meant he didn't sleep very well and, consequently, neither did she. Hospitals were amazingly noisy places, she decided, and with the nurse checking Bobby's observations every two hours they weren't exactly restful either!

The two of them were rather relieved the following morning when the consultant decided Bobby could go home, that his bruised head and knee could be better dealt with there.

In fact, Bobby went straight back to bed for a long sleep as soon as they reached the house, leaving Laura, with Amy to keep an eye on the sleeping Bobby, to check in at the office.

'Oh, and a Janey Wilson from the *National Daily* has rung three times already this morning,' Ruth informed her, once the immediate mail had been dealt with. 'She wouldn't say what it was about, but asked if you could call her back if you came in to the office today.' She handed Laura a slip of paper with the reporter's telephone number on before returning to her own adjoining office.

Laura looked down at the telephone number. She wasn't familiar with the reporter, although the newspaper she worked for was known for its sensationalism. What on earth could Janey Wilson want to talk to her about?

'I'm interested to know if you have any comment to make about the rumour that you're going to publish the new, long-awaited Liam O'Reilly novel?' The female reporter came straight to the point when Laura returned her calls.

Laura's hands began to shake. Rumour? Started by whom?

'Mrs Shipley?' Janey Wilson prompted sharply at her continued silence.

She had been completely thrown by this woman's opening question, and her stunned silence would not have helped the situation!

'I have no idea where you came by such information, Miss Wilson,' she finally came back smoothly, 'but—'

'My source is extremely reliable, I can assure you,' the other woman put in determinedly.

How reliable? Who could it be? More to the point, what was Liam going to say, after his forceful comments concerning no publicity, about this breach of confidence?

'I'm sure you believe that it is,' Laura dismissed lightly. 'But I have to inform you that we have no plans—immediate or otherwise—to publish a Liam O'Reilly novel. Always supposing he's actually written one,' she added brightly.

All the time her thoughts were racing! Liam was going to be absolutely furious if it became public knowledge that he had written a new novel. It didn't take too much intelligence to know who he was going to blame for this security breach.

Ruth, as her secretary, knew that Liam had been to her office, but would have had no idea why. Which left only Perry and herself aware that the manuscript they had received almost a month ago was in reality a Liam O'Reilly novel.

Well, she knew for certain that *she* wasn't this woman's extremely reliable, source, which only left Perry. Could Perry have—? She knew he was ambitious, that he wanted this Liam O'Reilly novel badly, but there was no way Laura could believe her senior editor would have stooped to such a level to achieve it. Besides, making the novel public was likely to have the opposite effect; Liam would simply take his manuscript and disappear back to Ireland with it!

'My source also tells me that you are actually going to be Mr O'Reilly's editor.' Janey Wilson softly interrupted her thoughts.

Laura drew in a sharp breath. 'That is a very definite lie,' she refuted.

'Do I have your permission to quote you on both those comments?' the reporter came back eagerly.

Did she? At the moment, not having had time to speak to Perry yet today, Laura had no idea whether or not they even still had Liam's manuscript on the premises!

'You have my permission to quote me as saying no comment to both those questions,' Laura came back cagily. The newspaper this woman worked for might deal in sensationalism, but there was no way Laura was actually going to contribute to it!

'Interesting,' the reporter drawled thoughtfully, in a way that Laura definitely wasn't happy with! But what else could she have said? She really didn't have any idea whether or not they still had Liam's manuscript.

'"No comment" will do just fine,' Janey Wilson told her politely. 'And thanks for taking the time to return my calls.' The reporter rang off.

If Laura had known what those calls were about—!

She slowly replaced her own receiver, wondering what she should do next. Much as she didn't relish the idea, she knew she would have to warn Liam of the reporter's interest. Because if Janey Wilson managed to track him down to the hotel, bombarding him with questions about his new novel, Laura had no doubt whose blood Liam would be after!

But before she committed herself to talking to Liam again she decided to check with Perry. The completely blank look on her senior editor's face when she told him of the reporter's interest was answer enough; Perry wasn't Janey Wilson's source either.

Laura frowned. 'Do we still have the manuscript of *Josie's World*?'

Perry gave a smile. 'Well, O'Reilly hasn't demanded it back yet, if that's what you mean.'

That was exactly what she meant. Although after Liam's statement yesterday—that he hadn't given up on the idea of having her as his editor—amongst other things!—she had somehow thought Shipley Publishing would still be in possession of the manuscript.

Her mouth quirked without humour. 'After that telephone call from Janey Wilson it can only be a matter of time, I'm afraid.' She grimaced, standing up to leave. 'I'm sorry, Perry. I know how much you wanted that manuscript.'

Even if she hadn't.

And still didn't.

But neither did she relish the idea of telling Liam of a reporter's interest in the novel he was ambiguous about— to say the least!

However, as there was no one else who could tell him, she had little choice in the matter!

Not that that made her feel any better as she waited in the lounge of his hotel for Liam to come down from his suite and join her.

She'd had Paul drive her here on her way home. She'd arrived a few minutes ago, ordering a pot of coffee for two to steady her nerves before asking the receptionist to call

Liam's suite and tell him she was waiting downstairs to see him. She had no doubt that it would be far from a pleasant meeting.

If any meeting with Liam could be called pleasant nowadays!

'Well, this is a surprise!' Liam drawled as he appeared in front of her.

Laura hadn't even bothered to look at the lift or the stairs as she waited for him this time; this man's appearances were just mysterious!

She swallowed hard as she looked up at him. 'Would you like to join me for coffee?' She indicated the second cup on the tray.

Dark brows rose over those mocking blue eyes. 'An even nicer surprise,' Liam murmured as he sat down in the chair next to hers, not having bothered to put on a jacket, today wearing black denims and a black shirt.

Appropriate colours? Laura grimaced inwardly.

'You remembered,' he said appreciatively. 'How I like my coffee,' he explained at her questioning glance, taking the cup of coffee she had just poured for him.

Black, with no sugar. Not such a big thing for her to have remembered. And yet she was irritated with herself for having done so; she had tried so hard the last eight years to forget everything about him!

She shrugged. 'I thought you could add your own cream and sugar if you wanted them.'

Amusement darkened his eyes now. 'Did you?' he said, sipping the black unsweetened brew. 'It's good to see you, Laura, but I had the distinct impression, when we parted yesterday, that you had no wish to ever see me again,' he remarked conversationally.

Laura felt her stomach perform a distinct somersault and wished herself far away from here. And Liam!

She moistened dry lips. 'Circumstances change.'

'They certainly do.' He nodded with a grin, obviously enjoying himself.

At her expense! Oh, how she wished she could wipe that self-satisfied smile off his face. Well...she could. But the method of achieving it wasn't guaranteed to let her escape without feeling the razor-edge of Liam's anger.

'There's something I need to discuss with you, Liam,' she began determinedly.

He relaxed back in his chair, feet crossed at his ankles. 'Discuss away,' he invited.

'I—it's a little difficult to know where to start,' she said awkwardly, not relishing the anger that she knew was to come.

'The beginning is always a good place,' he observed.

Her eyes flashed with sparkling colour as she glared at him. 'Very funny,' she snapped. 'In this case I have no idea where the beginning is. You see—'

'Did you have a good time last night?' Liam cut in abruptly, eyes suddenly narrowed with speculation.

'A good—? Liam, I didn't come here to discuss my private life,' she stated irritatedly, all the more impatient because she felt at a disadvantage in this particular situation.

'A few of the social niceties between us might not come amiss.' He shrugged broad shoulders.

'I don't have the time for social niceties—'

'In a hurry again, are you?' he asked speculatively, blue gaze narrowed. 'Your relationship might benefit from keeping him waiting once in a while.'

So they were back to that imaginary man in her life. 'Liam, I've come here to discuss business—'

'I thought you had decided not to publish my book?' He raised dark brows.

'I have never said that,' she replied tersely. 'Only that your choice of editor is unacceptable.'

'Still feel the same way?'

After she had finished telling him about the reporter's interest in his novel Laura didn't think it would matter much to Liam *how* she felt!

'I'm sure we could work something out...' she began cautiously.

'You *have* changed your mind,' he pounced triumphantly. 'I—'

'Liam, you're going way too fast,' Laura interrupted him. 'I said we *could* have worked something out, not that we are! You see...' She moistened dry lips, not quite able to meet his eyes now. 'There's been a development—and I want you to be aware from the onset that I do not hold any employee of Shipley Publishing responsible—'

'Liam! What luck! Sorry for interrupting.' The young woman who had arrived unexpectedly beside them turned to give Laura an apologetic smile. 'I just need a few words with Liam, and then I'll leave the two of you in peace.' She turned back to Liam. 'I thought you would like to know that—'

'Would you excuse us for a few minutes, Laura?' Liam stood up, his expression grim as he took a firm hold of the other woman's arm. 'This is private, I'm afraid.'

It always had been when a pretty woman was involved. And the newcomer was definitely that: tall and long-legged, in denims and a sweatshirt, a mane of curling blonde hair cascading down her back, beautiful face bare of make-up. Liam obviously hadn't lost his touch where beautiful women were concerned!

'Please, go ahead,' Laura invited, turning her interest to pouring herself another cup of coffee.

But that didn't mean she wasn't completely aware of

Liam and the beautiful blonde as they moved out into the reception area, their conversation quietly intense. Although the other woman—probably aged in her late twenties, like Laura—didn't look particularly concerned at having found Liam drinking coffee with another woman.

Probably because she knew she didn't have anything to fear from her, Laura acknowledged heavily. If things had been different, if she hadn't so much to lose by letting Liam too close to her now, she might possibly have allowed herself the indulgence of the brief relationship with him that he seemed to want—if only to finally rid herself of the ghost of the past!

But, as it was, there were too many things about her that Liam didn't know—must never know. So, even to a complete stranger, like the beautiful blonde Liam was talking to, it must be obvious that Laura's body language was all wrong for there to be any intimacy between herself and Liam.

Laura was unable to resist looking across at the other couple from beneath lowered dark lashes, analysing their own body language. Friendly, she would guess, but not intimate. Not yet, anyway!

The beautiful blonde was glancing across at Laura too now, as she continued to talk to Liam. Laura instantly turned away. But that didn't stop her wondering exactly what explanation Liam was giving the other woman for finding him here with her. Knowing Liam, it would sound plausible, whatever it was!

Laura turned back just in time to see the blonde woman reach up to kiss one of Liam's cheeks, then raising a hand in parting to Laura as she turned and hurried towards the hotel exit.

'Sorry about that,' Liam said as he rejoined Laura in the

lounge. 'An old friend just wanting to say hello,' he added as he dropped back into the chair beside hers.

A 'hello' he definitely hadn't wanted Laura to witness too closely!

'Really?' Laura murmured dryly.

'Really,' he echoed. 'I was at university with her brother.'

How nice for him that his university friends had such beautiful sisters!

Bitch, bitchy, Laura instantly rebuked herself. Liam had always liked beautiful women. Besides, it was none of her business.

'You were saying...?' Liam prompted, obviously also of the opinion that the sister of his old university friend was not Laura's business.

And compared with what Laura had to tell him now— albeit reluctantly—he was right!

'I may just as well come straight out with it,' she said flatly. 'You're going to be furious no matter how nicely I try to break the news to you!'

Dark brows rose over mocking blue eyes. 'I am?'

'Undoubtedly,' Laura sighed. 'Although I do reiterate, none of my employees is responsible for what I'm about to tell you.' She looked at him challengingly.

'I believe you,' Liam replied, holding up defensive hands. 'If I'm ever in a fight, Laura, I hope I have you on my side; at the moment you look like a lioness defending her cubs!'

Probably because she felt like one! She was also using the tactic, she acknowledged ruefully, that attack was better than defence!

'Very well.' She nodded. 'I received a telephone call from a reporter earlier today. She wanted confirmation that

Shipley Publishing is to print the next Liam O'Reilly novel, with me as your editor!' There, she had said it!

Light the blue touch-paper and stand well back. She inwardly grimaced.

Except nothing happened!

The blue touch-paper had definitely been lit, was probably still smouldering inside, but outwardly there was no sign of it...!

Liam continued to look at her with narrowed eyes, a nerve pulsing in his cheek, his mouth grim, his eyes unfathomable.

As with a smouldering but unexploded firework, Laura was left with a question: did she go and check that it was alight, or did she continue to stand well back in case the explosion was only delayed?

She didn't know!

Her nervousness only increased as the seconds ticked by with no reaction from Liam. Why didn't he say something? Anything!

Finally she could stand the suspense no longer. 'Liam—'

'And what—' Liam's voice was icily controlled '—did you reply to such an enquiry?'

She gritted her teeth. 'No comment.'

That silence again. She couldn't bear it. Why didn't he just scream and shout, demand an explanation? Which she didn't have!

'Well, that's...unoriginal, if nothing else,' he finally drawled sarcastically.

'What would you have had me say?' Laura countered, stung into being defensive after all. 'You have to agree this situation is unusual—to say the least. Subterfuge just isn't my style!'

'Implying that it's mine?' Liam prompted mildly.

Angry colour darkened her cheeks. 'You're the one insisting on secrecy!'

'Then it appears I've been wasting my time, doesn't it?' he replied. 'What are you going to do about it?'

'Me?' she responded. 'What can I do about it?'

'Well, for one thing, you could stop being so stubborn about agreeing to publish my book!'

It wasn't just a book, and they both knew it. It was an assured bestseller. 'And the second thing?'

'Well, as we seem to have been presented with a *fait accompli*, why don't you stop being so difficult about acting as my editor, too?'

There was something very wrong with this conversation, something that didn't add up. What? Ah, she had it. Why *wasn't* Liam screaming and shouting, demanding an explanation…? After being absolutely adamant concerning the need for secrecy concerning his novel, he would be perfectly within his rights to be blazingly angry. And yet he wasn't…

Three people knew about Liam's book: herself, Perry, and Liam himself. She had already eliminated the first two—which only left Liam…!

No, Liam couldn't have given that information to a reporter himself! It didn't make sense—

Why didn't it? A *fait accompli*, he had just said. And she was the one, not Liam, who had been presented with it…

But why?

It just didn't make any sense. She had to be wrong. Liam—

'What are you thinking?' He watched her with narrowed eyes.

Nonsense. Utter nonsense. There was absolutely no reason why Liam should have leaked the information to the press about his book himself. It went against everything he had previously told her he wanted concerning the publication of *Josie's World*.

'It isn't important.' She shook her head dismissively. 'So, you're saying you would still like Shipley to publish your novel?'

Liam shrugged. 'I never had a problem with it. Only with your choice of editor,' he added pointedly.

'And the publicity this reporter's article may incur?'

He shrugged again. 'I'm sure you're more than capable of dealing with it.'

'I may be,' she conceded. 'But what about you? It's the one thing you've maintained you definitely don't want.'

'I still don't,' he agreed. 'But if it's handled properly—' he gave her a sharp look '—the whole thing will just become a nine-day wonder. It may resurface once the book is published—'

'There's no may about it,' Laura warned him determinedly.

'Hopefully by that time I shall be safely back in Ireland, my whereabouts unknown by anyone except my lawyer,' he confirmed pointedly.

Because their only address for him was that post office box in London...

Laura gave him a narrow-eyed look, still not convinced. 'I must say,' she said slowly, 'you're taking all of this much more calmly than I expected.'

Liam grinned. 'I am, aren't I?' he agreed.

Laura's earlier suspicions weren't in any way lessened by this reply. If Liam had decided that publicity wouldn't hurt him after all, despite what he had earlier maintained to the contrary, then there was absolutely no reason why he couldn't have been the one to leak the information to the press. And neatly present her with that *fait accompli*.

It did seem a little extreme just as a means of achieving his own way. But, in a warped sort of way, it also made sense. Much more sense than the information having been leaked from anyone at Shipley Publishing.

And what more extremely reliable source could there be than the author himself...?

Laura sat back in her chair, looking across at Liam with narrowed eyes. Would he really have gone to that extreme just to ensure he got his own way—having her as his editor?

It seemed unbelievable, and yet...

'What is it?' he demanded, watching her closely.

Laura had been aware of that scrutiny, but her thoughts remained her own. 'I'm not sure,' she answered softly. 'Tell me, Liam, the young lady who was just here—'

'I told you, she's the sister of an old university friend,' he cut in harshly.

Laura nodded. 'And her name would be...?'

Liam was scowling now, sitting tensely forward on his own chair. 'What does her name have to do with anything?' he rasped.

She wasn't sure. Yet. But Liam had made no attempt to introduce the two women earlier; in fact he had seemed anxious to keep them apart. Which had been extremely rude of him. Although perhaps understandable if the other woman were a current romantic involvement in his life. But it might have another explanation...

Also, though she could be imagining it, now that Laura thought about it, the leggy blonde's voice had sounded vaguely familiar...

Laura drew in a sharp breath. 'Her name wouldn't happen to be Wilson, would it? Janey Wilson? As in Janey Wilson, reporter for the *National Daily*?'

She watched Liam closely for his reaction to her suggestion noting the way the pupils of his eyes widened and then contracted, the slight increase in grimness about his mouth, the nerve pulsing in his throat.

Her mouth quirked disgustedly. 'I can see that it is,' she bit out, shaking her head. 'Why, Liam?' She frowned.

But she already knew the answer to that. Liam was determined to have his own way concerning his publisher and editor, and had decided, after meeting her again, that she was to be both those things. He was even willing to sacrifice his own privacy to achieve that objective—had hoped to use Janey Wilson's newspaper article as a means of pressurising Laura into accepting those conditions.

'Don't bother to answer that,' she said, before he could even attempt to do so, turning to pick up her shoulder bag before standing up. 'I have to go now; I've already wasted enough of my day on this—' She broke off abruptly as Liam reached out and grasped her wrist to prevent her leaving. 'Let go of me, Liam,' she told him with cold determination.

His hand tightened about the slenderness of her wrist as he too stood up, at once dwarfing her. 'I did warn you yesterday not to believe you had got rid of me so easily.'

Her brows rose. 'And today has proved that you carry out your threats.'

His face darkened. 'It wasn't a threat—'

'Then you must have just managed to make it sound that way,' Laura scorned.

'And your decision?' His eyes were narrowed.

'Concerning your neatly engineered *fait accompli*?' she clarified derisively. 'I'm not sure,' she admitted heavily.

And she wasn't. She needed time and space—away from Liam!—to consider what she should do next. For everyone's sake, not just her own.

'Laura!' His hold on her wrist relaxed slightly, his thumb moving caressingly against the base of her own thumb now.

Laura snatched her hand out of his grasp, angry when she still felt that slight caress against her skin. 'I'll let you know, Liam,' she said tonelessly.

'When?'

'When I'm good and ready!' she returned hotly. 'You may have set this scene, Liam, but you don't have the power to dictate everyone else's moves now that you've done so! I need to think about all of this.' Definitely away from him—far away! 'When I've reached a decision I'll call you.'

He studied her flushed and angry face for several long seconds before slowly nodding his head. 'Just don't leave it too long, hmm?' he finally murmured.

Her eyes flashed in warning. 'As long as it takes! You've engineered a situation here, Liam—for your own reasons,' she added as he appeared about to protest. 'But none of us—including you!—know what the repercussions might be once this story appears in the newspaper tomorrow.' She shook her head resignedly.

Laura *didn't* know what those repercussions might be, but she could certainly take an educated guess.

She only hoped Liam was ready for it!

She hoped she was too!

CHAPTER EIGHT

PREDICTABLY, the telephone at Laura's home began ringing before eight o'clock the next morning. And continued to ring.

Laura had answered the first call, found herself talking to a reporter on a different daily newspaper from the *National Daily*, and quickly ended the conversation—only to have the phone ring again seconds later. To go unanswered. As the following dozen or so calls went unanswered, too. Until Laura decided to actually take the receiver off the hook. It meant she couldn't receive any genuine personal calls either, but in the circumstances it was a small price to pay.

How members of the press had got hold of her private home number she had no idea; she never ceased to be amazed by the amazing network that fed them.

To say she was annoyed by this intrusion was an understatement! Thank goodness Bobby was still fast asleep, no doubt exhausted by events; Laura wasn't sure how she would have answered his questions about the fact that the telephone receiver was being left permanently off the hook!

When the doorbell rang shortly after nine o'clock Laura opened the door to find one of the more determined reporters standing on her doorstep, vaguely waving his press card in her face before launching into a series of quick-fire questions. Questions Laura had no intention of answering. After telling him the inevitable 'no comment', she quietly and firmly closed the door in the young man's face.

But she could see several other reporters, some with

cameras, hovering at the end of the pathway as she did so, and her irritation turned to anger as she realised she would probably have to run the gauntlet of them if she wanted to leave the house at all today.

Her only consolation was that Liam was probably faring just as badly!

Not that she had expected her own privacy to be invaded in this way. It was Shipley Publishing the press should be talking to, not Laura Shipley herself.

Liam!

This was all his fault. If he hadn't been so determined to have his own way none of this would be happening.

The doorbell rang again.

And again, when Laura didn't move to answer it.

And yet again as she continued to stand in the hallway, glaring at the closed front door.

The incessant noise would wake Bobby in a minute, and then she was going to be really angry!

She wrenched open the door. 'I thought I told you— Liam!' she recognised, startled, as she found he was the one now standing on her doorstep, and groaned her dismay as several cameras flashed in her face. 'Come inside,' she instructed furiously, grabbing his arm to drag him into the hallway and close the door against those intruding cameras. 'What on earth are you doing here?' she demanded accusingly, knowing his presence here at her home was only going to add fuel to the fire.

Liam didn't look any happier than she did, scowling down at her darkly. 'Your telephone has been constantly engaged for the last hour,' he rasped. 'What else was I supposed to do, if I wanted to talk to you, but come over here?'

'My telephone hasn't been engaged all morning—I've taken it off the hook! A case of self-preservation,' she snapped in explanation. 'The first reporter rang here at eight o'clock this morning.' She glared her displeasure.

Liam relaxed slightly. 'They started ringing me at seven-thirty!'

Laura's eyes flashed blue-green. 'Is that supposed to make me feel better?'

He grimaced. 'If it was, it obviously hasn't succeeded.' He ran a distracted hand through the darkness of his hair. 'Are you going to ask Amy to bring us both a cup of coffee into the sitting room, or do you intend to keep me standing out here in the hallway all day?'

What she wanted to do was tell him to leave!

But he was right about the inappropriateness of them standing here in the hallway—though not for the reason he said. Even though this was a large house, their voices were no doubt carrying up the stairs to the bedrooms. And the last thing she wanted was for them to wake Bobby and for him to appear!

'Go through to the sitting room; you know the way,' she said ungraciously. 'I'll go and ask Amy for the coffee.' And check on Bobby while she was about it!

Liam was standing in front of the unlit fireplace when Laura joined him in the sitting room a few minutes later, his expression grim, although he seemed to shake that off as he turned to smile at her.

'You look much more like the old Laura in those denims,' he murmured huskily.

She felt the colour enter her cheeks. She didn't want to be reminded of the old Laura! But, as Liam had just pointed out, she was dressed casually today, in denims and a soft green jumper. Unless there was an emergency she had no intention of going in to the office today, was going to spend the time with Bobby instead.

Thoughts of her son still asleep upstairs gave a sharpness to her answer. 'Appearances can be deceptive!'

Liam raised dark brows, smiling slightly. 'Ever on the defensive, Laura.'

She gave an acknowledging inclination of her head before asking, 'Why are you here, Liam?'

His expression became grim once again, his eyes narrowed. 'Have you seen the *National Daily* today?'

She gave a disgusted snort. 'Do I need to?' She waved her hand towards the front of the house. At least half a dozen reporters and cameramen were gathered out there now.

Liam winced. 'I think so.' He pulled a folded newspaper from the pocket of his dark blue jacket, the usual denims and a tee shirt worn beneath. 'Here.' He held the newspaper out to her.

Laura sensed a certain wariness about him now, as if he already knew she was not going to like what she read in the newspaper he offered her. Her own unease deepened considerably.

'Page four,' Liam indicated as she took the newspaper.

She gasped as she turned the double-page spread to find a photograph of Liam and herself. The photograph had obviously been taken the previous afternoon at the hotel—without either of them realising it! The two of them were seated in the hotel lounge, smiling across at each other in what looked like a very friendly manner.

Laura couldn't imagine at what part of their meeting *that* had been, but nevertheless the evidence was there in front of her eyes.

She looked up accusingly at Liam. 'Your little friend was very busy yesterday afternoon! Did you know about this photograph being taken?' she accused.

'Certainly not,' he replied in a voice that brooked no arguments on that score. 'But, damning as the photograph is, I think you should read the article that goes with it before making further comment,' he suggested.

Laura shot him another narrow-eyed glance before turning her attention to the newspaper article, the colour slowly leaving her cheeks as she read.

Mrs. Laura Shipley, head of Shipley Publishing, preferred to make no comment on the suggestion that she would shortly be publishing a new, long-awaited novel by Liam O'Reilly. But the couple, photographed together yesterday afternoon, certainly seem to have a close relationship. Perhaps it could soon be wedding bells for the widow of the late Robert Shipley, mother of the Shipley heir, Robert Shipley Junior, and the world-famous Irish author, Liam O'Reilly...?

Laura felt sick, her hands shaking so badly she had to put the newspaper down on the coffee table. Where had Janey Wilson got all that information? More to the point, look what she had done with it. This was worse, so much worse, than she could ever have imagined.

She swallowed down her nausea, half afraid to raise her head and look at Liam. So much for her not wanting Liam to even know she had a son!

'I'm sorry, Laura.' Liam was the one to finally speak.

'*You're* sorry?' she flashed, looking up to glare at him. 'How do you think I feel?'

Liam winced at the unmistakable anger in her voice. 'I had no idea Janey intended printing something like that.' He looked disgustedly towards the open newspaper.

'She may be the sister of an old university friend, Liam,'

Laura told him sternly, 'but she is obviously first and fore-most a reporter!'

Anger was a much easier option than the tears she really felt like shedding. Tears of sheer frustration. How dared that woman print those private details about her life?

'Obviously.' Liam sighed. 'I—' He broke off as Amy arrived with the tray of coffee. 'Laura might need a brandy to go with that?' He looked at her enquiringly.

'At nine-thirty in the morning? No, thank you,' Laura refused. 'Thank you, Amy.' Her voice softened as she spoke to her housekeeper before Amy returned to the kitchen.

'Shall I pour?' Liam offered as Laura made no effort to do so.

'Go ahead,' Laura invited uncaringly, pacing the room as her thoughts raced.

There was no way Liam could have overlooked that mention of Bobby in the last sentence of the newspaper article. Not that it really told him anything except that she had a son, but she would have preferred that he didn't even know that much!

And as for that reference to wedding bells for Liam and herself—!

No wonder celebrities got so angry at some of the things the press wrote about them. She and Liam had only been drinking coffee together, and yet Janey Wilson's article implied so much more.

'Here.' Liam put a cup of coffee into her hand now. 'I know you don't take sugar, but I've put some in anyway. I think you need the energy boost.'

So he remembered how she took her coffee too. Strange, it afforded Laura no satisfaction that he had shown his own remembrance of their past relationship.

The sweetened coffee tasted awful, but Liam had been

right about the energy boost making her feel slightly better. She now felt she had enough strength to administer the slap on the face he deserved!

'Uh-oh.' Liam eyed her warily over the rim of his own coffee cup as he pretended to back away. 'Perhaps I put a little too much sugar in your coffee; I certainly recognise that light of battle in your beautiful eyes!'

Laura couldn't help it—she laughed. He really was the most irritating, arrogant, attractive man she had ever met in her life. His blue eyes had darkened teasingly; the hard strength of his face had softened in amusement. Even if she had no intention of being affected by that attraction!

'This isn't funny, Liam,' she rebuked. Although even to her own ears she sounded less than convincing.

'No, it isn't,' he agreed heavily. 'I've already spoken to Janey, told her exactly what I think of her half-truths and innuendos—'

'For all the good it will have done you.' Laura sighed. 'She'll probably print another story tomorrow along the lines of you doth protest to much!'

Liam scowled. 'I think I've made it more than clear to Janey that if she prints another word about the two of us I'll personally wring her neck for her!'

Laura grimaced. 'I don't think silencing Janey Wilson will have achieved much.' She glanced pointedly towards the front of the house, where the reporters were still gathered. 'I believe they already have several photographs of you arriving at my home to spice up another article for tomorrow's newspapers!'

'I really had no idea this would develop into such a circus.' He shook his head disgustedly.

'The press are even more vociferous now than they were eight years ago,' she opined.

'Obviously, if even a friend like Janey can make something out of nothing,' Liam replied.

Laura gave the ghost of a smile, nodding ruefully. 'Perhaps you should have told her she's eight years out of date where we're concerned.'

As soon as she had made the remark she wished she could take the words back. The atmosphere had suddenly changed between them, charged with an awareness now that hadn't been there before. An awareness of each other, of what they had once been to each other...

Liam put down his empty cup, taking a step towards her. 'Is she?' he said as he stood only inches away from Laura. 'I'm not so sure about that,' he said softly, one of his hands reaching up to cup the side of her face. 'You're more beautiful than ever, Laura,' he groaned.

She was barely breathing, her gaze locked with Liam's. The ticking of the clock that stood above the fireplace suddenly seemed very loud and intrusive. Her heart, she knew, was beating a much quicker pattern.

She shook her head. 'I don't think this is a good idea, Liam,' she murmured throatily.

'You're not a child any longer, Laura—'

'I never was a child where you were concerned,' she protested.

'Oh, yes, you were.' His gaze moved slowly over the perfection of her face, the darkness of her hair, before returning to the softness of her mouth. 'But you're a woman now, Laura. A mother, too,' he added gruffly, looking down at her with gentle enquiry. 'I knew there was something different about you when we met again, something that couldn't just be attributed to eight years' maturity. Obviously being a mother suits you.'

It didn't suit her; it was what she was. It was all she really wanted to be, and Bobby was the centre of her life.

'Why didn't you tell me about your son, Laura?' Liam prompted softly.

'I didn't want to bore you; you've made your views on children more than plain,' she scorned to hide her rising panic. She did not want to discuss Bobby!

'Only having any of my own,' Liam refuted. 'How old is Robert, Laura? Does he look like you?'

Her mouth had gone very dry, and the beating of her heart sounded louder than ever. She didn't want to answer any of these questions. Wouldn't answer them!

'We call him Bobby. Robert was too confusing when it was his father's name too,' she responded.

Only to witness the tightening of Liam's mouth, that nerve pulsing in his throat once again. Obviously he didn't like this reference to Bobby's father, Laura's late husband.

But even though Robert hadn't been Bobby's biological father he had been in every other sense there was. Robert had been beside her during her pregnancy, with her during Bobby's birth, and had involved himself totally in Bobby's babyhood and infancy, often reaching the baby's cotside quicker than Laura if Bobby had wakened in the night. Robert *had* been Bobby's father!

Laura moved determinedly away from Liam, turning as his hand fell back to his side. 'I believe we have much more important things to discuss than my son.' She felt an inward jolt at the possessiveness in her tone. But Bobby *was* her son, and with Robert gone she felt he was hers alone!

'I would like to meet him,' Liam suggested.

She turned to him sharply. 'Why?'

'Why not?'

Calm down, Laura, she told herself steadily, breathing deeply. 'It's been a difficult time for Bobby since his father died,' she reasoned. 'Losing a parent at such a young age has made him all the more attached to the one he has left; I don't like to confuse him with transient friends.' Even to her own ears that sounded like a deliberate slap in the face, and she could see by the tightening of Liam's mouth and the narrowing of his eyes that he had recognised it as such.

His head went back challengingly. 'Is that why you keep the man currently sharing your bed as a separate part of your life?'

A retaliatory slap! Probably deserved after her own remark, Laura accepted. But it wasn't one she was going to give him the satisfaction of reacting to!

Her lips pursed. 'Surely, Liam, that's a contradiction in terms?' she countered. 'If this mythical man were sharing my bed, then I wouldn't be able to keep him as a separate part of my life?'

His eyes had narrowed questioningly. 'Mythical?' he prompted softly.

She had fallen into his trap yet again! Trust Liam to pounce on the one word that was of any real interest to him!

She changed tack. 'You're the one who keeps insisting there has to be a man somewhere.'

'Only because I don't believe it's a woman,' Liam responded. 'And you are far too beautiful to have been completely on your own the last two years. Unless those were the ''transient friends'' you were referring to earlier?' he added derisively.

Oh, this man was so insulting! And under any other circumstances she would have told him exactly what he could do with his rude remarks. But here, in her home, with Bobby only feet away and likely to appear downstairs without warning, her one real wish was to have Liam leave as soon as possible.

'I'm not even going to qualify that remark with an an-

swer, Liam,' she returned. 'Now, if you've quite finished...? I have things to do today.' Although none of them
involved leaving the house; she had no intention of running
the gauntlet where those hovering reporters were concerned!

Liam's eyes were glacial. 'Like explaining to the current
man that this newspaper report is an exaggeration?' he challenged.

Laura eyed him coolly. 'I very rarely explain myself to
anyone these days, Liam.' And especially not him! 'And
that newspaper article isn't an exaggeration; it's an outright
fabrication!' she stated firmly.

'It needn't be,' Liam told her gruffly, suddenly close to
her once again.

Too close!

He shouldn't be here in her home at all, let alone standing only inches away from her. She was actually able to
feel the heat given off by his body.

A body she had once known more intimately than she
knew her own...!

Where had that come from? She groaned inwardly. She
didn't want to remember the intimacies she had shared with
Liam eight years ago!

Sometimes in the night, with sleep sweeping away her
defences, those memories came back in her dreams, and the
ecstasy she had once known in his arms was undeniable
then. And when she woke in the morning, much as she
hated herself for it, her body would still burn and ache from
that remembered pleasure.

'Laura...!' Liam whispered now, his arms moving about
the slenderness of her waist as he drew her close to him,
his eyes searching on the flushed beauty of her face before
his head lowered and his mouth took possession of hers.

Senses already heightened by those thoughts of the past,

Laura was instantly swept away on a tide of pleasure, her body arching into the hardness of his, her lips opening as Liam deepened the kiss, his tongue moving searchingly.

They fitted together like two halves of a whole!

Laura's height was no match for Liam's six feet four inches, but the softness of her curves fitted into the muscular hollows of his body, her breasts against his chest, thighs pressed into the hardness of his.

And her body remembered, as she remembered, the pleasure of that hardness. She felt a warm rush between her thighs even as Liam continued to sip and taste her lips.

His hands moved restlessly across the slenderness of her back, fingers seeking the warm flesh beneath the green jumper, moving round to cup the softness of her breast against the silky material of her bra, the nipple instantly hard, throbbing hotly as a thumbtip gently caressed her.

Liam moaned low in his throat as his own body hardened in response, hands shaking slightly now as they tightened about the narrowness of her waist, pulling her even closer against him.

His lips left hers to trail over the creaminess of her cheek, before travelling down the column of her throat to the sensitive hollows below.

Laura was now feeling dizzy with desire. Her hands clung to the width of his shoulders to stop herself from falling. She was aware only of Liam and the moist caress of his lips, his teeth gently nibbling an earlobe, sending arrows of warm ecstasy to every part of her body.

'Mummy? Mummy, where are you?'

The sound of Bobby's voice calling out to Laura from the hallway had the same effect on her as having a bucket of ice-cold water thrown over her would have done!

She sprang guiltily away from Liam, the pleasure she had known in his arms only seconds earlier completely obliterated as she heard the soft pad of Bobby's slipper-clad feet as he approached the sitting room.

Any second now, Liam and Bobby were going to come face to face with each other. And in her slightly befuddled state Laura couldn't think of a single thing she could do or say to prevent it happening!

CHAPTER NINE

'MUMMY!' A relieved Bobby appeared in the doorway, obviously pleased to have found her at last, although his dark blue eyes instantly moved curiously to the man in the room with her.

'Hello, darling.' Laura smiled, moving to his side, totally ignoring Liam—and what had just occurred between the two of them!—as she bent down to give her son a hug. 'Feeling better now?' she prompted gently, looking at Bobby searchingly.

Apart from a little bump on his head, and a slightly sore knee, he didn't seem to have suffered too much harm from his accident. His long night's sleep had obviously refreshed him too; this morning there was colour back in the previous paleness of his cheeks, and his eyes were bright and alert.

Eyes that were fixed now on the man who stood in front of the window. Bobby's expression was slightly shy as he looked at this stranger.

Laura drew in a deep breath before turning, her arm protectively about Bobby's narrow shoulders as she held him to her side, her expression slightly challenging as she looked across at Liam. A Liam whose expression was totally unreadable as he looked not at her, but down at Bobby.

Laura tried to see the little boy through Liam's eyes. Still dressed in his pyjamas, Bobby was tall for his age, with a thinness that resulted from an abundance of energy and not lack of food. His hair was dark and slightly curly, dark blue eyes fringed by lashes of the same dark colour.

114

Colouring that could just as well be her own, Laura decided stubbornly.

But could she also claim the facial features that already promised to look so much like Liam's as Bobby matured? Or the mischievous grin that could be so like Liam's?

If challenged, she would have to!

'Your mother seems to be temporarily speechless, Bobby.' Liam was the first one to speak, only the huskiness of his voice giving any indication of the passion they had so recently shared. 'So I had better introduce myself. I'm Liam O'Reilly.' He moved forward to hold his hand out formally to the little boy. 'An old friend of your mother's.'

'Robert William Shipley Junior,' Bobby told him with shy pride as he shook the proffered hand.

Laura felt an emotional catch in her throat as father and son faced each other for the first time. They were so alike. Liam *must* realise who Bobby was!

Or maybe it was just her, with her inner knowledge, who could see the likeness? She certainly hoped so...!

Liam released Bobby's hand as he smiled down at him 'Your mother tells me you prefer to be called Bobby,' he said softly.

The little boy shrugged narrow shoulders. 'I don't mind Bobby or Robert. The teachers at school call me Robert.'

Laura looked down at her son in some surprise. Bobby had never told her that before. But perhaps now that his father, also Robert, was dead...

'I think I quite like Bobby, if that's okay with you?' Liam spoke to the little boy, but his narrowed gaze was fixed on Laura. As if he was well aware of how perplexed she had just felt.

And maybe he was, she inwardly conceded; Liam, as an author, was a people-watcher, had always been able to intuitively read other people's emotions.

Which was yet another reason for guarding her own emotions when around him!

She straightened her shoulders. 'If that's all, Liam,' she prompted distantly, wanting him to leave. 'I would like to go and share some breakfast with Bobby now.'

'Breakfast sounds like a good idea,' Liam came back smoothly. 'I didn't feel much like eating earlier this morning,' he elaborated, as Laura gave him a frowning look.

Because he had been bombarded with reporters at his hotel even earlier than she had!

But, even so, her suggestion about breakfast had not included Liam. And he knew it!

'We're only eating cereal and toast,' she told him flatly.

'Sounds good,' Liam replied. 'As long as you have those cornflakes with the sugar already on them; they're my favourite,' he told Bobby conspiratorially.

'Mine, too,' Bobby told him with a gappy grin. He was missing his two top front teeth, being at the age when he was starting to lose his milk teeth in favour of permanent ones.

Laura looked down in puzzlement at her son; this was the first she had heard of that particular cereal being Bobby's favourite. But, with no permanent male figure in his life, she accepted that Bobby was likely to suffer a few cases of hero-worship over the following years. It was just that Liam was the last person she wanted Bobby to see in that role!

'It looks like it's sugar-coated cornflakes all round, Laura,' Liam told her with satisfaction, already following Bobby towards the kitchen.

Laura followed much more slowly. Did Liam know who Bobby really was? If he did, he was giving no indication of it. Which was even more disquieting.

Amy raised surprised brows in her direction when Laura

entered the kitchen. Liam was already seated at the pine table in there as Bobby got out the cereal, bowls and milk, putting them on the table before sitting down himself.

Laura gave the housekeeper a resigned shrug. There was really nothing else she could do; she couldn't exactly throw Liam bodily out of the house. Besides, she was still uneasy about how much Liam might or might not have guessed about Bobby's parentage...

'Shouldn't a big boy like you be at school today?' Liam asked Bobby once the two of them had their bowls of cereal.

'I fell over two days ago and bumped my head,' Bobby said. 'I had to stay in hospital overnight. But Mummy stayed with me.' He looked up at Laura for confirmation of this momentous event in his young life.

'I certainly did.' She ruffled the darkness of his hair with gentle affection, looking up challengingly at Liam as she sensed his gaze on her.

So that's where you rushed off to two days ago, his eyes clearly said.

Laura gave him a withering glance before turning away. She had told him the man in her life he kept referring to was mythical; it was Liam's own fault if he hadn't believed her.

'Sit down and eat some breakfast.'

Angry colour flooded her cheeks at Liam's dictatorial tone. She would eat breakfast when she was good and ready, not when he told her to. Who did he think—?

'Please?' he added cajolingly, blue gaze on her flushed cheeks.

Laura sat. Until she had spoken to him alone, found out whether or not he had guessed that Bobby was his son, then she didn't particularly want to antagonise him. Although his manner seemed rather too pleasant for that of a man who had just realised he had a son he knew nothing about...

It was impossible to tell with Liam. Able to read and gauge other people's emotions, he also had the ability to completely hide his own behind an inscrutable mask. That mask was firmly in place at the moment!

Liam continued to talk to Bobby as Laura drank her coffee and ate a slice of toast, encouraging the little boy to talk about school, and his friends there.

Laura's own troubled thoughts drifted as her wariness increased.

'—think you would really like Ireland, Bobby.' Liam's suggestion brought Laura's wandering attention back to their conversation.

What did he mean, Bobby would like Ireland? She had no plans ever to take her son there!

Liam turned to look at her with expressionless eyes as he sensed her renewed attention. 'Bobby was just telling me that he likes it when you and he go out for a drive at weekends so that the two of you can go for walks in the countryside,' he explained. 'There's nowhere quite like Ireland for beautiful countryside and peaceful walks,' he opined.

That might or might not be true—Laura had no intention of visiting Ireland to find out! 'I think after Bobby's accident our walks will have to wait for a while,' she replied—firmly stamping on any suggestion that Liam might join them this weekend before he even made it!

'Your mother is probably right,' Liam told Bobby as the little boy looked about to protest. 'Mothers usually are,' he added enigmatically.

Laura gave him a sharp look, surprised that he had actually agreed with her concerning the walks, but equally puzzled by his last remark, although she could see no mockery or sarcasm in his expression.

She stood up abruptly. 'If you've finished breakfast, I think it's time I took Bobby upstairs for a bath...'

'Oh, but, Mummy—'

'Remember what I said about mothers.' Liam teasingly interrupted Bobby's protest, standing up as he did so. 'It's time I was going anyway. But I'll come and see you again, Bobby, if that's okay with you?'

Laura gave him another look. She didn't want Liam and Bobby becoming any closer than they were...!

'Great!' Again Bobby gave Liam that toothless grin.

'Upstairs, young man,' Laura told her son firmly. 'While I see Liam to the door.'

Bobby followed them out into the hallway, running up the stairs with all the exuberance of his youth.

'There doesn't look too much wrong with him now,' Liam remarked as he watched Bobby disappear up to his bedroom. 'What happened?' he prompted, turning back to her.

'A fall at school. Nothing's broken, though, so he should be back at school on Monday.'

'He's a fine-looking boy, Laura.'

She swallowed hard, reluctant to look up into the hard handsomeness of Liam's face. A face that, after seeing the two of them together like this, was so obviously—to her, at least!—a mature version of Bobby's...

She drew in a deep breath, lifting her head in defiance. 'I like to think so.'

'You must be very proud of him.' Liam gave an acknowledging inclination of his head.

'Very,' she confirmed curtly, still uncertain of where this conversation was leading. If Liam had seen Bobby's likeness to him, guessed that he was actually his son, why didn't he just say so?

'Have dinner with me, Laura,' Liam said instead.

Her eyes widened in alarm. 'I can't leave Bobby—'

'Not tonight,' Liam interrupted. 'I realise that at the moment Bobby is your first priority, that for today, at least, he needs all your attention. But tomorrow is Saturday; I'm sure by then he'll be settled enough for you to leave him with Amy for a few hours. By that time you will probably welcome the break too,' he added as she would have protested once again.

Laua's mouth closed with a snap. Since when had Liam become so attuned to another person's feelings? He was certainly showing more sensitivity than she had ever known from him before.

But did she want to have dinner with him, tomorrow or any other evening?

The answer to that was a definite no! But there was much more at stake than her own feelings...

'In that case...thank you. Dinner sounds fine,' she accepted tersely. 'But could you find somewhere discreet for us to eat? I don't relish the idea of having reporters leering all over us!'

Liam's face tightened at this reminder of the reporters waiting outside the house. 'Don't worry, I'll make sure it's somewhere no one will recognise us.'

Very few people would recognise her anyway—at least, until that photograph of the two of them had appeared in the newspaper today they wouldn't have done!—but Liam was another proposition altogether. But he had issued the invitation; it was up to him to find the venue.

Not that it was a dinner Laura was particularly looking forward to. She just felt in the circumstances, until she had ascertained exactly how much Liam had guessed about

Bobby's true parentage, that it might be better to meet Liam halfway. Dinner together sounded harmless enough.

Although, as she had discovered only too well this morning, what sounded harmless didn't always turn out that way. Who would have thought, when Liam had arrived so unexpectedly this morning, that the two of them would end up in each other's arms before he left again...!

'It will be a business dinner, Liam,' she told him firmly.

His brows rose mockingly. 'Will it?'

'There's no other reason for the two of us to meet.'

'If you say so.'

Laura frowned darkly. 'Liam—'

'Your son is waiting upstairs for you to bath him,' he cut in dryly, reaching out to lightly grasp her shoulders. 'If mothers are usually right, then little boys shouldn't be kept waiting!'

She was very aware of the warmth of his hands on her shoulders. 'How about big boys?' she teased.

Liam shrugged, his mouth thinning grimly. 'We're just as impatient for what we want, but we've learnt to hide it better!'

'And what do you want, Liam?' she prompted softly.

He grimaced. 'Like most people, what I apparently can't have.' He sighed heavily. 'Tell me, Laura, do you hate me very much?'

She drew in a shocked breath at his words. Hate him? Of course she didn't— Well...maybe eight years ago for a while she had, she accepted. But that was so long ago, and her successful marriage to Robert, Bobby's birth, had more than compensated for that.

'I have too much in my life that's good to feel hate towards anyone,' she answered truthfully.

Liam looked down at her with assessing eyes. 'Did you love Robert Shipley?' he ground out harshly.

Her face softened with the remembrance of that love, eyes glittering with unshed tears. 'Very much,' she responded.

'He must have been quite something.' Liam nodded, his hands dropping away from her shoulders. 'I would like to know more about him.'

Laura looked up at him warily. 'Why?'

'Because you loved him!' Liam rasped harshly.

'I see no connection between the two things.' She shook her head uncomprehendingly. 'I certainly see no point in the two of us talking about my husband.'

'No?' Liam glanced up the stairs. 'From the little Bobby said about him over breakfast, he obviously adored him too.'

'Why shouldn't he have done? He was his father!'

Too defensive, Laura, she instantly rebuked herself with a pained wince. But she couldn't help it. There was much more to being a father than the mere act of bringing a child into being. And Robert had more than filled all those other roles necessary for being a father.

'Yes, he was,' Liam conceded gruffly. 'I'll call for you here tomorrow night about eight o'clock, shall I?'

The sudden change of subject threw Laura for a few seconds. Would she ever be able to keep up with this man's change of moods...?

'I don't think that's a good idea.' She shook her head. 'If, as I suspect, there's going to be more speculation about the two of us in tomorrow's newspapers, then it would be better if we weren't seen leaving my home together tomorrow evening.'

'Good point,' Liam conceded. 'Okay, I'll telephone here tomorrow with the name of the restaurant. If you don't mind meeting me there...?'

'Why should I mind?' she replied. 'As I've said, as far as I'm concerned it's business.'

His mouth twisted into a humourless smile. 'There's no need to belabour the point, Laura; I heard you the first time.'

He might have heard her, but she just wanted to make sure he understood!

'I won't come to the door, if you don't mind,' she said. 'I think the press have enough photographs of the two of us together for one day!' And she hated to think what they were going to do with them!

Although that was the least of her troubles as she walked up the stairs a few minutes later. Dinner with Liam tomorrow evening definitely headed that particular list!

'When I said somewhere discreet, Liam,' she snapped, 'I did not mean your hotel suite!'

She looked around them pointedly, at the dining table in the sitting room of his suite elegantly set for two people to dine, the crystal glasses, the cutlery gleaming silver, a vase of red roses in the centre of the highly polished table.

Liam had telephoned the house earlier and spoken to Amy, as Laura and Bobby had gone out to buy Bobby a toy, asking Laura to meet him at his hotel at eight o'clock. Laura had assumed—mistakenly it now turned out!—that the two of them would be going on to a restaurant from there. One glance at that elegant set dinner table had shown her how wrong she was!

'Don't look so accusing, Laura,' Liam responded impatiently. He was wearing a black dinner jacket, snowy white shirt and black bow tie, his hair still damp from the shower he had recently taken. 'I don't have an ulterior motive for deciding it was easier to eat here; I tried all the restaurants

I thought fitted your description and they were all fully booked.'

She gave him a scathing glance, very aware that her glittering figure-hugging gold dress, with its short length that showed the long expanse of her slender legs—chosen as a boost to her own confidence rather than any sort of come-on!—seemed slightly out of place in the intimacy of this hotel suite. *Liam's* hotel suite!

'Didn't you explain that you're Liam O'Reilly?' she threw back totally put out by the fact that she was expected to eat here alone with Liam in the intimacy of his hotel suite.

His expression darkened at her deliberate antagonism. 'I've never worked that way,' he rasped coldly. 'Look,' he sighed, 'I know you aren't happy with this arrangement—'

'You have no idea how unhappy it makes me,' she muttered grimly.

'But the alternative was to cancel the whole thing—and to me that was no alternative at all!'

Her eyes sparkled angrily as she glared across at him. 'Maybe you should have given me the benefit of choosing for myself!'

His mouth twisted furiously. 'And we both know what choice you would have made!'

She was breathing hard in her agitation, not at all pleased at the thought of spending the evening here alone with Liam.

She was still uncertain as to the reason for this dinner invitation, had been uneasy about it all day, and feeling herself cornered like this, without even the distraction of other diners to alleviate some of the awkwardness, had not improved those feelings of unease.

'This is impossible, Liam.' She shook her head.

'Why is it?' he reasoned impatiently.

'Don't be deliberately obtuse,' she returned. 'Did you see the newspapers this morning?'

Liam sighed, picking up the opened bottle of chilled white wine to pour some of the fruity liquid into two glasses. 'Of course I saw them,' he said evenly, handing her one of the glasses before taking a sip from his own. 'They would have been hard to miss.'

As Laura had guessed, photographs of Liam arriving at her home yesterday morning had appeared on the front page of several of the more sensational tabloids, and speculation about their relationship, both professional and personal, was continuing.

'Then you must see,' she said impatiently, 'that the two of us having dinner together in your hotel suite will only add to the rumour that we're—that we're—'

'We're what, Laura?' Liam interrupted, dropping down into one of the armchairs to look up at her with mocking blue eyes.

'Involved!' she spat the word out angrily.

He raised dark brows. 'And...?'

'We aren't!' Laura bit out through gritted teeth. Liam wasn't just being obtuse now, he was being deliberately awkward!

He shrugged broad shoulders. 'Not through lack of trying on my part.'

She gasped, colour heating her cheeks. 'You—I—'

'Yes, you and I,' Liam repeated softly, standing up to put his glass down on the coffee table before slowly walking towards her. 'Is that such an awful idea?' He came to a halt only inches away from her, his eyes navy blue now as he looked down at her.

'Awful?' she repeated incredulously. 'It's ludicrous!' she told him heatedly.

Liam's mouth tightened, his eyes narrowing. 'Why?' he prompted huskily.

'Not again, Liam!' She moved sharply away as he would have reached out and grasped her shoulders, moving to the other side of the room. 'Yesterday morning was a—a mistake. With maturity I've come to try not to repeat my mistakes,' she added challengingly.

'Believe it or not, I'm trying, in my own way, to do the same thing.'

Laura gave him a sharp look. Exactly what did he mean by that remark?

'Through my own stupidity I let you slip through my fingers eight years ago, Laura,' he said quietly, answering her unasked question. 'I don't intend letting it happen a second time.'

Laura could feel her cheeks paling as she stared across at him with wide disbelieving eyes. She might have told him this was a business dinner, but she had really come here purely to discover what he might or might not have realised about Bobby's parentage, and for no other reason.

Hadn't she...?

As she looked at Liam, so handsome in his evening attire, the warmth in his eyes for her alone, she began to question her own self-honesty. Had part of her, the part of her that also remembered how good they had been together eight years ago, ached to know whether it would still be the same between them? If their response to each other yesterday morning was anything to go by, then she could have no doubts about that!

But had she been aware of that when she'd dressed to come out this evening? Had her motives in wearing this gold dress, a dress that she knew suited her dark colouring and the slenderness of her figure, been as self-orientated as she had told herself they were at the time?

As she looked up into Liam's face, her own gaze locked with mesmerising blue eyes, she didn't know any more!

She moistened dry lips. 'Liam—'

'Laura, won't you give me a chance to make up for the past?' he cut in. 'I was an idiot; I freely admit that. But don't even idiots deserve a second chance?'

A second chance to do what? Ruin her life once again? To just disappear when it suited him, never to be heard from again?

She shuddered just at the thought of going through that again. Not again.

Never again!

'Laura!' Liam reached her side in two long strides, having watched the emotions flickering across her face, reaching out to grasp her shoulders, shaking her slightly as she refused to look up at him. 'Won't you at least give me a chance to try to make amends for—?'

'No!' she finally gasped, shaking her head in firm denial as she glared up at him. 'I like my life just the way it is, Liam. I do not want you around, with your egotistical arrogance, cluttering it up!' She was deliberately nasty, wanting to put an emotional barrier between them even if, with Liam's close proximity, she couldn't get a physical one.

He became very still, looking down at her searchingly. 'You lied to me yesterday morning, Laura,' he finally said heavily, his hands slowly dropping away from her shoulders.

She shivered involuntarily at the removal of that warmth. 'In what way did I lie?' she challenged hardly, afraid of what his answer might be. If he were referring to Bobby—!

He drew in a harsh breath, grim lines beside his nose and mouth. 'You do hate me,' he said tonelessly. 'But I can assure you it's no more than I hate myself for the idiot I was eight years ago.'

He wasn't talking about Bobby! Her relief at this realisation superceded everything else.

'I didn't lie, Liam,' she told him, almost gently. 'I really don't hate you. But neither do I wish to be involved with you again,' she added with finality.

Even if she might have some residual feelings left for Liam—and after the way she had responded to him yesterday morning she must have!—she must never lose sight of the fact that any involvement with him was a possible danger to her own relationship with Bobby.

'Fair enough.' Liam held his hands up in supplication.

Laura eyed him uncertainly. Had he accepted her decision just a little too readily to be sincere...?

Or was it her hurt pride that was reacting now? Surely she didn't really want him to keep up this personal pursuit?

As she had already told Liam, there was no point. It might just be that part of her that was still smarting from his desertion eight years ago that felt a certain sense of satisfaction in the knowledge that their roles had now been reversed; Liam obviously wanted a relationship with her now, and she was the one repulsing him.

Not very nice sentiments, she inwardly rebuked. Not nice at all.

She put up a hand to her temple, which had begun to pound painfully. 'I think, in the circumstances, I'll give dinner a miss, if you don't mind...?'

He nodded abruptly, eyes reflecting nothing but the room about them, his expression also unreadable. 'I think that might be a good idea.'

Laura bent to pick up her evening bag from the table she had placed it on when she arrived. Such a short time ago.

But a lot had happened in that half an hour or so. Primarily, Liam was once again going out of her life.

She should be glad. Should feel nothing but relief at having the pressure of his presence removed from her life once and for all.

She paused beside the door. 'What do you intend doing about the book, Liam?' She looked at him with inquisitive eyes.

He shrugged. 'You've assured me Perry is an excellent editor; I have no reason to doubt you.'

Her eyes widened. 'You're agreeable to his being your editor now? To Shipley publishing your book?' She couldn't quite believe this easy acquiescence. It wasn't like the Liam she knew at all!

His mouth twisted into a humourless smile. 'I'm not as completely unreasonable as you seem to think I am.'

No, but he had gone to so much trouble to try and achieve his own way, had even involved the newspapers—something he had told her he didn't want under any circumstances. There was definitely something not quite right about this!

'Liam—'

'Laura?' he came back smoothly.

Her feelings of unease increased. He was too smooth, too calm, too everything! 'You'll come in to see Perry on Monday?'

'I will,' he agreed, sounding very Irish. 'After which I have to return to Ireland.'

Not only was he agreeing to accept Perry as his editor, but he was removing himself from London—and her life—as well. There had to be a catch in this somewhere!

'I wish you had looked this pleased to see me again!' Liam chuckled self-derisively at her obvious relief at his going. 'I will be back, Laura. There are still things to do concerning the book.'

Yes, but she didn't have to be involved in them now…

Why didn't she leave? She had said she was going to, and yet she had made no effort yet to open the door and go.

Possibly because she felt that once she left here tonight she would never see this particular Liam again. The professional writer Liam O'Reilly, yes, but not this man who had pursued her so relentlessly the last few days.

Oh, she didn't know what she wanted any more! She had been telling Liam for those same few days that she wasn't interested in renewing their past relationship, yet now that he had accepted her decision she hesitated about leaving him.

She set her shoulders determinedly. 'Goodbye, Liam,' she told him firmly.

'Goodbye, Laura.' His expression was still unreadable.

Her feet felt as if they were weighted down by lead, her movements slow and sluggish. But finally she managed to open the door and walk out into the hotel corridor, closing the door firmly behind her.

And closing the door to that compartment of her heart that contained her repressed feelings for Liam—the door he had been trying so hard to prise open…!

CHAPTER TEN

'I CAN'T believe I slept until this time!' Laura exclaimed self-disgustedly as she entered the kitchen at ten o'clock the next morning to find Amy already preparing the vegetables for lunch.

Amy turned to give her a warm smile. 'You obviously needed the rest,' she volunteered.

No, it hadn't been that at all. When Laura had arrived home shortly after nine o'clock last night she had gone straight to her bedroom. But not to sleep. Not that she hadn't tried to sleep, to push everything but Bobby and her work from her mind. But memories of Liam, both from the past and the present, had kept intruding, making it impossible for her to relax enough to go to sleep. Consequently it had been the early hours of the morning before she'd fallen into a fitful slumber, resulting in her completely oversleeping this morning.

'Where's Bobby?' She had checked his bedroom before coming downstairs, and the morning room on her way past, expecting him to be in there watching television. The only other place she could think of him being was the kitchen, with Amy, but he wasn't in here either...

'Mr O'Reilly called in at nine o'clock—'

'Liam did?' Laura questioned sharply, a terrible sinking feeling developing in the pit of her stomach.

'He brought a kite with him,' Amy went on, frowning at Laura's obvious shock. 'He thought Bobby might like to go with him—'

'You've let Liam take Bobby out?' Laura gasped, paling.

'Into the garden to fly it,' Amy finished. 'I would never let anyone take Bobby out without your permission,' she added with gentle rebuke.

Laura sank down into one of the kitchen chairs, some of the colour returning to her cheeks. 'Of course you wouldn't,' she realised self-disgustedly, her colour receding again as the full import of Amy's words sank in. 'Liam is out in the garden—this garden!—flying a kite with Bobby?'

The housekeeper nodded. 'As Mr O'Reilly said, it's a nice windy day for it.'

It certainly was—but what was Liam doing here at all? Hadn't they decided last night that the less they saw of each other the better?

Not exactly, she realised slowly. She had told Liam she didn't want to become personally involved with him again. A statement, she remembered thinking at the time, that he had seemed to accept too readily... A statement he had taken to its literal limit; she hadn't included Bobby's name!

She stood up hurriedly. 'I think I'll just go and check on the two of them.'

'They were having a great time when I looked out at them a couple of minutes ago,' Amy assured her. 'Have a cup of coffee before you go out; you always say you need a couple of cups to be able to start the day properly.'

What Laura had actually said was that she needed a couple of cups of coffee in the morning to help her feel human!

She raised dark brows at Amy, her mouth quirking self-derisively. 'You think I'm overreacting?'

The housekeeper hesitated. 'That depends on what you're reacting to...'

Laura swallowed hard, sitting down abruptly as Amy placed the cup of strong coffee on the table in front of her. 'How long have you known?'

The housekeeper smiled. 'I'm not sure that I do know.

Not really. Of course I've always known that Mr Robert wasn't Bobby's father. We both know that was never even a possibility. But as to who Bobby's biological father really is...' She shrugged. 'In every other sense of the word Mr Robert *was* his father.'

'But...?' Laura prompted warily.

'I was struck by the resemblance between Bobby and Mr O'Reilly from the moment I first opened the door to Mr O'Reilly earlier in the week.' Amy admitted gently. 'That's the reason I was unsure about whether or not to let him wait to see you.'

Laura had thought that unusual at the time...

'What must you think of me, Amy?' She buried her face in her hands.

The older woman's arm came about her shoulders. 'I think you, and Bobby, helped to make the last five years of Mr Robert's life the happiest he had ever known,' she told her emotionally.

Laura looked up through a haze of tears. 'Did we? Did we really?' She so much hoped so, after all that Robert had done for her.

'Don't ever doubt it,' Amy said with certainty. 'A family, a child of his own to love and care for, were things Mr Robert had long ago accepted he would never have. I know that he looked on both of you as a gift,' she said. 'A gift he wasn't sure he deserved, but one that he cherished above everything else.'

Laura swallowed hard. 'If anyone deserved a loving family, Robert did.'

'And you gave him that, Laura; never doubt it for a moment,' the housekeeper told her firmly. 'As to Mr O'Reilly, I'm sure you had your own reasons for not marrying him eight years ago.'

Laura gave a humourless smile. 'A very good reason, Amy. He never asked me!'

The older woman raised blonde brows. 'Some men aren't very good at responsibility—'

'He never knew about Bobby, Amy.' Laura felt compelled to defend him.

The other woman looked concerned. 'That would no longer seem to be the case,' she observed ruefully, looking in the direction of the garden, where Liam was now flying a kite with his son.

Laura looked up at her. 'You think Liam knows?' her voice was hushed.

'Don't you?'

'I have no idea,' she burst out. 'If he does know, he hasn't said anything. And it isn't the sort of thing I can come straight out and ask him!' Especially as she would prefer it if Liam *didn't* know! 'If Liam does know, Amy, then why hasn't he said anything?' she asked emotionally.

The housekeeper paused, straightened, and then replied, 'I think you would have to ask him that.'

But she couldn't, not without revealing the truth herself. And it was a truth she still wasn't sure Liam knew...

Amy returned to peeling the potatoes. 'Will there be two or three for lunch?' she prompted lightly.

'Two! No—three. I don't know, Amy.' She sighed wearily. 'I'm not sure I know anything any more.'

Last night it had seemed so cut and dried: Liam was going to stay out of her personal life but continue to let Shipley publish his book. Liam turning up here this morning to play with Bobby made a nonsense of all that.

The housekeeper gave her a sympathetic smile. 'I know this isn't much comfort to you at the moment, but things do have a way of working themselves out.'

But not always as one would like them to!

Could Amy be right, that Liam did know Bobby was his son? And, if he did, why hadn't he challenged her about it?

She was no nearer knowing the workings of Liam's inner mind now than she had been eight years ago!

'I think I'll go out and say good morning,' she decided firmly, draining her coffee cup before standing up. 'That should be harmless enough.'

Amy nodded. 'And I'll prepare lunch for three. Just in case,' she added with a glint in her eyes.

Laura watched the two males in the garden unobserved for several minutes. Bobby was wrapped up warm in his winter coat; Liam was looking lithely attractive in denims and a thick blue chunky sweater.

Both faces were lit up with boyish pleasure as they gazed up at the red kite high in the sky above them, dark hair ruffled, blue eyes glowing. Bobby was holding on to the string but Liam was standing behind him, helping to guide the kite away from entanglement with neighbouring trees.

Laura felt an emotional pain in her chest as she watched them. How different their lives could have been if Liam hadn't walked out of her life eight years ago...

But by the same token, as Amy had already said this morning, if Liam hadn't gone Robert would never have enjoyed five years of family life.

Besides, what was the point of regretting something that was already a fact? Liam had left, and Robert had become her husband and Bobby's father. Nothing could ever change that.

'That looks like fun,' she called out to the two kite-flyers.

'Mummy!' Bobby cried excitedly, grinning from ear to ear as he looked at her. 'Look, Liam bought me a kite.'

Liam glanced over his shoulder at her, his expression slightly wary. And with good reason, Laura thought crossly, all her old resentment resurfacing at sight of him! Bringing her son presents, stopping to play with him, had not been part of their agreement the evening before.

Her gaze met Liam's questioningly. 'That's nice,' she said challengingly.

Liam met that gaze unflinchingly. 'Did you have a good sleep?' he enquired.

Almost as if he knew it had been the early hours of the morning before sleep finally claimed her! 'Very good, thank you,' she said tersely, going down the steps into the garden.

Liam watched her progress down the lawn as she walked towards them, his eyes narrowed on her slenderness in the black denims and deep blue jumper. She knew soft wisps of her dark hair were framing the paleness of her make-upless face.

Well, she hadn't realised they would have a visitor so early on a Sunday morning!

Laura met his gaze unflinchingly. 'Enjoying yourselves?' she asked.

'Isn't it great?' Bobby was the one to enthuse, obviously thrilled with his new toy, 'I've always wanted a kite of my own,' he explained with a grin looking up at Liam.

Laura felt that pain in her chest again as she looked at the two of them. How could they possibly have become so close in the hour or so Liam had been here? A natural gravitation to each other...? Whatever it was, that ache in her chest was starting to become a permanent feature!

'I trust you thanked Liam for his gift?' she asked Bobby, completely avoiding looking at Liam now.

Anyone looking at them, Laura knew, who was unaware of the real circumstances, would have assumed they were a family: mother and father with a much-loved son. But anyone would be wrong. Very wrong!

'Of course I did,' Bobby replied with obvious surprise; one thing he had known from an early age were good manners.

Her resentment at Liam's presence here was starting to show, even to Bobby, Laura realised guiltily. But how else was she supposed to feel? Liam should not be here!

'All little boys love to have a kite of their own to fly,' Liam chuckled.

But it felt like a slap in the face to her that Liam had been the one to realise—and rectify!—the lack of a kite in her son's life. It seemed to bring into glaring focus her own inadequacies as a single mother, concerning the upbringing of the little boy. A father would have realised about the kite. Robert, for all he had lacked experience in the role until the late arrival of Bobby into his life, would have realised.

Laura couldn't help wondering what other oversights, as a lone female bringing up a male, she might have made...

'Don't start beating yourself with a stick,' Liam said softly at her side, his gaze soft on her face now as Bobby moved off down the garden, holding tightly to the string of his kite. 'I would be just as lost if you happened to have a daughter rather than a son,' he assured her.

Laura looked up at him. 'That situation will never arise,' she told him distantly.

Dark brows rose over mocking blue eyes. 'You aren't even thirty yet, Laura!'

Old enough to know she would never have any more children. After her earlier mistake she knew she would have to be married for that to happen.

The only man she had ever loved in a romantic way had walked out of her life without even a glance backwards. The man she had married, although she hadn't loved him in the same way, had been the most wonderful man she could ever hope to meet. To expect she could ever find both those things in another man was just expecting too much...

'Old enough to know better,' she retorted.

Liam seemed to have lost interest in the subject as he turned his attention back to Bobby.

At least, it seemed that he had until his next remark.

'Would you have married me, Laura, if I had asked you eight years ago?'

Laura gasped at the unexpectedness of the question, all the colour draining from her cheeks as she looked up at him with widely hurt eyes.

She had told Amy that Liam had never asked her to marry him, but would she have married Liam eight years ago if he had?

Like a shot came the instant answer. She had lived for him eight years ago, would have done anything for him. *Had* done anything for him. If he had asked her to marry him she would have become his slave for life!

She breathed deeply and evenly, desperately trying to regain control over her shattered composure. He had no right! No right at all to say things like this to her!

'I was very naïve and inexperienced, Liam,' she finally answered.

'That's no answer, Laura,' he responded. 'Besides, you assured me—only yesterday, wasn't it...?—that where I was concerned you were never a child.'

'It's possible to be naïve and inexperienced at any age, Liam,' she came back. 'But to answer your question...' She drew in a sharp breath. 'I suppose it would have to be yes,' she bit out with distaste. 'And what a pretty mess that would have made of both our lives!'

Liam looked down at her searchingly. 'Do you really believe that?' he finally asked.

She gave him a pitying look. 'Don't you?' she derided. 'Liam, I meant so much to you then that you were married to someone else within weeks of leaving England—'

'A mistake I definitely wouldn't have made if I had already been married to you!' He reached out to grasp the tops of her arms. 'You might just have been what I needed to keep my feet on the ground!'

Laura shook her head ruefully. 'And I might just have got myself trampled to death in your stampede to get out of any marriage between the two of us!'

Liam gave a perplexed frown, shaking his head. 'You don't regret a thing, do you...?' he realised slowly, his hands dropping away from her arms.

In a word—no. If she had never been involved with Liam then she could never have given Robert, a man she had already owed so much, the family he had so desired. Her marriage to Robert was something she would never regret. If she regretted anything at all, then it was meeting Liam again—

Was it?

Did she really wish that had never happened?

She looked up at him searchingly, at the changes in him, the obvious signs of physical maturity. But hadn't he changed in other ways too? Hadn't he shown concern for her yesterday morning over that newspaper article? An article he was completely responsible for, though, she acknowledged hardly. But he could have had no idea of how far Janey Wilson would play up the possibility of a personal relationship between the two of them.

More to the point, much as she might like to try to deny it, even to herself, hadn't she responded to Liam yesterday morning? Hadn't she forgotten everything but the two of them, totally lost in the aching need, the long forgotten emotions Liam had roused in her? What would have been the conclusion of that meeting if Bobby hadn't interrupted them?

She swallowed hard, her eyes meeting Liam's unwaveringly. 'There's no point in regrets, Liam,' she told him flatly. 'The past is gone, never to return. The future is unknown, for all of us. Which only leaves the present. I'm quite happy with my present exactly the way that it is.' She looked across at Bobby, her eyes shining with pride.

'Then you must be one of the lucky ones,' Liam rasped. 'Because I don't like any of my life!'

Laura turned back to him slowly. 'Then do something about it.'

His face darkened angrily. 'I'm trying to! I—'

'Uncle Liam, the string's got caught in the tree!' Bobby's distressed wail interrupted them.

'"Uncle" Liam...?' Laura repeated with soft fury, her hand tightly on his arm, holding him back as he would have gone to her son's aid.

Liam turned back to her impatiently. 'He didn't know what else to call me.'

'*Uncle* Liam...?' she bit out furiously, annoyed beyond reason by the intimacy of the title.

'Come on, Laura.' Liam shook off her hold on his arm. 'He's a polite child. He didn't feel comfortable calling an adult by their first name. I couldn't see any harm in the title of uncle.'

'I'm sure you couldn't,' she replied. 'I happen to feel differently—'

'Why?' Liam turned fully back to face her. 'I seem to remember you have an honorary uncle of your own...?'

Laura became very still, the anger draining out of her as quickly as it had risen. She didn't want to talk about her own 'uncle'—!

'Where is he, by the way?' Liam continued scornfully.

'I've been here several times now, and he hasn't been in evidence once. Which is surprising, considering eight years ago you never stopped talking about the man! Don't tell me Mrs Shipley has become too high and mighty to bother with her beloved uncle any more?'

Laura was very pale now, her throat moving convulsively. 'Stop this, Liam,' she choked. 'Stop it now!'

'Why?' he challenged. 'What is it, Laura? Don't you like being reminded of your more humble beginnings?'

She swallowed hard. 'You don't know what you're talking about.'

'I know that you hurt me just now by your obvious aversion to having your son call me uncle—'

'And that gives you the right to hurt me in return?' She looked up at him with tear-wet eyes. 'You have no rights here, Liam, no rights at all, and—'

'Uncle Liam!' Bobby was becoming increasingly distressed at the sight of his kite entangled in the branches of the tree.

Laura glanced across at her son. 'You had better go and help him,' she said flatly. 'And then I would like you to leave.'

'And what you want you always get?' Liam countered.

'Almost never.' She shook her head sadly. 'Go and help Bobby,' she said dully, turning on her heel to walk back into the house.

Too close. Liam was getting far, far too close.

To everything...

But especially to the truth!

CHAPTER ELEVEN

'SO NICE of you to join us.' The sarcasm in Liam's tone was unmistakable as he looked across the restaurant table at Laura.

The meeting this morning between Liam and Perry had gone very well, and the two men had decided to go out to lunch to celebrate the settling of the deal and the signing of the contract. For reasons of her own, Laura had decided to join them.

The true fact of the matter was that after yesterday morning she didn't dare leave Liam alone socially with anyone who knew her! He was arrogant enough to question Perry about her personal life. Not too openly, of course, but she knew Liam well enough to realise he would find out what he wanted to know without Perry even realising he had given him the information.

Liam had done as she'd asked yesterday morning, and left as soon as he had finished flying the kite with Bobby. But, as Laura now knew only too well, his acquiescence counted for nothing; Liam would do exactly as he wanted when he wanted!

She shrugged dismissively. 'It's always nice to personally welcome a new author into the company.'

Liam smiled without humour. 'Even this one?'

'We're all really excited at welcoming you on board.' Perry was the one to answer him enthusiastically. 'You have a sure-fire number one bestseller in *Josie's World*, Liam.'

Liam raised dark brows. 'Now he tells me,' he drawled

mockingly. 'Is that your considered opinion too, Laura?' he prompted, his guarded gaze giving away none of his inner feelings.

Considered opinion...? She wasn't sure she had those any more! 'It's going to do very well for you,' she told him non-committally.

'And Shipley Publishing,' he pointed out.

She shrugged again. 'It would be madness to allow a bestseller to slip through our fingers; so many publishing companies are in financial difficulties nowadays.'

'But not Shipley,' Liam said with certainty. 'I checked before sending in the manuscript.'

'And decided to hitch your star to a winner?' Laura returned sharply.

His mouth twisted scornfully. 'It seems we have more in common than we realised.'

Colour brightened Laura's cheeks. So Liam was back to implying that she had married Robert for his position and money! Well, even that was probably preferable to him learning the truth...!

Perry, Laura saw with some dismay, was listening to the exchange with a slightly puzzled look on his face.

And no wonder; the antagonism between Liam and herself was tangible, seemed to fill the very air about their luncheon table!

She sat forward with deliberation, lifting the glass of champagne that had been poured for her minutes earlier, encouraging the two men to do the same. 'Success,' she toasted.

'I'll certainly drink to that!' Perry touched his glass lightly to hers before turning to do the same with Liam's.

'And a peaceful life,' Liam added as he touched his glass against the side of Laura's.

'Do the two go together?' she came back sceptically.

Another photograph of Liam and herself, as Liam had arrived at her house on Sunday morning, had appeared in the newspapers today. Laura had taken one glance at the photograph before throwing the newspaper in the bin. As she had warned Liam at the time, the situation was out of his control now.

He nodded grimly. 'If you want it badly enough, yes.'

'I hope you're right,' Laura returned dryly.

There had been more reporters camped out outside her home this morning. Disappointed reporters as they'd seen she was alone in the back of the car with Bobby, on her way to dropping him off at school before continuing on to her office. Her son, at least, seemed to have suffered no ill-effects from the last few days!

'I'm returning to Ireland tomorrow,' Liam put in. 'Can I come and see Bobby before I leave?'

Laura gave him a sharp look, aware of Perry's quiet interest in the conversation. No doubt he had seen those photographs in the newspapers too!

Her own relief at Liam's first statement had definitely been ruined by his second!

'I don't want Bobby to think I've just disappeared out of his life,' Liam continued.

Why not? He had just disappeared out of her own life eight years ago!

'You have changed,' she replied.

Liam's gaze was glacial as it met her challenging one across the width of the table.

'Shall we order?' Perry prompted lightly as a waiter appeared beside their table.

Laura felt as if food would choke her! But she had to stay here and eat her lunch without making a scene. Besides, her reason for being here in the first place still existed...

'You didn't answer my question?' Liam persisted once their order had been taken.

She took another sip of her champagne. She didn't want Liam anywhere near Bobby. Didn't want him anywhere near either of them, come to think of it!

'On condition you don't stay too long,' she finally answered. 'It's a school day, and Bobby has homework to do before bedtime,' she added in explanation—resentful at having to make one at all! She owed this man no explanations. About anything!

Liam gave an abrupt inclination of his head. 'I'll try not to interfere with that.'

He might try. But, as Laura knew only too well, he was unlikely to succeed; Bobby had taken an extreme liking to the man he called 'Uncle Liam', had talked of little else after Liam had left yesterday. Much to Laura's dismay. Bobby would be very reluctant to let Liam leave again once at the house.

Lunch was a stilted affair, despite Perry's many attempts to lighten the atmosphere, and Laura, for one, was more than glad when it was finally over. She had eaten little anyway, drunk several glasses of champagne instead, and her head felt more than a little light.

'Steady.' Liam grasped her elbow as they went outside, the fresh air seeming to have a dizzying effect on her. 'You really should eat more, Laura,' he admonished, keeping a firm hold of her as he guided her over the road to where Paul had parked the car, holding the door open as he waited for her.

'When I want your opinion I'll ask for it,' Laura snapped back, her irritability audible only to Liam as she settled into the back of the car. Perry had gone round to the other door and was now seated beside her. 'Can we drop you anywhere?' Preferably on his head, she thought childishly!

She had drunk too much! Which was most unlike her; she had never been a big drinker, and since Bobby was born, when she had needed to be mentally alert twenty-four hours a day, she had only ever drunk the occasional glass of white wine with a meal. Three glasses of champagne at lunchtime was definitely out of character. It would be a relief—to her, at least!—when Liam returned to Ireland!

Liam's expression changed, almost as if he were able to read her thoughts and was amused by them. 'No, thanks, the walk will do me good. Is five-thirty okay for calling in to see Bobby?'

Perfect; as they always dined at six in the week, she would have a good excuse for asking him to leave. Unless Bobby, in his youthful enthusiasm, decided to invite his new friend to stay to dinner with them...?

'That's absolutely fine,' she agreed firmly. 'That way I'll be able to sit down and do Bobby's homework with him before we have dinner at six.' She couldn't say any clearer than that that Liam wasn't invited to join them for the meal without being extremely rude—and only Perry's presence stopped her being exactly that!

Blue eyes glittered with hard amusement before Liam turned to smile at Perry. 'I'll call you when I intend coming back to London.'

Laura kept her face averted as the car door was finally closed. Paul manoeuvred the car out into the early-afternoon traffic, her sigh of relief as he did so audible only to herself. She hoped.

'Well, that went off better than expected, don't you think?' she said lightly to Perry.

'I'm not sure what I expected,' Perry answered slowly. 'You and Liam are obviously old friends, but—'

'I was referring to the business aspect of the meeting,' Laura put in quickly.

'Oh, that.' Perry nodded his satisfaction. 'Yes, that went very well.'

Laura turned to him, her brows raised. 'But…?'

Her senior editor hesitated. 'Maybe there isn't a but.' He grimaced. 'I just have the feeling that—well, that—'

'Yes?'

'I think it's a good idea that you persuaded Liam to accept me as his editor—'

'*I* persuaded him?'

'Well, didn't you?' Perry said.

She had completely lost track of who had persuaded who to do what! She did know that she still felt she had been manoeuvred into this situation by Liam. And she probably had!

'Not that I recall, Perry,' she said dully. 'Although I do approve of the arrangement.'

He nodded. 'It isn't a good idea to mix business with pleasure.'

Pleasure? With Liam? The man had been nothing but a thorn in her side from the moment she'd met him again!

'I think you've misunderstood the situation between Liam and myself, Perry,' she answered evenly.

'Hey, I wasn't criticising,' he instantly assured her. 'I have no right to do that, anyway. However, if you don't mind my saying so, it's good to see you have someone in your life again. You've been on your own too long, Laura.'

She *did* mind him saying so! But with those wretched photographs in the newspapers, and Liam's request to call at the house later this evening, she was only going to make the situation worse if she protested too much.

Perry's remarks did not put her in a particularly good humour for welcoming Liam into her home later that evening. She scowled at him as Amy showed him into the sitting room, where Laura stood alone beside the unlit fireplace. Bobby was upstairs changing in anticipation of Liam's arrival.

'Champagne worn off?' Liam queried once they were alone, as he took in her glowering expression.

The fact that that could be half the reason she felt so irritable did not elevate her mood one little bit! 'How like you to pass the blame on to something other than yourself,' she snapped scathingly. She was still wearing the black suit and cream blouse she had worn to work today, very conscious of Perry's comments concerning business and pleasure; she wanted to make it clear that for her part this association with Liam was solely business!

Liam's own expression darkened. 'You really should try to put your bitterness behind you, Laura,' he advised. 'After all, you did all right for yourself in my absence.' He looked about them pointedly at the obviously luxurious comfort of her home.

Angry colour darkened her cheeks at his obvious accusation. 'Making snide remarks about me isn't going to change the fact that you deserted me eight years ago—'

'Deserted you?' Liam repeated in a steely voice. 'Isn't that rather an odd way of putting it...?'

It was the way she had thought of Liam's departure for so long. But that didn't change the fact that it must sound odd to someone who didn't know all the circumstances...

'Perhaps,' she conceded non-committally. 'It isn't important, anyway—'

'I happen to think it is,' Liam interrupted. 'You—'

'Uncle Liam!' An ecstatic Bobby burst into the room, launching himself at Liam.

Liam picked him up under his arms and swung him round. 'Hello, *spalpeen*.' He grinned up at Bobby as he held him high.

'*Spalpeen?*' Bobby repeated with a puzzled frown.

'Rascal,' Liam translated lightly, putting Bobby back on the ground. 'Had a good day at school?' He ruffled the darkness of Bobby's hair.

'It was okay,' the little boy replied. 'Can we go outside and fly my kite again?'

'I'm not sure... I can't stay long, Bobby,' Liam added gently, after a brief glance at Laura. 'I have an early-morning flight back to Ireland tomorrow,' he explained softly.

Laura hadn't told Bobby the reason for Liam's visit this evening, had felt it would be best coming from Liam himself. From the look of tearful disappointment on her son's face maybe she should have spoken to her son first.

'Bobby—'

'When will you be back?' Bobby completely ignored Laura's soothing tone, staring intently up at Liam.

Liam's expression softened as he went down on his haunches beside the little boy. 'A few weeks, possibly,' he answered, reaching out to touch Bobby's arm.

Laura watched in dismay as her son wrenched away from Liam, his face dark with rebellion.

'You won't! I know you won't!' Bobby was rigid with resentment, blue eyes sparkling angrily.

Laura could only stare at her son; she had never seen him behave in this way before. She knew he had grown fond of Liam the last few days, but this was completely unexpected.

Liam glanced up at her, frowning darkly. 'Of course I'll be back, Bobby. And when I do—'

'You'll never come back,' Bobby cried, shaking his head, his face flushed with emotion. 'My daddy went away and he never came back!' He was breathing hard in his agitation.

Laura swallowed hard, feeling tears sting her eyes.

'Bobby, this isn't the same at all.' She made a move towards him, only to come to a halt as he began to back away from her towards the door. 'Daddy was ill, Bobby. You know that,' she told him huskily. 'He didn't want to go away. He just didn't have any choice,' she said emotionally.

'Liam has a choice—and he's still going away!' Bobby accused stubbornly, glaring at Liam now. 'I thought you liked me,' he declared chokingly.

Liam had straightened, frowning his consternation at Bobby's reaction. 'I do like you, Bobby. I'll only be gone for a short time, I promise you—'

'No.' Bobby was shaking his head in disbelief, his hand on the doorhandle now. 'Take your old kite with you! I don't want it any more!' came his parting shot as he wrenched open the door. The sound of his feet running up the stairs could be heard seconds later.

Laura was stunned. Shocked. Dismayed.

Where had all that come from?

She had spent hours with Bobby after Robert's death, explaining about his father's illness, how Robert hadn't wanted to leave them, that his heart had just given up under the strain. From Bobby's outburst just now she felt she couldn't have got through to him at all.

She dropped down heavily into one of the armchairs before her shaking legs refused to hold her up any more. 'I—' She swallowed hard, holding a hand up to her stricken face as her lips began to tremble. 'Oh…!' She buried her face in her hands as the tears began to fall.

This was too much, just too much, after the strain of the last few days!

'Laura!' Liam came to sit on the arm of her chair, gathering her up into his arms, holding her tightly against his chest. 'Bobby didn't mean any of that, you know,' he soothed, after letting her cry for several minutes. 'He's just hurting right now, hitting out.'

She shook her head. 'I had no idea he felt abandoned after Robert's death. I—I thought he understood.' She sighed shakily. 'I must go to him.'

Liam's arms tightened about her as she would have got up. 'Leave him for a few minutes,' he advised. 'At the moment he's so angry, at both of us, that he might say something in the heat of the moment that he will bitterly regret.' Liam looked down at her ruefully. 'One thing's for sure, your decision concerning transient friends in your life seems to have been the right one!'

Laura felt a jolt in her chest. Transient friend? Was that what Liam was?

'No, it isn't,' Liam firmly answered her unasked question. 'You know that isn't what I want at all.'

Did she? Not really. Liam had shown her—all too clearly!—that he would like to resume some sort of relationship with her, but she had no idea what he had in mind!

He was right about one thing: she had been right to try and protect Bobby from being hurt again by coming to care for a man who was simply going to walk out of his life when he felt like it...

Although until the last few minutes she had been completely unaware of how Bobby felt deserted by Robert.

'I really must go up to him,' she said firmly, releasing herself from Liam's arms to stand up, smoothing down the shortness of her hair before turning back to him. 'I think it might be better if you had already left when Bobby comes back downstairs.'

Liam looked up at her searchingly. 'I will be coming back, you know, Laura,' he told her.

Her mouth quirked humourlessly. 'Well, I suppose that

possibility is more than you gave me eight years ago,' she said bitterly.

His expression tightened, his eyes flashing deeply blue. 'Is it…?'

She eyed him warily. 'Isn't it?' she challenged defensively.

He stood up abruptly. 'I have some business to attend to in Ireland—'

'Business, Liam?' she echoed tauntingly. 'Would that be business of the female kind?'

He drew in a harsh breath at her deliberately insulting tone. 'I realise you're upset at the moment, Laura.' Otherwise she wouldn't be getting away with this so easily, his own tone implied! 'And as it happens, yes, it's of the "female kind"; it's my mother's sixtieth birthday on Wednesday. We're having a surprise family party for her. Obviously I have to be there,' he added dryly.

'Obviously,' Laura echoed, wondering how Mary O'Reilly would react if presented with the biggest surprise in her life: her grandson, Bobby!

'You could always come with me.'

She looked up at Liam sharply, wondering if her own thoughts could possibly have been reflected on her face. Liam steadily returned her searching gaze, giving away none of his own thoughts.

'And Bobby, of course.'

'I don't think so, thank you,' Laura replied dismissively, her hands clenched so tightly at her sides her fingernails were digging painfully into the palms. 'As you said, it's a family party.' She looked across at him challengingly.

'As I said…' He gave an acknowledging inclination of his head. 'In view of Bobby's upset, I'll be coming back on Thursday, Laura. And when I get back I think we need to talk. I mean really talk.'

'I—'

'Don't you?' he queried pointedly.

No, she didn't! But if she knew anything about Liam—and she knew a great deal!—she knew she wouldn't have much choice in the matter!

Did he know Bobby was his son? Did he know, one hundred percent certain, that he was Bobby's father? And, if he did, why didn't he just come right out and say so?

Now was the perfect time for Liam to launch into his attack, when she was already feeling utterly defeated by Bobby's emotional outburst. So why didn't he...?

Liam shook his head as he watched the emotions flickering across her face. 'I'm not the man you thought I was eight years ago, Laura,' he told her. 'Then I tried to act noble—and ended up being completely the opposite! This time around I'm determined to succeed.'

'Noble?' Laura repeated dazedly; it wasn't a word she had ever associated with Liam! 'I don't know what you're talking about.'

'No, I know you don't.' He gave a humourless smile. 'But that's part of what we need to talk about. I'll get here on Thursday in time to speak to Bobby before he goes to bed; keep the rest of the evening free for me, Laura.'

She moistened dry lips. 'I—'

'Go up and talk to Bobby now,' he continued firmly. 'Tell him I'm coming back. And make him believe it,' he added grimly.

How could she be expected to do that when she wasn't sure she believed it herself...?

CHAPTER TWELVE

'FINISHED?' She looked questioningly at her son as he left half the pizza that she had ordered for him on his plate.

Since their talk on Monday evening Bobby had been very quiet. He had seemed to accept what she'd said about Robert, and why he had died, but at the same time had not quite believed what she'd said about Liam's intention of coming back today.

Maybe because she still wasn't sure she believed that herself...!

Liam had telephoned her from the airport on Tuesday morning before his plane took off, wanting to know how her talk with Bobby had gone. Not that she'd been able to reassure Liam too much on that point; Bobby just wasn't giving away his feelings at the moment.

Other than that brief telephone call from Liam she had heard nothing from him the last three days, had no idea whether or not he still intended coming to the house this evening. It was a point Bobby was well aware of; the first question he had asked when he'd woken up this morning was had she heard from Liam? Which she hadn't. And still hadn't, as the day progressed.

Which was one of the reasons she had decided to take Bobby out for a pizza after school, hoping to take his mind off Liam's proposed visit. Although, from Bobby's lack of appetite, she might as well not have bothered!

'Finished. Can we go home now?' he asked eagerly.

She gave a weak smile. 'Of course.' She stood up to pay the bill, feeling an ache in her chest at Bobby's obviously suppressed excitement; he was just too afraid to dare to outwardly anticipate that Liam would keep his promise.

Laura knew the feeling.

Only too well!

But this bewildered pain was exactly what she hadn't wanted for Bobby, was the reason she would have preferred Liam and Bobby never to meet. Of course, she couldn't have anticipated the invisible bond that had come into existence between the two of them from the moment they had met, but she had known enough not to want even to take the risk of the two of them forming an attachment. Because it *was* a risk. To Bobby's fragile emotions...

But, after doing everything in her power to prevent the two of them ever meeting, she had bowed to the fact that they had, that there was nothing she could do about the fact they actually liked each other. What she would do was personally strangle Liam if he let Bobby down this evening!

Bobby could barely contain his excitement on the drive back to the house. Laura was relieved at having the concentration of driving herself, for a change, to keep her own mind from dwelling on the possibility of Liam's arrival. In fact, she had chosen to drive herself for that very reason.

Bobby waited barely long enough for her to bring the car to a halt in front of the house before jumping out and running in, leaving the front door wide open as he did so. Laura followed at a more leisurely pace, reluctant to feel the sting of her own disappointment as well as Bobby's.

'What kept you, Mrs Shipley?' drawled an achingly familiar voice as she entered the hallway.

She couldn't help it; her pulse rate quickened at the sound of Liam's voice, her eyes glowing with pleasure as she looked up at him standing only feet away with a grinning Bobby held up in his arms.

Her breath caught in her throat as she realised how right

they looked together. But it wasn't with that wariness she had felt from the moment she met Liam again over a week ago, this was something completely different...

She was still in love with Liam!

Had she ever stopped...?

She had thought she had, had believed, when she'd finally accepted Liam had left her eight years ago, that her love for him had died too. But looking at him now, so achingly familiar, his eyes smiling into hers, their son held in his arms, Laura knew that she had never stopped being in love with Liam, that she had only buried that emotion deep in her heart, never to be looked at again.

Except Liam was back...

'He came back, Mummy.' Bobby's words echoed her chaotic thoughts.

She swallowed hard, inwardly struggling to behave naturally, even if she did feel like screaming at the painful discovery she had just made. 'So he did,' she acknowledged lightly, concentrating on putting her bag down on the hall table so that she no longer had to look at Liam.

How could she have continued to love him all this time?

How could she not? came the next instant thought; every time she looked at Bobby, the son she loved above everyone and everything else in life, her love for Liam, the man he resembled so strongly, became more deeply entrenched in her heart.

'Okay, Laura?'

She looked up to find Liam looking at her concernedly. But how could everything be okay when she had just realised her love for this man?

She swallowed hard, avoiding that searching blue gaze. 'If you don't mind, I'll leave you two to chat while I go up and change.'

Liam continued to look at her frowningly for several long

seconds before giving a barely perceptible shrug. 'Don't be long; I've brought you back a piece of my mother's birthday cake.'

Wonderful—it would probably choke her!

She fled up the stairs, throwing herself dazedly down on her bed once she reached her room. She was still in love with Liam! Unbelievable. Incredible. Impossible!

Oh, Liam had made it more than obvious that he still found her attractive, that he would be happy for the two of them to have some sort of relationship. But too much had happened in the last eight years, to both of them, for them ever to be able to start all over again.

Besides, there was still Bobby...

Bobby was Liam's son, as well as her own. When Liam had left her life so suddenly eight years ago...had married another woman within weeks of leaving...Laura had known, once she found out, that she couldn't contact him to tell him she was pregnant; she simply hadn't wanted him in her life, in any guise, under those terms.

But what of Bobby's life? Her decision had meant that neither Bobby or Liam knew of the other's existence.

There was no doubting that Robert had been a wonderful father to Bobby, but, given a choice, would Bobby rather have had his own father, even on a part-time basis? More to the point, how would Liam see, in the light of his unknowing absence in America, what she had chosen to do eight years ago?

He should never have left her in the way he had!

This wasn't solving anything, she acknowledged heavily. She might still be angry with Liam for deserting her in the way that he had, but Liam might be just as angry with her at not being told of her pregnancy. Hadn't he made a comment last week along the lines of not having made the mistakes in his own life over the last eight years if she had been his wife when he went to America...?

Laura sighed heavily, having no idea what she was going to do now. She was in love with the father of her son. Under other circumstances it would be the most natural way in the world for her to feel. Under these particular circumstances, it might be just as disastrous for her as loving Liam eight years ago had been.

What was she going to do?

Liam had told her that they needed to talk this evening, once Bobby had gone to bed. She was starting to dread what that conversation might be about!

'Come and have some cake, Mummy,' Bobby invited as soon as she entered the kitchen. A pot of coffee, and a plate of cake, were laid out on the wooden table. 'It's delicious!'

'One of my sisters made it,' Liam supplied, his expression indulgent as he watched Bobby enjoying his slice of cake. The little boy's appetite had obviously returned.

'Domesticity has never been my forte,' Laura heard herself snap in reply, instantly cringing inwardly. It wasn't Liam's sister's fault Laura had just discovered she was still in love with him!

Liam raised dark brows at her sharpness. 'Tough day?' he sympathised.

Laura felt the sting of tears in her eyes at the gentleness of his tone. The last thing she could cope with right now was Liam being kind to her! Especially when she had just so obviously been a bitch.

She gave an uninterested shrug, having changed into denims and a loose blue jumper. 'No tougher than usual. Where's Amy?' She frowned at the absence of her housekeeper.

'She said to tell you she had to pop out for a couple of things,' Liam explained, still frowning slightly.

Probably because Laura had forgotten to mention to Amy there was a possibility of Liam being here for dinner this evening! Because she hadn't wanted to end up looking a fool when he didn't arrive.

'You're looking tired, Laura.' Liam looked at her concernedly. 'Do you have to work so hard?'

Her eyes flashed her resentment as she glared across the room at him. 'I have a business to run!'

He nodded slowly. 'And a child to look after and a home,' he elaborated.

None of those things were the reason she looked so tired; the truth of the matter was she hadn't slept well since Liam had left on Monday evening. And she hadn't even realised she was still in love with him then!

'Liam, in this day and age lots of women have a bigger workload to cope with than I do,' she replied.

'But probably not as much lone responsibility,' he persisted. 'From what I've observed you're a working single mother, and Shipley's is a big company to run—'

'The art department have started work on the cover of your book, by the way,' she interrupted brightly. 'I think you'll be pleased with it.'

'I'm sure I will,' he dismissed uninterestedly. 'Come and sit down, Laura, and I'll pour you a cup of coffee.'

Laura sat. Not because Liam had told her to, but because she was still deeply shaken by the realisation she was in love with him.

Bobby, she could see at a glance, looked happier than he had in days. Obviously because of Liam's presence. What was she going to *do*?

'Stop worrying so much,' Liam murmured at her side, reaching out to briefly squeeze her hand with his. 'Things will work out.'

Would they? Would they really? Somehow she didn't

feel that Liam would still feel that way once he learnt the truth. And a part of her said she now owed him and Bobby that, at least...

It was at times like this that she wished she had an older sister she could talk to, or a close friend she could confide in. But, as Liam had already pointed out, her life was kept busy enough being Bobby's mother and running Shipley Publishing. The closest she came to having a female friend was Amy, and because Amy had worked for over twenty years for Robert Laura knew she would feel slightly disloyal talking to the other woman about her feelings for Liam.

'I'll go upstairs to my room and get my kite,' Bobby said excitedly, having devoured two slices of birthday cake.

Laura watched her son leave the room, all the time wishing that he hadn't. She had no idea what she was going to say to Liam now that they were alone.

She sipped her coffee, warming her hands around the cup; for some reason she felt incredibly cold. 'Did you have a nice time with your family in Ireland?' She tried to pick an innocuous subject to talk about; they had hours to get through before Bobby went to bed and the two of them could have that talk.

'I missed you and Bobby,' Liam came back—instantly turning the conversation back into intimacy.

Laura looked down at the table-top, wondering how she was going to get through this without breaking down.

'I'm sure your family were pleased to see you,' she said. 'Was your mother suitably surprised with her party?'

'She appeared to be.' Liam smiled indulgently. 'Although I'm sure she knew exactly what was going on. My mother is a woman who sees a great deal that isn't actually said,' he replied appreciatively. 'She saw the photographs of the two of us in the newspapers,' he added gruffly.

Laura winced. Oh, no, she hadn't given a thought to the fact Liam's family might see them too. And wonder... 'Did your family give you a hard time over them?' she attempted to tease.

He shrugged broad shoulders, having discarded his outer coat, wearing a black shirt and blue denims. 'Not particularly. I think my mother took one look at me and warned them off the subject. She would like to meet you,' he added gently.

Laura took in a hard breath. 'Didn't you explain to her that those stories in the newspapers were just publicity nonsense dreamed up by the reporters?'

Liam's mouth quirked into a smile. 'There would have been no point; my mother has always been able to tell when I'm lying!'

Laura raised startled lids, those different coloured eyes, one blue and one green, shining brightly with confusion.

Liam shrugged. 'Of course, she doesn't realise you're the same Laura from eight years ago yet, but—'

'Your mother knew about me then?' Laura gasped, her eyes wide.

'Oh, yes, she knew.' He nodded slowly.

'But—'

'Here we are.' A happy Bobby bounced back into the room with his kite. 'Can Liam and I go outside for a while Mummy?'

Almost as if Liam were Bobby's own age, and the two of them were going out to play in the garden!

'If Liam wants to,' she answered non-committally.

Liam stood up, grinning. 'I've thought of doing nothing else the last three days!'

Somehow Laura found that hard to believe, but if it made Bobby happy—which it most assuredly did, as his face lit with excitement when he and Liam went outside—then who was she to question the statement?

Besides, she was glad of this brief respite. Too much seemed to be happening too soon. And once Liam learnt how she had deceived him about Robert and Bobby it might just be going nowhere!

Liam had told his mother about her eight years ago…

Laura found that incredible. Admittedly their relationship had lasted over six months, but for most of that time Liam had treated her like another one of his sisters—someone to be patted on the head when she did something right, or shouted at when she did something wrong.

Why on earth would Liam have told his mother about her?

Yet another fact from the past that needed explaining. By the time the two of them had finished explaining themselves, there would be nothing left!

'That was absolutely delicious, Amy,' Liam told the housekeeper warmly as she took away their used plates before putting cheese and a pot of coffee on the table.

'Thank you, Mr O'Reilly,' Amy accepted before turning to Laura. 'I'll clear away in the kitchen, check on Bobby, and then call it a night, if that's okay with you, Mrs Shipley?'

It wasn't okay with her, it meant she would be left on her own with Liam, but, like her, Amy had had a long and tiring day and deserved some time to herself.

Bobby had been bathed and in bed for over an hour now, having insisted Liam join them for his story. Just as if they were a real family, Laura had realised. This situation was definitely getting out of hand!

And maybe the sooner it was settled—in whatever way!—the better it would be for all of them.

Nevertheless, Laura felt her stomach give a nervous lurch as Amy closed the dining room door softly behind her as she left.

'You should know me well enough by now, Laura, to know that I don't bite!'

She looked up at Liam, instantly looking away again as she saw from his teasing expression that he had meant the remark in a double-edged way; he wasn't about to verbally attack her just because they were now alone, but at the same time he was reminding her of the fact that he had been a passionate but gentle lover eight years ago...!

'It never occurred to me to think you might,' she lied—having no idea how the rest of this evening was going to go!

'No?' he mocked lightly. 'I don't know about you, but I don't care for any cheese... Shall we take the coffee through to the sitting room, then?' he suggested after she confirmed she wanted nothing else to eat either.

Why not? It might only delay the dreaded moment for a couple of minutes, but it would delay it...

Liam didn't sit down once they were ensconced in the sitting room, but prowled around the room, as if he were reluctant to begin this conversation too.

He came to a halt beside the dresser at the back of the room, lifting one of the many photographs from its surface, looking down to study the picture intently.

Laura squeezed her eyes shut, knowing exactly which photograph he was looking at; it had been taken shortly after Bobby was born. Laura was sitting on the arm of one of the chairs in this room, Robert was seated in the chair and Bobby nestled contentedly in his arms.

'You look a happy family.' Liam spoke gruffly.

Laura opened her eyes to look across at him, but found

herself unable to read anything from Liam's closed expression. 'We were,' she confirmed quietly.

Liam gave an abrupt inclination of his head. 'Robert was a good father?'

She swallowed hard. 'He was,' she confirmed, aware they were both talking around the real point at issue. But at least they were talking.

'And a good husband?'

Her head rose challengingly. 'I've already told you that he was,' she answered.

Liam nodded slowly, replacing the photograph. 'I'm glad.'

Her eyes widened. 'You are?'

His gaze was shuttered as he gave her a considering look. 'Didn't you think I would be?'

Laura shook her head. 'I don't know,' she told him truthfully.

He gave a rueful smile. 'I've never wished you anything but happiness, Laura. Never. Do you believe me?'

How could she? He had become the sole reason for her happiness eight years ago, and six months later he had cruelly walked out of her life!

'Obviously not,' Liam acknowledged at her silence. 'Laura, eight years ago you were still a child—'

'I was over twenty-one,' she protested.

'Sixteen going on twenty-one,' Liam corrected softly. 'When your parents died they left you in an emotional time-warp of the age you were when they died—'

'That's utter nonsense, Liam, and you know it,' Laura declared.

'No, I don't?' He gave a firm shake of his head. 'Sixteen is a terrible age to lose both your parents. Admittedly you had a guardian who could take over the financial side of your life, but emotionally you had been left in wilderness.'

He gave another shake of his head. 'I had no idea of any of this when I first met you; how could I? But it rapidly became obvious to me that you were badly in need of someone to love. And for someone to love you.'

'And that wasn't part of your immediate plans, was it?'

'Laura,' he began patiently, 'you have no idea how I felt eight years ago. You weren't mature enough—'

'Oh, please!' She stood up impatiently. 'Don't try and blame any of what happened then on my so-called immaturity. I didn't see that stopping you when you made love to me!'

Liam drew in a harsh breath. 'Nothing could have stopped me the night—that one and only night!—I made love to you,' he admitted 'You had been in my life, every part of it, for almost six months. There, with your sensual allure, your undoubted beauty, your complete acceptance of who and what I was. Once I began to touch you that night, kiss you, I could no more have stopped either of those things than I could have stopped breathing!'

'You said it had been a mistake.' Laura shakily recalled his words of rejection the following morning. 'That it must never happen again.'

And it hadn't. It hadn't needed to. Bobby had been conceived from that single night of physical love between Liam and herself.

And Liam had left her life before she had even had a chance to share that knowledge with him...

'Obviously you'd had what you wanted, found it unsatisfactory, and simply moved on,' she bit out caustically, the words cutting into her like knives.

Liam's expression was dark with anger. 'Obviously you don't know a thing about how I felt after that night!' he shot back.

She eyed him scathingly. 'Triumphant, I expect.'

Liam stepped forward, grasping the tops of her arms. 'You were a virgin until that night, Laura. And I—I had taken that precious gift from you. Triumph didn't even enter into how I felt the next morning when I woke to find you beside me in my bed!'

Laura closed her eyes against the fury of Liam's face.

They had been out to celebrate that evening, Liam having signed the contract that day to go to Los Angeles and write the screenplay of his book. They had drunk too much champagne, already high enough on Liam's success. It had seemed the most natural thing in the world that the two of them should make love with each other when they returned to Liam's apartment. At least, it had seemed natural to Laura…

'I should never have drunk as much champagne as I did.' He scowled.

She opened her eyes to look up at him frowningly. 'What happened between us had nothing to do with the champagne.' She shook her head protestingly. 'It was always going to happen. I'm just surprised it took as long as it did,' she added, knowing she had fallen in love with Liam, had wanted him physically, from their second time of meeting. Liam had always been the one who held back.

Was this way? Had he really believed her too young and vulnerable to know what she was doing?

Liam's expression was grim as he thrust her away from him. 'It wasn't supposed to happen. I had told myself it wasn't going to. I was too old for you—'

'You're only ten years older than me, Liam, not Methuselah,' she said, her arms tingling where he had held her so tightly.

'In terms of experience I was totally out of line continuing my friendship with you at all!' he told her grimly. 'And I don't just mean physical experience,' he added at her derisive expression. 'I left Ireland when I was nineteen, came to live in London, found success with my writing. Those years before I met you I lived my life to the full. In every way.'

'And then stupidly naïve me came into your life,' Laura realised. 'Following you everywhere. Worming my way into every part of your life.'

'It wasn't like that at all, and you know it.' His eyes glittered dangerously. 'I liked having you there, came to look forward to the time we spent together. Too much! Because I was aware that you already had a blinkered adoration for your guardian, the man who had come to your rescue when you were left alone in the world. I also knew that I was rapidly taking on that same untouchable role in your eyes, of someone you thought could do no wrong—'

'Liam, that is utter nonsense,' Laura cut in incredulously.

'I was far from perfect,' he said.

Laura frowned. 'How I felt about you bore no relation to how I felt about—my guardian,' she said awkwardly. 'Yes, I adored him. How could I not? I had known him all my life; he was a friend of my parents. I told you he had always been an honorary uncle,' she added exasperatedly as Liam continued to look unconvinced.

'I know I learnt to be jealous of the man; you talked about him incessantly,' Liam said. 'Uncle Rob this and Uncle Rob that.'

'I loved him!' she cried exasperately. 'He was the kindest, most wonderful man I've…' Her voice trailed off as she saw Liam look at her sharply, a dawning recognition appearing in those intelligent blue eyes.

Liam swallowed hard. 'I seem to have heard that description somewhere before…' he said slowly.

Laura was flustered now, remembering all too well where

he had heard it before! The question was, was Liam remembering it too...?

He was breathing shallowly, his searching gaze never leaving the paleness of her face as he obviously tried to come to grips with a realisation that just seemed too incredible to take in.

'I've been a fool, haven't I?' He finally spoke slowly. 'A complete and utter damned fool.' His voice hardened angrily.

She hadn't meant him to find out like this, had wanted to explain the situation to him quietly and calmly. Unfortunately, those two things had never been too near the surface in her dealings with Liam!

'I can't believe how stupid I've been,' he continued self-disgustedly. 'I was just so bowled over when I met you again. I didn't connect— Guardian Uncle *Rob*. Husband *Robert*. They're one and the same person, aren't they?' he breathed incredulously.

Laura stared at him wordlessly, feeling the colour slowly drain from her face.

'Aren't they?' He moved swiftly, grasping her arms again. 'Answer me!'

His face was only inches away from her own, bombarding her with the full force of his anger.

She shook her head. 'You don't understand, Liam—'

'Robert Shipley was your guardian, wasn't he?' he ground out fiercely. 'The adored Uncle Rob you talked about all the time?'

'Yes!' she burst out forcefully, the tears beginning to fall hotly down her cheeks now.

Liam thrust her away from him, staring at her disbelievingly. 'I thought—believed— I've been making an idiot of myself, haven't I?' he exclaimed impatiently as he moved away.

'Where are you going?' she choked as he strode over to the door.

He looked back at her with glacial eyes. 'As far away from here as possible!'

'But—'

'Don't say another word, Laura,' Liam bit out in a dangerously controlled voice. 'Not another word. I won't be held responsible for the consequences if you do!'

She watched mutely as he swung the sitting room door back with a bang. The slam of the front door seconds later told her that he had gone. Never to return, probably.

And with that realisation came the knowledge that she still hadn't told him about Bobby, his son...!

CHAPTER THIRTEEN

SHE hadn't told him anything that mattered!

That, much as she had loved Robert, it hadn't been in the way she loved Liam. That Robert hadn't loved her in a romantic way either. That, as well as trying to help her once she had told him she was expecting Liam's baby, Robert had seen their marriage as a way of having the family he would never have had otherwise.

Liam had left before she could tell him any of that. Before she could explain.

She sat down, wondering what to do next. That Liam would never willingly come near her again she was certain. And he had to know the truth. No matter what the consequences, he had to finally know that. After the last few days she knew she owed that to Bobby as much as anyone else...

It didn't take long to organise herself—to check with the hotel Liam had stayed at previously and find that he had booked in there again earlier today, to knock on the door to Amy's flat and ask her to mind Bobby while she just popped out for a short time, to get her car out of the garage and drive to Liam's hotel. Before she lost her nerve!

That Liam would be reluctant to see her she didn't doubt. But he had to hear what she wanted to say. Not because she thought there was any chance left between the two of them, but because Bobby, without even knowing who Liam really was, had grown to love him. Her marriage seven and a half years ago had been to give Bobby a father, and, no matter what it cost her, she couldn't do less for him now.

'I believe I saw Mr O'Reilly go through to the bar a short time ago.' The pretty hotel receptionist answered her query brightly.

Laura was sure that if that was what this young lady believed, then it was true; Liam's attractiveness certainly hadn't dimmed over the years!

'Thank you.' She smiled distractedly, her steps reluctant as she walked towards the hotel bar. If Liam was drinking again…!

Do it, Laura, she told herself firmly. You came here to talk to him, and that's what you're going to do.

He sat alone in a corner booth of the dimly lit bar, a glass of what looked like whisky in front of him. Untouched whisky, if the high level in the glass was any indication.

Laura came to a halt beside his table, managing to remain unmoving as, sensing her presence, he looked up at her, his gaze instantly fiercely angry.

'What do you want?' he demanded unpleasantly, the lines about his eyes and mouth more pronounced.

What she really wanted was for him to sit there and listen while she talked, saying nothing in response to anything she said, and then for him to let her leave again!

'Can I join you?' she said quietly.

'Why not? It's a free country. Although there are plenty of empty tables if you just want a drink.'

'I don't.' She slid onto the bench-seat opposite his in the booth. 'You left earlier before I had finished talking,' she explained softly.

His gaze was scathing as he straightened, one hand reaching out, the fingers curling about the glass of whisky. 'Don't look so worried,' he derided as she gave a wary glance at the glass. 'I ordered this twenty minutes ago and

I haven't touched any of it yet!' But there's still time, his words seemed to imply!

Laura sighed heavily, shaking her head in the direction of the young barman as he came over to see if she would like a drink; she already knew she wasn't going to enjoy the next few minutes, and Dutch courage wasn't going to help!

She drew in a deep breath. 'Liam, there are—things about my marriage that you can't possibly be aware of,' she began carefully. 'Circumstances that—'

'Are we talking about Bobby?' he cut in harshly.

She swallowed hard. 'What about Bobby?'

'Maybe these will help,' Liam ground out, reaching into the breast pocket of his jacket to pull out several photographs. He placed them carefully, side by side, on the table in front of her.

Laura moved forward slowly, looking down at those photographs. Apart from the fact that the clothes were all wrong, dating the photographs at thirty years or so ago, the little boy smiling into the camera in all of them could have been Bobby!

'You?' she managed to croak.

'I asked my mother for them when I was in Ireland,' Liam confirmed, gathering up the photographs to put them back in the pocket of his jacket.

Laura moistened dry lips. 'How long have you known?'

'That you must have been pregnant when I left eight years ago?' Liam paused. 'From the first moment I set eyes on Bobby.'

Her eyes widened incredulously at the admission. 'Then why—?'

'Why didn't I say something?' Liam finished raggedly. 'I've been waiting for you to tell me! Again I was being stupid.'

'I was going to tell you—'

'When?' he demanded.

'Tonight. But before I could—'

'I realised that your husband had been your beloved Uncle Rob!'

'We decided when we got married that it would be better for everyone if I called him Robert in future,' Laura put in inconsequentially.

'Convenient,' Liam drawled.

She shook her head. 'Why are you making this so hard for me, Liam?' she choked.

'"Hard for you"?' he repeated savagely. 'What I would really like to do is break your pretty little neck! I have no idea why you've come here, Laura.' He drew in a deeply controlling breath. 'I really think it might be better if you just left again.'

'Better for whom?' She was becoming angry herself now. 'Just what do you think happened eight years ago, Liam? Do you think I lied to Robert, tried to pass Bobby off as his son? Is that why you're so angry? Because I can assure you Robert was never in any doubt about the fact that he wasn't Bobby's father. He couldn't have been,' she added emotionally, her hands clenched tightly together.

Liam became very still, looking at her through narrowed lids. 'Why couldn't he?' he finally said slowly, obviously not seeing any of the answers in her face.

She turned in her seat, opening up her handbag. 'I brought a photograph of my own to show you, Liam.' She placed it in front of him, much the way he had done to her seconds ago.

Liam glanced down. 'I've already seen it, thanks,' he said, pushing away the photograph he had looked at so intently at the house a short time ago.

She nodded. 'What you can't see, what you can't possibly know, is that slightly out of this picture is a wheelchair. Robert's wheelchair,' she explained shakily. 'The wheelchair he had been confined to for twenty years.'

Liam reached out to slowly pull the photograph back towards him, peering down at the images.

Laura knew exactly what he would see on closer inspection; the way Robert's legs were bent slightly unnaturally, his awkwardness as he held baby Bobby in his arms. Robert had injured his lower spine playing rugby twenty years earlier, had been completely paralysed from the waist down.

'It never stopped him from doing the things he wanted to do.' Laura spoke tearfully. 'He was very supportive while I was pregnant, was present at the birth, would get up in the night and feed Bobby. He played with him for hours, never tired of being with him. Just looking at him...' she recalled brokenly. 'He cried the first time Bobby called him Daddy. He never believed he would be lucky enough to become a father, you see.'

Liam swallowed convulsively, looking down at the photograph once again. 'Were you in love with him?' he asked gruffly. 'Tell me, Laura!' he insisted harshly as she hesitated.

'I've tried to tell you how I felt about him, but you don't seem to be listening.' She sighed. 'I loved Robert very much. But I wasn't *in* love with him.' How could she have been, when the only man she had ever loved was sitting opposite her?

Was she getting through to him? Did Liam understand? Could he see—?

Liam straightened. 'I don't think this is the place for us to discuss this, Laura,' he said abruptly, pushing the glass of whisky away untouched.

'Will you come up to my suite with me?' He looked across at her with narrowed eyes.

He no longer looked dangerous, just weighed down with a sadness Laura didn't completely understand. But she would like to...

'Yes, I'll come with you,' she answered softly, picking her bag up in readiness for leaving.

Liam took a light hold of her elbow as they walked across the reception area to the lift, but the two of them moved apart once they had stepped inside, neither of them speaking.

Laura's tension started to rise again. So much depended on this conversation. So very much!

'Very nice,' she murmured dismissively once they were in the luxurious comfort of the sitting room in his suite.

Liam moved to the mini-bar, taking out a small bottle of whisky to pour the contents into a glass tumbler. 'For you,' he offered dryly, holding the glass out to her as she looked at him warily. 'You look as if you need it!'

She didn't like whisky, had never liked strong alcohol, but Liam was right; at the moment she felt in need of it! The first sip made her wince initially, but it was quickly followed by a warming sensation, seeming to settle those quivering butterflies in her stomach too.

'Let's sit down,' Liam suggested gently. 'At least, you sit down,' he amended once she had done exactly that. 'I think better standing on my feet,' he acknowledged ruefully.

Laura wasn't sure she wanted him to be able to think better; she would rather he just listened.

'I realise you haven't yet told me all you feel you want to,' Liam said softly. 'But maybe it will help if I first tell you a few things about my version of what happened eight years ago. What do you think?'

She thought that at the moment she was coward enough

to welcome putting off her own version if that was what Liam wanted her to do!'

'Go ahead,' she assented, taking another sip of the whisky. It really was quite relaxing.

Liam drew in a ragged breath. 'Well, I've already explained what I thought of you and your emotions eight years ago. What I haven't told you is that I—Laura, eight years ago I was in love with you! One hundred per cent completely in love with you!' he stated evenly.

Laura stared at him. He hadn't— He didn't— He couldn't have been!

Liam took in her dumbfounded expression. 'Sometimes, still, your emotions are so transparent,' he said. 'I was in love with you, Laura,' he repeated firmly. 'But, as I've already explained, I was ten years older than you, felt you had a lot of growing up, a lot of living still to do, before it would be fair for any man to ask you to devote your life just to him.' His expression was grim now.

Laura moistened dry lips. 'You said, when we met again last week, that you wished I had been this Laura eight years ago...' she remembered slowly, that remark perhaps starting to make more sense to her now.

Perhaps...

She gave a firm shake of her head. 'You couldn't have loved me eight years ago, Liam,' she said. 'You could never have left me in the way that you did if that had been the case. Certainly never have married someone else within weeks of leaving England. And me,' she added painfully.

He gave a heavy sigh. 'After that night, when we made love, I knew I had to get out of your life, give you chance to grow up without my influence. I didn't go straight to America when I left England; I went home to Ireland first. Perhaps you remember my telling you earlier today that my mother isn't yet aware that you're the same Laura from eight years ago...? I talked to her about you then,' he continued at her affirmative nod. 'Told her everything—'

'Everything?' Laura echoed.

'Everything,' Liam repeated. 'My mother agreed with me that your parents' death must have been a terrible blow for you, that you were bound to still be emotionally immature, that my making a clean break from your life was probably for the best—'

'I wasn't too immature to become a mother!' Laura reminded him tautly. 'Don't you think that you—and your mother—should have let me be the one to decide whether or not I was mature enough to know my own mind?' she demanded impatiently. 'And heart,' she added huskily.

'I always intended to come back, Laura,' Liam told her gruffly. 'It was never meant to be for ever.'

She looked up at him disbelievingly. 'You married someone else, Liam,' she reminded him.

'I missed you so much when I got to America, Laura. Drank too much,' he stated flatly. 'Sometimes I would lose days at a time,' he remembered. 'I'm making no excuses,' he assured at her sceptical expression. 'Diana was beautiful, obviously willing. I—It only happened the once. A few weeks later she told me she was pregnant. What can I say? I married her. Only to discover within weeks of the marriage that she had apparently made a mistake, that she wasn't pregnant, after all. It's the oldest trick in the book.' He groaned. 'And I fell for it!'

How ironic. How utterly, awfully ironic! Because back in England Laura had been genuinely pregnant with Liam's child.

Her expression hardened. 'What do you want me to say, Liam?'

'About my marriage?' He shrugged. 'Nothing. It's a mistake that I have to live with. But it was also a mistake that made it impossible for me to come back here to you. I knew you would never forgive me for marrying someone else, never believe that it was you I loved the whole time. But when I saw you again last week—!'

Laura had tensed, staring at him intently. 'What did you think then, Liam? How did you feel?'

'Initially? Stunned. Quickly followed by euphoria; I thought I was being given a second chance! But then you told me you were someone else's wife!' He shook his head. 'Seven years ago, after my divorce, I had no right to come back and tell you how I felt about you; the fact that you were married to someone else would have made the whole thing impossible. But then I found out you were a widow, that your husband had been over thirty years older than you—'

'You believed I had married Robert for his money,' Laura recalled dryly.

'I couldn't think of any other reason why— The age gap seemed too vast for it to be a love-match. The man was almost twenty years older than me, for goodness' sake! Then, at first, when I saw Bobby and realised—I had to rethink it all. I thought perhaps you had married Robert Shipley to give the child a name,' he admitted raggedly. 'At least, I began to hope that was what you had done. And then today I learnt that Robert had been your Uncle Rob. The man you had obviously adored eight years ago.'

'Of course I adored him,' she confirmed emotionally. 'He picked me up and put me back on my feet again when my parents died, was always there for me. Always!' she added shakily, remembering all too vividly her own euphoria, quickly followed by heartbreak on learning of Liam's marriage to another woman, when she had discovered she was expecting Liam's child. Robert had cared for her. 'But I wasn't in love with him, Liam. Nor he with me. Our marriage was that of two very good friends, each caring deeply for the other, joined together by the love we both had for an innocent child.'

'How you must have hated me all these years.' Liam looked ashamed.

'Yes.' She wasn't about to lie to him; she *had* hated him—for leaving her, for marrying someone else, for not being there when their son was born. 'For a while I did,' she agreed. 'Until Bobby was born, probably. There was too much love in my heart then to feel hatred for anybody.' Least of all, she realised now, the man who had given her Bobby, given *Robert* Bobby.

'I love him, too, you know,' Liam told her huskily.

'I know you do.' She nodded understandingly. 'At first, when I realised I was pregnant, I didn't know what to do. It was Robert who said I had to tell you. He was even willing to go to America with me so I could tell you. He hated all the fuss that was made when he had to fly anywhere,' she recalled affectionately. 'But he was willing to do it to help me find you. Then we saw the photographs of your wedding in the newspapers,' she said bleakly.

'Oh, Laura...!'

'No.' She put up a shaky hand to stop Liam as he would have come down on his haunches beside her chair. 'It all has to be said, Liam,' she told him flatly. 'The truth told at last.' She drew in a ragged breath. 'I was twenty-one years old, in my last year of a university degree, and pregnant—and the father of my baby had just married someone else! Robert knew that I—I wanted to keep my baby. He—he offered to marry me, to take care of both me and the baby. Now we come to the difficult bit, Liam.' She looked up at him with tear-wet eyes.

He squeezed her hand. 'If it's any consolation, Laura, I know I deserve whatever you're going to say next.'

She stood up, putting down the glass of whisky she had only sipped at. 'It isn't a question of deserving anything, Liam,' she told him. 'If I had been different eight years ago, perhaps none of this would have happened. But the fact of the matter is we are both who we are, what we are. And if you had asked me to marry you eight years ago, Liam, then I would have said yes.' She again answered the question he had once put to her. 'But, with hindsight, I—I have to say that I wouldn't change a single thing about what actually did happen the last eight years!'

His throat moved convulsively. 'Because you married the man you loved after all...?'

'Haven't you been listening to a single thing I've said, Liam?' she challenged impatiently, her expression one of exasperation now. 'I loved Robert; I wasn't *in* love with him. But...' She paused, drawing in a deep breath. 'I have to be honest with you, Liam, and tell you that I can't regret my marriage to him. He was a wonderful husband and father; neither Bobby or I could have had better.' There, she had said it!

Because it had to be said. If there were to be any future relationship at all between Liam and herself, even that of friendship just for Bobby's sake, then Liam had to understand she regretted making none of the choices that had been open to her, that she would never have a denigrating word said about Robert, on any subject, within her hearing.

She hadn't been in love with Robert, but she had loved him deeply, and she knew that Bobby felt the same about the man he had known as his daddy. How Liam, with the knowledge that he was Bobby's biological father, intended dealing with that she had no idea. But he would have to deal with it in a way that was acceptable to her. Otherwise she would fight all the way any claim he tried to make on Bobby. She owed Robert that, at least.

Liam looked across at her with narrowed, thoughtful eyes. 'You asked me a short time ago why I hadn't told you that I knew I was Bobby's real father,' he began slowly. 'My answer was I was waiting for you to tell me. But there's a lot more to it than that, Laura,' he continued firmly as she would have spoken. 'Being a father isn't about impregnating a woman. It's being there for her during the sometimes scary days of pregnancy, being at her side during the birth, helping to care for and nurture the child once it's born. All the things that Robert did, in fact,' he acknowledged. 'The deep affection you had for him once frightened the hell out of me—eight years ago I thought you felt more for him than you did for me! But it doesn't frighten me any more, Laura. Now I'm just grateful to him. For being there for you, and Bobby, when I couldn't be or simply wasn't,' he admitted sadly.

The tears were swimming in Laura's eyes now. 'Do you really mean all that?' she breathed.

'Of course I mean it,' he replied. 'I'm not expecting to just walk into Bobby's life, announce that I'm his real father and take over that role as if it's my right! Because it isn't. I have to earn that right. In the same way I have to earn the right to tell you I'm still in love with you,' he carried on. 'That I've never stopped being in love with you,' he added emotionally.

'Oh, Liam…!' she choked tearfully.

'Is that, Oh, Liam, you'll never be able to convince me of that?' he asked. 'Or is it, Oh, Liam, I'll let you try if it's what you really want to do?' He looked at her with narrowed eyes.

Laura drew in a deep breath; it was now or never! 'It's, Oh, Liam, I do love you,' she admitted shyly, holding her breath as she waited for his response.

He became very still, eyeing her warily. 'Is that, I love you, Liam, or is that, I'm *in* love with you, Liam?'

She gave a shaky laugh. 'Which do you think?'

He raised his eyes heavenwards. 'After the confusion of the last week—I have no idea!' he admitted. 'Although I'm hoping it's the latter,' he added. 'You have no idea how much I'm hoping that!'

Oh, she thought she did—if it was anything like the way she felt!

'I love you very much, Laura. I've never stopped being in love with you,' he assured her. 'And, if you'll give me the chance, I would like the time to convince you of that.'

She took a step towards him. 'Don't you think we've wasted enough time already?' She took another step.

Liam covered the short distance that was left between them, sweeping her into his arms, holding her so tightly against him he was in danger of snapping her in half. 'I love you, Laura! I love you so much it hurts!' He groaned into the softness of her throat. 'I never want to be without you again!'

She could feel him shaking as she put her own arms about his waist and held him just as tightly as he was holding her. 'You won't be,' she promised. 'Not ever again!'

As his mouth claimed possession of hers, lips moving passionately against her, sipping, tasting, Liam desperate to make her a part of him, Laura knew that this time they wouldn't be parted by anything, or anyone.

This time it was for ever...

EPILOGUE

'OH, LOOK how tiny she is.' Bobby glanced up excitedly at Liam as they stood side by side looking down into the tiny hospital crib. 'Isn't Hannah beautiful?'

Liam glanced at Laura as she lay in the hospital bed, the two of them sharing a smile of complete love as Bobby enthused about his hours-old baby sister, Hannah Mary.

'Gorgeous. But not as beautiful as your mother,' Liam answered Bobby huskily, raising Laura's hand up to his mouth as he kissed the softness of her skin. 'Thank you,' he mouthed silently.

'When can we take her home, Mummy?' Bobby pressed excitedly.

Laura smiled at her beloved son, so pleased that he had taken this new addition to their family so well.

She and Liam had been married for a year now—a year of complete happiness, but also of necessary adjustments for all of them. Bobby most of all. He had had to learn to share his mother with 'Uncle Liam'. Now he had to share her with a baby sister too...

'Tomorrow, probably,' she answered sleepily. The labour with Hannah had been much shorter than with Bobby, but very tiring.

Liam had been with her this time, every day of her pregnancy, all through the hours of labour. As she had no doubts he would be with her every day for the rest of her life.

During Laura's maternity leave Perry was in charge of Shipley Publishing. Liam's book had been published three

183

months ago, had been at the top of the bestseller list for two of those, and was looking likely to remain there for some time.

Laura knew she had never been so happy, knowing herself completely loved, and completely in love with Liam in return. And now they had a daughter as well as a son.

Liam had told her at the outset of their marriage that he thought Bobby should continue to think of him as 'Uncle Liam', in the hope that one day Bobby would decide to call him Daddy, simply because he wanted to. Telling Bobby the whole truth about his birth, they had decided together, could wait until he was older.

'Can I hold her?' Bobby asked softly. 'Can I, Mummy?'

Laura smiled. 'If you sit in this chair next to the bed I'm sure Dad—er, Uncle Liam will pick her up and give her to you.' She blushed slightly at the slip she had just made.

But it was how she always thought of Liam now. He had become Bobby's father, loved him, played with him, scolded him slightly if it were necessary, listened to him. Everything a father should do. And she knew if Robert could see them all now that he would be happy that Bobby and Laura had someone who loved them both so deeply.

'Will you, Daddy?' Bobby looked up almost shyly at Liam. 'Please?'

Laura watched as Liam swallowed the lump in his throat, her own eyes swimming with tears. It was the first time Bobby had called him Daddy...

But as she watched Bobby cuddling Hannah, Liam bending solicitously over both of them, Laura knew it wouldn't be the last time.

They were a real family now.

Complete.

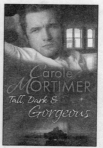

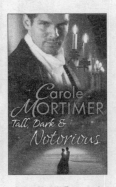

Nights Collection

Introducing the Nights Collection

On sale 5th July

On sale 2nd August

On sale 6th September

On sale 4th October

Mills & Boon® Modern™ invite you to step into a world of intense romance...after dark!